Karen's Stories

Ted Kuzminski

Pocol Press
Clifton, VA

POCOL PRESS
Published in the United States of America
by Pocol Press
6023 Pocol Drive
Clifton, VA 20124
www.pocolpress.com

Publisher's Cataloguing-in-Publication

Names: Kuzminski, Ted, author.
Title: Karen's Stories / Ted Kuzminski.
Description: Clifton, Virginia: Pocol Press, 2016.
Identifiers: ISBN 978-1-929763-68-9 | LCCN 2016933094
Subjects: LCSH Short stories, American. | World War, 1914-1918--Fiction. | World War, 1939-1945--Fiction. | Europe--Fiction. | United States--Fiction. | Love stories. | BISAC FICTION / Short Stories (single author).
Classification: LCC PS3611.U97 | DDC 813.6--dc23

Introduction and Dedication

During the fall season of our first year of marriage (1973), Karen and I discovered that I had amassed enough points, while still a bachelor, with Book-of-the-Month Club. Naturally, we decided to redeem them for a book of our choosing. And so Karen selected a book of Christmas stories. That, of course, was fine with me.

When the book arrived, she quickly opened it and scanned the table of contents. I could tell by the expression upon her face that she was unhappy.

"Theodore," she said. I knew she was very unhappy because she called me Ted at all other times in our relationship. "We have already read all of the stories in this book."

"That's too bad." I was already thinking of someone to bestow the book upon on Christmas Day.

"Well, you have written a novel, haven't you?"

"Yes, I have." Over a period of five years, I wrote a novel, which presently sat in a box in the attic.

"If you've written a novel, you can write me a short story for Christmas."

I earnestly thought about the request. A few days later, I sat down and wrote "To Tell or Not to Tell" and then placed it under the tree on Christmas Eve.

That was only the first of forty-two stories that I have penned for Karen. And since all of the tales in this anthology actually belong to Karen, I decided to entitle this book *Karen's Stories*.

I also wish to take this opportunity to dedicate this book to Karen and the following people: Bonnie Deisher, Clara Kuzminski, Jonathan Deisher, Russ Sitlinger, Judith Deisher, Mirella Deisher, John Kuzminski, Jim Deisher, ClaraRose Deisher, Ruth Sitlinger, and Jaime Deisher.

TABLE OF CONTENTS

Doughboy on the Run

On April 6, 1917, the United States declared war on Germany. The following day thousands of Americans volunteered for the United States Army. I, for one, was not among them. It wasn't that I was unpatriotic. Far from it. I was a true patriot. My family's roots, in this country, went all the way back to 1609 when the first Stefanski, a glass maker, settled in Jamestown. Did you know that shortly after his arrival, he built the first factory in America? He also organized the first labor union.

And, by the way, don't let anyone tell you that Abner Doubleday invented our game of baseball in 1839. Stefanski brought the game of baseball to these shores from his native Poland. He called it *pilka plantowa*.

If some Bolshevist argues that your information is bogus, send him to me. I'll set him straight.

Now ... back to my personal dilemma. My reason for not enlisting in the Army immediately after Wilson declared war was quite simple.

At that time in history, I was a student at the Tioga Conservatory with a scant two months left on the calendar until graduation. After considerable thought, I decided that the war would still be raging in Europe when I graduated.

General John Pershing, the Commanding General of the American Expeditionary Forces, and his staff arrived in France on June 13, 1917. I received my diploma the following day at the school's commencement. Two days later, I offered my services to the United States Army.

Clad in my only suit and my Sunday shoes, I proudly marched down Main Street to the Recruiting Office. I expected to see hordes of young men milling about the post office, waiting to sign up. Much to my surprise, there wasn't a crowd lined up in front of the post office. The only people in the area were a couple of pensioners loitering about the flag pole.

I guessed that the prospective doughboys had all swarmed into the post office once it opened for business. Boldly and proudly I threw open the post office door and entered. Much to my dismay, the only occupant in the post office was Harry Waters, the Post Master. Undaunted, I marched downstairs into the very bowels of the building. Surely, there I would find a gaggle of young men in the Recruiting Office. All would be clamoring to be sworn into the Army.

When I slowly turned the door knob and peeked into the dimly lit room, my jaw dropped. The room was empty, save for a solitary sergeant, sitting at his desk. He continued to scan the front page of the *Tioga Times*, even after I entered.

"May I help you," he said, finally glancing up. Tossing the newspaper aside, he crushed his cigarette butt in an ashtray.

I saluted. "Yes, sir, I'd like to enlist." I clicked my heels together, stood tall, and saluted once more.

The sergeant saluted and then offered his hand. "I'm Sergeant Homer Reynolds." He stood back and studied me as if he were about to paint my portrait.

After shaking his hand, I assumed a rigid position as I had seen soldiers adopt on recent military posters. "Sir, I'm Paul Stefanski."

"Well, Paul, if you'll fill out these papers, we'll get started." Sergeant Reynolds handed me several papers, a pen, and pointed to a nearby desk.

I took the papers and sat in a desk that was too small for my frame. Twenty minutes later, after I had checked my answers and signed on the dotted line, I handed Sergeant Reynolds my enlistment papers.

"Am I now in the Army?" I asked in all seriousness.

He glanced at my papers before he spoke. "Err ... not yet, Paul." He briefly tinkered with his collar disks. "You need to pass a physical examination before you're sworn in." I nodded, thinking it only proper for the government to know just how healthy I was.

"Your physical is scheduled for Camp Biscayne next Thursday morning." I nodded. "If you pass your physical, you will be sworn in at that time. Then you will be sent to your next duty station." I shook my head again. "Now, are there any questions?"

Since I knew nothing about the military, I visited Willie Hawkins, an old Union soldier, prior to my visiting the Recruiting Office. Willie listened to my concerns and was only too happy to offer me some sage advice. "Never loan nobody no money. Never do no volunteerin' for anything, and never neglect your rifle," Willie said firmly.

Though Willie's advice was sound, it didn't apply to my present situation. I hadn't been accepted into the military as yet.

Recently I had read an article in the *Tioga Times*, which explained that all enlistees were entitled to choose their line of duty: infantry, artillery, or the newly formed armor division.

The article went on to say that conscription for all males between the ages of twenty-one to thirty was only a matter of time. And since those men were not volunteers, they would be assigned to branches of the United States Army as the government saw fit.

After reading the article, I decided that I was entitled to choose my fate. And so I said to Sergeant Reynolds, "Sir, since I'm joining up, do I have a say in the branch of service I serve and what I do?"

From the startled expression upon the sergeant's face, I knew that my question hadn't been posed too often. Before speaking, he pored over my papers once more. "What would you like to do?" he finally asked.

After clearing my throat, I looked him straight in the eye before addressing him. "Sir, I am a graduate of the Tioga Conservatory." I pointed to my enlistment forms. "As you can see, I can play the piccolo … ugh … the clarinet, and the piano." I shifted my feet slightly and grew bolder. "I would like to play in the band for the troops."

After blurting out my request, I was sure that Sergeant Reynolds would dismiss my request as insane. However, he merely nodded and took his pen in hand. "Mmmmm … let me see." His finger traced an imaginary line across my papers. "I … errr … see that the Army Air Service has a need for musicians. How about if I add Army Air Service to your enlistment papers?"

"That would be fine."

Sergeant Reynolds smiled. I saluted. He returned my salute. Happily I left, knowing that I would continue my musical career in the United States Army.

As soon as I returned home, I informed my parents of my enlistment. Outwardly, both supported my decision to enlist. However, I knew better. Both were concerned with my immediate safety.

Martin Stefanski, Dad's uncle, had been mortally wounded in the Battle of Antietam. And in a ten-week conflict known as the Spanish-American War, Mom's brother was killed charging up Kettle Hill with Teddy Roosevelt.

However, when I told them that I had been assigned to play in the band for the troops, both breathed a sigh of relief and wished me success in my endeavor.

Ever since war was declared, I knew that I would either volunteer for the military or eventually be drafted. Prior to my graduation, I discussed my plans for enlistment with Lucy Logan, my girlfriend of many years. Our friendship actually dated back to elementary school. It wasn't until we entered high school, though, that we began dating on a steady basis.

After high school, I entered the Tioga Conservatory. Lucy stayed home and kept house for her widowed father. Though we never openly discussed marriage, it was a forgone conclusion that once I earned my diploma and found gainful employment, we would tie the knot.

When I informed Lucy of my enlistment, she insisted that we marry at once. I, on the other hand, explained that even though I would be playing in the band, there was still a remote chance that I could be killed. I told her, in no uncertain terms, that she was much too young to become a widow. It took some convincing on my part, but Lucy finally agreed with me. And after a chocolate malt down at the local drug store and several tender pecks on the cheek, Lucy affirmed her love for me. However, as soon as the war ended and I returned home, we were to be married. I, of course, consented to that arrangement.

I expected the days to creep by at a snail's pace before I left for active duty. I quickly discovered that each day was filled with pressing obligations. And the evenings found me bidding farewell to family and friends or attending a social function with Lucy.

When the day of my departure finally arrived, I arose at 4:00 A.M.. I still had to pack clean underwear, my toiletries, and my clarinet. I was still searching for a new reed for my clarinet when Lucy arrived to accompany me to the station. After much searching, I found a fairly good reed atop my chiffonier. Finally I was set to leave.

As the four of us strolled down Main Street, our talk centered on such whimsical topics as the Rotary's impending Blueberry Festival, the annual church picnic, and the misfortunes of the town's baseball team.

I really didn't comprehend the magnitude of my decision to enlist until we rounded the corner and I spied the sleek Greyhound bus standing before me.

"Morning, Paul," said Sergeant Reynolds, approaching me with a clipboard and pencil in hand.

"Good morning," I said and introduced the sergeant to my parents and Lucy.

Once the sergeant checked my name off the list, I realized that my life was about to change greatly. I seemed to fall into a stupor of some sort. Much later I recalled shaking my father's hand and kissing my mother on the cheek and embracing Lucy. But that was it. I don't remember lining up with the recruits or marching to the bus. And I certainly didn't recall hanging out the window and waving goodbye to anyone.

Once the bus was underway, I discovered that I had left my toiletries, clarinet, and clean underwear behind. So much for all my planning.

Two hours later, the bus pulled into Camp Biscayne, a military installation dating back to the Civil War.

Over the years I had received many physical examinations from Dr. Burton, our family physician. None of his examinations, though, were as thorough as the military physical I underwent at Camp Biscayne.

Of the fifty men who traveled with me to Camp Biscayne that morning, forty-five passed the physical. Luckily, I was one of the forty-five who passed. Ten minutes after receiving notification of our passing the physical, we were ushered into a crowded gymnasium. There we all raised our right hand and were sworn into the United States Army.

After a hardy lunch of meatloaf, mashed potatoes, stewed turnips, and hot coffee, we all received our assignments.

Of course, the five rejects boarded the Greyhound bus and returned home.

Another large contingent was loaded into ten trucks bound for Camp Allan. I joined a smaller group of men who boarded a train for Camp Carson in Illinois.

Finding the first three Pullman coaches quite crowded, I strode into the fourth car and settled into an empty seat near the window. I was quickly joined by a ruddy-faced youth, wearing a threadbare suit jacket and dungarees.

Outside, a whistle blew three times. The train suddenly lurched forward. A conductor and a sergeant promptly strolled through the coach to see how we were getting along.

I suppose it was some ten minutes later, after things settled down, that I retrieved a piccolo from my coat pocket and softly played "Over There."

"That was very good," said my companion. He held out a bag of pralines and offered me one, which I graciously accepted.

"Paul Stefanski," I said and offered my hand.

"Greg. Greg Burns." Taking my hand, he wrung it as if it were a pump handle. "Just think." He rolled his large head toward the sky. "Next week at this time we'll all be flying."

My eyes widened, my throat tightened. "F-f-flying!"

"Yes, Camp Carson is where you go to learn how to fly." Greg good-naturedly slapped my knee. "What did you think they did there?"

Suddenly I felt somewhat nauseous. "I'm a musician. I joined the service to play in the band. I saw the recruiter write Army Air Service on my enlistment papers." I held out my open palms in bewilderment. "I vomited every time I rode the carousel at the county fair."

"Motion sickness?"

"Yes, I suppose." When Greg offered me another praline, I declined. "If I go up in a plane, I'll heave my lunch all over the place." Very quickly I saw my military career unfolding badly. "Then what will they do with me?"

"Probably reassign you to an infantry outfit and ship you to the trenches in France."

"Maybe when we get to Carson, I could request a transfer to the band."

"Maybe, but don't count on being transferred to the band."

Totally depressed, I settled back into my seat and watched the telephone poles whiz by. In all honesty, I watched a lot of poles fly by. It took the train more than two days to reach Wanaka, the tiny hamlet down the road from Camp Carson.

All that night I tossed and turned on my cot. I wrestled with several questions. Should I tell someone in authority that I volunteered to play in the band? Should I mention, that as a child, I was afflicted with motion sickness? Or ... should I wait until I flew in a plane and upchucked all over the place?

The following morning I decided to stay the course. A Stefanski never quit. If I retched all over the airplane and was transferred to the infantry, so be it.

After we received our inoculations and military clothing, a sergeant marched us across camp to a set of rickety bleachers. There we met Lieutenant Winston Sloan, our company commander.

Lieutenant Sloan, a recent graduate of West Point, welcomed us into the military. He then explained that, as cadet pilots, we would follow the Bingham Plan, which was a three-phase program.

He said that the first phase would consist of weaponry, military drill, airplane mechanics, meteorology, and astronomy.

Actual flying would comprise the second phase. And, if we succeeded to the final phase, we would be sent to Europe for advanced flying instruction.

Being a college graduate, I enjoyed the classroom instruction. But as the days passed, I knew that eventually I would have to fly in an airplane.

On a balmy Midwestern morning, that fateful day arrived. As soon as we completed our calisthenics, Lieutenant Sloan and the First Sergeant, a fellow who actually served in the Spanish-American War, marched us to the airfield.

While the First Sergeant called out the cadence, we marched smartly over hill and dale. I had actually grown quite fond of my comrades and would miss them when I washed out of aviation training. I quietly prayed that I would be sent away to my new assignment in the middle of the night when everyone was asleep. So great was the attachment I had forged with the likes of Greg and Sonny and Lefty.

The First Sergeant guided us to the bleachers, where we sat in rows of four. And while we filled our nostrils with the smell of castor oil, Lieutenant Sloan hiked across the field to one of the hangars.

I prayed that the instructor was delayed by pressing family business over in De Kalb County. However, ten minutes later Lieutenant Sloan appeared with not one, but two flying instructors.

The instructor to Sloan's left was a tall, rangy man with a rather handsome face and a kind smile.

Whereas, the instructor to his right appeared to be a cretin with Tartar features and a perfidious snarl on his face.

I decided right then and there that I would rather fly with the smiling chap than with the cretin from hell.

Though I had only been in the service for a short period of time, I had learned that the military did everything alphabetically and by the numbers.

Since my surname *Stefanski* began with the letter *S*, I knew that it would take several days before I was summoned to fly. Taking comfort in my temporary reprieve, I sat back and relaxed. "I won't have to pack my bags tonight," I said to myself.

In the meantime, while I was congratulating myself for my sheer good fortune, Lieutenant Sloan and the two instructors huddled before us. I noticed that Sloan handed each instructor a slip of paper. Probably a list of names I reasoned.

When I glanced over at Glenn Abbott, who was, in all probability, the first cadet to take to the air, I noticed that he squirmed considerably.

Andy Addison fared no better. He nervously gnawed upon his palm.

"Cadet Stee-e-e-e-fanski," bellowed the cretin. I glanced around, not realizing that my name had been called. "Cadet Paul Stee-e-e-e-fanski."

I finally rose on wobbly legs and descended the bleachers. Across the field I strode to where the cretin awaited me.

"Cadet Stefanski ... eh ... reporting, sir," I said and saluted the cretin.

"Relax, Paul. You don't hafta salute me." The cretin chuckled. "I'm not in the military. I'm just a civilian instructor."

"Yes, sir."

"You don't hafta call me *sir* either." He slapped his thigh with his leather helmet. "Relax ... and just call me Joe. My name's Joe Tylka from Cairo." He smiled and revealed a set of crooked teeth. "You related to the Stefanski family over in Cairo?"

"Distant cousins." Since Dad had a brother living in Michigan, I supposed that the Stefanski clan in Cairo was also related.

Joe chuckled once more. "Can't wait to tell the wife that I'm teaching one of her cousins how to fly. Always says the Stefanskis are pretty sharp."

As we approached the closest Jenny, a mechanic squirted gasoline into the cylinder. Another mechanic replaced a plug before removing one of the wheel chocks.

"Do I sit in the front?"

"Yes, you do. Once we're situated, I'm going to talk to you over a one-way speaking tube." After slipping on his sweat-stained helmet, Joe helped me climb into the front cockpit, where I slipped on my shoulder harness and tightened it. Next I donned my helmet and awaited further instructions. "If you can hear me over the tube, nod or raise your hand?"

"Gottcha." I nodded and raised my right hand.

"Good. Now, relax and enjoy the ride."

I did just as Joe instructed. In a moment one of the mechanics removed the final wheel chock. His companion approached the wooden propeller and wound it as if it were a clock. All at once he swung the prop. *Whrrrrrrr* screamed the engine. The Jenny vibrated. Blue smoke blew into my face. The mechanic backed away and gave us the thumbs up sign. Proudly, I returned the sign.

"Here we go, Paul," called Joe through the tube. I nodded. "I'm going to take her up to a safe altitude. And … once we're high enough, you're going to take over. Got that?" I raised my hand. "Good."

The Jenny shimmied as we gained speed and raced across the grass. The smell of castor oil grew stronger. In the distance I spied a copse of fir trees. When the wind watered my eyes, I closed them and lowered my goggles. Opening my eyes, I watched the majestic fir trees draw closer. The pine cones loomed larger. The Jenny raced on. I now detected a bird's nest in one of the trees. *Whrrrrrr!* Suddenly the nose lifted, and the Jenny cleared the top of the nearest tree. I swallowed, breathed deeply, and exhaled. We were safely airborne.

"Good takeoff," I said, remembering that Joe could not hear a word I said.

Gaining courage, I peeked over the side of the fuselage. Below everything looked smaller and more remote and quite serene.

"You operate the control stick to fly the Jenny," announced Joe above the roar of the engine. Until then, I hadn't thought much about flying the plane. But upon closer inspection, I realized that the stick was similar to the tiller on Dad's Curved Dash Oldsmobile, which I learned to drive at age fourteen. I recalled that I encountered little difficulty with the tiller. And Dad, always a stern taskmaster, said that I was a pretty good driver after just one spin around the block. But that was an auto. And this was an airplane.

I judged our air speed to be about seventy miles an hour as we climbed higher and higher into the blue sky. I now brazenly glanced over the side of the cockpit. All land features looked much smaller than when I initially stole a peek.

"If you feel comfortable, you may take over the stick," Joe's voice boomed in my ears as if he were sitting next to me.

I nodded and reached for the control stick. Much to my surprise, it felt as if I were driving Dad's Oldsmobile. I tingled with sheer excitement.

"Good, Paul. Very good." I nodded. "Take her around the field about three times." I shook my head and complied.

I surmised that after I circled the field three times, Joe would take over the controls and land the Jenny.

You can imagine my reaction when Joe said, "You know, Paul, you have a very nice touch." I wanted to nod, but I thought Joe might construe that gesture as a boast. So I did nothing. "How would you like to take her down and land her?" I nodded emphatically even though I was frightened as hell. "To slow down, cut the engine." I nodded and did as instructed. "Push the throttle forward." I did. The plane not only slowed down, but it descended. "Excellent. Keep the nose above the horizon." I nodded several times. Slowly the plane glided down to the earth. "Not too steep." I nodded. "Good." I cut the fuel again as the Jenny approached the field. Judging my altitude, I cut the ignition slightly and eased back on the stick. The Jenny hit the grass with a bump, jumped up, and then landed safely. "Wanna taxi over to the troops?" I shook my head several times and then followed Joe's directions.

Once the engine shut down, I extricated myself from the harness, climbed out of the cockpit, and jumped down to the grass. Beaming from ear to ear, I awaited Joe, who I considered one of my best friends.

In the moments that followed, all I could think of was writing home to my parents and Lucy. I simply had to tell them about my exploits in the sky. Remembering that today was Friday, I should have received two letters from home -- one from Lucy, which would be scented with lavender, and one from Dad and Mom.

I wasn't disappointed at mail call. I received my two letters. Lucy's wasn't scented, but I figured that she either forgot or ran out of perfume.

Because Lucy's letters were always so mushy, I decided to read Mom's letter first. As was her custom, she briefed me on the local news. She then informed me that Uncle Phil suffered another bout of the gout and Cousin Emmy found a squirrel in her attic, which caused quite a bit of damage. Sadly, she also stated that Willie passed away. In ending, she asked me if I had heard from Lucy. I thought it a strange question. Mom knew that Lucy wrote to me three or four times a week.

I set Mom's letter aside and took up Lucy's. In addition to the lack of a scent, the letter felt lighter. Lucy always wrote at least seven pages. I also noticed that it was postmarked from New York City.

Tearing open the envelope haphazardly, I read the first line and discovered it was a Dear John letter.

Lucy had married Sergeant Reynolds, the recruiter, and moved to New York City to begin a new life.

Stunned, I folded the letter and returned it to its envelope. Somehow, I went about my duties as best I could. After supper, I bought two bottles of Schlitz beer and drank them under the shade of a gigantic chestnut tree.

After much reflection, I decided that Lucy just wasn't meant to be my wife. Since I was no drinker, I returned, quite sober, to the barracks and turned in for the night.

The following morning, however, I experienced a pounding headache. I also discovered that my reflexes were not as acute. Certainly I could not fly an airplane if under the influence of alcohol. On the spot I promised myself that I would never drink the night before I was scheduled to fly.

With Lucy's departure from my life, I immersed myself in my new career -- flying. Not only was I the first cadet pilot in my class to land a Jenny, I was also the first to solo. And I followed that feat up by being the first to hurl a sandbag several hundred feet onto a target below.

Slowly but surely all my feelings for Lucy vanished. There was no other woman in my life. And, in all honesty, I saw no prospects for a meaningful relationship until I returned from Europe.

In the near future I did, however, see myself fighting for my country. And so on a rather windy morning in September, I joined my classmates in the rickety old bleachers one more time. After a less-than-rousing speech by the base commander, Colonel Horace Donneley, the squadron received their wings and were commissioned Second Lieutenants in the United States Army.

Though my parents were unable to attend the ceremony, Joe Tylka and his wife Florence, sat in the audience. Once the festivities concluded, Joe introduced me to Florence, who gave me the name of a Stefanski family residing in Wales. I promised Florence, an avid genealogist, that if I ever found my way to Wales, I would call upon our distant cousins.

Throughout the week, rumors abounded that the squadron would be disbanded. We would then be assigned as substitutes to various units already in action. I, for one, thought that highly unlikely, for we had not yet received our advanced flight training.

Later that evening we were all ordered to pack our duffle bags for an unknown destination. Ten o'clock came and went. We were still waiting for a train at eleven. The old army saying of "Hurry up and wait" was never more apropos. We never boarded the train until 2:00

A.M.

Of course, we knew our destination was the port of New York because all transport ships sailed from the New York Harbor. Four days later the entire squadron sailed for Europe on the transport *Knoxville.*

It is not my intention to bore the reader with minutia concerning the seven-day odyssey across the Atlantic Ocean. But on midnight of September 17, 1917, the squadron disembarked at Warmouth Crossing and boarded a train for our advanced flight training at Harrington. Built six months before our arrival, Harrington was closer to Glasgow than it was to London.

Under the careful eye of Major Peter Thomson, our new squadron leader, we mastered the intricacies of flying the Sopwith Camel, a very skittish biplane. After learning to fly the Camel, our instructions in strafing, acrobatics, and aerial combat were humdrum by comparison.

Before I left Camp Carson for Europe, Joe informed me that the Jenny's top ceiling was 6,500 feet. The Camel's ceiling was 21,000 feet. At such an altitude, I needed to dress warmly, or I would pay the price.

I made a mental note of Joe's information and relayed it to Dad in my next letter. Since Dad was an engineer, I expected him to arrive at a solution. Unfortunately, Dad had no answer. He, however, sought the advice of Ludwig Brenheiser, the town tailor and an immigrant from Austria. Old Ludwig thought about the conundrum for a long time. Finally, he requested my measurements from Dad.

On one of my last days at Harrington, I received a sizeable package from home. I had a good idea of the contents. When I rushed back to my tent and opened the box, I discovered a tailor-made flying suit of wool that was lined with rubber.

The following morning I wore my new flying suit. I discovered that when I took the Camel up to 16,000 feet, I was as snug as a bug in a rug.

Now every solution to a problem might not be perfect. As far as warmth was concerned, the suit passed the test. However, since Ludwig once served in the Austrian militia, he patterned the suit after that worn in his native Austria. I looked more like a German officer than an American airman. Greg took to calling me *the Keiser.* Others in the squadron poked fun at me. I didn't care. I was warm, and that is all that counted.

As soon as our advanced training ended, the entire squadron packed up and headed for France aboard the troop ship *Arcadia.*

When General Pershing arrived in France, thousands of Frenchmen turned out to greet him. In contrast, when we marched down the gangplank in Amand at 2:00 A.M., two chippies, their bully, and a mangy mongrel welcomed us. The dog even had the audacity to yelp at us.

Once we reached the dock, we were hustled into Fiat trucks and transported some fifty miles inland to our permanent base near St. Itta.

The following morning Major Thomson delivered a speech about our commitment to fight and destroy the Hun as soon as possible. He promptly sent ten Camels soaring into the sky to seek out and destroy the enemy.

I was not one of the pilots called to arms. Of course the snub upset me. But I reasoned that there would be other occasions. In the meantime, I was assigned to standby duty, which meant that if an emergency arose, I would be summoned.

Along with Greg and Eddie Wilks, I drifted over to the Mess Hall to drink a cup of coffee and grab a smoke. No sooner had we finished our coffee and Fatimas, when Corporal Sanders burst into the building. "There's a couple of Gotha bombers headed for Paris, and you guys gotta intercept them … pronto," he said, flailing his hands wildly.

"Coming," I said, and tossed my butt away.

Excited, we raced out the door and across the field. In the distance, I spied three khaki-colored Camels. With our heads slung back and our legs pumping, we dashed across the grass. I was the first to reach my ship and climb aboard. As soon as I seated myself in my wicker chair, I glanced at the mechanic below me. "Contact!" I screamed. The mechanic nodded and swung the propeller. Immediately, the rotary engine roared to life. As I adjusted my goggles, a plume of gray exhaust swept past the cockpit. I coughed. The engine screamed louder. The odor of castor oil filled the cockpit. Dust covered the nearest mechanic. I checked the panel and then waved to the mechanics. They quickly pulled the chocks away. Someone gave me the thumbs up signal. I responded. Two other mechanics released the wings and tail. I nonchalantly flipped the blip switch. The spinning propeller blew dust into my mouth. Cautiously I taxied onto the cinder runway. Pushing the throttle up, the Camel raced down the runway and leaped into the sky.

When I craned my neck, I noticed that Greg and Eddie were right behind me. "In my first taste of action, I get to defend Paris," I said to myself above the din of the engine. "Wait until the folks back home hear about this."

Since there were only three of us, we formed up into a three-bird flight. Ten minutes out of St. Itta, Eddie's engine began to cough and ping. Two minutes later he began to lose altitude and speed. The only action a pilot can take in such a situation is to return to base. And that's exactly what Eddie did.

Greg and I climbed to fifteen thousand feet. No sign of any enemy craft. When we reached seventeen thousand feet, I spotted one Gotha bomber directly below us. I signaled to Greg. He nodded. Calmly I dove at the lumbering bomber. Greg followed.

Diving out of the sun, the rear gunner spotted us when we dropped to sixteen thousand feet. "Wait until you're closer to fire," I said to myself. I closed upon the bomber, my jaw set. The frigid wind lashed my face unmercifully. The guy wires shrieked. On I dove.

Pop! Pop! Pop! Bullets raced past my head. *Pop! Pop! Pop!* Flexing my fingers, I waited. Ahead I noted the German gunner's frightened features. He shook his right fist at me. Apparently his machinegun had jammed, for he was pounding it with his left fist.

I zeroed in on the hapless gunner. *Rat-a-tat-tat! Rat-a-tat-tat!* My volley struck the man in the chest. Blood gushed from his mouth. He grabbed at his tunic and then slumped forward. *Rat-a-tat-tat!*

Whr-r-r-r bawled my engine. *Whr-r-r-r!* I settled in behind the Gotha. Sweat poured down my face and felt refreshing.

I knew that the gunner in the front cockpit would soon man the rear machine gun. I waited. When he appeared, I squeezed off several rounds. *Rat-a-tat-tat-tat!* The second gunner simply collapsed and dropped out of sight.

Rat-a-tat-tat! Rat-atat-tat! Smoke snaked out of the front cockpit. Flames lapped the wings. Down plunged the bomber end over end. Mesmerized, I watched it descend until it crashed in a fireball.

Glancing around for Greg, I spied him off in the distance. He dove at the Gotha as soon as I dove. But I didn't recall seeing him fire. Perhaps his guns jammed, and so he broke off contact and headed for home.

Since the Camel had sufficient fuel, I decided to search for the other bombers. Corporal Sanders had mentioned that there were several bombers headed for Paris. I only encountered one. Were there other bombers lurking about? I didn't know, but I decided to scout around the area. I pushed upon the throttle and climbed to seventeen thousand feet. There was no activity in the vicinity. All was very serene.

Satisfied that the second or third Gotha bombers had headed for home, I set a course for home myself.

As soon as I landed, I reported to the Squad Room to be debriefed. A beaming Major Thomson rushed up and shook my hand. "Good hunting, Paul," he said and handed me a piece of canvas with a Maltese cross painted upon it.

"What's this?" I asked and studied the frayed canvas.

"That confirms your kill. Some doughboy cut it off the bomber and sent it back here."

"I don't know what to say."

"You don't have to say anything. By the way, we bagged two Fokkers, but we lost Rogers."

"I'm sorry to hear that." Bruce Rogers and I were bunkmates back at Camp Carson, which now seemed as if it had been a long time ago.

"Where's Burns?"

About then I realized that I had not seen Greg. "I don't know. He dove with me, and then he disappeared. I believe that his machine guns jammed, and so he decided to head home."

. I saw a concerned expression grip the major's long, lumpy face. "He should have returned by now."

Suddenly the roar of an airplane engine filled the air. We all rushed outside and scanned the sky. Out of the eastern sky a lonely Camel appeared. In addition to listing, it approached the field at too high a speed. "Go around again," I shouted to Greg. "You're coming in too fast."

"Maybe he can't slow down," said Major Thomson. "Corporal Sanders, get a meat wagon and a fire engine out to the field pronto."

"Gottcha," cried Sanders as he turned and trotted away.

It was apparent that Greg was not himself. Despite his speed, he was going to land come hell or high water. In all honesty, he gained more speed as he cleared the tree tops and descended.

Out of a hangar sped the fire truck. Over the hill raced the ambulance. We all glanced at each other and then chased after the ambulance.

"Keep her steady!" I screamed and watched Greg touch down, promptly rise, and hover about for several seconds. He then corkscrewed the Camel into the turf as if it were a bottle of wine.

The ambulance arrived first. And then the fire truck. We all got there just as the ambulance driver and his assistant were stepping over the struts and a severed wing to get at Greg.

"How's he look?" called Major Thomson.

"He's alive," said the taller ambulance driver, "but I don't think he's gonna make it."

While someone set the litter upon the ground, the drivers freed Greg and lifted him from the cockpit. "Mo, what do we do with his leg?" asked the shorter driver.

"Leave it. He ain't got no use for it no more."

As soon as Greg was secured inside the ambulance, the vehicle rumbled past us and headed for the hospital.

The following morning we engaged the Hun once more. Bradley and Kunkle went west, meaning that they died in action. Lenny Davis was also shot down in no-man's land but rescued by a horde of doughboys.

That afternoon we took to the skies again. Our ten Camels pounced upon six Fokkers. We lost Anthony Webster. They lost two ships.

Two days later we jumped a gaggle of Rumplers flying at two thousand feet. Major Thomson bagged his fifth Hun, making him an Ace. I got my second confirmed victory.

When we returned to the base there was more good news awaiting us. Greg was out of danger. And though he lost his left leg, he would make a total recovery. I requested permission to take a train into Paris to see him. Major Thomson immediately granted my request.

When I asked for directions to the hospital, Corporal Sanders informed me that the hospital was down the street from the train station. Actually the station was across the street from the hospital.

Dodging traffic, I dashed across the street, bounded up three steps, and entered the brownstone building. From the number of students' desks on display, I suspected that the hospital was a school prior to the onset of the war.

Gazing around the crowded corridor, I wondered if I would have any difficulty finding Greg. I didn't. At once I spotted him in a bed directly across from a lavatory. I guessed that the wards were so crowded with casualties that there was simply no room for him in any of the rooms.

"Paul," shouted Greg as soon as he spied me. "How are you doing?" Though battered and bruised, he appeared to be in good spirits.

"I'm fine. The major and everybody else sends their best wishes." I reached into my pocket and retrieved the Maltese cross from the bomber. "Here's a souvenir from that bomber we chased the other day."

"Cripes! You didn't hafta do that."

"Paul!" called a sweet-sounding feminine voice behind me.

When I turned, my eyes widened. My mouth went dry. The hackle hairs on my neck rose. "Elizabeth Ma--a-a-adison!" I stammered as if a schoolboy. "W-what are you doing here in Paris?"

Elizabeth struck an erotic pose in her Red Cross Volunteer uniform. "I'm helping to win the war … ugh … just like you."

Elizabeth and I were classmates back at the Tioga Conservatory. She was an accomplished actress and a gifted singer. I believe that Elizabeth starred in all the theatrical productions Tioga staged during our years at the school. Many men vied to win Elizabeth's heart. But as I recall, she gave her heart to Malcom Bloomstein of the Bloomstein Cosmetics fortune.

Remembering that they were engaged during our senior year, my eyes immediately sought out her left hand and ring finger. No engagement ring. No wedding ring. No ring of any sort. Hoping to conceal my obvious delight, I lowered my eyes to her shiny boots and casually raised them gaze upon her starched collar and lastly her finely chiseled face.

Elizabeth smiled coyly. "I couldn't help but notice that you spent an awfully long time scrutinizing my left hand." She raised her left hand and spread her fingers. "See. No ring of any sort. I'm as free as a bird."

"I -- I wasn't checking out your hand."

"Yes, you were." Her blue eyes twinkled mischievously. "Liar! Liar! Pants on fire."

I reddened. "Well, maybe I was ... a little."

Elizabeth inched closer to me, her brows arched. "Are you married to Lucy?"

"No, we parted." The scent of her jasmine perfume aroused me. "Hmmm ... she married someone else."

"Malcom and I separated soon after graduation." She folded her arms across her chest and tapped her foot upon the floor like a drummer keeping the beat. "I found him in a compromising situation with another woman ... er ... one night. And that was it for Malcom Bloomstein." She pointed to Greg. "Now ... how do you know Greg here?"

"We're in the same squadron." When I glanced over at Greg, I could see from the dreamy expression upon his face that he was in love with Elizabeth as so many other men had been. "And I came down to Paris to see him."

"Wasn't that nice. Same old thoughtful Paul."

Just then there arose a clattering of wheels upon the marble floor. The din grew louder and louder until an orderly appeared before us with a wheelchair. "Monsieur, iss time vee go to see zee doctor."

"Already," said Greg, sounding despondent. "My friend just got here."

"No, vee ... mus' go now. Zee doctor vait for you."

"I'll be back to see you again," I said and assisted the orderly in seating Greg in the wheelchair. We then shook hands before the orderly whisked Greg away.

"In five minutes my shift is over," said Elizabeth. "Would you like to take a walk and get something to eat?"

"I'd love that."

Within three minutes I was strolling down the street with Elizabeth on my arm. Since I had never been to Paris, I allowed Elizabeth to show me the sights. And she did.

Though it was a cold, blustery December day, we trudged up one boulevard and down another. We didn't get to see the Eiffel Tower because of time. But we did end the day with a fine meal at Chez Robespierre, a very fine restaurant near the train station.

No sooner had I purchased my train ticket when the approaching train whistled in the distance.

"Thank you for a great time," I said, looking into Elizabeth's sparkling, emerald eyes.

"Thank you," she said.

"Oh, what the hell!" I swept her up into my arms and kissed her tenderly. She sighed and ground her body against mine. I then kissed her passionately.

"Wow!" She clasped her hands around my neck. "That was some smooch."

"I'm sorry ... ehh ... that I got carried away."

"Don't be sorry." She closed her eyes and inched closer if that were possible. I kissed her again, more passionately than the first time. "Hon, write to me when you get back."

"I shall write to you tonight."

"If I don't see you for a while ... there's a Christmas dance at the hospital."

"It's a date."

"I'll be waiting for you under the mistletoe."

"Wild horses couldn't keep me away." I kissed her again. We finally parted, and I boarded the train back to the base.

I was smitten by Elizabeth Madison. And now as I sat back and watched the telephone poles scoot past, I knew that my life would never be the same.

As soon as I reached the barracks, I sat down and wrote to Elizabeth, telling her that I loved her more than anything in the world.

The following morning I ate a hearty breakfast of Spam and powdered eggs before I attended the usual briefing. "Today, men, we're going to destroy the submarine pens," said Major Thomson, and an hour later the entire squadron took to the air.

Ten minutes out of St. Itta, Bertie Faircraft and Frank Lymaster turned back when their Camels began to run roughly.

Outside of Millette, the archie (anti-aircraft flak) grew intense. *Whump-whump-whump* screamed each shell. My Camel bucked as high explosives burst around me. Shrapnel tore into the Camel's skin. To my right Andy Michelson's ship caught fire and exploded in the sky.

Above a dozen or so Fokkers dove at us out of the sun. Major Thomson climbed up to meet them. We all followed.

I fingered my throttle and headed straight for an oncoming Fokker. The Hun approached quickly. *Ping! Ping! Ping!* The Fokker's bullets whizzed past. Get a little closer," I said to myself and did.

When I was fifty yards from the Fokker, I squeezed off a burst. *Rat-a-tat-tat! Rat-a-tat-tat!* The volley struck the pilot. His ship turned over and flamed.

I climbed and then dove upon the tail of another Fokker. *Rat-a-tat-tat! Rat-a-atat-tat!* I was sure that I had hit the Hun, but he somehow managed to climb into a cloud. I followed.

Out of the cloud, I sped. I looked around for the Fokker. He was nowhere to be seen. To my right, I spotted another Fokker heading for home. I gave chase. For some unknown reason, he had no idea that I was tailing him. I closed quickly. He still was unaware of my presence and took no evasive action.

"Don't be too anxious, Paul" I set my jaw and pursued. Finally, when I was within spitting distance of the Fokker, I opened up with a short burst. *Rat-a-tat-tat! Rat-a-tat-tat!* The Fokker suddenly caught fire and exploded before me. Ducking, I flew through the carnage. The dismembered Hun hurtled past. Then the propeller. And finally the remnants of the fuselage.

I craned my neck to the right and then to the left. In the far distance, I spied tiny specks chasing each other. But in the immediate area, the sky was empty. I was the sole occupant of the air space.

I checked my gauges. My fuel was low. It shouldn't have been. But it was. I decided to head for home and banked the ship.

When I glanced at the fuel gage again, I noticed that it was nearly empty. I was deeply concerned. I wondered if shrapnel had hit the fuel line or the tank. I grew anxious. I knew that I was flying over enemy territory. And if I went down, it was all over.

"Don't panic, Paul. Stay calm." Perhaps I could magically nurse the Camel back to friendly lines. Seconds later the engine coughed and went dead. I flipped the blip switch *off* and *on*. Nothing. "No Christmas dance with Elizabeth for me. Damn!"

I decided to glide to earth and so eased back on the stick. The Camel soared through the sky as if a large bird. When I glanced over the side, I noticed that the terrain below seemed somewhat flat. That was ideal for a forced landing. In one last-ditch effort, I tried to restart the engine. No luck. The fuel tank was certainly empty.

Looking upon the bright side, I figured that if I landed with an empty tank, there would be less chance of a fire. That was good. I might be killed by the impact, but I wouldn't burn to death.

When I peeked over the side again, I saw the distinct features of the immediate area. I braced for a rough landing. "Easy, Paul. You can land this thing." I crossed myself and uttered a prayer. I didn't want to hit the ground with my nose. And I didn't. The Camel belly flopped, tilling a sizeable amount of verdant land.

As soon as the Camel came to a rest, I tore off my seat belt, grabbed my survival kit, and jumped out of the cockpit. If I harbored any thoughts about escaping back to my base, reality quickly set in. Over in the distance, a black automobile screeched to a stop, and a German soldier jumped out with a rifle poised at me. In the woods behind me, a group of soldiers appeared and ran toward me. "Oh, nuts! Prison camp, here I come." I lit a cigarette, drew a puff or two, and tossed the butt into the cockpit. Within seconds, the wicker seat caught fire. And by the time the first soldier confronted me, the Camel was engulfed in flames.

"*Kamerad,*" shouted the pocked-faced soldier, gesturing with his rifle.

"Yea! Yea! Yea!" I exclaimed and handed over my Colt pistol. "I surrender." Raising my hands above my head, I walked toward the automobile.

When the corporal nodded, I opened the door and slid inside beside a German captain. "I am Captain Karl Mittenbaum," said the German in perfect English. "From zee expression on your face, you are amazed dat I speak English so goot."

"Yes, I am."

"Vell, I live in New York for many years un vork at Macy's … ehh … before zee var." The captain promptly tapped the corporal upon the shoulder. "*Wir gehen.*" The driver engaged the clutch, and the Opel crawled away at a snail's pace before bouncing along the pitted road.

"Where am I?"

"Ahhh … so. Vee are in Belgien. Not so far from zee Hollanisch border."

"I see." My face must have expressed concern for my safety, for Captain Mittenbaum offered me a cigarette, which I accepted. "Ughhh … what happens to me now?"

"After vee eat goot lunch … errr … of *gesdhnetzeltes* un *jagertee,* you go to St. Quentin."

"Would you please be so kind as to send a note over to my base … ugh … to tell them that I'm safe."

"Yes, of course."

Satisfied that my immediate fate was firmly sealed, I sat back and relaxed as best I could. In a few minutes I heard a distinct sound. Very low initially. But then it grew louder. It was the squeal of an engine. A Camel engine. I slouched as best I could. And then the roar of the Camel's engine thundered in my ears. *Rat-a-tat-tat! Rat-a-tat-tat-tat! R-r-r-rat-a-tat-tat!* The bullets raced up the hood of the Opel. It tore the windshield into shards, it hammered the driver and the captain into bloody masses of pulp.

Neither man knew what struck him. I braced myself and hoped for the best. The Opel took flight and soared through the air. *Thump!* It nose dived into a gulley.

"Damn! That was close." Stunned, I sat on the floor of the auto for a full minute before I regained my senses. "Gotta get the hell out of here." When I tried to open the door, it was jammed. Marshaling all my strength, I kicked at the door and pried it open. Once I crawled outside, I brushed myself off and breathed a sigh of relief. With the exception of the hum of one of the spinning wheels, all was silent. I lifted my eyes toward the sky. "Thank you, dear Lord."

I realized that I had to evacuate the area at once. But I also knew that I needed to take along anything that might aid me. Growing bolder, I examined the inside of the Opel. The glove compartment yielded several maps. I stuffed them into my pocket. On the seat, I saw a sack of some sort. When I examined it, I discovered two sandwiches, an apple, and a flask. I pried off the cap and sipped. "Booze!" I also pocketed the flask. "My pistol. Gotta have it." I found my Colt on the floor next to the captain's service cap. Naturally, I confiscated both.

Glancing about the brush, I saw nothing but an emaciated fox. Nodding to the fox, I climbed up the steep bank and set out for the Netherlands. I walked on for about a mile when I spotted the burned-out hulk of a tank. Famished and tired and in need of a cigarette, I crawled inside the tank and sat against the wall. I immediately inspected my surroundings and noted some French words written upon the brown walls. In high school and at the conservatory, I studied German. No French. And so I had no idea what the writing said. As for the brown walls, they weren't really brown. They were blood stains from the former inhabitants -- probably French.

Back in flight school, a flight instructor informed us that if we found ourselves behind enemy lines, our primary goal was to return to our unit, regardless of the distance. Under no circumstance were we to engage the enemy. And no sabotage.

I whispered another prayer and then treated myself to a sandwich and the apple. I didn't touch the liquor. I might need that later.

Next, I emptied the contents of my survival kit upon the floor: a pocket knife, a compass, French money, some beef jerky, gum, matches, a pencil, clean socks, and a map.

While it was still light, I needed to study and memorize the map. I guessed that I was somewhere between Trudo and Colette. If I traveled northeast, I should cross into the Netherlands.

I sat back and thought about my trek through Belgium. I suddenly recalled that Captain Gumpert, the Intelligence Officer, said that we should stay off the roads and only travel at night. I decided that he knew best. I was still a free man, and I wished to remain free. No German prison camp for me. With about an hour or two before darkness set in, I stretched out and closed my eyes. Within minutes, I was fast asleep.

About two hours later, I awakened. It was pitch-dark outside. A biting wind whistled through the tank. "Well, Paul, you better get going." Before gathering my things, I muttered a prayer. "Dear Lord, take care of me."

I crawled out of the tank as I had entered and glanced into the sky. "Good night for a walk," I said, noticing that the heavens were crowded with stars. In addition to the compass, I could use the stars to find my way.

"Stay off the road, Paul." And I did. I stayed in the gully, which may have been a dried-up creek and traveled north. With the exception for the sighing wind, I heard nothing. No explosions. No voices. No animals howling.

And for a long time, I saw nothing. Then I spotted two figures approaching. At once I dropped to the ground and concealed myself in the gully. The men paused. I hugged the ground and prayed.

"*Es kalt,*" said one of the soldiers.

"*Hmph,*" said the other soldier.

"Der *wind konnte mir die ohren wegblasen.*"

"Ja."

They continued on. Twigs snapped. Frozen thistle crackled. And then my index finger popped when one of the soldiers tread squarely upon my extended hand. At that second, excruciating pain exploded inside my brain. I ground my teeth. I prayed. But I lay as still as humanly possible.

After what seemed like an eternity, the soldier lifted his boot from my hand and walked on with his companion. I lay there for several minutes, not risking detection.

Finally I sat up and examined my hand. My three fingers and thumb pointed north, which was normal. However, my index finger pointed east. That was not good.

Searching about in my pocket, I found the pencil, put it into my mouth,and bit down upon it. I then took my free hand, grasped the damaged index finger, and bent it back into place. Tears welled in my eyes. When I flexed the injured hand, I no longer felt a throbbing pain. I had actually set my own finger into place. Right then and there, I wondered if a musical career was out of the question for me. Wincing, I took the flask from my pocket and sipped. The liquor soothed me somewhat. I then sat for another five minutes before I resumed my journey.

I walked all night. At about three o'clock, I decided to begin searching for somewhere to rest for the day. And at four o'clock, I spied a barn silhouetted against the sky. Since it was still dark, I headed for the barn, sure that no one had spotted me.

As soon as I pushed the barn door open, it creaked. A cow lowed in one of the three stalls. With my night vision at its best, I surveyed my surroundings. "One cow in the far stall," I said offhandedly. "No other farm animals." I searched about, looking for straw. "A little straw in that stall. Not enough to hide in." I raised my eyes and lo and behold -- the mother lode. The entire second floor was filled with straw.

Surreptitiously, I climbed a narrow ladder to the second landing. I realized that once the sun rose, my movements would be severely restricted. Living in a rural setting back in Pennsylvania, I knew that sooner or later the farmer or his wife would happen into the barn to feed the cow and perform other chores.

Any activity, such as eating, had to be accomplished before daylight. I sought the far end of the loft, where I figured the farmer had no need to visit because of the abundance of straw in the forefront.

I squatted and ate ravenously. The thick-pork-sausage sandwich filled my stomach beyond expectation. And, of course, I washed it all down with the *schnaps*.

Just as I was about to burrow into the straw, I heard the barn door creak. I cocked my ear and listened. Whoever it was, slipped into the barn as quietly as I had done. However, the ever-alert cow greeted the interloper as it had me.

I shifted my position and sat in the very corner, where I commanded a view of anyone who reached the landing. After some thought, I decided that the nocturnal visitor could not be the farmer. It was much too early to begin his farm chores. I also dismissed the thought that the caller was a German soldier. The Germans occupied the country and had no need to slink about at such an ungodly hour. The only reasonable solution, therefore, was that the visitor was an American soldier on the lam as I was.

The intruder coughed and promptly spat upon the dirt floor. He then investigated his surroundings as I had done so recently. Arriving at the same conclusion as I had, he found the ladder and ascended to the hay loft.

Whereas I had quickly and quietly climbed the ladder, this man struggled mightily to clamber up the rungs. And when he reached the loft, he wheezed and coughed. "Damn gas," he whispered, confirming his identity as an American soldier.

"Who's there?" I asked, giving notice of my presence. "Identify yourself."

"M-m-my ... w-w-word ... another Yank." The man coughed. "Sergeant ... Homer ... Reynolds."

"T-the ... recruiter?"

"Y-yes." He coughed again. "How ... do ... you ... know ... me?"

"I'm Lieutenant Paul Stefanski of Tioga. You married Lucy Logan."

"Ahh ... yes. Lucy ... was ... your ... girlfriend."

"Yes, she was."

"I'm ... sorry ... about ... that."

"That's history. I have a new girlfriend." Though Elizabeth and I hadn't really discussed our relationship, I didn't think she'd object to being called my girlfriend. Besides ... it made me sound as if I were a real hustler. "What are you doing here?"

"Got ... gassed ... three ... days ... ago and ... taken ... prisoner."

"And you escaped?"

"Yes."

"How do you feel?"

"Lousy." Reynolds crawled closer to me. "Eyes ... water. Chest ... pain. Headaches."

"Hungry?"

"Haven't ... eaten ... since ... my ... capture."

Reaching into my pocket, I retrieved some beef jerky and the *schnaps*. "Here's some food and drink."

When Reynolds reached out for the food, I placed it in his hand and found it cold to the touch. I wondered if the clammy skin was a result of the frigid temperature outside or his gassing by the Huns.

"Do ... you ... have ... a plan?" he asked between bites of the beef jerky.

"We stay up here until it gets dark tonight. Then we make our way to the Netherlands."

"Good ... plan." I heard him drink heartily and wipe his mouth on his sleeve.

"Now ... if you don't mind, I'm going to burrow into the straw and go to sleep. If anyone comes up here, I don't want to be spotted."

"I'm ... gonna ... do ... the same."

Without another word, I dug deeply into the straw, relaxed, and fell asleep.

I had no idea how long I slept initially. But since I was not a sound sleeper, I heard the barn door open once. And on that occasion, the cow mooed loudly. Hours later, I awoke and reflected upon the preceding day's events. Like Reynolds, I had been taken prisoner and escaped. But unlike my companion, I hadn't been gassed.

Eventually I grew restless and crawled out of the straw. Judging from the shadow cast upon the near wall, I guessed that it was midday. When I glanced over to where Reynolds lay, I noticed nothing unusual and assumed that he was fast asleep under the straw.

Below the cow lowed once more. I took his mooing as a sign of someone approaching the barn. At once I scurried back to my refuge in the straw. And not a second too soon. Seconds later, someone entered the barn, fed the cow, and departed.

Though the afternoon dragged by, neither Reynolds nor I quit our hideout. When I finally poked my head out of the straw, it was very dark. "Sergeant," I whispered, crawling over to his area.

"I'm ... here," called Reynolds, peeking out from his concealment. By degrees he surfaced like a frog from its winter hibernation and brushed away the straw.

"Let's go."

"Right."

I descended the ladder first. Reynolds followed. The cow mooed and swished his tail when I walked across the room and clutched the doorknob. Cautiously, I opened the door and peeked out into a foggy, damp evening.

"Excellent time for a stroll."

"Y-yes."

Without another word, I pulled upon my collar, led the way down the pitted lane, and headed north for the Netherlands.

Having rested for many hours, I experienced no difficulty marching along the narrow lane, which lead to a forest. Reynolds, however, lagged behind from the very beginning of our journey. When the path grew steeper and the temperature dropped several degrees, he coughed and gasped for air.

I had no recourse but to slow my pace considerably and rest more often. My strategy immediately agreed with Reynolds's constitution. His coughing subsided. His breathing improved. But most important of all, he was able to keep pace.

According to the map, I had studied earlier in the day, Waltrude, a small town, dating back to the Middle Ages, would appear on our right within the hour. It didn't. Even after I allowed for the revision in our timetable, the hamlet didn't materialize.

I didn't panic. I was deeply concerned, though, because I didn't know where we were.

Reynolds must have sensed my anxiety, for he hastened his step and caught up to me. "Lost?" he asked, sounding casual.

"I don't know. We should have passed a small town a while ago, but I sure as hell didn't see any signs of a village."

"D-don't … w- worry … about … it." He slapped me across the back good naturedly. "Go … w-with … your … instinct. Everything … will … fall … into … place."

And so it did. Just ahead of us the fog lifted. And ten minutes later, we spied the village of Waltrude.

Back at Camp Carson, a veteran pilot informed me that if I ever found myself behind enemy lines, I should avoid passing through any settlement. "Go around it," he said. Naturally we bypassed the village.

A short distance later, Reynolds lagged behind once more. I decided to rest. But when we resumed our journey, he walked for only a short distance before he collapsed.

"Leave … me," he begged. "I … can't … go … no … more."

"Like hell," I said and sat down next to him.

"I'm … holding … y-you … b-back."

"Nonsense!" Rising, I prayed for physical strength and fortitude to continue our journey. "Let's go, Homer."

"I … can't."

When I extended my hand, he took it. I slowly pulled him to his feet and slung him over my shoulder. "We're a team, and we're going to make it to the Netherlands together."

I guessed that it was quite a distance for me to carry the sergeant. But, what the hell, I was young and in excellent health.

After a while, it seemed as if Reynolds had grown lighter. Buoyed by the fact that we were moving in the right direction once more, I trudged on in silence. Our objective was the Netherlands, and with God's help, we would reach it and become free men.

About twenty minutes later, I thought that I saw a yellow light flicker on the horizon. I was certain that the Dutch border was not that close. And the map I had studied earlier showed no settlement of any sort in the vicinity.

Was the light a mirage? Perhaps, it was. I inhaled the fresh, frigid air and tramped on.

"Homer, how are you doing?"

When Sergeant Reynolds said nothing, I knew that he had dropped off to sleep.

Up ahead the light disappeared. I was sure that it was, in fact, a figment of my imagination.

On we trekked. And then it began to flurry. Big, white flakes fell like goose feathers from heaven. Under any other circumstances, I would have taken the piccolo into my hands and played a Christmas carol. However, the possibility of a German patrol lurking about made it unsafe.

25

"There it is again," I said to Reynolds when the light appeared again. And then, to my surprise, a second light appeared. And a third. "That's no mirage. There's something up ahead." I quickened my pace. "Maybe it's the border."

As I staggered onward, I beheld some sort of a building with a cross protruding from a steeple. "It's a church." Back in the eighth grade at St. John's School, Sister Mary Irene told us about each Catholic church offering sanctuary to anyone who needed a safe haven from danger. Hell, Reynolds and I sure were in need of a safe place to rest. I would enter the church and request sanctuary for my companion and myself. The priest had no alternative but to grant our petition. "Hang on, Homer."

When we approached the site, I noticed that more lights flickered. I also discovered that there was more than one building. Several buildings were situated around the main church. "I think we happened upon some kind of abbey," I said to myself.

I paused and gazed up at the sign next to the massive wooden door. *Abbaye de St. Piatus* said the sign in Gothic script. With Reynolds becoming heavier as I mounted the three steps to the door, the pain in my muscles and back intensified.

While grasping Reynolds with my left hand, I rapped upon the door several times with my right hand. Nothing. I waited, and then I rapped again -- harder. After several seconds, I detected the sound of approaching feet.

The Judas hole slowly opened in the heavy paneled door. Two large, black eyes peered out from under a monk's cowl. "Holy man, we are two American soldiers fleeing the Germans," I said. "Please ... assist us."

Instantly, the cumbersome door squeaked open, and the diminutive porter waved us into the foyer. While I set Reynolds down, the monk held up a gnarled finger. He then turned and disappeared down the dark corridor.

Before I could unbutton my coat, the monk appeared with a tall, robust associate. "Velcome, my son," said the man with a distinctive French accent. "I am Francois Redon, zee abbot of zee monastery." He bowed piously.

"It's an honor to meet you," I said.

"You friend iss ill? Yes." The abbot glanced at Reynolds and then knelt to check his pulse.

"He was gassed by the Germans several days ago."

"He no sleep. He iss dead."

"Dead!" I screwed up my face in disbelief. "He can't be. We're going to the Netherlands together."

"No, Lieutenant, he iss dead." Abbot François kindly made the sign of the cross and patted Reynolds upon the head. "You go wid me … tonight … to zee border. Him … errr … vee bury in zee cemetery outside … umph … tomorrow."

"Tonight … we're heading to the Netherlands?"

"Yes, you un me." Abbot Francois rose and smiled warmly. "Iss … how you say … goot night to cross border. Iss snowing … und … zee guard be cold un tired."

"What ever you say."

After a hardy bowl of lentil soup, crusty, black bread, and a cup of scalding coffee, Abbot Francois and I slipped out a side door and headed for the border.

With our heads bowed against the howling wind and the drifting snow, we walked parallel to a frozen river and past the wreckage of a German field ambulance. Once we reached a stand of mature fir trees, Abbot Francois held up his hand and then pointed to a silouhette on the horizon. "Zee guard no see us here." He then reached into a sack and produced several wrapped items and a bottle. "Cheese un bread un beer … eh … for zee guard." He then handed me the sack. "You stay here un no go no place until zee guard un me go to his shack to eat and drink." He extended his hand, and I shook it firmly. "Den you walk across zee field un climb up zee bank un you be safe."

"Thank you for everything."

"Merry Christmas un go wid God."

And while Abbot François walked silently toward the German guard, I held my breath and watched from behind the stoutest tree available. Within no time the abbot reached the guard, who, from all appearances, knew him. After conversing for several minutes, both men walked away. I watched until they disappeared. And only then did I emerge from my concealment and stroll toward the Dutch border.

When I reached the exact spot where Abbot François encountered the guard, I paused and looked to my right. I spotted the guard shack approximately a hundred yards away. A light suddenly showed in the night, and two figures bobbed on the shade.

With sack in hand, I walked steadily, never glancing back. In time the snow ceased, the wind died down, and a cluster of stars twinkled as if sapphires in the night sky.

On I marched for another hour. I guessed that I was now safely inside the Netherlands, but I had seen no sign of man or beast. And then there arose before me a gigantic ground-sailer windmill. I stopped and doffed my cap to that magnificent structure.

I was finally safe from the Germans. Furthermore, I would spend Christmas with Elizabeth at the dance. And in all reality, I would probably never fly in combat again. Since I had been a Prisoner of War and had escaped from the Germans with the help of Abbot François, I was, according to General Billy Mitchell's directive, grounded for the duration of the conflict. General Mitchell reasoned that if a repatriated pilot flew in combat and was captured again by the Germans, he might be tortured to reveal the names and places of those partisans who had assisted in his escape.

I guessed that I would be dispatched to Toulan or be assigned a desk job in Paris. If I had my druthers, I would accept the position in Paris, where I could see Elizabeth every night.

The Judge

After almost four years of studies at Montauk College in Portage, I looked forward to student teaching at the local high school. However, since the Portage Junior and Senior High School only needed two student teachers, I found myself assigned to the West Moreland School District, which was fifty miles north of Portage.

Immediately, panic set in. I had no means of commuting between Portage and West Moreland on a daily basis. Professor Hinkle, the head of the student teaching assignments, however, came to my rescue. He contacted the principal at West Moreland High School and explained my situation to him.

The principal, a Mr. Jordan, explained to Professor Hinkle that there were several citizens in the community who were quite willing to let a room or even an apartment to a student teacher at a reasonable rate.

As a matter of fact, he knew of a local judge who had contacted him earlier that morning concerning a newly renovated bedroom in his spacious Victorian mansion.

And so my dilemma was satisfactorily resolved. The following day I sent my trunk ahead by train. I followed three days later by bus.

West Moreland was a tiny hamlet nestled in the mountains between Grayhall and Cambry. During the Civil War, many homes in the area served as stations or safe houses for slaves escaping to Canada.

My initial impression of the tree-lined streets, which surrounded the main square, was positive in every respect. I was even more impressed with the judge's Victorian mansion, which displayed an historical marker on the spacious front lawn. This marker designated the house as being on the National Register of Historic Places.

The judge and his wife treated me as if I were a member of the family from the very first moment I set foot inside the spacious foyer.

As for the student teaching assignment, it could not have been more enjoyable. I spent the initial nine weeks in the junior high school wing. I then packed up my books and sashayed around the corner to the senior high school area.

Much to my delight, I found the senior high school experience even more enjoyable. In all honesty, the last nine weeks passed all too quickly.

On the morning of my last day of student teaching, the judge's wife flew down to Tampa to see the new grandson. The judge was supposed to go too. Supposedly something came up in court. I don't know what it was.

Since I enjoyed teaching so immensely, I dawdled in the building as long as possible, savoring my memories. I only departed when Lucy Hospidor, another student teacher, stopped by and literally dragged me out of the school and down the street to grab a bite to eat with several other student teachers. Over burgers and fries, we rehashed our student-teaching experiences, exchanged our home addresses, and finally parted. It was well after six o'clock when I strolled up the path to the mansion.

As soon as I entered the house, I heard the judge humming some old show tune in his office down the hall. "Have a good time, Susan?" he called in a very friendly voice.

"Yes, I did," I said, feeling warm all over from the one and only whiskey sour I had ever drunk. "Good night." With my last semester of college concluded, I needed to pack my things in order to leave for home the following morning.

"Don't go." As I headed for the stairs, the judge, a tall, portly man with a slanting forehead, approached me with two glasses in his hands. "Here's to your successful career as a teacher." He held out a glass to me. "I never like to drink alone." He smiled in a fatherly fashion, revealing his new dentures. "And since you're not a drinker, I made you a sloe gin."

Growing warmer, I unbuttoned my coat. "I don't know ... ehh ... I already had my first ever whiskey sour tonight."

"Here ... try this." I could see in his cobalt eyes that he was lonely and sought company.

I shrugged my shoulders. "Oh, why not." I accepted the glass and sipped. The cool liquor tasted delicious. "If I get a bit loopy, I don't have far to go to bed." I drank more and felt very relaxed.

"Take your coat off. It's pretty warm in here."

"Yes, it is, isn't it?" I set my drink down, removed my coat, and dropped it on the sofa. "Have you heard from Eva?"

"Yes, I have." At once he collected my coat and hung it in the closet. He then crossed the room and drew the drapes. "She's having a good time." After retrieving my drink and handing it to me, he latched onto my upper arm and rolled his head toward his office. Down the hall, we walked. My spiked heels thundered upon the hardwood floor. His slippers shuffled along silently.

"You're right. This is good." Inside his spacious office, I glanced about at the plaques on the walls. All honored him for his judicial service and civic work in the community. "I can see why Eva and the kids are so proud of you."

"I'm just trying to be an honest judge and a good neighbor ... err ... to those who ... uhmm ... are less fortunate than I am." He took a scrapbook from a drawer and nodded for me to take a seat.

As I paged through the book, I grew hotter. "Why am I so

warm?" I paused and fanned myself with my open palm.

"Maybe you're feeling the effects of the Mickey Finn I put into your drink."

"Y-y-you ... w-what?" I knew what a Mickey Finn was. Sitting up, I realized that the sooner I got out of that room the better off I'd be. But when I tried to rise from the armchair, the entire room spun. And when I plopped myself back down, the room grew darker.

"Ever hear of Trierotate?"

"N-n-no." When I tried to speak, my throat grew parched.

"It's a drug used as a sedative."

"Ohhh!" Again I tried to rise. But I couldn't. My legs felt cramped. My feet were too heavy to move.

"I happened to get some from a friend of mine." The judge stood over me, reached down, and took me by the hands. "Up you go." With his assistance, I rose and stood unsteadily. "Trierotate is also used as a date rape drug."

"An' ... you're gonna rape ... me?"

"Not yet." Taking me by the arm once more and squeezing it, he escorted me across the room. "But I'm going to have my way with you after I snap some pictures of you in the buff." He removed a book from a shelf and pressed a concealed button. Suddenly, the book shelf moved, and a secret entrance appeared.

"Gonna ... un ... dress me?" Though I had been drugged, I understood what the term rape meant. "P-p-please ... don't ... hurt ... me." I began to sob. "R-rape me ... an' ... an' I'll tell ... the cops."

"Tell the police." He chuckled. Nobody's going to take your word over mine." He tapped his chest repeatedly. "I'm a Common Pleas judge." He cruelly twisted my arms behind my back and exerted pressure. Excruciating pain immediately coursed through my body. I yelped in agony. He merely applied more pressure as he frog-marched me down a dimly lit corridor and into a secret room. "You know ... you've not only got bedroom eyes, but you've got a hot little body. Been waitin' to strip you and check your oil ever since I met you."

"Oh ... my ... word!" I exclaimed when he switched on the lights, and I noticed that I was inside some sort of dungeon. "Ahhh!" Against the far wall stood a forlorn army cot. It was the same kind of cot I had slept in at Girls Scout camp. And immediately before us stood the largest wall mirror I had ever seen.

The judge pointed to my image in the mirror. "When I look into the mirror, I see the reigning Miss Lincoln County." He shoved me closer to the glass. "She's dressed to the nines in a very tight, seductive dress. Know what?"

I shook my head.

31

"There's not an ounce of fat on her body. Doesn't she look ravishing?"

"Yu-u-um," I said, trying to say the word *yes*.

"Well, we have to make her look and feel more comfortable by undressing her." Cackling like a hen, he tugged at the sleeves of my dress and slid them off my shoulders. "Now sit down and be a good little girl so I can take your picture."

Without waiting for my response, he lowered me to a stool and pulled the hem of my dress up to my thighs. I decided that once he turned his back, I would rearrange my dress. And so I did with great effort.

The judge soon found the camera he needed and returned to face me. When he noticed that I had rearranged my dress, the vein in his neck bulged. Without warning, he slapped my face. "That's for lowering your dress." He drew closer until his jaundiced face was only inches from mine. "You are no longer a beauty queen. You're now a common slave and have no rights as a person. You will do as I command." He hiked my dress up once more. This time to my panties. "Touch the dress again, and I shall punish you more severely." He seized my bare shoulders and shook me. "Understand?"

"Yuuum," I said, now aware that in addition to slurring my words, my voice had deteriorated to a mere whisper.

"The first picture I want is with you fully clothed."

"Yuu-uh."

With my dress hiked up past my garter belt and my hands folded in my lap, I sat while he stood and snapped several pictures of me from different angles. "Now ... some cheesecake."

"Uhhh!" Though I had led a sheltered life, I knew what cheesecake was.

Setting his camera aside, the judge dropped, with great effort, to his knees and gazed into my face. He smiled once more — demonically. He then unclasped one of my stockings from the garter belt and rolled the hose seductively down my leg. "Nice legs." He paused to study my face for a reaction. "Let's take the nylons off your gorgeous legs." I watched as he rolled a nylon stocking down my thigh, over my knee, and down to my ankle. He then unhinged the mate and repeated the procedure. "Now the spiked heels. You're a small-town girl, and small-town girls like to traipse around barefoot, don't they?"

"Nuuu!" I decided to kick out with all my strength. Something, however, told me that the judge would certainly retaliate. And so I decided that being barefoot wasn't the worst thing in the world. "M-m-m-m!"

He glanced up and stroked my thigh. "Does that mean that you don't want to be barefoot?'"

"'"Yu-u-u-u!"

"You really don't have any say in the matter. Besides ... I'm dying to see you in the nude. And I can't boff you with your clothes on."

"Uuuuuhhh!"

The judge took the four-inch stiletto heels into his hands and tugged. I scrunched my toes in order to keep my shoes on my feet. However, in the end, the shoes slipped off my feet like butter off a cob of corn. Carefully he set my heels aside. "Now ... those pesky nylons. Roughly, he seized one of the nylons and slipped it over my heel and off my icy-cold toes. He promptly took the stocking in both of his massive hands and stretched it beyond use. "Let's get the other nylon off."

"Nuuuu!"

"You do like being barefoot, don't you, you little slut." Using both hands, he quickly pulled the hosiery off my other foot. "Taa-daa!" He held up the gauzy stocking before he tossed it aside. "More pictures."

"Nuuuu!"

"Now ... I want a real close-up of those beautiful legs."

"Mmmmm!"

"Lift your feet ... err ... so that only your toes touch the floor." The judge arranged my feet so that my heels left the floor. He then snapped away once or twice. "Now ... the dress comes off." He jerked me to my feet, pulled down the zipper, and tugged upon the hem. Up, up, and up my dress rose as if a window shade. He paused momentarily once it reached my frilly bra. And then he yanked it over my head, leaving me clad in my undergarments. "My, my, my! Look at you." After tossing my dress onto the floor, he seated me once more upon the stool.

"Uhhhhrrr!" I could feel my face redden and hoped that suddenly the door of the dungeon would burst open, and I would be spared further humiliation. But since I was a slave in captivity, as the judge explained, my shining knight never appeared.

"Just one or two pictures in your undies, and then ... well ... we'll strip you down to your birthday suit." He knelt down upon the floor and snapped away ... once ... twice ... three times. "That's enough." He rubbed his hands together gleefully. "Now let's get those knockers out in the open."

"Uhhhh!" Though I was now twenty-one, I had experienced sex only once. And, since neither of us knew what we were doing, it was not enjoyable.

With a sadistic smile etched upon his face, he reached down, grasped my hair, and pulled. "Up!" When I was slow to rise, he smacked me across the face once more. "Up, damn it!" I rose, but he still smacked me again – harder. He then pulled me closer and whacked my *derriere*. "Discipline!" Taking my shoulders, he spun me around like a top. "That's what you need." Reaching behind my back, he teasingly played with the clasp before he unhinged my bra. Of course, the garment fell away immediately. My large breasts sprang forth and jiggled as if Jell-O on a spoon. Embarrassed, I sobbed. He slapped my breasts several times. I wobbled. He promptly cuffed my breasts again, leaving the imprint of his hand. I screamed. But no sound came out of my mouth. The Trierotate apparently worked as it was intended. He slapped me again. Reaching down, he rolled my panties over my buttocks. They slid past my thighs and puddled around my ankles. "Damn nice!" Though gooseflesh appeared on my arms, I stood stark still like a scarecrow in a farmer's field.

I mouthed a few words of anger and hate and objection. But nothing came out. For all intents and purposes, I was mute and would be until the drug wore off.

"You got one hell of a body, Skyclad," he said as he turned me around and around. Hearing the word *Skyclad*, I turned my head and arched my brows inquisitively. "Don't look at me like that." Tousling my hair, he studied me in the mirror. And then he mussed it up some more. "Susan Gale no longer exists. You're now Skyclad. It's a Wiccan name ... uhmm ... means *in the nude*." He now turned his attention to my jutting breasts and fondled them. "And you certainly are in the nude."

I wondered if he would now rape me as he boasted. However, he decided that he wanted more pictures of me in the buff. One of the walls was painted white. And against that white backdrop, he sat me upon the floor. After drawing my knees up to my chest and placing a kepi upon my head, he promptly snapped the initial picture. More hats and pictures followed. All in various poses. Finally when he snapped a picture of me lying upon my back with my legs perpendicular and my toes crooked like a bishop's staff, the picture session ended.

"The night is still young, Skyclad, and you have much to learn." He ushered me across the room to the cot and forced me to recline upon my back. He then tied my hands to the rail above my head. "That'll keep you." He stepped back and studied me. "With your hands above your head, those big boobs of yours really stand out." Though restrained, my hands did not hurt. "We gotta do something with your feet." He sounded as if he were searching for a remedy. But we both knew damn well what he was about to do. Within seconds he tied my feet to the top of the other bed rail. That posture hurt. I also discovered that it took great effort to simply crook my toes, wiggle my buttocks, and twitch my fingers.

All of a sudden, I realized that with the exception of my breathing, there was no other sound in the chamber. Since I could raise my head, I did so and searched about for the judge.

Several minutes passed in perfect silence. And then the door to the dungeon creaked open. I arched my head. Craned my neck a mite. But saw nothing. Then a sound of rolling wheels arose. The wheels abruptly stopped, and the judge appeared. If the muscles in my face had not been numbed by the drug, I would have chortled. As it was, I could only stare. Before me stood the judge in an outlandish costume — bare, flabby chest, tights, slippers, and a black mask such as worn by the Lone Ranger. I guessed that he was dressed as some sort of medieval dungeon keeper.

Once more the wheels clattered. Being a normal human being, my curiosity was piqued. I turned my head. There next to me stood a mannequin atop a wagon. My eyes bulged in their sockets. The mannequin wore my dress and shoes. I blinked in disbelief. Its mask was the exact likeness of my face, including the tiny scar above my eye. My jaw slackened.

"Beautiful ... isn't she, Skyclad?" The judge stroked the mannequin's blonde curls. "Meet Susan." He promptly positioned the mannequin on the other side of the dungeon. "I am Liderc, your jailor ... your master ... and your executioner."

"Trierotate has afflicted you with aphonia ... ugh ... which is the temporary loss of your voice." He took an ostrich feather from a nearby shelf and brandished it as if it were a saber. "Trierotate also relaxes the muscles ... er ... makes the body hypersensitive to touch."

"We shall now continue your training as my sex slave." With a fiendish smirk on his lips and sweat beaded upon his large, bald head, he drew the feather across my armpit. Of course, I screamed. But the only sound emitted was a faint groan. He proceeded to tickle my upper lip. In response, I tossed my head from side to side. He then traced the feather across my breasts. Up and down went the feather. Very methodically. My mouth fell open, my fingers grasped at the air. But up and down traveled the feather. "You're very beautiful, especially when aroused." When I glanced down at my feet, my large breasts hid them. On and on the feather journeyed. Across my stomach. Over my thighs. Between my toes. Up my soles. I closed my eyes as the sweat rolled down my armpits and onto the paper-thin mattress. And then the judge tired of his sport.

I guessed that he was about to rape me. And I was correct. Wheezing, he staggered towards the cot and untied the nylon stocking around my feet. He then spread my legs. I whispered a prayer and awaited his assault. As he crawled between my legs, I glanced up and decided that he was the most hideous creature I had ever known. His putty-colored stomach fell over his sash and shook uncontrollably. I let out a sob and peeked at his hairless chest, which was covered with warts and boils. I cringed in disgust. His breathing sounded like a locomotive. "Lift your feet." Once more I did as commanded and waited. When he reached into his tights and fumbled about, I shuddered. "Ohhhh … my … God!" I closed my eyes as he sought his tool. "M-m-mercy!" I watched, horrified, as he raised his arms to the ceiling, threw back his enormous head, and mumbled incoherently in a foreign tongue. Arching my body, I threw him off balance. Or so I thought. He suddenly breached like a whale, and thrashed violently at the air with his pudgy fingers. I watched, my mouth ajar. His cavernous mouth trembled. His eyeballs rolled to the back of his head. His heart thumped audibly. And then he vomited and collapsed upon me. "Ahhhh!" I kicked his legs with my toes. "Up! Get up!" He only smothered me more. "Get … off!" Vomit slithered out of his mouth and onto my stomach. I heaved a sigh and kicked again. When he failed to move after my latest kick, I realized that he was dead. "The creep had a heart attack and died on top of me." The stench from the vomit was revolting. "Help! Someone … help." I cocked my ear. Dead silence. I realized that no one could hear me because the house was empty. "Think, Susan! Think."

Again I kicked with my feet in an attempt to dislodge him. And again I failed. While his torso was firmly lodged between my legs, his face reclined upon my breasts. I kicked again with all my strength. And with the same results. I decided that these were drastic times, and drastic measures were needed.

"Don't panic, Susan." I needed to evaluate my situation in great detail. Within moments I decided that the judge was dead weight in more ways than one. And secondly, I could not dislodge him with a kick or two. He was far too heavy. Thirdly, though my mind raced. I could devise no immediate plan. I screwed up my face and knew that I needed a miracle – immediately.

My hands were immobilized above my head. My feet, though free, were of little help. Now I knew how a frog felt when pinned to a dissection table. In frustration I wiggled my sweaty buttocks. The springs groaned under the weight. I squirmed again with more effort. The springs responded with more enthusiasm. I suddenly remembered Ann Novak and Girl Scout camp. Little Ann, somewhat of a hellion, constantly used her bed as a trampoline. She spent hours jumping on her cot. If Ann could cavort on her cot, why couldn't I do the same? For

36

the first time since my captivity, I saw a flicker of light at the end of a long, dark tunnel.

"You'll have to get rid of him rather quickly because your strength will wane after a few attempts," I said to my smelly armpits. I inhaled and filled my lungs with the fetid air. "Here ... goes." Marshaling all my strength, I planted my buttocks firmly upon the mattress and rocked slowly. The springs squeaked like a litter of hungry pigs. The judge's head moved slightly. His bulbous nose landed directly upon the right breast. "It hurt, but at least he moved." With my spirits buoyed, I increased my gyrations. Nothing. No further movement by the judge. "Damn!" I lifted my feet and prodded him. Still nothing. "Dear God, please help me." I continued to perspire like a ripening cheese. On I rocked. "Move!" Feeling my strength ebb, I kicked him in disgust. Ever so slightly he listed to the right. I uttered another prayer. This time to St. Jude (the patron saint of hopeless cases). No more movement. Well, I reasoned, it may take some time for God to assess my predicament and answer my prayer. But, in my situation, time was not my ally.

Perhaps it was the incessant pitching of the springs or the rank odor hovering about the cot or the heat from my body. I didn't know what it was. But I knew that something was stirring on the cot beside me. "Ouch!" There was something nipping at my ankle. Lowering my eyes, I spied a small, flat, oval blood-sucking bed bug marching toward my calf. "Shoo-o-o!" The bed bug paused. And then another and another paraded across my black sole. "Scra-a-a-am!"

Again I reflected upon my stay at the Girl Scout camp and the bed bug infestation. Though all the cots were infected with bed bugs, the vermin seemed to enjoy my blood best of all. I had suffered some twenty bites, resulting in severe rashes upon my legs and feet.

I needed no further incentive. "Bed bugs ... be ... gone!" As a light-brown bug led a platoon of comrades toward my inner thighs, I bounced my buttocks and my upper torso as well as I could. *Umph* shrieked the springs. "Kee-e-ep ... going." The undulation angered the bugs. Ten more poured out of the mattress. Another squad goose-stepped over my foot. "Shooo!" I heaved myself time and again. The springs squawked angrily. On I bounced. And finally the judge moved another iota. I lowered my right leg and kicked with the left. He swayed. I breathed deeply, raised my left foot, and dug my toes into his ribs. "Go-o-o pervert!" I felt my face turn hot and crimson. I kicked again. He slouched like a catcher blocking a pitch in the dirt. And then – and then miraculously, he crashed to the floor in a heap.

I sighed expansively and thanked the Lord. My celebration was short lived. Another legion of bugs swarmed out of the mattress and assaulted my feet. "Shooo!" I kicked. I cursed. I wiggled my toes. But on they came, wave after wave. With the judge finally dispatched, I was free to make my stand against the bugs. And so I did. I shimmied with my buttocks toward my bound hands. "Here goes." I raised my feet and repeatedly stomped upon the mattress. Angry bugs scattered in every direction. And those, which paused to assess their situation, fell dead to the fury of my dirty, bare feet. I stomped. I tread. I squashed. My feet ultimately turned the tide of the battle. Only one or two of the bugs escaped into the mattress to reorganize their efforts. The vast majority fell prey to my avenging feet.

"Now, Susan, turn your individual attention to your bound hands." I breathed and stretched my neck in the hope that I could rip the nylon with my teeth. No luck. I just couldn't reach the stocking. Letting out a loud sigh, I decided to just sit and think.

After several minutes of serious thought, I arrived at the conclusion that I was a woman with sixteen years of formal education. I knew the capital of every state in the Union. And I could tell you the year William the Conqueror invaded England. I even knew that Eddie Rickenbacker shot down twenty-six planes during World War I.

However, I couldn't preserve fruit or vegetables. Nor could I cook. And I certainly proved, beyond a doubt, that I couldn't defend myself against a mugger.

All my learning was book knowledge. I actually had no practical knowledge or training that was of use in the real world.

Again I tried to untie my hands by undoing the knot that bound me. Again … I failed. "Susan, if you don't free yourself, you're going to starve to death because there's no one in the house to help you. And Eva's not due back from Tampa for another week."

I slumped down upon the cot and sobbed, as had become my habit since my strip to the buff. Closing my eyes, I screamed and beat my feet upon the mattress. I suppose that I had hoped that someone would hear my pleas and come to my assistance. But after several minutes, I still sat alone with my hands bound above my head.

And then I felt a stabbing pain in my hand. "O-o-ouch!" Craning my head, I glanced up at my hands and watched a reddish-brown bed bug feeding upon my hand. "Oweeee!"

Instinctively I somehow managed to put my hands together. Don't tell me how I did it, but I accomplished the unbelievable. At once I remembered that I had been very submissive when the judge bound my wrists. Perhaps my passiveness had been to my advantage. "Relax, Susan." Now that my hands were together, I rotated my right wrist clockwise. "Good! Very … good." I promptly rotated my left wrist counterclockwise. Gently and slowly I slipped my left wrist out of the nylon stocking. "Free-e-e-e!" I had actually freed myself from the restraint. I massaged my sore wrists as I sat up and then vacated the cot.

Glancing down at the judge, I suppressed the urge to kick him with all my strength. In the end, I said a prayer for his soul and stepped over his prostrate body.

I decided that I would leave the house of torment as soon as I physically could. Quickly I stripped the mannequin of my shoes, dress, and mask. I also collected my nylons from the cot. With my clothing in hand, I left the area as I had found it and climbed the winding stairs to my room.

Since I had sent most of my belongings home by trunk, earlier in the week, I had only a few articles to pack into my suitcase. But before I could take my leave from the house, I needed to shower and dress in warm, traveling clothes.

At a few minutes after nine o'clock, with my suitcase in hand, I found myself walking briskly up Main Street to the bus station. I had no idea if there were any buses leaving town so late. However, much to my delight, a bus departed for home in ten minutes. And fifteen minutes later, I boarded an Algonquin bus and was headed home for Christmas.

Poppa's Chest

On August 18, 1939, *The Wizard of Oz* premiered, and on that day Dorothy and Toto returned to Kansas, the Tin Woodman received a heart, the Cowardly Lion gained courage, the Scarecrow acquired his brains, and my mother gave me life.

I was born at 8:30 P. M. to Mr. and Mrs. Hans Himmelreich at their home on Henne Court, which was across the street from Gruber's Dairy. Many people at that time were delivered at home. Poppa told Momma that they were too poor to have their son delivered in the hospital, where according to Poppa only the rich people could afford to bear their children.

Momma agreed with Poppa that I would be born at home. Poppa also told Momma that there was no money for a doctor. However, if she desired Krueger, the old crone, to deliver her baby, Poppa might be able to afford the fifty cents that Krueger charged for her services as midwife.

Momma again agreed with Poppa. And, come to think of it, I don't ever recall an occasion when she didn't agree with his wishes. That's how Momma was reared -- servile obedience to the husband without question. It was the manner in which her mother was reared and her mother before that.

While Momma was born in this country, Poppa came to America from the old country to make his fortune. But, to tell you the truth, all our lives we lived near or below the poverty level.

When Poppa arrived in New Hannover, he spoke no English, possessed no trade, and knew no one. Luckily, when he came to town, he met old Ludwig Yoder, who offered Poppa room and board for a dollar a week.

The meals were prepared by Ludwig's sixteen-year-old daughter. She also laundered the clothes and cleaned the house. Ludwig, an illiterate man with a keen appetite for liquor, lost his left arm as a boy in an hunting accident. With such a profound impairment, it was difficult for him to secure employment or even learn a trade. Therefore, he bought a horse, a rickety wagon, and set himself up as an entrepreneur. From sunrise to sunset, for six days a week, he would patrol the alleys of New Hannover, collecting old newspapers, discarded clothing, and anything else he could lift onto his wagon. Later he would sell his junk at Wegmann's Junk Yard -- three cents for a pound of paper, two cents for a pound of rags, and six cents for a pound of scrap metal.

"R-r-r-a-a-a-gs ... pa-a-a-a-puh ... r-r-r-rags," Ludwig sang, pausing to spit a mouthful of tobacco juice upon the cobblestones, turning them a glistening brown.

When Poppa couldn't find work after several days, and his funds were exhausted, his fortune changed. Ludwig offered him a job as his laborer. He informed Poppa that he was getting too old to lug a cast-iron stove by himself from someone's yard to his wagon and then to Wegmann's scale.

Poppa enjoyed working for Ludwig. In no time, he learned the English language and mastered his job. He also made friends at the local *Bund*, a pro-Nazi organization, with Fritz Wegmann, the owner of the scrap yard. Each night after Helga, the one-eyed horse, was fed, Poppa and Ludwig sat down to a simple meal of scrapple, boiled potatoes, and turnips with Ludwig's daughter. It wasn't that Poppa couldn't have more friends as it was that he enjoyed sitting in the kitchen and watching Ludwig's daughter, a buxom teenager, scrub the dishes, mend the socks, and iron Ludwig's spare shirt.

In time Ludwig detected the interest Poppa showed in his daughter. One night in the beginning of June, when the evening air was as astringent as alcohol, Ludwig called Poppa into the parlor, which was completely furnished with furniture that had been reclaimed from the junk yard.

"Hans, how old yous iss?" asked Ludwig, stuffing a chunk of Red Man tobacco into his crooked mouth.

"Vhy ... uh ... t-tirty f-four," stammered Poppa, arching his bushy eyebrows into triangles.

"Ludwig spat into the coal scuttle, spraying the floor in the process.

"Ah man who so olt ... um ... shoult be marry." Ludwig paused to stroke his unshaven jowls. "Und me see ... er ... how yous vatch ... uhm ... my Gerta." Rising stiffly, he waddled across the room to the china closet, seized a bottle of homemade dandelion whiskey, and poured two drinks into mismatched glasses. "Vood yous ... ehh ... like marry her?"

"Vhy ... vhy I tink so."

"Ahhh! Goo-o-o-t." Ludwig drank and smacked his lips. "Den it be." Smiling broadly, he revealed a solitary gold tooth. "Gerta, come here. Me tells yous goot news."

Two weeks later, while the blue arms of rain reached down from the sky, Momma and Poppa were married. Almost a year to the day, Ludwig died of a massive heart attack. Of course, he left his business to my poppa, the new ragman of New Hannover.

"R-r-racks ... papuh ... r-r-r-a-a-acks," crooned Poppa from atop the perch on his wagon. "S-s-scarup ... me-e-e ... dull."

41

During the Great Depression of the 1930s, many Americans were unemployed, but not Poppa. Although his business fell off because others were competing with him for paper, rags, and scrap iron, he managed to earn enough money to support Momma and himself.

Fritz Wegmann raised the prices he paid to Poppa. A pound of paper rose to four cents; rags jumped to three cents a pound. Scrap iron soared to eight cents a pound.

Fritz also disclosed to Poppa that Japan was buying all the American scrap metal it could purchase. In turn, it was manufacturing tanks, airplanes, bombs, ships, and rifles for a great war that would pit Japan and Germany against the rest of the world.

At heart Poppa was always loyal to the old country. Therefore, it was not difficult for Fritz to convince Poppa that he must become more active in the *Bund*, which held its meetings in the rear of the Bismarck Tavern.

Whenever the *Bund* held a meeting, Poppa quit work early so he could take his weekly bath and attend the gathering on time. Whatever business was conducted at those meetings was held in the strictest of confidence. Poppa never mentioned the organization's activities to Momma, who he considered socially, intellectually, and culturally inferior to himself.

By 1939 the war that Fritz had forecast erupted in Europe. Germany, under Adolph Hitler, was on the march. The Nazi blitzkrieg had already swallowed huge tracts of real estate. And in Poppa's mind, nothing human could stop the *Führer*, as Hitler called himself.

Bund meetings increased from one a month to one a week. Then on August 18, 1939, Fritz sent a personal messenger to our house, informing Poppa of an urgent meeting to be held in Fritz's home that night.

"Me be beck vhen me be beck," called Poppa over his shoulder to Momma as he hurried out the door that night. One hour later Momma experienced her first contractions.

"Eva!" she shouted across the fence to Mrs. Fenstermacher, her neighbor. "I'm going into labor. Get Krueger."

Within ten minutes, Krueger, a roly-poly woman with a purple birthmark in the shape of a toad on her mottled face, arrived, wheezing and perspiring.

"Now, Mrs. Himmelreich, you're gonna be fine," said Krueger, lathering her hands. "I've delivered hundreds of babies. She smiled assuredly and brushed a wisp of graying curls from her emerald eyes. "Where's your husband?"

"H-he's … out," whispered Momma between clenched teeth.

"They're always out when you need them most." Krueger shook

her head as she dried her hands in the dish towel. "Me and you don't need him anyhow." She patted Momma's arm. "You're gonna see."

An hour later Momma gave birth to a baby girl (Poppa wanted a boy) with the aid of Krueger, who was astounded by the birth.

"Missus, I always charge fifty cents for my work, but I don't want no money from you because your baby girl was born with a special gift."

"What?" asked Momma, blinking repeatedly.

"Your little girl was born with a veil on her face." Krueger fingered a mole on her cheek nervously. "It … it ain't no real veil. It's skin that I peeled away." She opened her chapped hand, revealing a handful of fetal membrane. "See! It means that your little girl was kissed by God, and … and because of her veil, she's gonna be a famous person." Krueger slipped the membrane into her pocket. "Your daughter will be able to see the future. Jus' you wait and see."

"Oh, go on." From the tone of Momma's voice, it was obvious that she was proud.

"What are you gonna name her?"

"I … urr … really didn't have a name picked out for a girl. Hans and me had dozens of boys' names picked out, but no girls' names." Momma sat up and sipped some broth from a chipped cup. "How about Ann?"

"That sounds nice, Missus." Krueger pointed a gnarled finger at Momma. "But you mind me, little Ann is gonna be able to tell the future before it ever happens."

When Poppa returned from his meeting, he was quite surprised by my birth since I wasn't expected for another week. He was also overjoyed with the news that Krueger didn't accept her usual fee. "If dat voman no take da money, me puts it in my pocket." Rubbing his hands together gleefully, he snatched the fifty cents from the table and deposited it into his coat pocket. "One more ting. Ve name 'er Nelly."

So instead of being baptized Ann Himmelreich, I was christened Nelly Geli Himmelreich. Where the Geli came from I never learned. But Momma always succumbed to Poppa's wishes in order to keep peace in the home. The baptism was almost canceled when Poppa refused to pay Father Lutz a dollar for the baptismal certificate saying, "Vhy ve pay fer such ting?"

"Because, Hans, the baptismal certificate is printed in old-world script," rejoined the priest diplomatically.

"Hmmmm," grunted Poppa as he reluctantly handed over a dollar to the smiling priest.

On December 11, 1941, the United States declared war on Germany. And on December 12, 1941, Fritz Wegmann was arrested as a Nazi spy by the FBI. That night, under the cover of darkness, Poppa burned his Nazi flag, his picture of Adolph Hitler, and his *Bund* membership card.

I was too young to comprehend the enormity of war, but Momma swore that I predicted the exact date of the Japanese surrender. I think it was all a figment of Momma's over-zealous imagination. As a tot I truly had no idea who the Japanese were, much less the day when they capitulated to the United States.

When the Japanese did surrender, I was too busy contemplating my entry into the first-grade class at St. Boniface Grammar School. Since Momma was Catholic and St. Boniface was only a city block away from our home, it was decided that I would attend the parochial school. Poppa, who said that there was no such thing as God, only agreed that I could attend the Catholic school after Momma assured him that the school taught old-world traditions.

I may not have had any premonition about the Japanese surrender, which ended World War II, but I did have a feeling of foreboding one morning during the last days of Advent.

Prior to the beginning of Advent, Father Lutz visited each of the respective grades and distributed canisters to all of the children. Each can had a picture of the Nativity scene on it, and we were instructed to show our love for Jesus by dropping our spare pennies into the can. Near the end of Advent the cans were to be collected.

Our family was so poor that Poppa hardly had enough money to give Momma to buy food, let alone supply me with extra pennies for my canister. All during Advent I carried grocery bags for the neighbors, putting the pennies they gave me into the canister.

On the morning that we were to give Sister our cans, I ran downstairs to claim mine from atop the kitchen, where I kept it. Much to my surprise, however, my can was empty. A gaping hole existed near the picture of Jesus' head.

"Poppa," I exclaimed, "my money for the baby Jesus is gone."

"Me take it," said Poppa, blowing into his coffee cup. "Priest no need so much money. Priest gots lotsa money."

"Poppa, you stole my money, and ----"

"Vhat!"

Poppa's open hand lashed out, cuffing me across the side of the head, sending red, green, and blue stars shooting to my brain.

I climbed from the floor slowly, said nothing, and ran to the bathroom. Diligently I washed away Poppa's fingerprints from my face. I dawdled as long as I could and hoped to put off the eventual confrontation with Sister Brunnhilde, my teacher.

As soon as we pledged our allegiance to the flag and recited the morning prayers, Sister called on the first student, Otto Herbein, and asked him to produce his can, which he did.

"Very good," she said. With all the gusto of a successful Neanderthal hunter, she slit the can with a bowie knife, poured out the money, and counted it. Her thin lips moved silently, prompting the black hair sprouting from the mole on her chin to bob. "Sixty cents." She dropped the coins into a leather pouch. "God will reward you in heaven, Otto, for your gift." She then noted the amount next to his name and glanced over the top of her horn-rims. "Nelly, bring me your canister."

"Y-yes, Sister," I stammered and reached inside my desk for the empty can. "H-here it is." I placed it on her desk, aware that every eye in the room was focused upon me.

She picked up the canister, suddenly angered by its weight. "What is this, Nelly Himmelreich!" Her face reddened. "You have nothing to sacrifice for Jesus?" A dark-blue vein protruded from her florid forehead and disappeared into her wimple. "Answer me!"

"Ragman's daughter ain't got no money," called Thomas Hartman from the second row.

"Silence!" The faint moustache under Sister's hawked nose quivered. "What kind of a person is it that has not even one penny for Jesus?" She stuck her bony finger into the opening. "You stole the money from Jesus."

"I'm sorry, Sister," I apologized, lowering my eyes and hoping the earth would open and swallow me up for being such a sinful person.

"You must learn that you should give to Jesus that which belongs to Jesus." Taking a ruler from her desk, she approached me. "Put out your hand." Fear like the quick, hot touch of the devil shot through me. Nevertheless, I did as commanded. Within seconds there was a loud hissing sound as the ruler flailed out, cracked me across the bare knuckles, and send slivers of pain racing to my brain for the second time that day. "Now ... go to the front of the room, kneel before the statue of Jesus, and pray for the forgiveness of your sins."

I may have been young, but I quickly learned that life could be intolerable both at home and at school. I vowed that no human would ever humiliate me in such a fashion again.

The following year I devised a strategy that would successfully see me through my remaining years at St. Boniface. When Sister Sieglinde passed out the canisters, I carried mine home and hid it under the kitchen sink with the mouse trap. There it remained empty for the entire Advent season.

Under no circumstances would I be abused again by Poppa or by a nun. However, I also decided that toting heavy shopping bags for several blocks in return for a few pennies was sheer folly and not very profitable. One day before Poppa arrived home from work, I stole down into the basement and counted over eighty-five cast-iron dogs, cats, lions, turtles, squirrels, bears, panthers, and horses. Poppa collected them on his route, repainted them, and sold them on Sundays at Hinkle's Picnic Grounds. If one was missing, he'd never miss it. I decided to claim a dog because he had more dogs than any other animal. Besides I liked dogs. Over the course of a few days I rubbed away the rust as I had seen Poppa do, and I painted it black. Because there was no yellow paint available, I settled upon red eyes. Much to my surprise, I created a dog which looked possessed.

When completely dry, I carried it to school and displayed it to my classmates. Many were delighted with its demonic eyes. Mary Ellen Wartluft, the prettiest girl in the class, offered me a quarter for it on the spot. I declined her offer because I had a more creative idea. During recess, I announced that I would chance off the dog. Each chance cost one penny. Word of my scheme spread throughout the school. In a few days I sold over three-hundred chances. On the Friday before Christmas the drawing was held, and Felix Hottenstodt's number was selected. I wasn't particularly happy that he won because Felix was one of the boys who always called me *Rags*, but business was business.

On the day that the cans were due, I thoughtfully deposited fifty pennies into the canister and presented it to Sister Sieglinde.

In addition to satisfying my Advent obligation, I had, for the first time in my life, money to buy milk during recess. For the next ten weeks I drank heartily. With each swig, I wondered which of Poppa's animals would be next to fall prey to my paint brush.

I realized that if Poppa had ever discovered my enterprising scheme, I would have received the thrashing of my life. However, these were desperate times, calling for derring-do heroics on my part. Each year until I reached the sixth grade, I repeated my escapade.

Prior to the beginning of sixth grade, rumors surfaced among my classmates to the effect that they were growing weary of purchasing tickets for my cast-iron lawn ornaments. When the rumors persisted in September, I knew that I needed another promotional gimmick. But when Thanksgiving arrived and I had conceived no new idea, panic arose. Dejectedly I plopped myself upon a chair and pored through a comic book that Poppa had found in an abandoned house. There on the rear cover was my salvation. It was a full-page advertisement promoting Dr. Zinkoff's Magic Hemorrhoid Salve. I had no idea what a hemorrhoid salve was, but Dr. Zinkoff declared that any person who sold one case of his ointment would receive a gold-plated necklace.

I immediately ordered a case of ointment and sold it in its entirety within a week. I didn't realize that so many people suffered discomfort in the rectum. Old Mr. Wentzel, the church sexton, bought three jars on the spot.

The second case took longer to sell. But in two weeks I sold its contents. Ten days after my last sale, I received the necklace and an authentic Gene Autry cap pistol and holster from Dr. Zinkoff.

I now had two prizes for my game of chance, and both items were received with enthusiasm. My classmates, paying five cents for each chance, supported my project to the tune of five dollars.

Of course, I couldn't neglect the primary purpose behind my venture. And so on the morning my canister was due, I stuffed fifty-six pennies inside. That left me enough money to buy Poppa a box of handkerchiefs for Christmas and Momma a box of chocolates.

Dr. Zinkoff served me well for two more years, enabling me to fill my canister and also purchase Christmas presents for my parents.

After eight years at St. Boniface, I graduated and prepared to enter the local high school. I wanted to attend St. Jude's, the Catholic high school, but tuition cost ten dollars, and I knew we were too poor to raise the money.

Sister Espronce, my eighth-grade teacher, and Father Lutz knew of my predicament. One day during the summer Father Lutz called me into the rectory and informed me that Joe Hussman, the druggist, needed a girl to help stock the shelves, sweep the floor, and occasionally dip a cone of ice cream for one of his customers.

Since Father Lutz had dealt previously with Poppa, he stipulated that I would have to attend St. Jude's in order to maintain the job at Hussman's. Initially Poppa balked at the papist terms. When I brought home ten dollars the first week and gave it all to him, he quickly reconsidered his untenable position.

When I turned sixteen, Mr. Hussman promoted me to full-time waitress. That move allowed me to triple my wages and still remain in school. Poppa, however, decided that I should quit school and work full time because then I could earn more money. Both Momma and I pleaded with him to no avail. He marched me into the principal's office and withdrew me from school, much to my displeasure. Though I was a good student, I knew that our family was too poor to send me to college. But I had always hoped to graduate from high school.

"Now ve gets job at factory," said Poppa, waving my withdrawal papers high in the air. "Ve gets lots pay."

Finding a good-paying job was not as easy as Poppa thought it would be. Eventually, I found myself laboring as a feather plucker at Angstadt's Chicken Farm. I earned forty dollars a week, which elated Poppa. But unlike the drugstore, where Mr. Hussman exacted no taxes from my wages, I carried home less money from Angstadt's than I had earned at the drugstore. Less money saddened Poppa.

In addition, I now had to pay Amy Zigenfuss, a girl I worked with at the plant, fifty cents each week for a ride to work. After a week Amy, seeing how poor I was, reduced the fare to twenty-five cents. I never said anything to Poppa about Amy's kindness because I knew that he would never let me keep the extra quarter.

I decided to save my quarters and buy something beautiful for Christmas for my parents. I truly had no idea what I would purchase. But on the Saturday after Thanksgiving as Momma and I were walking into the business district, Momma stopped in her tracks and said, "Look, Nelly, at that beautiful Christmas tree. It's artificial, and it's made from aluminum."

There in the store window rose up to the ceiling a shiny, aluminum Christmas tree. As multicolored panes rotated around a spotlight, it changed its color.

At once I knew what I would purchase with the money I had saved from my carfare ---- an aluminum Christmas tree. And as the weeks passed, my savings increased.

Since we were so poor, Poppa never allowed me any spending money, but I had almost enough money for the tree. One night, as I was sitting on my bed counting my quarters, Poppa burst into my room. His red eyes bulged at the sight of my quarters.

"Vhat!" he screeched. "Mo-o-o-o-oney! Vhere dat money cum from?" His thin nostrils flared in anger as he approached the bed. His fist doubled. "Yous ... yous steal from me."

"N-no, Poppa, no," I stuttered, ducking his punch but falling backwards. Striking my head on the radiator, I slumped to the floor like a rag doll.

I had no idea how long I lay on the floor, but when I regained consciousness, Poppa and my quarters were both gone. Staggering to my feet, I grasped the bed post to keep the room from spinning. My head throbbed. Light flashed before my right eye, erasing a portion of the image. I inhaled slowly. After taking one step, I collapsed upon the bed. Only when the neighbors' rooster crowed the following morning, did I awake.

I knew that I couldn't tell Momma what had happened. She might believe that Poppa had tried to hit me, but she'd turn away, lower her eyes, and mutter, "Poppa is always right. We must do as Poppa wishes under his roof."

I must have looked peaked because Amy's jaw dropped when she saw me. "Holy cow!" she said. "What happened to you?"

"I ... uh ... slipped in the bathroom and hit my head," I explained, hoping that I spoke convincingly. Closing my eyes, I breathed deeply, wishing that those little particles would stop floating before my eye.

"You'll be fine," she said, chomping on her Dentyne just like one of Farmer Moll's cows chewed its cud.

I knew that she was correct. I'd be fine in a day or two. But three days later the headaches intensified. And those pesky little creatures kept floating in front of my eye, too.

The pain interfered with my work. Since I was the best worker on the line, Mr. Angstadt, the owner, grew concerned. Against my strongest complaints, he drove me home before the shift ended. I expected him to tell me that I was fired. But he escorted me to the stoop, rapped on the door, and waited for Momma to answer.

When Momma opened the door and spied me in the company of a stranger, her forehead knit in agitation. Mr. Angstadt, a true gentleman, tipped his fedora. "Mrs. Himmelreich, I'm Joseph Angstadt, the owner of the place where your daughter works." He took me under the arm and led me into the house. At once his firm jaw slackened at the sight of the primitive décor, which Grandpa Yoder had collected to furnish the house. "I don't make a habit of bringing one of my employees home, but your daughter is my best worker." He cleared his throat and stared at the springs protruding from the sofa. "The girl has a bad bump on her head, and her vision is blurred." When he turned and pointed to the bruise on my scalp, I detected a glint of pity in his eyes for our predicament. "She has to see a doctor and bring me a note which states that she's fit to work." He turned to me and smiled warmly. "When she's feeling better, her job will be waiting for her." Reaching into his vest, he produced a business card. "Here is the name of my personal physician. I want you to call Dr. Watkins for an appointment." His gray eyes narrowed. "I'm going to telephone him later to ask if you made an appointment."

Since Poppa had always commanded Momma in such a fashion, she knew no other way. As soon as Mr. Angstadt departed, she telephoned Dr. Watkins from a neighbor's house. And within an hour, we were sitting in the doctor's office. My head still thumped, but the tiny particles were now dive-bombing at some distant target instead of merely floating.

Dr. Watkins, a sword-thin man, ushered us into his office, examined the contusion, and shined a light into my eyes. "Uh-huh," he said softly each time I winced. "Look straight ahead, Nelly." I didn't think there were so many ways to examine an eye, but he seemed to know them all.

When Dr. Watkins concluded his examination, my head still throbbed. But the particles in my eye had settled down to simply floating once more. ""Doctor, what's wrong?" I asked.

"Young lady, you have a slight concussion that will go away." He pulled his mouth in at the corners. "I'm not worried about the bruise. What I'm concerned about is the retina in your eye is separating from the choroid and the sclera." Drumming his fingers on the desk, he studied me. "If we don't operate soon, the retina will detach. Sight will be lost."

"I'm gonna be blind." Tears welled in my eyes.

"Doctor, how much does such an operation cost?" asked Momma, wringing her fingers.

"It's expensive, but cost is a minor concern," said the doctor, sighing. "If the operation isn't performed, Nelly will lose her sight."

Momma nodded. "We are very poor, but I will talk it over with my husband." Biting her lip, Momma swallowed hard.

"It has to be done. Worry about the money after the operation."

It was the Christmas season and should have been the happiest of time. Instead, I was extremely depressed. First, I had been forced to quit school. And to compound matters, there was now a distinct possibility that I would lose sight in my eye through no fault of my own.

"Humbug," I whispered as we trudged home. Passing Bender's department store, where the aluminum Christmas tree shimmered in the light, I felt the chill of the salty tears stream down my face. I knew darn well that we were too poor to pay for an operation of such magnitude. Besides, Poppa would never comprehend the urgency of the situation. When we reached the corner of Haley Street, I watched a platoon of wind-blown leaves, dry to the stem, disregard the traffic light and scurry across the intersection like a colony of penguins en route to the ocean. For no logical reason I hated those leaves for being so carefree.

By the time we reached our home, I was no longer angry at those leaves. But I did curse the life that fate had dealt me. As soon as we crossed under the transom I knew that Poppa was home, judging from the scent of musty paper, oily rags, and cheap whiskey. Poppa professed that the latter kept him warm and soothed his rheumatism.

I had never been able to predict the future as Krueger had announced I would, but I knew that Poppa would never approve of the eye surgery because of our poverty. True to form, Poppa's first word echoed throughout the dreary parlor, "Vhy yous need two eye?" He flailed at the drafty air with his fist like a madman. "Me knows men in var got no eye. Dem still live." He ran a greasy hand through his sparse, graying hair. "Yous no need two eye."

Poppa squinted and staggered towards me with menacing, yellow eyes. His unsure gait prompted me to touch the bruise on my head and recall how I had incurred his wrath over a handful of quarters. When he spied the fright in my eyes, he guffawed and backed off. As usual there was no support from Momma. Silently I retreated to the safety of the kitchen. Heaving a deep, long sigh, I resigned myself to a life with one eye.

With Dr. Watkins's note in hand, I returned to work. I had to admit that the headaches disappeared as he predicted. The eye was an altogether different problem though. The light flashes persisted. And gradually I experienced more loss of image. It was scary, but I had no recourse other to lose total sight in the eye.

On the anniversary of the bombing of Pearl Harbor, Mr. Angstadt gathered all of the workers around him and spoke of the supreme sacrifice that so many people endured during the recent war in order for us to live in a free, democratic country. I reflected upon his words, and suddenly my personal problems seemed minuscule.

After work Amy drove me as far as Elm Street, leaving me a distance of two blocks to walk in sub-frigid weather. In my current state of mind, the bone-chilling cold failed to dampen my spirits. As I tramped past Ziegler's Grocery Store, I noticed a sleek, black Buick parked next to our house. I wondered who the caller was.

Quickening my pace, I slid across a patch of ice in the alley. "Nelly, you'd better get home," called Mrs. Hinkel, craning her head out the door. From behind her curtained windows, she saw everything that occurred on the block. "The doctor man has been in your house for a long time."

Perspiration trickled down my temples despite the numbing cold as I trotted past the sedan. Onto the stoop I bounded just as Dr. Watkins brushed past me, tugging at the collar of his topcoat. "Your father had a severe heart attack. He's not good," said the doctor, protecting his fedora against the arctic blast that bowled over several garbage cans. I nodded as the contents of the garbage cans blew past his automobile and up the street.

Throwing open the door, I darted upstairs, skipping every other step. I only paused when I reached the bedroom, which reeked of a mixture of Ben-Gay and cigarette smoke.

Momma, her eyes red and swollen, stood by the bureau, dabbing her nose with a worn handkerchief. Poppa lay in the iron bed that once belonged to Grandpa Yoder. Poppa's chest heaved as his eyes followed me.

"Me ... die, Nelly," he whispered, his nicotine-stained fingers trembling.

"No!" cried Momma, clutching the bedpost.

"Gerta, bring ... chest," instructed Poppa. With great effort, he reached under his pillow for a key.

"What chest?" asked Momma, who seemed puzzled by the request.

"In ... closet." Poppa raised himself to a seating position and pointed across the room to the only closet in the room. His finger quivered like a palm frond in a breeze.

Momma tiptoed across the room to the closet, parted the curtain, and rummaged through a pile of rags on the floor. Finally, she spied a small chest. With some difficulty she lifted the chest and dropped it onto the bed, jouncing Poppa in the process.

Slowly, with deliberate care, Poppa slipped the key into the lock. *Tha-a-a-li-I-ip!* The lid popped up, startling Momma and me.

Our eyes bulged as Poppa slid his hand over the contents ---- piles of crisp one-hundred-dollar bills. "Money," said Poppa. "Money from vork. Fif-f-f-fy ... sousand." He caressed the notes tenderly. "Vhen me die ... put money ... in coffin, Gerta, vit ... me."

"Yes, Hans," said Momma as obedient as ever.

"What!" I shouted. "We've been living like beggars all these years because you've been too cheap to give us a decent life." I felt the hairs on my neck rise. My cheeks smoldered with anger. "You steal a couple of quarters from me, and ... and almost kill me ... while you're hoarding fifty grand."

"Me ... money," he shouted, stuffing the money inside his tattered shirt.

"Hans, I promise that I will put the money in your coffin," said Momma calmly.

Momma gently tried to usher me out of the room. Not to be denied, I dove onto the bed. "I want to keep my eyesight, that's all."

"Me ... die ... vit money," Poppa shouted and then fell back against his pillow ---- dead.

Even though Poppa didn't believe in God, Monsignor Lutz agreed to conduct a graveyard service for Momma's sake, which she deeply appreciated.

Friends, neighbors, and distant relatives accompanied us to the parish cemetery as a hard wind knifed lungs and tingled bare skin. The church bell tolled solemnly as the coffin, the cheapest rough box at the funeral parlor, which was all Momma could afford, was borne from the hearse to the grave by six stout men.

Momma, bundled in a black coat that Poppa had resurrected from the junkyard, stared blankly at the coffin while Monsignor Lutz blessed the casket and mumbled something about ashes to ashes and dust to dust.

I cried profusely, prompting Momma to embrace my shoulder.

When the coffin was lowered into the grave, I dove after it, hearing some of the mourners console me about being a good daughter. Of course, they didn't realize that fifty grand was being earmarked for a worm farm.

I returned to work on Christmas Eve, saddened by Poppa's greed, which had done none of us any good. The plant shut down after lunch for a party, which Mr. Angstadt always threw for his employees.

I was particularly relieved that we quit early because the light flashes had been incessant that day. But I was sure that more of my vision hadn't been stolen.

Instead of attending the party, I pulled on my coat, thrust my hands deeply into my pockets, which were two holes, and ducked under the mistletoe and out into the fading day.

Since I had no money for bus fare, I walked briskly. Occasionally I bowed my head against a wind as cold and as vicious as syrup. On several street corners Salvation Army personnel stood, shifting their weight from one foot to another in order to stay warm. I felt bad about not depositing a penny into the box, but I was destitute.

When I reached Sticker's Hardware Store, a howling wind rushed around the corner with snow on its breath. It stalked me and blew beneath my skirt. By the time I reached our stoop, the snow had created a sonata in winter white.

Dusting myself off, I pushed open the door. Much to my surprise ---- there guarding the center of the parlor was the aluminum Christmas tree in all its splendor. Beneath its silver branches were piled Christmas packages addressed to Momma and me.

"Momma, what's the meaning of this?" I asked, my ears still numb from the flesh-cutting snow.

"It's Christmas, and I want you to enjoy it because I contacted Dr. Watkins." Momma clasped her hands with excitement. "And ... and he's going to fix your eye the day after Christmas ...so that you can go back to school after the holidays."

"Momma, you didn't." I threw my arms around her. "Where did we suddenly get the money for a tree and the operation and for all the presents?"

"On your poppa's deathbed I promised him that I would bury him with his money, and I kept that *last* promise to him." Momma smiled and breathed deeply. "After I picked out his coffin, I came back home, took all the money, and carried it to the bank. I then had the teller lady deposit all the money in an account. Later I wrote a check in the amount of fifty-two thousand dollars, took it to the funeral parlor, and slipped it into Poppa's pocket."

Back to the Bronze Age

I was an ace in World War II. Shot down five enemy aircraft. One Betty and four Zekes. Actually I shot down six planes. The sixth, another Zeke, couldn't be confirmed by my gun camera. And no one else, flying with me that day, saw it go down. Therefore, according to the regulations, since the kill couldn't be verified, I didn't receive credit for it. Ironically, I shot down all six planes during my first three months of combat in the Pacific theater.

Shortly thereafter there were few opportunities to engage the Japanese aviators in any dog fights. It wasn't that they weren't courageous pilots and shied away from us. Far from it. To a man, they were very brave. According to Captain Novak, our unit's Intelligence Officer, it was more a question of resources. The Japanese had simply exhausted their supply of airplanes and fuel and pilots, especially skilled pilots.

Since we seldom encountered any Zekes in the skies over the South Pacific, our squadron flew submarine patrols or support missions for the ground troops, slugging it out with the Nips, on New Musse. But when and if targets of opportunity presented themselves, we were more than ready for the challenge.

Between May and August we had relocated our base of operations from French Seusst to Ebellu to Ladua. And now as December drew to a close, we were flying out of Papooga. The island, once a Dutch colony, had been bombed relentlessly by our offshore batteries. After the Army landed, it was pulverized some more. It took the Army over a month of intense, bloody fighting to finally secure the island. There were, however, still Japanese soldiers holed up in the caves in the rugged mountains. The Army brass decided that it wasn't worth the effort to flush them out and so left them in those caves to starve.

Personally, I never encountered any of those Nips, but every once in a while one of them would tramp down from the mountains, fire a random shot, and promptly sneak back into the jungle. Someone, I don't know who it was, named the interloper Pistol Pete. Old Pete never hit anything or anybody. We went about our business and considered him nothing more than a petty nuisance.

However, Major Campbell, our Commanding Officer, considered Pete a major threat to our safety and morale. He put up a bottle of Jack Daniels as a prize for the man or men who either captured Pete or killed him. But a month after he tacked the notice on the Ready Room's bulletin board, the bottle still lay unclaimed in his desk drawer. It wasn't that a bottle of Jack Daniels wasn't desirable; it was. Pete, though, wasn't regarded as much of a nuisance as were the blood-thirsty mosquitoes, the incessant heat, and the lousy grub.

I realized there was nothing that could be done about the mosquitoes and the weather. But the food was an altogether different matter.

Almost everything we ate originated in the powdered state -- milk, gravy, eggs, mashed potatoes, and even the chocolate pudding. Everything. And then there were the endless meals of Spam. Sergeant Brooks, the chief cook, served Spam as our chief staple at all three meals. We ate it at breakfast with eggs. For our midday meal it was covered with gravy and served with mashed potatoes. Finally, at supper the Spam was wedged between two pieces of bread.

It wasn't the Japanese who were destroying out morale; it was the food. I'm sure Major Campbell was aware of it. He realized that he had to act quickly, or the unit's military spirit would reach rock bottom.

As Christmas rapidly approached Major Campbell vowed publicly that a turkey dinner with all the trimmings would grace our plates. We all poo-poohed his latest bluster. Back in November he had guaranteed us a turkey dinner for Thanksgiving. The birds never materialized. Not a one. Instead we ate Spam, swimming in black grease, along with slimy, green eggs.

When we questioned the Major about our turkeys, he hemmed and hawed before he informed us that the Navy had mistakenly delivered them to the Marines fighting on Konupoia. Though we bemoaned the loss of our birds, we all agreed that the leathernecks, who were sustaining heavy casualties on that rock, were more than welcome to them.

Being a brash young lieutenant, I cornered Major Campbell one day as he was leaving the mess hall and asked him how he could promise us turkeys on Christmas when he couldn't produce them on Thanksgiving.

"Stork's going to scrounge them up for us," replied the Major without any inflection in his voice.

"Oh, really!" I said, sounding rather skeptical. While he droned on matter-of-factly about his faith in Lieutenant Stork's ability to barter twenty cases of Tooheys, a fine Australian beer, for forty canned turkeys from the hospital on Port Ritchie, I grew more dubious with his every word.

Every outfit had someone who was adept at scrounging anything from a phonograph player to an ice cream maker to booze. Most of those men, for obvious reasons, were attached to the quartermaster units.

To the best of my knowledge Stork had no experience trading one commodity for another. He was, however, a small-time souvenir hunter.

Definitely nothing big. A few tin helmets, all with bullet holes in them, a Japanese flag in deplorable condition, and a blood-stained pamphlet, which no one could read because it was printed in Japanese.

"Lieutenant Stork," said Major Campbell, lighting up a cigarette with the butt he had just removed from his mouth, "will get those turkeys for us. I have confidence in him." Campbell puffed enthusiastically. "Just look at how imposing the man is. His striking figure should count for something when he sits down to negotiate for those birds."

"Imposing! Striking figure," I soliloquized to myself and decided that Major Campbell was hallucinating.

Yes, it was true that Stork stood well over six feet tall. But, at the same time, I doubted if he weighed more than 130 pounds. He looked more like Ichabod Crane than Attila the Hun. Imposing?

Because of his height he was too tall to fit inside the cockpit of the P-38, which our squadron flew. I knew, for a fact, that he was barely able to stuff his frame inside the Piper Cub he flew from island to island, delivering mail.

"Where's he going to get twenty cases of Tooheys?" I asked, pausing to slap at a stout mosquito sitting on my forehead.

"I don't know, but you can ask him." Major Campbell pointed to a Piper Cub approaching the landing strip from out of the setting sun in the west.

While Major Campbell strolled on toward a patch of grass behind the Officers Club, where the weekly movie was shown, I watched Stork execute a not-so-perfect landing and taxi his craft up the runway. Once he reached the tin-roofed hangar, where several mechanics were refitting a canopy on a P-38, he shut down the engine, threw open the door, and ducked out of the Cub. As soon as he spotted me, he waved. But before he slammed the door shut, he reached inside for the mailbag and two metal canisters, containing the night's feature motion picture.

"Got a good one tonight," said Stork in a nasal twang. He paused, stepped over a puddle of brackish water, and marched briskly toward me.

"Is it the same Abbott and Costello flick we saw last week?" I asked with a tinge of sarcasm in my voice. For some bizarre reason our outfit had already seen Abbott and Costello in *Buck Privates* four times. I was sure that most of the guys not only knew the plot very well by now, but the dialogue as well.

"No Abbott and Costello tonight." Stork's floppy mouth curved into a smile. "*Flying Tigers* with John Wayne."

I stopped in my tracks and crinkled my brows. "Great! Who's the broad in the flick with Wayne?"

Stork pursed his lips and scratched his head, obviously searching in his mind for the female co-star's name. "M-m-m-m … I think it's Anna Lee. Yep, that's it."

Nodding, I half smiled. Stork flashed a broad grin at my approval, which for some unknown reason he always sought. "She's not bad to look at."

"No, she's not."

"I heard you're gonna get us forty turkeys for Christmas dinner."

"Gonna try." Stork held up his index finger. "Wait for me here. I gotta drop the mail off."

While Stork strolled across the compound to a Quonset hut, which served as our headquarters, I took a cigarette from a pack of Lucky Strikes, jammed it into my mouth, and lit it. Drawing heartily on the cigarette, I expelled a plume of gray smoke through my nostrils. I took two more drags on the butt before Stork, still carrying the film, backed out of the Quonset hut and strolled across the rutted road toward me.

"You have a plan for getting those turkeys?" I asked, expecting Stork to admit that he hadn't given the subject much thought.

"Sure do," he said, pausing at a card table to place the canisters next to our ancient, but reliable, movie projector.

"What's your plan … er … if I might ask?" Since the area was already quite crowded with personnel, waiting for the movie to begin, we searched high and low for some place to sit. Finally I spotted two empty ammo boxes directly in front of a bed sheet attached to two charred tree stumps. Needless to say, the sheet served as the movie screen. Stork, bobbing his head, led the way toward the boxes. From prior experience I knew that we would sit and wait for quite some time until someone properly threaded the movie projector with the film.

"My plan is very simple."

"Really."

"Yep. Nothing to it."

"Oh!"

"The hospital at Port Ritchie has a surplus of turkeys … eh … about forty-two birds to be exact."

"No kidding." My interest was piqued. I was sure that my dormant taste buds awoke and listened to our conversation. "How'd the hospital come by those extra birds? Probably our Thanksgiving turkeys."

"I don't know." Stork glanced at his watch and then at the card table, where Sergeant Kluski was busily threading the movie projector. "But the hospital wants beer … Tooheys in return for their turkeys."

"And … pray tell … er … where are you gonna get the Tooheys?"

"That's not a problem." Stork, who had stretched out his long, skinny legs, withdrew them when the cook and his native boys, who labored in the kitchen in return for their meals, plopped down on the grass in front of us Indian style. "A Sergeant Bumgardener over at the 126th has the beer."

"How'd he get it?"

"Don't know. That's not the point."

"Oh!"

"No, the point is that this Bumgardener collects souvenirs."

"Ohhhh!" I nodded. "So you gotta come up with the trinkets he wants."

"Right." Stork raised a bony finger and counted the natives before him. "Last week Brooks had four boys." Stork counted again. "This week he has five." When I offered him one of my horehound mints, he reached into the bag, took one, and shoved it into his mouth. "I already put up my valuable Nip helmets."

"Valuable!" After slipping a horehound into my mouth, I sealed the bag and dropped it into my pocket. "Every one of those helmets is rusty and has a bullet hole in it."

Stork tapped repeatedly upon my knee. "That's what makes them so valuable."

"Yeah, I'll bet." I sat up, sniffed the fetid air, and turned up my nose. One of the natives reeked of body odor, and when the wind shifted direction, I was overwhelmed by the stench. "What else do you have? I'm sure Bumgardener won't settle for only those tin helmets."

"Of course not." Stork screwed up his nose and gestured in the direction of one of the natives. "I gotta give up my Japanese flag and that pamphlet I prize."

"That's it?"

"Oh, no. Major Campbell has graciously donated his Nip bugle to the cause."

"That should be enough."

"It's not."

When I glanced at Stork, who was sucking loudly on his candy, I detected a glint of desperation in his large blue eyes. "Don't look at me like that. No, I won't do it."

"Come on."

"Nope. I'm not gonna give you that *Samurai* sword. Damn it."

"Bumgardener ... eh ... in particular ... er ... asked me if I had a *Samurai* sword."

"Well, you don't."

"I know. I know."

Just then the assemblage let out with a loud whoop, a few boos, and a scant ovation. When I looked up, I saw the logo of Republic

Pictures displayed upon the sheet. The movie was beginning.

As soon as John Wayne's face projected upon the white bed sheet, a smattering of jeers erupted from various sectors of the audience. Many of my fellow servicemen held a low opinion of Wayne because, while they were putting their lives on the line daily, he was enjoying the good life in Hollywood and earning millions of dollars in the process.

Though I always felt that Wayne played himself on the silver screen and was a mediocre thespian, I never booed him.

I guessed that Wayne was approximately forty years of age when the Japanese attacked Pearl Harbor. In all honesty, he was too old to serve as a private in the Army. Hell, I struggled through flight school at the tender age of twenty-one. There was no way that Wayne would have successfully completed basic training at his age. Besides, the man was declared 4-F by his draft board. Had a perforated ear drum.

I was particularly interested in the footage of Wayne supposedly engaged in aerial combat. And I wasn't disappointed; it was fairly realistic. One of the native boys in front of me was also impressed by the action. He became so engrossed in the drama unfolding on the screen that he stood and shook his fist. He shouted encouragement to Wayne, but since I didn't understand his language, I didn't comprehend a word.

"Sit down," I said firmly to him. He was now jabbering quite loudly. "Your father wasn't a glass maker."

My remark set the man off. After glaring at me, he dashed forward and slashed at the sheet with some sort of knife. "Yon Way … die," he screamed. Thrusting again at the sheet, he slit it into half.

While the audience sat in stunned silence, Stork jumped to his feet. Sprinting after the demented man, he seized him by the scruff of the neck. The man retaliated by butting Stork in the stomach. Down they went in a heap. Entangled in each other's embrace, they thrashed about in the dirt. Over and over they rolled, punching each other and grunting.

When Stork, who seemed to be gaining the advantage, cursed the man, I rushed forward to assist him. Suddenly lights flashed somewhere. The air raid siren, atop the Quonset hut, wailed. Most of the men took leave and fled to the air raid shelters. A few, the more fool hardy, followed me with intentions of intervening in the melee.

In the irregular shadows cast by the floodlights, I watched Stork finally pin the man, who was still cursing John Wayne to the highest, to the ground.

Major Campbell, strolling into view from amidst a small band of onlookers, shined his flashlight upon Stork. I could see that Stork's face was grimy, and he had suffered a laceration on his forearm. Steadying his light, the Major slowly lowered it upon the crazed native boy.

"Cripes!" I shouted. My eyes bulged. "H-he's not a native. He's … he's a Japanese soldier."

"It's Pistol Pete," called Stork, panting. He pinned the man's wrists behind his back and thus held him at bay.

"Lieutenant Stork, you've captured Pistol Pete," said the Major, looking and sounding quite relieved.

"No Pis'ol Pee," cried the half-naked, foul smelling Japanese soldier. "Kamamoto … Shuji … Yapanese … Army."

By and by the more inquisitive movie goers straggled back to the area in small groups. Probably to get their first look at a live Japanese soldier. Minutes after the air raid siren announced that the area was safe, the Military Police arrived en masse. Unceremoniously they hauled Shuji Kamamoto, also known as Pistol Pete, away to a better life than he led in the jungle of Papooga. No sooner had the Military Police and their prisoner disappeared over the hill, the crowd dispersed to the Officers Club.

"I guess this means that you win the bottle of Jack Daniels," I said to Stork, who had become an instant hero with his fearlessness.

"It sure does," said Major Campbell, patting Stork upon the back. "If you follow me to my office, I'll get you the hooch."

"Thank you, sir," said Stork, tucking his torn, soiled shirt back into his trousers. "I'll be over as soon as I wash up and put some iodine on my arm." Stork held up his forearm. "The damn monkey bit me while we were wrestling."

"Break the skin?" The Major peered over his eyeglass at Stork's arm.

"Yes, sir."

"That means I'm puttin' you up fer a Purple Heart. Wounded in combat."

While I looked on, Stork followed Major Campbell across the road and then veered off to his tent. I then strolled off to my own quarters. I had sufficient excitement for one evening.

Earlier in the day I had received a seven-page, scented letter from Bessie. Once more she affirmed her love for me. I wanted to read her words one more time before I turned in for the night. Tomorrow, I was scheduled to fly submarine patrol up the coast. And when I flew, I liked to be alert.

In addition to all the local news, ranging from the Tuesday night bingo held at the Grange to the new stop sign on Third Street to the unveiling of a statue of General George Armstrong Custer in Wolverine Park, Bessie, who was the town librarian, informed me of all the new books she had recently catalogued and stacked on the respective shelves.

I had just gotten to that part of her letter where she told me how much she missed me when the tent flap rustled and then parted. In strode a smiling Stork with a bottle of Jack Daniels in his hand. The bottle was practically empty. Since he wasn't much of a drinker, I knew that he had shared the whiskey with anyone and everyone he had encountered on his journey from the Major's office.

"Get your cup," he said, holding up the bottle and shaking its contents. "I saved a little for you." Taking my canteen cup from a web belt, which I never wore, I dusted the inside with my towel and held it up for Stork. "Say when."

"Whoa!" I said as soon as Stork poured and covered the bottom of the vessel with the liquor.

"Gee!" Stork held the bottle up to the light. "You didn't take much."

"I gotta fly tomorrow morning, and I don't need a hangover." I raised my cup. "To our health."

"And may this stinkin' war end soon." Stork lifted the bottle to his mouth and drained the contents. "Maybe then we can all go home to our families."

"Amen." Outside someone was playing "The Beer Barrel Polka" on an accordion. I listened and longed to be home.

Stork extended his hand. I clasped it firmly. "See yah ... tomorrow." After dropping the bottle into my wastebasket, he turned to leave.

"Ed!"

"Yeah."

"Take it."

Stork paused and pivoted on his heels. "Huh!"

"The sword."

"Really!" His face lit up like the proverbial Christmas tree. "You mean it?"

"I wouldn't have said it if I didn't mean it." I tossed him my keys. "It's in the foot locker."

Stork bowed before my locker as if he were a *shogun* venerating the emperor. Slowly and deliberately he turned the key and lifted the door. Pausing, he held his breath momentarily.

The *Samurai* sword, which I had accidentally discovered in the bushes near our latrine, was buried under several of my khaki shirts. Stork handed me the shirts before taking the sword and placing it upon my bunk.

When I stumbled across the sword, I honestly believed that it was the most beautiful thing I had ever seen. However, as I glanced down at its rusted handle and chipped blade, I wasn't so sure. It no longer fascinated me. Actually, there was something about it that repulsed me.

"Take it," I said and handed it to Stork. "I know that I'll enjoy a slice of turkey much more than any pleasure I'd ever get out of that ... that thing."

Stork held it up to the naked light bulb overhead. "This sword's gonna make our Christmas a little better."

"Good."

"You flyin' sub patrol tomorrow?"

"Yep." I slipped a cigarette into my mouth. "While you're negotiating with the doctors and the pretty nurses over at Port Ritchie, I'll be skimming above the whitecaps, searching for submarines, which I never find."

I was always searching for periscopes, conning towers, and suspicious shadows. Never spotted anything. Not even a whale or a porpoise.

Weather wise, the following morning proved to be no different from any other day I had spent in the South Pacific. Though it was the first day of winter according to the calendar, it was unlike any Winter Solstice morning I remembered in the Upper Peninsula of Michigan. No snow. No ice. No biting wind. Soon after breakfast I took off and flew north. Of course, I saw nothing but the coral-green waves below me. All was peaceful. When I reached the westernmost tip of Quientisus, I banked the P-38 and set a course for Papooga, completing another milk run.

"Red Rover, this is Black Baron ... over," announced a gravelly voice over my radio. When the static grew harsher and louder, I frantically fine-tuned the set. Just as quickly as the grating sound registered, it vanished. I didn't know if the static had disappeared because of my deft fingers or because of some natural phenomena.

"Black Baron, this is Red Rover ... over," I drawled into my mouthpiece. From prior missions in the area, I recognized Black Baron as the call sign of an Army unit battling the Japanese on New Musse.

"We're pinned down by a Nip machine gun. Taking heavy casualties. Need for you to wipe the nest out ... over."

"Give me the coordinates ... over." I took a map of the island and placed it upon my lap.

Several seconds elapsed before Black Baron responded. "Er ... coordinates are ... let me see ... mmmm ... five ... eh ... six ... two-o-o ... er ... seven ... eight ... thareeee ... over."

"Am presently cruising at two angels ... eh ... off to the east of your present position. Will make a house call immediately ... out."

After checking my machine guns by firing several short bursts, I veered abruptly and climbed steadily. Within seconds I spotted New Musse, a tiny dot on the horizon. It was a volcanic island, resembling a burnt pork chop.

I breathed deeply and exhaled slowly, deliberately. Banking sharply to the left, I checked my harness as I approached the target in a steady, steep glide. Gaining speed by the seconds, the P-38 suddenly dove as though an eagle in pursuit of an elusive salmon. *Whr--r-r-r-r* roared the twin engines. My mouth, open and distorted, felt dry as the desert. Gravity forced my weight forward against the harness. The plane bucked as it accelerated. I tensed and then relaxed my grip on the stick. When the wind screamed at a higher pitch, the change of altitude pained my ears terribly. "Ahhhh!" I shouted and swallowed to relieve the pressure. I began to attract fire that was well off the target. "E-e-easy. Don't rush it. Make sure you bring ... the target into the bombsight." The bullets whizzing past the cockpit failed to unnerve me. "Easy." As I neared the earth very quickly, I spied the Japanese pillbox dead ahead. "Don't jerk the trigger. Sque-e-e-eze." *Rat-a-tat-tat* chattered my machine guns.

A tracer from the Japanese machine gun flew past my right wing. Once more I squeezed the trigger. The guns roared and spat death. The machine gunner's assistant spun around like an Olympic ice skater before toppling out of the bunker. I could now distinguish the machine gunner's features -- high cheek bones, beaked nose, and bovine lips. His black eyes widened with fear as I neared. Holding the stick for an instant with my sweaty hand, I waited until the last possible second. "Now!" I screamed and dropped my bombs. Just as I pulled up in a steep bank, I glanced back. *Kabo-o-o-mb!* The earth shook and split open. A geyser of dirt and debris spewed in every direction. A ball of red-and-yellow fire jumped into the sky. The barrel of the machine gun somersaulted toward me. It was followed by a limp torso. "Got 'im!"

Icy-cold sweat streaked down my forehead and seeped into my eyes. Shivering mightily, I tugged on the stick and climbed into the sky

"Good job ... Red R-r-r," transmitted someone from the Army unit on the ground. Then my radio went silent. Patiently I tried calibrating it once more. That didn't work. I promptly smashed it with my fist. That didn't remedy anything, but it hurt my hand.

"Damn! No radio," I said to myself." Stretching my cramped legs, I repositioned them. "Don't worry." Though I didn't have a radio, I knew that I could still get back to the base. Intuitively I checked my gauges. They all appeared to be operating perfectly. "I'll fly by compass. No problem." Without warning, the fuel-warning light blinked. "Damn! Now what?" The propeller on the right engine immediately stopped turning. "I can still make it back with only one engine." When I looked up, I noticed that the light on the fuel gauge no longer blinked intermittently. It now glowed a bright red.

"Oh, shoot! I'm outta fuel." I gently tapped the dial. But the red light only seemed to burn brighter. "Musta taken a hit in the fuel tank."

Panic had not set in, but I was deeply concerned. I realized that there was no way I would get the craft back to Papooga. Either I bailed out, or I tried to land the plane … somewhere. But where?

I flew on for several minutes before the second engine conked out. Though I was now out of fuel, the airplane glided along effortlessly, magically. Was it possible that I might successfully land the craft?

Desperately needing some place to set the plane down, I glanced to the right and then to the left. Nothing. I sniffed and thought that I smelled smoke. I sniffed again. I did smell smoke. A trace of gray smoke drifted up from the floor. I lowered the side window on the canopy to allow the smoke to escape. And when I gazed out the window, I spotted an atoll below my left wing and the island of Maldovia just beyond.

When I joined the squadron, Captain Novak informed me, during my initial briefing, that Maldovia, a dense jungle of trees, foliage, vines, and thicket, was inhabited by tribes of cannibals. According to him they lived in a Bronze Age culture. And all practiced head-hunting. No white man had ever set foot on Maldovia. It surely looked as if I might be the first.

After checking my crash straps, I banked to the left and sought a place to land. "Cripes! Nothing but jungle down there." In a last-ditch effort, I fiddled with the radio. Dead.

Somehow the jungle looked beautiful in its own macabre way. Suddenly my eyes glowed. Off to the right I spied a sandy beach, and immediately I knew where I would set the plane down.

Since nothing seemed to be going right for me, I didn't expect the landing gear to deploy. But down it came. Smoothly. Precisely. My spirits rose. I knew that my chances of survival increased if I could avoid a belly landing.

The smoke in the cockpit had not intensified. But by the same token, it had not lessened. The pundits of the world exclaimed that a drowning man saw his life march past him. Well, I wasn't a drowning man … yet. However, strange unexplainable incidents occurred inside the cockpit. First, the red light on the fuel gauge expired. My spirits soared. Could it be that the fuel tank was not empty? Frantically, I tried to start the engine. Nothing doing. The fuel tank was, indeed, empty. Next, I believed that I detected a faint hum emanating from the radio. "Mayday! Mayday!" I barked into my headpiece. "This is Lieutenant Moose Kanty … er … I'm about to crash-land on the eastern shore of Maldovia. Damn it! Somebody!" For the second time within the hour,

I beat my bruised fist against the radio. The radio was quite dead.

I totally resigned myself to my fate, whatever it might be. In a few short minutes I was going to crash-land on an island populated by fierce, flesh-eating savages.

Back in flight school I was taught to fly straight in a full-stall when crash-landing. "Humph! Full-stall," I mumbled into my transmitter. "The engines are dead." Checking my shoulder harness once more, I shoved the balky canopy open with some effort. Peering out over the side of the fuselage, I couldn't help but notice how serene the jungle appeared. Everything was some shade of green. "Pull back on the stick. Bring the nose up." I swallowed hard and licked my parched lips. "Good. Aim for the beach. Goo-o-od." From experience on Lake Michigan's shores, I knew that it was easier to walk on the wet, packed sand, rather than the loose, sunbaked sand. And, I reasoned, if walking was easier on wet sand, landing an airplane must also be an easier task. "Gotta get the rear wheel down first." Perspiration glistened on my upper lip. "You can do it. Relax." I pulled back on the stick to slow the craft down. "Too fast. Slow ... down!" I grit my teeth and bit my lower lip. "The plane's traveling too fast." With wind swirling in my face, I strained every muscle to slow the plane down and avoid flipping it over. *Whrrrrrr* screamed the front tires upon touching the pristine sand. "Damn! Get the rear wheel down first." Fire shot out from both the floor and the nose of the craft. Without rhyme or reason, one of the front tires collapsed, pitching the airplane in a helter-skelter fashion. "Whew! Getting hot in here. Gotta get out." As the damaged tire plowed into the sand, it slowed the craft quickly. Before it completely stopped I was able to climb out of the cockpit and leap to safety. The plane slid along the sand for another ten feet before grinding to a sudden stop. Springing to my feet, I watched the voracious orange flames lap at the wings and the cowling. "So much for a perfect landing." Shielding my eyes from the scorching heat, I thought that I heard the booming thump-thump-thump of a bass drum. Owing to the excitement of the moment, I attributed the pounding to a figment of my vivid imagination. I stepped back from the fire. And not a second too soon. *Bavoo-o-oom!* A radiator on one of the tail booms exploded into the sky and then landed in the surf. I was sure that the fuel tank was empty, but the Browning machine guns were still armed. It was simply a matter of time before the ammo detonated. As I edged closer to the ocean, the sound and splash of the breaking waves intensified. The drumbeat also magnified. I paused in my tracks and cocked my ear. It quickly became apparent that the drumming was not taking place inside my head. The tattooing echoed throughout the tree tops. Its source, I judged, was several miles inland.

In all honesty I had no game plan. All that, however, changed quickly. *"Saso-o-o-onu!"* shouted a voice above me. When I turned and glanced past my shadow, I spied a band of aborigines standing poised atop a grassy knoll. Their naked bodies were painted with red-and-white stripes. All clutched spears decorated with feathers and shells. *"Sasoonu!"* called the leader, a paunchy fellow, wearing a headdress of brightly colored feathers. Unlike his followers, he sported no spear. He menacingly waved a scepter with some sort of ball on the tip of it. Upon closer inspection I noted that the ornament on the end of his scepter wasn't a ball at all. It was a human skull. *"Sasoon-u-u-u!"*

"Sasoonu!" screamed his cohorts. At once the entire mob, yelping and waving their weapons, raced down the hill and headed straight for me.

Not especially desiring to be slowly roasted upon a spit, I fled down the beach. With my knees pumping and my arms swinging, I dashed like a sprinter, not knowing where I was running.

"Sasoonu!"

Having been a member of the high school track squad, I was certain that I could outdistance a motely pack of brutes. But stealing a look over my left shoulder, I discovered that the cannibals were, in fact, gaining on me. My comfortable lead had been narrowed considerably, but I chugged on.

"Sasoonu!" chortled a tall, lean warrior. The man had separated himself from the pack and was catching up to me, slowly but surely.

"Damn cigarettes," I muttered to myself, listening to my raspy, hollow breathing. "Dear God, if you get me outta this pickle … huh-huh … I'll never smoke again."

I no longer heard the fleet, pounding feet of my pursuer upon the wet sand. A set of foreign sounds, which my brain failed to absorb and process, reverberated in my ears.

When I hazarded another peek, I discovered that the tall fellow had purposely stopped in order to plant his foot, reach back, and hurl his spear at me. *Whooooosh!* The spear sailed wide of my head and fell harmlessly in the sand.

Without breaking stride, I reached down, grabbed hold of the spear, and continued on my way.

"Saso-o-o-o-onu!" cried the spear chucker.

"Sweating like a block of ripening cheese, I paused to suck in as much oxygen as my bursting lungs would tolerate. Though supposedly in the prime of my life, my breathing sounded like an ancient bellows that had been infested and then chewed to shreds by hordes of rats.

To add insult to injury, the warrior had run back to the main force, commandeered another spear, and nonchalantly resumed his chase.

Perhaps if I reached the jungle, I could hide in the thick brush and avoid capture. Certainly with my vast Boy Scout experience, I could subsist off the earth, couldn't I? I took about two steps toward the tree line when I spotted a phalanx of tribesmen storming out of the undergrowth. I quickly reconsidered my strategy.

Stumbling and then tumbling to the sand, I unsteadily clambered to my feet just as my airplane exploded. While the natives stopped to watch the craft burn, I threw my head back and raced toward the ocean. I could swim, and I recalled sighting an atoll just before I ditched my airplane. I certainly couldn't keep running around the beach. Eventually the natives would catch up with me. And then, as they say, the jig was up.

Heartened by the cannibals' decision to stop and gape at the pyrotechnics and my proximity to the ocean, I redoubled my efforts and plowed on. Meanwhile the tribesmen, who recently quit the jungle, effortlessly loped along, parallel to me. They seemed quite intent upon denying me access to the thicket. It now became obvious that my capture was commissioned solely to the man behind me. And he appeared to be running faster than ever.

Would I reach the ocean before he overtook me? My head throbbed with the taunts of the headhunters, the staccato beat of the tom-tom, the pounding of the surf, and a strange new buzzing.

With tongue hanging out, I trotted. No, that's not correct. I was staggering as if drunk. I coughed, retched upon the sand, and coughed some more. "Another ... ten steps ... and ... and I'll ... reach ... the water." All around me the noises of the moment melted into one dull pitch.

Reeling from side to side, I fell and then climbed to one knee. "Moose!" called a strident voice. Blinking, I wiped the vomit from my chin and the tears from my cheeks. Looking around, I sought the source of the voice. There, some fifteen feet to my left, snorted a Piper Cub. "Get in," called Stork, throwing open the door.

Marshaling all of my strength, I trudged over to the airplane, dove inside, and slammed the door shut.

"How'd ... you ... know ... I was here?" I asked, plopping myself into the seat.

"Heard your Mayday call on the radio."

"Really!"

"Yep."

"I see ... you ... got the turkeys." I turned and fingered a silver can.

"Yep." Stork gunned the engine. The plane cooed and shimmied like Little Egypt before the wheels actually freed themselves from the sand. "Let's get outta here."

"Truer words were never spoken." I closed my eyes, aware that within seconds the Piper Cubwould be airborne, leaving the Bronze Age behind.

After an inordinate period of time, the plane was still lumbering along the beach. When I glanced at Stork, I detected a pained expression scrawled upon his long, narrow face.

"We got a problem, Moose." Stork shoved the throttle forward, but the Cub reacted no differently. The engine simply throbbed and whined.

"W-what's the matter?" Glancing out the door, I saw that my old nemesis, the spear chucker, was still running close behind us. In fact, he seemed to be gaining on us. And his tribesmen were right behind him.

"Too much weight."

"Huh!" I closed the door, slumped down into my seat, and swore.

"With all those turkeys back there, we have too much weight to lift the plane off the ground."

"Cripes!"

"I was all right until you came along."

"Well, I'm not getting off." I sighed and folded my arms across my chest resolutely.

Stork chuckled. "Then start tossin' the turkeys out the door."

Reluctantly, I grabbed hold of a canned turkey and kissed it before flinging it out the door. The can hit the sand and became embedded like a raisin in vanilla pudding.

"More. One can's not gonna do it."

"Damn."

Like a lobster fisherman, casting his traps, I tossed the turkeys out the door. Can after can thumped in the sand, puzzling the inquisitive headhunters. To a man they had stopped running. Retrieving the cans from the sand, they studied them from all angles and scratched their heads in bewilderment.

Only after I had jettisoned the last can, did the Cub's engine spring to life. The fuselage no longer shook as if palsied; the tires lifted from the quagmire of sand. With his jaw set in determination, Stork taxied down the beach and tugged upon the yoke. *Wrrrrr* roared the engine. "Hang on," instructed Stork, and I did. Suddenly, as if on cue, the airplane lifted off the sand and soared into the wild blue yonder.

"Know what?" I said, glancing out the window at the charred, smoldering skeletal remains of my airplane.

"No, what?"

"As soon as I get back, I'm gonna have a Spam sandwich."

"Me, too."

The Safecracker, the Pug, and the Cupcake

Me and Duffy have been sidekicks ever since we both served time in the canneroo up in Landisburgh.

I got two to five for safecracking, while Duffy got sent up for robbing a gas station.

During my entire career I worked solo, relying upon my wits and skills to earn a living. But the one time I teamed up with this yegg from Steubonville, I got busted.

Frank the Chicken, that was his moniker, set the job up at the First Farmers and Miners Bank in Chesterville. He said that the main crate was a piece of cake, and it was. I peeled it open minutes after we entered the bank. But then things went bad. The first problem popped up when I cracked it and found it was a bloomer or an empty crate. The second difficulty, a more serious setback, was the fuzz waiting for us as we left the building.

"Guilty as charged," bellowed the judge, a slight man with a hawk-like nose and jaundiced skin, at my trial.

I had done time before. So I knew what to expect -- shake downs, tunnels, rabbit fever -- but Landisburgh was much tougher than any canneroo I had done time in before.

I guess -- no, I know -- I had just completed my second tour of duty in the icebox for brawling when I met Duffy, an ex-prizefighter with a glass jaw and one cauliflower ear. Why only one ear was deformed, I never learned.

Duffy was a chain smoker, but cigs, of any type, even the hand-rolled kind we called fast burners, were difficult to come by.

In all canneroos, cigs are used as currency among the inmates. Since I was a pretty good card player, I often won a large number of cigs, which I traded for Hershey bars. I do not remember a time when I did not have a craving for chocolate.

Duffy knew that I always carried my cigs with me in my coat pocket. And one day, while I was working in the laundry room, I took off my jacket because it was quite warm and hung it on a nail. Well, while I was folding a pair of coveralls, Duffy decided to avail himself of my smokes. Though he was quite sneaky about it, I caught him lifting a Camel out of my pocket. Now that really made me mad.

"Hey, what do you think you're doing?" I said, tossing the coveralls aside. Boldly, I marched right up to him. Though he was a head taller and fifty pounds heavier that I was, I still looked him square in the eye and never backed down.

"I thought it was my jacket," he said, "and I was jus' getting' a coffin nail."

"Yeah. Yeah." I shoved him away. I knew that surprised him because his jaw dropped and his eyes bulged. "Lousy crook." I shook my finger right in his face. "If you wanna bum a cig ... jus' ask me."

He swaggered up to me with menacing eyes. Immediately I saw anger flash in his long, weather-beaten face. At once I assumed a boxer's stance and began to bob and weave just like Joe Lewis. Duffy cocked his fists, two hams, and snarled, revealing a mouth of missing teeth. I danced and feinted. Duffy watched curiously. Then he lashed out with a hard right. Of course it landed on my jaw and sent me sprawling across the floor into a pile of smelly socks. I staggered to my feet. Down I went again when he busted my nose with his left hook. Clenching my fists, I sucked in the blood. I stood unsteadily, squinted, and saw two of him. Hell, that was not fair. Two of him against one of me. I growled and charged him. He merely smashed a right-cross into my eye, closing it instantly. "Stay down, yah bum. I can kill yah ... If I wanna."

I clutched the washing machine and struggled to my feet. Glowering out of one eye, I now saw him three times. The guy certainly had no sense of fairness at all. "You can beat me to a pulp ... but you're still a stinkin' crook."

"I ain't gonna hit you no more. You're crazy." He dropped his fists, turned, and walked away.

"Humph! You're yeller."

"No, I ain't," he called over his shoulder. "I don't wanna get the chair fer murder. Don't need a weed that bad."

It suddenly dawned upon me that Duffy was right. He could have very easily beaten me to death. I also realized that we were both addicts -- he to tobacco and I to chocolate. "Hey, Duffy!"

"Yeah."

"You're right. You could have sent me to the bone yard." Duffy stopped in his tracks and pivoted to face me. "Help yourself to my cigs."

He smiled crookedly, looking like a jack-o'-lantern. "Only if yous let me buy yous a cup of java."

"Deal."

We shook hands there amidst the smell of bleach and detergent and the piles of soiled laundry on the floor. And while the Maytag washing machines grunted like football linemen, I offered him a light for his cig. I guess it is true that opposites attract. In the next few weeks, we became fast friends. When we were both paroled, within hours of each other, we decided to strike out together. Our destination was

Martinville, where Duffy's granddaddy once operated a gin mill. According to Duffy, the still produced the best Jersey lightning in the area. The still was long gone, but the family homestead still stood on three acres of wooded land.

The five-room, clapboard shack, whose frames were once steel-gray, had become bleached to the color of long-exposed bones. Resting forlornly at the bottom of a ravine, it was accessible only by means of a gravel path. And this path meandered among patches of blueberry bushes and coarse, leafy-stemmed sow thistle and hawkweeds.

Though vacant for several years, the structure was basically habitable, save for a leaky roof and a missing stove pipe, running from the chimney to the wood-burning stove in the parlor. On our second day there, Duffy nailed some discarded Mail Pouch signs onto the warped shingles. And while he was busy with the roof, I went to the hardware store in town and purchased a length of pipe. Once I installed the pipe, the stove was completely serviceable.

With our funds almost exhausted, we knew that we needed to find employment. However, the only skills we possessed were outside the scope of the law.

I was a master safecracker, but I owned no tools to ply my trade. Furthermore, Martinville had no bank. The closest bank was located in Skyport, and that was thirty miles downstream.

Duffy, a palooka, who took more dives than Esther Williams, had few marketable skills. For a short time, he worked as a dishwasher after he retired from the ring. When that didn't pan out, he tried robbery, once, and got busted. Actually, the robbery went well. He held up a gas station, collected a grand in small bills, and escaped through the front door. Trouble was that he robbed the only gas station in town, where his best friend worked. The attendant informed the fuzz about the robbery. In about ten minutes, Duffy was apprehended.

"Gotta take you down to the gas station for a positive identification," said the policeman.

"Suit yourself," said Duffy, holding out his wrists as the fuzz cuffed him and led him to the squad car. Five minutes later, when Duffy and the cop arrived before the gas station attendant, Duffy blurted out, "Yep, that's the guy I robbed."

Shortly thereafter Duffy was tried in court, sentenced to prison, and there we met.

With the last of our money in my pocket, I set out for town to buy some grub for the coming week. I also wanted to fill the Chevy's gas tank at Mitch's Emporium.

Mitch's was a combination general store and gas station. It was also the town's social center, where a select group of farmers, tradesmen, and pensioners gathered each day to solve the world's problems, exchange gossip, play chess, and warm their hands over the potbellied stove.

Being an eavesdropper by nature, I gravitated to the circle of captains' chairs near the stove. I immediately noticed a well-dressed, elderly gentleman, who I later learned was the mayor. From his facial expression, I surmised that he was pondering the vulnerability of his rook. As I watched him finger his rook, he explained to his opponent that he was thinking of purchasing a diamond ring for his wife for Christmas.

At the mention of a diamond ring, my ears perked up. I simply had to hear more about the diamond ring and the mayor's finances. But since the ever-efficient Mitch had filled my order, I knew that if I lingered about too long, my interest in the mayor's conversation would be obvious to the gaggle of onlookers.

My brain raced helter-skelter. As soon as I maneuvered the Chevy away from the curb, I had formalized my plan. I planned to kidnap the mayor's wife with Duffy and hold the old biddy for a sizeable ransom. Then we would skedaddle with the money.

I knew that Duffy would agree to the abduction as long as it did not include murder. Later, when I revealed my scheme to him, he staunchly opposed the plan.

"Robbery, big cons … errr … safecracking are … hmmm … all legit business dealings, but," Duffy paused to exhale slowly, "kidnappin' goes against my religion. What if the old gal has a heart attack and croaks on us? Then we're guilty of something' real big."

Since Duffy only ever recognized his personal and immediate needs, I reached into my pocket, withdrew a sawbuck, and tossed in onto the table. "This is all the dough we got between us. Snatch the old broad for a nice ransom, buy some tools with the dough, and … uhm … I'll be in business again … crackin' any crate in the country."

Duffy merely grunted and gestured with his hands, saying, "Since you put it that way … I guess we gotta snatch the old hag … though I don't like grabbin' some old geezer in brogans and a babushka."

If Custer had planned his campaign strategy at the Little Big Horn as meticulously as we devised our plan, the 7th Cavalry would not have been decimated by the Indians.

We knew the complete layout of the mayor's Tudor home and his daily routine. We even knew that his wife attended the local church's choir practice, alone, each Wednesday evening.

On the third Sunday in December we made a trial run. We noted how long it took us to drive into town and the best area for concealment. We even found the darkest streets to drive upon after the seizure.

The drill went off so well that we unanimously declared ourselves fit for the undertaking and eagerly anticipated our adventure.

When Wednesday arrived, I had no qualms about snatching somebody's grandmother. As the day wore on, I began to have real serious reservations about the abduction.

However, there was no turning back. Later that night, when the Chevy lurched away from the grove of oak trees and bounced along the pitted, dirt road, I looked forward to the caper.

"Sky's as black as a crow's wing," said Duffy, negotiating a hairpin turn in the road. "Good night for an old-fashion kidnapping."

"Ain't that the truth?" I felt my kidneys moan as the Chevy bottomed out in a ditch before Duffy shifted gears, and we crept onto a sleek, smooth macadam road. "Gonna be real easy snatchin' the old gal."

Twenty minutes later Duffy was still sure the abduction would go as planned. "Piece of cake," he said as he joined me behind an overgrown English holly. Strategically planted, the holly guarded the walk, leading to the mayor's somber house at the back of the lot.

"Shhhh---h-h-h. Here she comes."

"Remember ... we'll snatch her when she's on top of us."

"Gottcha."

We parted the holly branches and watched her traipse up the hill. With bated breath and our palms clammy, we waited. Suddenly, she paused and stopped. Puffing on a butt, she blew out a cloud of smoke. She then nonchalantly tossed the butt into the gutter and resumed her journey.

"Now!"

Together we sprang from our cover like two bobcats attacking a doe. Duffy clasped his huge hand over her mouth, while I reached for her ankles. "Um-mp-p-phhh!" I cried when she kneed me in the groin. "Geee-e-e-e-!" Down I went to my knees, clutching myself.

"Uh-h-h-mm!" she grunted, while Duffy dragged her to the Chevy. "L-let ... me!"

Pain raced through my brain. I believed that I would either pass out or vomit or both within a few seconds. With all the strength I could muster, I climbed to my feet. Onward to the Chevy I staggered and opened the trunk.

Duffy, a massive man with the strength of a bull, picked her up. But she kicked and thrashed about. Falling to the grass, she quickly recovered and sprang to her feet. Duffy seized her from behind. "Ahhhh-h-h-h-h!" he moaned as she sank her teeth into his hand and stopped only when she reached bone. She spun and kicked at me. Luckily I caught her ankle and tugged, sending her sprawling with a thud.

Dazed, she looked up at me. Before she could lash out, I hauled her to her feet and tossed her into the trunk, slamming it shut.

"Let me go!" she screamed and pounded on the trunk.

"Let's go," said Duffy. Cautiously, he wrapped a rag around his hand. And while he attended to his wound, I massaged myself and limped along, puffing and gasping.

A light flickered in one of the front windows in a home across the street as we sped away. "Whew! Glad that's over."

"For an old geezer ... she put up some fight."

"Duffy, she ain't no old lady."

"Huh!"

"Look." I held up a high-heeled shoe and watched Duffy's silhouette fade to a saffron color as we passed under a street lamp. "She may be the old mayor's wife, but she ain't an old codger." I tossed the shoe onto the backseat. "She's a cupcake in the prime of her life." Despite the frigid air outside, I rolled down the window and let the arctic wind brush against my perspiring face and revive me. "I think we bit off more than we can handle."

"Too late to turn back now." When Duffy held out his arm, I tied the rag securely on his battered hand. "The cupcake needs a good talkin' to ... uhm ... after a little bath."

I had hoped that the cupcake would have tired of kicking and pounding on the trunk. However, the faster we drove, the louder she kicked. At Putnam's Gulch, Duffy eased the Chevy off the main highway and onto a winding, dirt road, which took us up into the mountains. Only then did the kicking and screaming stop.

"Cripes," I said as Duffy ground to a stop. "Are we here already?"

Duffy chortled. "I thought snatchin' the old guy's wife would be easy, but she beat the stuffin' out of us."

As the muffled screams and kicking resumed, the Chevy rocked like a baby's cradle. "Let's just sit here for another minute ... or two."

The sooner we deal with her and set her straight ... the easier it's gonna be." Slowly Duffy freed his body from behind the steering wheel and strolled to the trunk. Lifting it slowly, he reached inside and plucked the cupcake, swinging and kicking from inside.

"I -- I'll," she started to say from underneath the cowl of her parka when Duffy entwined his hand in her long, flowing hair. With a mighty yank, he forced her head back until it was parallel with the sky. "S-stop!" She flailed and gestured with her hands. Duffy only tugged more emphatically. Finally, she dropped her hands to her sides. When he shoved her, she hobbled along on one shoe, and then that shoe fell off.

"S-shoe ... my shoe."

"Here's her shoe," I said, retrieving the pump and handing it to Duffy.

"She don't need no shoes. From now on, she goes barefoot so she can't run away." Winding up like Dizzy Dean, he heaved the shoe through the trees, where it plopped into the bushes.

"B-b-barefoot?" she whimpered softly. "M-my ... new s-stilettos ... gone."

"After we give you a little bath and a good talkin' to ... and if you still don't behave ... errr ... we're jus' gonna keep you hogtied until your husband pays the ransom we demand."

"D-don't hurt me."

Somewhere over the hill, an owl screeched shrilly, reminding us that we were descending into the valley. Onward our little trio marched along the gravel path towards the shanty. Duffy wheezed loudly with each step. I hummed quietly. And the cupcake winced and muttered, "Ow-w-w-w ... o-o-ouch," when she tread upon an acorn or pine cone.

When we reached the stoop, Duffy thought that the cupcake might try to break his grasp and race off into the bushes, and so he tightened his grip. I opened the door and switched on the kitchen light, throwing the room into gloomy shadows and geometric patterns.

"Fill the tub," commanded Duffy, "while I show the cupcake to her quarters."

I nodded as he frog-marched her to a closet, shoved her inside, and locked the door.

"You two gorillas ... just better unlock this door and take me home ... pronto ... or -- or my husband will have every lawman in the state hunt you down."

"Yeah ... yeah," said Duffy while he removed the bandage from his hand and poured whiskey into the open wound. Though it burned like hell, there was no sound out of Duffy. He calmly bandaged it again with a clean cloth.

"I -- I mean it," she said and promptly pounded upon the door.

"I mean it ... too," said Duffy. He unlocked the door, latched onto the cupcake's neck, and marched her to the bathtub. Her eyes widened at the sight of the tub, filled with brown water. She rose on tiptoe and inched away from the tub. When she bumped into me, Duffy scooped her up and unceremoniously dropped her into the icy water. She thrashed about, trying to escape. Duffy was up to the task though. He snared a fistful of curls and submerged her head under the water, watching the bubbles rise to the surface. When he raised her head, she coughed and snorted. He promptly dunked her again. This time he held her head under for a full minute. Up she bobbed, and back down she went into the freezing water. After each immersion, she groaned more feebly than the last. Finally, when Duffy held her head above the water, her narrow shoulders quivered. Her back sagged. Duffy smiled and winked to me. "Had enough?"

She nodded meekly. When he hauled her to her feet, she huddled against him, her teeth chattering.

She offered no resistance when he stripped away her coat, which glistened in the dim light, and tossed it into the corner. "D-don't k-k-kill ... me." With nimble fingers, she tried desperately to cover her naked shoulders with her tattered dress.

"Behave yourself and do as we says," said Duffy. He took her under the arm, forcing her to rise up on her toes, and led her to the kitchen. There he poured whiskey into a mason jar and handed it to her. Without blinking, she gulped down the liquor. She then allowed Duffy to escort her to the closet, where he locked her inside.

I was sure that I would have difficulty falling asleep because of all the excitement. And I did. It was well after one o'clock when I finally dozed off. Several times during the night, I awoke and heard the faint sobbing of the cupcake. I felt sorry for her, but business was business.

Long before the sun climbed the eastern sky, the aroma of freshly brewed coffee wafted throughout the house. From the dour expression upon Duffy's face and the bags under his eyes, I knew that he had not slept well either.

Duffy, a barely adequate cook, was busily humming to himself and stirring a pan of fried spuds when I joined him in the smoke-filled kitchen.

"Wanna get the cupcake ... while I pour the coffee?" said Duffy, nodding to the closet, where all was quiet.

"Sure." Cautiously, I unlocked the door and peeked into the dark cubicle. The cupcake sat in a corner hugging her knees. "Breakfast is ready."

Sighing expansively, she pulled herself up. She then padded seductively into the kitchen. I followed. I often heard men talk about a broad havin' Rockette legs. Since I never was to Radio City Musical Hall, I never saw a Rockette's legs. However, I saw pinups of Betty Grable and Jane Russell and Rita Hayworth. All had fabulous gams. The cupcake, however, had nothing to be ashamed of. Her pins were absolutely stunning. And the ankles -- well -- since this narrative don't allow me to elaborate upon her attributes in detail, let me jus' say they were sculptured like those of a goddess.

Seating herself, she tossed her auburn mane over her shoulder. "I -- I take it ... I'm being held for a large ransom." She lifted her coffee cup with both hands and sipped slowly, studying us for a reaction.

"Ten grand," I said and offered her the sugar bowl, which she declined.

She blinked and fought back a large tear. "Well, Henry loves me deeply ... so-o-o I don't think I'll be here very long before you get your money."

"While you're our guest, we expect you to cook the meals, scrub the floors, clean the pots ... uhm ... and do the wash."

"Am I a hostage or a maid?"

"Either yous do as told ... or yous will go fer another bath ... errr ... this time ... ugh ... naked as a jaybird," said Duffy, rolling up his sleeves and flexing his biceps.

"Better do as Duffy says." I smiled at the cupcake. She merely turned her nose up and dabbed the corners of her mouth. "I'm going into town to scout around and see how the locals reacted to your kidnapping."

As soon as I stepped out of the shack, a Canadian clipper rushed down the slope and chilled me to the bone. The blast reminded me that my threadbare coat needed to be replaced as soon as we received the ransom money. "Brr-r-r-r!" I slapped my hands against my thighs and quickened my pace along the path, where a dusting of snow covered the tawny remains of the coneflowers.

"Don't drive too fast," I said to myself once the Chevy engine sprang to life, "because you don't wanna attract attention." A short time later, I entertained the same thought as I drove down Main Street. Slowing to a crawl, I peeked at the mayor's house. All appeared peaceful.

I decided to visit Mitch's Emporium and purchase a couple of Hershey bars. Perhaps there I'd find out how the locals responded to the kidnapping.

Mitch, a tall, barrel-chested man with deep-set eyes, was filling his potato bin when I entered the store.

"Morning," said Mitch looking up. "Hershey bars?"

"Two ... please." I nodded to the empty chairs surrounding the chess board. "Too early for chess?"

"Hell ... after that big Christmas party the mayor tossed last night ... over at the town hall ... everybody's still sleeping it off. Henry and the boys won't be in fer quite some time."

I paid for the candy bars and wandered up Main Street. Just past the town hall, I spied the Chief of Police, and Lester Kunkle, the town's only other policeman. Both were sitting in the squad car, reading a newspaper and sipping coffee.

A kidnapping had taken place in town. The ransom note was duly delivered. But no one seemed upset over the crime. And as the day unfolded, there was no visible change in the town's demeanor. How could a community be so apathetic to a serious crime?

In frustration I returned to the shack and learned that the local radio station failed to announce anything about the abduction.

"I don't understand it," I said, throwing up my hands in disgust. "We snatch a real gorgeous cupcake right from under their noses, and -- and no one cares." I nodded and cracked my knuckles. "Life goes on as if nothin' happened."

After a supper of fried scrapple, mashed spuds, and canned peas, we set up the eight-inch Magnavox television on a box in the parlor. We seldom played it because the reception was poor until after midnight. Johnny Carson always looked like the Ghost of Christmas Past. And whenever an airplane circled overhead, the picture vibrated, rolled, and then disappeared for several minutes. The audio, however, was always good. Therefore, we decided to listen to a Groucho Marx rerun, while the cupcake, now clad in one of Duffy's flannel shirts, which gave us a good look at her gorgeous legs, scoured the pots and pans.

We knew that Martinville had no radio or television station. As for the weekly newspaper, it was not due to hit the newsstand for another three days. But Skyport had a family owned television station, which broadcast the local news. We hoped that the station might carry some news of the cupcake's abduction.

After the local weather, the obituaries, and a story on Flash Coogin, a local bowler, the Martinville Police Chief appeared with Henry.

I glanced at the fuzzy picture of the mayor and then at the cupcake, who shuffled into the room and knelt before the Magnavox, revealing her ebony soles. After studying her features, I calculated that a difference of some forty-some years existed in their ages.

The cupcake brushed the snarled curls from her rosy cheeks and folded her hands like one of those saints on a holy picture. From the smug expression on her face, I knew she expected her husband to affirm his love for her. We all expected him to state that he would happily pay the ransom money for her safe return. However, he mumbled something about poverty. That statement rocked the three of us. He then addressed the cupcake personally. And after hemming and hawing for several seconds, he explained to the audience that he would pay no ransom for her release. He ended by requesting that she understand and accept his position. By the time the newscaster mentioned the F B I, the cupcake had scuffed away, sniffling.

"T-that creep!" she shouted, causing a blue vein to surface on her forehead and bulge. "He's got twenty grand in cash in a safe at home ... eer ... from kickbacks, and he doesn't want to part with ten grand to save my life."

Duffy followed her into the kitchen and patted her shoulder. "Sorry he feels that way about yous." If yous was my wife ... I'd pay anything to get yous back."

She gazed into his gray eyes and nodded. "I need a good stiff drink." She promptly poured herself a shot of whiskey and passed me the bottle.

"It ain't none of my business," I said, sipping the liquor, "but how did you get hooked up with that old goat? He don't seem like your type."

She poured herself another drink and slumped into a chair. "You're right. It's none of your business." She closed her eyes and rested her chin of her folded hands. "But just for the record ... I was a kootchy dancer in Vegas when I met Henry. He had just lost his third wife."

"Third wife?" inquired Duffy, who was now scrubbing the pots.

"Yep. The first wife died in some kind of boating accident." She held up her glass for me to fill. "I think the second wife died in Maryland while they were hunting." Duffy glanced at me, and we nodded in agreement. "The third wife forgot to open the garage door ... ugh ... while she was starting her car."

"Are yous thinking the same thing I am?" I asked Duffy.

"Three broads whacked by the mayor," he said and tossed a soapy Brillo pad into the sink.

"Yep."

The cupcake held her booze as well as any man. I believe it was well past midnight when the three of us finished off the last bottle of Four Roses and decided to turn in for the night. We relinquished the bedroom to the cupcake and slept on the floor before the crackling fire in the Franklin stove.

I slept much better than the previous night. As a matter of fact, I didn't awaken until I heard the dying embers hissing in the stove. Quickly I tossed the remnants of our wood pile into the stove in an effort to resurrect the fire.

Duffy, an early riser, was already preparing breakfast, judging from the smell of fresh biscuits, which permeated the shanty. I was sure that the cupcake was still fast asleep after a night of hard boozing. Minutes later, however, her bedroom door opened. The cupcake, her hair still damp from her morning shower, appeared with a radiant glow about her. I switched on the portable radio. After a barrage of commercials, I was greeted by Ace Conway, a local disc jockey. He announced the Mormon Tabernacle Choir's rendition of "Silent Night." Before the choir was finished singing the entire song, he interrupted to announce that Mayor Henry Snodgrass had agreed to pay his wife's ransom as demanded by her abductors.

When I glanced across the room at Duffy, he did not appear overly happy for a man who was about to become wealthy. In the other corner of the room, the cupcake was not exactly doing cartwheels either. As for myself, I felt as miserable as the time the Bums lost the World Series to the Yankees. I couldn't understand it. All three of us were getting what we initially desired. Yet, none of us was happy.

I knew that the mayor was a devious man and considered asking the cupcake to stay with us. Down the road, I was sure, old Henry would decide the cupcake was expendable. I said nothing though. Why? I guess because Duffy deserved to be rewarded for my half-baked scheme. As for the cupcake, she was old enough to choose her own destiny.

Later that morning, after the dishes were scrubbed and stowed away, the three of us climbed into the Chevy and drove in silence to the drop-off point. I still wished that the cupcake would ask us to grab the dough and then drive off to California or Texas or Florida with her and start a new life on the right side of the law. At Rummy Ditch I spied the drop-off point, a split maple tree. Stopping the Chevy, Duffy and the cupcake jumped out. Duffy quickly found the satchel and held it up for me to see. He then opened it up, while gabbin' and smiling to the cupcake. Growing impatient, I finally tooted the horn. They separated, each traveling his way.

I do not believe that we uttered two words to each other the rest of the morning. And all afternoon, we simply sat and stared at the money. It was only after we counted the dough for the sixth time and discovered that we were short a C-note that we discussed how we'd spend it.

"Ain't the same without her," I said and meant it. Switching on the Magnavox, I fiddled with the wire coat hanger, we used as an antenna. Perhaps our fortune was really changing because the picture was vivid and the audio crisp. I drew closer to the screen, squinted, and gasped. "They arrested her."

"Huh!"

"The cupcake!" I pointed to the screen. "She's wearin' bracelets."

After turning up the volume, we huddled closer to the Magnavox and listened to the reporter explain that the cupcake had been arrested as an accomplice in her own abduction.

It appeared that her husband found a marked C-note in her fist when she returned home. He then contacted the police. Upon interrogating her, the fuzz decided they had sufficient evidence to book her.

Angrily I switched off the set and stalked Duffy, turning him around. "So that's why we're a C-note short."

Duffy smiled sheepishly. "I took it out of the wad and ... eh ... slipped it to her fer a new dress ... uhmm ... seeing how I shred hers."

"We can't let her take the rap." I poured a cup of java and stared blankly into the murky liquid. "I gotta plan." Duffy looked at me quizzically. "Are you in ... even if it means we give up all the ransom money?"

"If it clears the cupcake ... I'm in."

"It's Christmas Eve." I repeatedly tapped Duffy's chest for emphasis. "The mayor ain't gonna be expectin' nobody to make a house call."

"We're gonna break into his house?"

"It's a desperate plan to save the cupcake, but I'd feel awful if we didn't try. Besides ... if it wasn't for us ... she wouldn't be sittin' in the can."

Though only five o'clock, the sun had already set behind the mountains, throwing the shack into a very depressing sight. In hopes of lifting my spirits, I switched on the radio and found Perry Como crooning "White Christmas."

The break-in, to be successful, had to take place late at night when everyone was asleep. I, therefore, listened to Perry sing while I planned the crime over and over again in my mind. For some reason I kept thinking of the cupcake sitting alone in the caboose. I was sure she wasn't listening to Perry sing "White Christmas."

Late that night, as I strolled down the street and approached the mayor's house, all dark and foreboding, I hummed "White Christmas" to myself and the English holly. I paused and recalled that this was the exact spot where we had snatched the cupcake only a few days ago.

I breathed deeply, exhaled, and shot out a cloud of vapor, which instantly disappeared. Nervously I fondled the picklock in my pocket, while surveying the silent house before me. Nonchalantly, I strolled up the path as if calling upon the mayor for a cup of eggnog. But when I reached the stoop, I paused and glanced about. When I saw no one in the area, I ducked under some sort of fruit tree and headed for the yard. I was quite pleased that the ground was as hard as iron and void of any snow because my gummers would leave no footprints.

From casing the joint I knew which door I wanted to pick. And from conversation with the cupcake, I knew exactly where the mayor's safe was located.

"The old coot's probably out boozing, while the cupcake's sittin' in the jug."

Ever since I decided upon the housebreaking scheme, I questioned my skills. I truly wondered if they had eroded. Much to my delight, however, none of my talents had vanished. I quickly picked the lock and let myself into a small mudroom, where an assortment of galoshes, mackinaws, shovels, and ceramic pots shown under my flashlight.

"So-o-o ... far ... so ... good." On silent cat's paws I crept down the gloomy hall. I paused when a grating noise off to the right startled me. Freezing, I listened. Just then the grandfather's clock coughed and tolled twice. "Scary ... place."

On I walked until I spied the drab mahogany door of the study, which was slightly ajar. Without touching the knob, I slipped into the tobacco-reeking room and was welcomed by the safe. It stood against the far wall and looked like a squat sumo wrestler.

The object of my quest was a Sears and Roebuck Acme crate. I judged, from the flanged door, that it was manufactured around 1900. I flashed my light upon the lock, but before I could study it more comprehensively, I heard the front door squeak. "Oh, crap!" With my night vision as acute as ever, I glanced about. The front door closed and heavy steps approached. Spotting a walk-in closet, I quickly and quietly concealed myself among mothballs and moth-eaten smoking jackets. I cocked my ear. The slow, ponderous steps grew more distinct. Suddenly a table lamp flashed dimly in the study.

Because of my seclusion I saw nothing. But I heard the mayor wheeze, the slurping of his tongue, and a loud burp.

Holding my breath, I fingered the blackjack in my pocket. If uncovered, I would baptize the mayor with the sap and let the chips lie where they fell.

Much to my relief, the old drunk merely poured himself a second shot. After gulping it down, he switched off the light, leaving me alone in the dark.

I slipped out of the closet only after I heard the toilet gurgle and the water race through the pipes. I then sprang into action.

I learned my trade on the Acme's combination lock, while I was still a pup in Chicago. I honestly believe that over the years I had peeled more Acme crates than I cared to remember.

Since I considered myself an innovator amongst those of my generation, I used a stethoscope to listen as the numbers registered. Most of the time, the combination was solved within minutes, and the heavy door swung open.

The spacious inside appeared empty, save for a big, brown bag. However, when I flashed my light on the bag, it pulsated. "Cripes! A snake. He keeps a stinkin' rubber boa constrictor inside his crate." The boa, a native of the Seattle area, was surprised to see me. It coiled its olive-brown skin around its head. When I reached to pet it, the boa ejected a pungent secretion, fouling the immediate air. "Not gonna hurt you." I lifted the two-foot long reptile and placed the ransom money inside. I then deposited the boa on top and sealed the door. "Good luck, Henry. I hope you can explain all that ransom money to the fuzz … when they show up."

For some reason I could not get that silly Christmas carol out of my head. I hummed it as I stole away from the mayor's house. I was still singing "White Christmas" the following day.

"Goose, turkey, or ham fer Christmas dinner?" asked Duffy. I found his words amusing because there were only four hotdogs, six spuds, and three eggs in the icebox.

"Goose," I said morosely, thinking of how we would never see the cupcake again.

Just then the wind wailed like an air-raid siren and swooped down upon the loose shutters. Of course it whipped them against the windows, creating dancing shadows on the floor. "Some wind out there."

I raised my finger to my lips. "Shhh-h-h. Hear that?"

"The fuzz?"

The wind subsided, but the soft tapping on the door persisted. "What else can go wrong?" As I strode to the door, my stomach churned. Throwing the door open, I beheld a beaming cupcake, framed in the doorway. She smiled and gently set down her suitcases.

"Got room for a cupcake?"

Balloon Reconnaissance

If I asked you what Alexander Graham Bell's most famous invention was, you would immediately tell me the telephone. And, of course, you would be correct.

However, if I asked you what Herman Snellen developed (during that same time period), you would stare at me with a blank expression upon your face. You might even ask, "Who is Herman Snellen?"

I mentioned Snellen because his contribution to society has affected my life greatly. But more about Herman Snellen later.

Ever since my dad took Paul Stefanski, who is my cousin, and me to the Hancock County Fair to watch a barnstorming pilot by the name of Tug Tucker execute barrel rolls, spins, dives, and even a loop-the-loop in his Jenny, I was hooked on flying. As for Paul, not so much.

Since Paul was a year older than I am, he graduated from the Tioga Conservatory in the spring of 1917. I didn't receive my degree until the following year.

Being very patriotic, Paul volunteered for the Army Air Service, hoping to continue his musical career in an army band.

Much to his surprise, however, a devious recruiter assigned him to Camp Carson to undergo flight training.

Since I never truly liked Paul (I don't know why), I chuckled gleefully at his predicament. I recalled that, as a child, Paul always experienced motion sickness when jarred even slightly. Of course an airplane in flight undergoes much agitation. Unbeknownst to anyone, I secretly counted the days until Paul was dismissed from flight school and transferred to latrine duty.

Much to my disappointment, Paul had outgrown his days of motion sickness and blossomed into a competent pilot.

Last week the *Tioga Times,* our local newspaper, reported that he shot down two or three German planes over the skies of France. And after being shot down himself, he managed to escape from his captors and returned to his unit in England.

Days after his debriefing, he was promoted to the rank of captain and installed as an aide-de-camp to General Billy Mitchell.

The story didn't end there. He promptly went out and married an enchantress by the name of Elizabeth Madison. The *Times* article ended with the statement that he had been recently recommended for the Distinguished Service Cross and the Silver Star.

Angrily I folded the clipping and thrust it into my pocket. Deep down, I knew that I could be a better pilot than Paul. All I needed was an opportunity.

Therefore, the day after my graduation, I paraded down Main Street to the post office to enlist in the Army.

Once inside the post office, a clapboard building built during the Civil War, I descended a flight of rickety stairs to the basement that reeked of old newspapers and formaldehyde.   Near several sacks of mail, I paused and studied my surroundings.   Glancing right and then left, I spied the Recruiting Office between Congressman Moses Bumgardner's Office and the Farm Bureau's kiosk.

With head held high and arms swinging like a Hussar, I marched down the dank and dismal corridor to the Army Recruiting Office.   At the door I paused momentarily to collect my thoughts before throwing it open.   And then I counted to ten before I strode inside and marched up to a roly-poly sergeant with floppy ears, from which sprouted tufts of coarse red hair.

In the space of a few seconds, I saluted crisply (the sergeant returned my salute nonchalantly), introduced myself, and unveiled my diploma in case verification of a college education was required.

"Sergeant," I said, clicking my heels together, "I wish to enlist."

"Good," said the sergeant, eyeing me from head to foot.   He extended his hand and shook mine.   "I'm Sergeant Sam Smathers." With the civilities completed, he handed me a pen, a stack of forms, and pointed to a card table littered with cake crumbs and bits of bread.

Unceremoniously I plopped myself into a chair.   With a flourish of my arm, I swept the crumbs upon the floor, much to the sergeant's displeasure.

Inside of twenty minutes, I completed the enlistment papers. After signing my name, I handed them to the recruiter.

The sergeant, judging from the scowl upon his sallow face, was still upset with my housekeeping initiative.   Nevertheless, he scanned the papers.   "Ste-fan-ski," he said, allowing each syllable to roll laboriously off his tongue.   "Are you, by any chance, related to Captain Stefanski ... errr ... who I read about in the newspaper?"

"No!"

The sergeant scratched his thinning hair.   "Well, if you was, he might be able to get you into flight school, but ... er ... right now we're not taking nobody on as pilots."

If I became a pilot, it had to be on my own merit.   I would accept no nepotism of any sort.   "No, we're not related."

From the look upon his face, I knew he had caught me in a lie. After all, in a small town such as Hancock it was obvious that all the Stefanskis had to be related to each other, if only remotely.   "As ... you ... say."   He tapped the papers against his thigh several times and then pursed his lips.   "We're not taking on any more pilots for airplanes, but

... we do need pilots for observation balloons. Would you be interested?"

For the first time since I read about my cousin in the *Times,* my lips curled into a smile. "Yes, if there's going to be danger and excitement and recognition?"

"If by excitement, you mean hanging from a hydrogen-filled balloon at three thousand feet with Germans shooting at you with machine guns "

I rubbed my palms together in delight. "Go on."

"And you're only armed with a pair of binoculars, a telephone, and a parachute."

"I'm your man."

"Good." The sergeant paced across the room, executed a nifty about-face, and shook a tobacco-stained finger at me. "There is one problem, Carl."

"Oh!"

"You wear glasses."

A lump arose in my throat. "My glasses are a problem?"

"Not once you're in training. If you have a vision problem while training, we'll work on it until it meets our standards."

My shoulders sagged. The sergeant took a long drag on his cigarette and slowly blew the blue smoke skyward. "That's where I come in."

"You."

"Yes, me." After setting his butt aside, he strode to his desk and withdrew a sheet of paper from a drawer. "Here's the answer."

"The ... answer." I accepted the paper and glanced at an eye chart. "An eye chart."

"Not any old eye chart. It's the Snellen Eye Chart."

"The Snellen Eye Chart."

"That's the chart the doctor is going to use next Thursday at Camp Biscayne when he checks your vision."

"My vision."

"Exactly. There are eleven lines. Study them."

"Gottcha." With his advice and encouragement, my career in the Balloon Service now looked promising.

"D ... E ... F... P ... O ... T ... E ... and C is the only line you're gonna hafta read."

"Why that line?"

"Because it's the line that denotes perfect vision."

"D ... E ... F ... P ... O ... T ... E ... C," I said aloud, smiling.

And the following week at 10:00 in the morning, I took a deep breath, looked straight at the chart on the wall, and recited in measured tones, "D ... E ... F ... P ... O ... err ... T ... errr ... E ... uhmm ... C."

"Correct," announced the ophthalmologist. "You're in."

"Dress and report to the auditorium to take your oath," instructed a chubby soldier in a tunic that gathered around his stomach.

"Thank you, Sergeant Smathers," I soliloquized and winked at the forlorn chart. "Thank you ... so much."

As I strode towards the auditorium, I wondered how Paul traveled from Camp Biscayne to Camp Carson. Suddenly I paused in my tracks and slapped myself upon the forehead. What I had just said wasn't true. I had fibbed again. I knew that Paul traveled by train. Aunt Sophie told me as much. She even pressed Paul's letter upon me. I had read all about his journey. Ever since Paul's good fortune, I had become a habitual liar. And ... that had to stop before I lied again ... uhm ... about my own travels to my next destination, which was Camp John Wise in Texas.

As soon as fifty-two of us were sworn into the United States Army, we were issued box lunches and assigned transportation to our various training sites.

Most of the boys climbed into buses for their journey. Those of us, who had hundreds of miles to travel, were issued train tickets. Along with a few other men, I crowded into a Pullman car at the local train station and rode the rails (a three-day trip) to Camp John Wise Aerostation in Texas.

Back in 1915 Major General Leonard Wood organized a summer camp at Plattsburg, New York, to provide military training for young men (such as me) at their own expense. My dad thought that it might be a good idea to participate since war was imminent. And I did. Paul's family saw no need for such training, and so he refrained.

That summer at Plattsburg was spent in daily drill, K. P., guard duty, map reading, celestial navigation, hand-to-hand combat, tactical training, and first aid.

At Camp Wise all of these subjects were taught in great detail. In addition, as the weeks progressed, we studied balloon fabric repair, hydrogen generation and storage, cordage and balloon rigging, basket repair, parachute rigging, and maneuvering a balloon.

About three days before our training concluded, while our platoon was engaged in bayonet training, I was informed by Sergeant Flowers that Captain Hooper, the Company Commander, wished to see me at once in his office.

Instantly I slung my weapon over my shoulder and jogged over hill and dale to the company area. Since I had been a model soldier and had even been made an acting squad leader, I knew that my performance was not in question. "What does Hooper want with me?" I asked a stand of scraggly conifers as I sped past. "I've done everything that they have asked me to do." Ahead an observation balloon, looking like a giant sausage, rose above the trees and hovered menacingly. "My eyes! That's it." When a company of doughboys marched toward me, I stepped aside and waited impatiently until they passed. Once they were gone, I returned to the road and spied the company area in the distance. "I'll bet they found out that I cheated on my eye exam. That damn Smathers ratted on me."

I knew that if charges were leveled against me for cheating, I would probably receive a summary court martial. I stopped dead in my tracks and reflected upon the lecture we attended on our second day at Camp Wise. If court martialed, according to Captain Keller, who delivered the lecture, I could lose pay, be reduced in rank, or be confined for thirty days.

The Army couldn't reduce my rank any lower. And so that punishment wouldn't be considered. As for reduction in pay. I only earned a dollar a day, but I spent almost nothing. I neither drank nor gambled nor visited the local brothels. In all honesty, I sent most of my pay home.

The confinement part did upset me. No one in the family had ever been imprisoned for any sort of crime. And as I recalled Captain Keller's words, it was a thirty-day confinement. Would they shackle me and send me off to Fort Leavenworth for hard labor? Gosh! I hoped not. The local poky would suffice. Perhaps if I stayed close to Camp Wise, the family wouldn't know anything about the incident.

With the thought of prison and the shame that my parents would be forced to bear in the community becoming realities, my knees wobbled, my hands grew clammy, and my left eye blinked uncontrollably.

I attributed the blinking and the wobbling and the clamminess to a type of hysteria I had undergone in the past. Ever since I was a child, my body reacted poorly to stressful situations. I hadn't experienced swelling of the face or chills or nausea since the championship game against Upper Wickton. And so I actually believed that I had learned to cope with my anxieties. However, the summons to see Captain Hooper triggered fear and tension throughout my body.

Though it was a cool day, I perspired profusely. "T-take it easy, Carl, and don't lie to Hooper," I told myself. "Every time you lie, you gotta tell five more lies to cover the first fib. Keep it up ... and one of these days ... your nose is gonna start to grow."

Though I believed in God, I never did much praying in my life. Not even when I attended church. That time was generally set aside for ogling all the young women. I paused before the Company bulletin board and asked for God's help.

Grabbing hold of the railing, I ascended the three steps of the Headquarters building. When I reached the landing, my eyes watered. "Da-a-amn h-h-hysteria," I stuttered and kicked over a butt can. "Ahh-ahh-ahh!" I sneezed violently. "Get a hold of yourself, Carl."

But in addition to the sneezing, my eyes now itched. My nose ran. As I groped for the brass knob, I grew congested. "R-r-relax, Carl." I breathed deeply and sneezed once more. Mucous dripped from my nose like water from a leaky faucet.

Determined to enter the building, I sought the knob. My hand trembled. But I grasped it and held on. I squeezed the knob until my knuckles turned ashen. And then I stepped inside.

At this time of day, the orderly room should have been void of any activity. And it was. Only Corporal King, the clerk, was present.

"Private Stefanski ... uhm ... to see Captain Hooper," I said between clenched teeth.

Corporal King, a towhead with acne, never glanced up from his comic book. "Captain Hooper is waiting to see you, Stefanski. Go on in."

With my rifle still slung over my shoulder, I mechanically strode toward Captain Hooper's office. I mouthed another prayer for good luck and then rapped upon the door.

"Enter," barked a gruff voice.

I began to shake uncontrollably. My head bobbed like a robin digging for worms. My knees vibrated more violently then previously. And my right hand trembled so badly I had to finally settle it with its mate. But I managed to turn the knob, causing the door to creak unmercifully.

With my feet refusing to budge, I grimaced and thrust the right foot toward the opening. Dutifully my left foot followed, and soon I was inside Hooper's office.

I knew that I had to hide my hideous appearance. Quickly and quietly, I shuffled into the shadowy area between the regimental flag and a coat rack.

The hysteria had caused me to commit a cardinal sin. I failed to salute Captain Hooper. He, however, merely stared past me with bloodshot eyes. I was certain that he didn't notice how my body shook along with the mucous covering my chin. Nodding, he dropped his hand to his side. I was now sure that he was about to announce my court martial. "Sir, Private Stefanski reporting as directed."

Captain Hooper, a burly man with a known penchant for alcohol, beckoned for me to approach his desk. "At ease, Stefanski."

"Yes, sir." With the strap of my rifle cutting into my shoulder blade and numbing my back, I took two steps and assumed the at-ease position.

"I called you in to discuss a very serious matter."

"Y-yes, sir." Since I knew that his next words were going to be about my cheating on the eye exam and the impending punishment, I braced myself for the news.

"According to your records ... and verified by the Secretary of the Army ... errr ... you attended summer camp at Plattsburg back in 1915."

"Yes, sir." This was going to be worse than I anticipated. Hooper somehow found out that I sneaked away from the camp one night at Plattsburg and walked into town for a burger and fries. And on another night, I slipped out of camp, met Amy Hodges (a townie), and went swimming with her in a local lake.

"Well, did you know that anyone ... uhm ... who attended that camp is entitled to a commission in the United States Army?"

"No, sir." I began to realize that Hooper knew nothing of my transgressions. He was jabbering about a commission.

"I didn't think so." Hooper opened his desk drawer, retrieved a mug, and sipped. From the smell filling the room, I knew that the mug contained something stronger than coffee. "I took the liberty to contact the Secretary and notify him of your Plattsburg training and your outstanding record here." Hooper rose unsteadily. After taking another sip, he took an envelope from his desk and opened it. "This came today." He smiled. "It's your commission as a second lieutenant in the Army."

"No-o-o!" My jaw dropped. I thought that I wet myself, but I wasn't sure.

"Yes, on Saturday, when your outfit departs for Europe, you will be leaving as Lieutenant Carl Stefanski."

"You did say a commission?"

"I did, Lieutenant Stefanski."

And so there was no court martial. On Saturday, before a sparse crowd, I not only received my Aeronaut Badge but my commission as a second lieutenant in the Army.

The only downside occurred when the guest speaker, a Mr. Baxter of the War Department, spoke. A hulking man with a booming voice, Mr. Baxter stated that the Allies' latest offensive was a huge success on all fronts. He insisted that the Germans would soon sue for peace. "You fellers may be home by Christmas," he thundered and pounded with his fist upon the podium.

With those words, the crowd applauded. Most of my fellow soldiers stood and cheered. I, for one, bit my lip and remained silent. If the war ended soon, as Baxter proclaimed, I would be denied the opportunity to distinguish myself with fame and glory. I wanted the war to continue. At least until I received my due recognition as a gallant soldier and leader of men.

Later that day and during the entire voyage across the ocean, rumors persisted that our outfit would become an army of occupation. Most of the troops believed that we would be stationed somewhere in France.

However, once we disembarked in France, we were transported to an area between the Meuse River and the Argonne Forest. I was happy to see that there were no signs of retreating Germans. If anything, the Huns were on the offensive. It was the Allies who were retreating.

On our second day in the area, Captain Snyder, the new commanding officer, received word that a German artillery piece was wreaking havoc upon a Canadian outfit on our right flank. Would he send up a balloon to locate it?

Captain Snyder sent up a balloon an hour later. No luck. Later in the afternoon another request. Another balloon. Again no luck. A third request came. "Stefanski, I want you and Peterson to go up and take a good look," barked Snyder.

"Yes, sir," I said. Silently I thanked the good Lord for the opportunity to make my mark in history. I also asked God to allow me to function normally under any stressful situation that might arise. "Let's go, Peterson."

"I'm ready, sir," called Private Peterson. From the tone of his voice, I wasn't so sure that he was ready.

After checking his body harness three or four times, he finally climbed into the basket. I followed and signaled that we were ready to ascend.

Minutes later the ground crew released the cable. Quickly the balloon climbed into the sky. I watched us climb and then waved to Captain Snyder. He nodded and then departed.

Once he vanished, scores of soldiers jumped into action. Some mounted antiaircraft installations. Others manned the wagon. And a smaller contingent attended to their machine guns.

With our launch a success, I turned my attention to the telephone and binoculars. Peterson was already checking the maps and chutes.

The balloon now rose swiftly, owing to the crew's rapid release of cable. I don't know if it was due to all the activity onboard or the tension of actually going into battle, but neither of us uttered a word. However, when Peterson buttoned his trench coat and pulled up his collar, I said, "Colder up here ... than back in Texas."

"Y-yes, sir," called Peterson above the howling wind.

Higher and higher we climbed. I took the binoculars and scanned the area below. No enemy troops. No convoys hauling supplies. No artillery pieces. Nothing.

Suddenly the gondola lurched. My stomach churned in response. Peterson's eyes bulged. Steading myself, I peered over the side. "My God! The cable broke," I cried and hoped that I didn't sound frightened.

"We're gonna die," screamed Peterson. When he attempted to call the ground, there was no answer. "What are we gonna do?"

"Nothing. Let's just ride this thing out ... for a few minutes."

The balloon continued to rise and drift. Taking a map, I noticed that we had passed over the Allied lines. Faster and higher we traveled. When we sailed over no-man's-land, I saw no sign of life. No vegetation. No troops. No standing structures.

Though I said nothing to Peterson, I grew concerned. In a matter of minutes we would be in German territory.

"I think it's time we abandoned ship," I said and pointed to the chutes.

"I'm way ahead of you." Peterson had already attached his harness to the nearest chute.

"You go first, and I'll follow."

Peterson nodded, climbed atop the gondola, and was gone. *Whump!* His chute jumped out of its bag, rushed after him, and opened.

Realizing that it was my turn, I attached my harness to the remaining chute. Wondering what sort of medal I might receive for my entry into hostile terrain, I nonchalantly climbed atop the gondola and jumped.

The parachute, however, never opened. Somehow the shroud lines became entangled with the silk chute. Then the mischievous wind caused the chute to coil several times around the cable. "Ohhh ... Shooot!" When I looked down, Peterson had grown smaller and smaller. "Ohhhhh, God!"

The wind dove and swirled around my head, tearing my spectacles from my face. "N-n-no!" I screamed and watched my glasses plummet, end over end, to the desolate earth below.

With the chute being torn to shreds, I free fell. Down, down, down I plunged, head over heels, to my certain death. "Dear God, save me, and I promise that I won't stare at Maddy McCormick in church. Really ... I promise." I closed my eyes and expected to see my young life rush past me. Instead, I saw only blackness and felt the frigid cold sting and slap my face repeatedly. "O-o-o-ouch!"

To add insult to injury, the tattered chute now enveloped me. "Ahh-h-h-h-h!" So this was how I was to die – shrouded in a parachute.

I tensed up every muscle in my body. At any second I expected to crash into the earth. And I did. *Thump!* I heard the crash very distinctly.

In death I was finally free of my chute. But how did I know I was free of my chute if I were dead?

Opening my eyes, I discovered that I had struck Peterson's chute. "W-w-what ... are ... you ... doing ... here?" he shouted above the wind. "You were supposed to use the other parachute. With you attached to me, we're falling too fast."

After I smiled sheepishly, we both glanced up. Peterson's chute had collapsed upon my sudden impact. His face turned white. I suppose mine did, too.

Peterson's mouth moved. He was praying. I joined him in praying for the same thing – a miracle. Soon after I mouthed, "Amen," the sky above us thundered with a roar. "It's Him."

"W-w-who?"

"God.'"

When we both glanced up, we noticed that the chute had mushroomed into a gorgeous umbrella. The Lord had delivered us from certain, untimely deaths. Tears welled in Peterson's eyes. I think I also sobbed.

Somehow my coat had become attached to Peterson's chute. I was certain that God had something to do with that.

Deciding that I needed to tell my grandchildren about the time I shared a parachute with another man, I grabbed hold of Peterson and held on for dear life.

Down we glided as taught at Camp Wise. The landing should not have been text-book perfect. And it wasn't. My six-foot frame landed squarely upon Peterson, who was barely five feet tall. As soon as we crashed to the earth (which I guessed was in no-man's-land) Peterson moaned for several seconds. Lying atop him, with our legs and arms jutting out, I wondered if we looked like Kafka's bug.

I attempted to extricate myself at once. However, our harnesses had become entangled with each other. "Peterson," I whispered, "are you okay?"

"I think so, sir."

"Good." In attempting to untangle our harnesses, I accidently poked him in the ribs. He winced, making me feel worse. "Sorry."

"That's okay. Can you get us free?"

"I'm trying." Reaching into my pocket, I fingered my pocketknife. Retrieving it was another matter. But after I elbowed Peterson in the chest several times, I finally produced it. And then I dropped it.

"W-w-why ... is ... your face ... turning white?"

"I ... err ... dropped the knife."

"Oh, my God! We're finished."

"No, we're not." When I gazed into Peterson's face, I saw nothing but despair. "Roll over."

"I can't ... unless you help me."

"Okay. On the count of three, we roll together."

"Gottcha."

"One ... two-o-o ... thareeee!" We each rolled in opposite directions and nullified our intentions. "Move the other way."

"Right."

"No, left! One ... two ... three." We rolled in the same direction but couldn't quite turn over. "Four!" I jammed my knee into Peterson's buttocks, gained leverage, and turned us over.

"Lieutenant, hurry. You're killing me."

"Sorry." Reaching out with my fingers, I touched the elusive knife. "Slowly I clutched the knife and retrieved it. "Got it."

"Good."

Upon pressing the button, the blade popped out. "Here we go," I said and hoped that I sounded optimistic. Getting to work, I busily hacked at the strap. "Presto!" Without much difficulty, I cut away the strap that joined us and promptly slipped it into my pocket. A souvenir to share with the people at home. That is ... if I ever made it home alive.

At once I climbed to my feet and looked down at Peterson. Though his face was bruised and his neck raw, he appeared none the worse for the ordeal.

"Whew!" he whispered when I helped him to his feet and brushed him off.

"Peterson, may I call you Edward?"

"Call me Ed, sir."

"And you call me Carl." I held out my hand. Peterson smiled and shook it.

"You saved my miserable life today, and I want to thank you from the bottom of my heart."

"Shucks." Peterson reddened. "It wasn't nothing."

"Yes, it was, and we both know it."

Just then, we heard the tread of many hobnailed boots approaching. "Germans?"

"We won't know until they march up out of that ravine."

Because of the risk of a fire and explosion aboard the balloon, we carried no weapons. And we couldn't run away. The woods were two football fields away. Our only alternative was to wait and see. The steps grew louder. I breathed deeply and waited for our visitors. If they were, indeed, Germans, I'd be sending my Christmas cards from Berlin this year.

"I hear them talking."

"What are they saying?"

"I don't know. Think it's in German."

I craned my neck and listened. "I don't hear anything."

"What kind of helmets do the Germans wear?"

"I think they look like coal scuttles. We want to see dishpan helmets like ours and olive-drab uniforms."

The steps ceased. Then resumed. I listened for voices but still heard nothing. Suddenly dishpan helmets appeared. And then the olive-drab uniforms.

"They're friendly troops."

"Yes, they are. Americans ... just like us."

We both waved to the approaching American troops. They smiled and waved back. From the number of doughboys I counted, I surmised that it was a squad. On they came. When they were twenty yards from us, they broke into a trot. Reaching us, they suddenly mobbed us and offered us cigarettes.

In battle no one saluted, and I liked that. The leader held up his hand for silence. "I'm Captain Rogers of the 28th Division."

"I'm Lieutenant Carl Stefanski, and this is Private Ed Peterson."

"I see only one chute. Where's the other parachute?"

"You're not gonna believe this, but we both came down on one chute."

"What!" Rogers walked over to the chute and examined it. "My ... word." He shook his head in disbelief. If I didn't see it, I never would have believed it."

"I guess that's a first."

"As soon as I get back to our lines, I'm gonna recommend the two of you for medals."

"I don't know about Private Peterson, but I don't want any medal. Just doing my job."

Rogers stooped and retrieved the chute. "I'm takin' this thing back for verification, and after the war, I'm going to hang it in my house." Rogers shook his head. "Dadgumit! Two doughboys on one chute."

With dusk fast approaching, we fell in with our rescuers and marched back to their lines. Peterson, who hadn't said much the whole day, suddenly found his tongue. I listened while he explained to another soldier about our haram-scaram adventure.

After he recounted his story, another soldier sidled up to him and asked him to repeat the tale. Of course he did. I smiled and thought about what I had said to Rogers concerning a medal. It was true. I no longer sought glory or fame. All I wanted to do was execute my duties as best I could and go home. I already had enough of war.

Taking the clipping about Paul from my wallet, I held it up to the fading light and then gently tore it into bits. I no longer hated Paul. In fact, I liked the guy very much. Anyone who flew thirty-five missions in a motorized kite was a true hero. I guessed that hundreds of Germans had shot at him during those thirty-five missions. And he must have seen quite a few dead Germans. As for myself ... I had never seen a live German or a dead one. Never fired a weapon in anger. And never spotted the enemy's howitzer, which was my assignment.

On the flip side, I believed that my bouts of hysteria were a thing of the past. If I could cope with a parachute that failed to open at three thousand feet and free us from it, I could handle anything the Fates tossed at me. In fact, I had acted very admirably under a very stressful situation. No excessive blinking. No facial twitches. No nose bleeds.

I decided that if I lived through the war, I wanted to personally thank Paul for his effort. I just had to tell him that he was a real American hero. But most of all, I wanted to be a part of his life ... if he'd allow me.

A Summer to Remember

The Great Depression severely impacted towns and cities that counted upon steel, auto production, construction, railroads, and coal mining for survival. The town of Hancock relied upon none of these industries.

It depended upon gambling, loan-sharking, narcotics, prostitution and racketeering for its existence. The town boasted no nationally known criminals such as Ma Baker or Bonnie Parker or Machine Gun Kelly or Pretty Boy Floyd. But it did have Luigi Pizelli and his well-organized syndicate.

In all honesty, though, the quality of life in Hancock was quite good during the 1930s. Crimes such as murder, robbery, vandalism, rape, and arson did not exist because Luigi would not tolerate them.

All of the social and fraternal establishments in the area offered slot machines, punch boards, and raffle tickets to their patrons. Luigi, of course, siphoned off a portion of the profits from these games of chance. But each organization earned sufficient money to sponsor a softball team or a bowling team or a float in the Christmas parade.

Luigi was also instrumental in funding the town's symphony orchestra, an amusement park, which rivaled Hershey Park, and a municipal swimming pool.

I don't know of anyone in the 1930s who grumbled about life in Hancock or talked about moving away to another area of the country.

As for my family, my parents, Felix and Sophie Skarbeck, immigrated to America in 1900 to build a better life for themselves and their children. And they did. Dad and Mom bought a farm outside of town and down through the years added acreage to the original plot. The fertile land allowed them to rear seven children, of which I was the youngest.

All seven children graduated from the local high school. I, however, was the most fortunate of the children because, in addition to being a high school graduate, I was able to gain a full-paid scholarship to The Tioga Conservatory of Music and Art.

That scholarship, by the way, was awarded to me through the persistent efforts of Mr. Stefanski, an alumnus of the Conservatory and the Hancock Symphony's assistant conductor.

I guess you might call me some sort of childhood prodigy because I played the trumpet in the symphony since I was twelve.

At Tioga, I play in the school's orchestra. To earn extra money, I toot the trumpet in my own quartet at socials in the area and perform magic tricks under the name of the Great Skarbeck.

With school recessed for the summer months, I resigned myself to milking cows and baling hay on the family farm. However, all that changed when Mr. Stefanski telephoned and informed me that President Roosevelt had recently created a federal program to employ college students for the summer months. "Was I interested?" he asked.

"You betcha!" I answered enthusiastically.

"Good. Report to the Court House tomorrow morning at eight o'clock."

And the following morning, I joined Brian Snodgrass, Lily Capsack, whom I escorted to the senior prom, and a petite blonde with captivating blue eyes in Mayor Higby's office.

Of my three companions, I knew Brian and Lily fairly well. Brian was the quarterback on our high school football team and currently attended St. Tuda's College on a football scholarship.

Lily, an Home Economics major at the local teachers' college, was the reigning Miss Hancock. She was also my assistant when I assumed the role of the Great Skarbeck locally. When we performed, I often felt that the audience was more interested in ogling the shapely Lily than in witnessing any of my sleight-of-hand tricks. But we always played to a full house. And that's all that mattered.

The blonde's name according to the name tag on her blouse was Theresa Nave. I personally knew of no Naves living in Hancock. And so I decided that the blonde resided in Pheasant Run, a settlement just outside of town.

As I studied her from across the room, I wondered why I hadn't known her at school. All the people from Pheasant Run attended Hancock High School. A conundrum to be sure.

I was about to introduce myself to Theresa when Miss Thompson, the mayor's secretary, suddenly appeared and announced our assignments.

Brian and Lily were assigned to the Tax Collector's Office on the third floor. As for Theresa and me, we were sent to Judge Anderson's chambers on the fourth floor.

Being a gentleman, I opened the door for Theresa and led her down the hall. "Err ... I'm Leo Skarbeck," I said very politely and extended my hand. Theresa nodded and smiled. She then took my hand, and for some reason, she held onto it for quite some time. "During the year ... ugh ... I attend the Tioga Conservatory ... where I play the trumpet and sometimes ... mmm ... accept gigs as the Great Skarbeck."

Theresa paused and arched her tawny eyebrows. "You're a magician?"

"Yes." I flexed my fingers as if I were about execute a feat of legerdemain.

"Do you make bunnies disappear?"

"I do."

"And hypnotize people?"

"Would you like to be hypnotized?"

"I'm already under your spell."

"Oh!" I stroked my chin and wondered exactly what Theresa meant by her comment.

When we reached the judge's chambers, I bowed and accompanied Theresa inside, where wood paneling covered the four walls and the ceiling. I had to admit that I hadn't seen so much wood since my wood shop class in the seventh grade.

"Good morning," said a chubby matron, wearing a print dress with padded shoulders. In all honesty, she looked like a tackle on a football team. "I'm Mrs. Potts, and you must be Theresa and Leo?"

"We are," we said simultaneously.

"And we're so pleased to have you." Mrs. Potts glanced to the right and then to the left, searching for something. "Theresa, you will occupy that desk over there and be our receptionist." She continued to search but apparently did not find what she was looking for. Finally she glanced at me with her bovine eyes and said, "Leo, you'll just hafta stand around and look handsome until I can get something for you to sit on."

Theresa nodded and immediately reached into a cloth bag and retrieved some sort of porcelain contraption with an electrical cord. When Mrs. Potts and I looked at each other quizzically, Theresa reddened. "I have asthma," she said apologetically. "This is an electrical nebulizer." She swallowed with some difficulty. "When I have an asthmatic attack, I … uhm … breathe in some of the aerosolized medicine." We both nodded sympathetically.

While I watched Theresa set up her nebulizer, Mrs. Potts explained that I was to replace the late Jake Arnold as the judge's tipstaff.

"A what?" I asked in complete ignorance.

"A tipstaff." Mrs. Potts folded her tiny, chapped hands before her and smiled faintly. "A tipstaff escorts witnesses and juries to and from the courtroom and uhh … does whatever jobs the judge assigns him."

"Like legal work?"

"Exactly."

While Theresa spent the morning fine-tuning her nebulizer and answering the telephone, Mrs. Potts sent me over to Kort's Dry Cleaning on Pine Street to claim one of Mrs. Anderson's dresses. Upon my return, I shined the judge's riding boots (of course he wasn't wearing them at the time) and trudged over to the Acme to pick up the judge's pre-ordered groceries.

When I returned to the Judge's chambers with the groceries, Mrs. Potts discovered that I had inadvertently been given the wrong groceries. Back I went to the Acme.

It was well past twelve when I returned with the correct groceries. Much to my surprise the chambers were empty. Everyone had departed for lunch. Being acquainted with foodstuffs, from all my years of eating, I rummaged through the bags, sought the items I deemed perishable, and stuffed them into the icebox in the judge's private office.

I had never known any judges (I hadn't met Judge Anderson as yet), and so I had never frequented their private haunts. I must confess that the average man on the street was truly suffering during the worst depression in the country's history. However, the judge's inner sanctum was elaborately furnished with everything from a liquor cabinet (fully stocked with Canadian liquor), to a private shower, to a unique bed, which I had never ever seen in a respectable man's bedroom.

Mom, always thoughtful, insisted earlier that morning that I carry a ham sandwich in my pocket. "Jus' so you eat somethin' ven you have no time to valk back to farm for cooked dinner," she said, stuffing a sandwich into my coat pocket.

And it was sound advice. For no sooner had I swallowed the last morsel of bread, when Mrs. Potts, slightly inebriated, returned from her liquid lunch. Off I went once more. Over to the vet to pick up Cuddles, the judge's poodle. Then down town to return three Agatha Christie novels to the library. And finally over to the post office to drop off several packages for shipment to California.

When I finally shuffled into the judge's chambers at five o'clock all was dark. A stout elm tree, outside one of the windows, cast shadowy figures upon one of the drawn shades. "Hello!" I called. There was no answer, for everyone had gone home for the day.

From all my day's activity, I should have staggered out of that building and crawled home much fatigued. However, I was young (twenty-one) and had earned a whole dollar for my efforts that day. Furthermore, I had a date that night. In a little over two hours, I would accompany Lily to the amusement park. Life couldn't get any better than that, could it?

As soon as I stepped inside the parlor of our modest farm house, the family greeted me with a barrage of questions. Who did I work with? What were my duties? Did Mayor Higby really wear a wig? Did I occupy a desk near a window?

The questions would have gone on and on, but, thankfully, Mom interrupted the interrogation to announce that supper was waiting on the kitchen table.

Even though I had an hour's walk to Lily's house, I showered once more (rather quickly) and changed clothes. The cold shower fully invigorated me, for I reached Lily's house in less than forty-five minutes.

"My word, you're a bit early," said Lily, her jade eyes flashing, as she welcomed me into the parlor.

"And you look absolutely stunning in that new dress," I said.

Lily blushed with pride. "It's something I designed and put together in one of my elective classes."

Since Lily lived in close proximity to The Whirlwind, the park's roller coaster, we heard the *chug-chug-chug* of the coaster climbing the steep incline as soon as we ventured outside. I couldn't answer for Lily, but I could feel my pulse quicken as we walked up the cobbled street.

Two hours ago I was toting a handful of packages up Main Street on my way to the Post Office, and now I was escorting the former captain of the Hancock High School cheerleaders to an evening of fun and excitement at Freedom Park.

Ahead I could see that the admission line was strung out around the bronze statue of General Winfield Scott Hancock, for whom the town was named. "Won't take long until we're inside," I said reassuringly and gently squeezed Lily's delicate hand.

She looked up into my eyes and smiled. "I know."

And it didn't take long for us to reach the front of the line, where a family of ten, eight children and their parents, stood in front of us.

I knew most of the people in Hancock, but I certainly didn't recognize the family standing proudly and quietly before us. I could tell that they were not wealthy by their clothes, which were not new but very clean.

While the father, a willowy, sallow-faced man, rocked on his heels, his wife held onto his hand and beamed proudly.

"Next!" cried the ticket lady in the booth.

The father cleared his throat and tipped his faded fedora. "I'd like two adult tickets and eight children's tickets." When he glanced at his wife, she nodded in agreement.

"That will be twelve dollars, sir."

Instantly the father's jaw dropped; his wife turned pale. "T-t-that … ugh … can't be." He looked at the children, who stood motionless. "Isn't admission twenty-five cents … err … per child and a buck … errr … per adult?"

"No, sir. Tonight there's fireworks and Johnny Cochoran and the Dreamliners are playing in the ballroom."

"Ohhhh." The father's narrow shoulders sagged.

"It can't be," said the mother, teary eyed. "W-we drove so far jus' to get here, and … and we're jus' gonna hafta turn roun' and go home."

I knew that I had to act and quickly. Without batting an eye, I slipped my hand into my pocket, withdrew ten dollars, and dropped it nonchalantly. "Oh, my," I said loudly. Bending over, I retrieved the money from the ground, rose, and handed it to the father. "You must have accidentally dropped this, sir."

Before the stunned man could utter a word, I slipped it into his hand, which trembled. The wife, looking on, sobbed and clutched her husband's arm. The glint in the man's twinkling black eyes told me that he appreciated the help. "T-thank you, young man. This night means so much to my family."

Lily and I watched the family happily walk through the turnstile and pass into the park. "That was so nice of you," said Lily, inching closer to the ticket booth.

"Uuuh! Lily," I said softly to the back of her head. "I don't have any more money."

"What!" Lily pivoted on her toes like Frankie Frisch (Cubs second baseman) trying to complete a double play and scowled at me with pure disbelief in her green eyes. "You … have … no … money."

"I thought you'd understand." I felt my face turn beet-red. "We could come back another time."

She marched up to me, stood on her tiptoes, and pounded upon my chest. "I don't want to come back another time, you idiot. I wanted to see Johnny Cochoran and the Dreamliners … tonight."

Holding up my hands, I noticed that several people had paused en route to the park and were watching us with interest. "I'm sorry. I'll make it up to you."

"No, you won't, buster." She shook a finger in my face. "And I'll tell you why."

"Please do." As she moved closer, I retreated slightly.

"Because I don't ever wanna see you again." As she grew angrier, a purple vein in her forehead surfaced and bulged. "I will no longer talk to you or … or be your assistant in that stupid magic act … which … I might tell you succeeded … because of my body. Without me … that … that act is kaput."

"I think you're wrong. I'm a pretty fair magician."

"No, you're not. You're nothing but a farmer."

"Really!"

"You're gonna spend your whole life milking cows and playing the bugle---"

"Trumpet. There's a difference."

"Trumpet or bugle. They're all the same to me. When you're

seventy-five, you'll still be playing in the town band with all the local yokels." She pointed to herself. "And, as for me, I'll be a famous fashion designer over in Paris." She stamped her foot, turned, and stormed down the street, still berating me.

"Well, I guess she told me a thing or two." Several people standing by, nodded in agreement. And when I turned in the opposite direction, I noticed that quite a crowd had witnessed our heated argument.

Crestfallen, I thrust my hands into my pockets and walked toward Main Street. Being a Friday night, the retail stores were open until nine o'clock, and so quite a few people were still busy shopping.

At the corner of Sixth and Bedford Avenue, I spotted Brian and Carol Angstadt, his steady girlfriend, exiting Miller's Ice Cream Parlor. They didn't see me. And I wanted to keep it that way because Brian knew that I had a date with Lily. When he saw that I was alone, I knew that I had some explaining to do. And explanations can sometimes be humiliating or worse. I, therefore, turned down Bedford Avenue and avoided a possible embarrassing situation.

Bedford Avenue, lined with stately sycamores, was quite dark and rather deserted. It was just the sort of thoroughfare I sought. I marched on for three blocks before I saw another soul. And then in the next block I spied two lovers, hand-in-hand, strolling along leisurely.

Up ahead I spotted a woman and her shadow singing quietly, "Once ... I built a-a-a-a ... rail ... road ... now ... it's done ---"

"Brother ... can ... you spare a ... dime?" We sang in unison. The girl, probably startled, turned. In the somber amber street light, I quickly recognized Theresa. Slowly we walked toward each other and met under the soft glow. "What are you doing here?"

"I live nearby."

"You do?"

"And what are you doing so far from home?"

I stopped in my tracks. "How do you know where I live?"

"I have my spies, and they tell me everything I want to know."

"Humph!"

"Well, since you're here, I think it's only proper that you escort me home."

"I agree." We took several steps before I asked Theresa a question that had been burning inside me. "How come I never knew you before today?"

Theresa slipped her slender fingers into my hand and paused. "Because I recently moved to Hancock from upstate New York."

"Oh!"

"My parents were killed a month ago in an automobile accident, and so-o-o-o I moved here to live with Aunt Maria and Uncle Luigi."

"Errr ... Uncle Luigi?"

"Yes, Luigi Pizelli. He's quite wealthy. Owns the Pizelli Furniture Store." From the tone of her voice, I could tell that Theresa was proud of her uncle and knew nothing of how he had accumulated his fortune. And I surely wasn't going to inform her that he was a gangster.

"Yes, I know of the store."

Suddenly we stopped in front of an unpretentious Tudor home. Squinting, I perceived a duffle bag lying on the front stoop. Upon closer observation, however, I noticed that it was a man, hunched over, sitting in front of the door.

Theresa squeezed my hand. That's Uncle Luigi. Come and meet him. You two have a lot in common."

"We do?" I took a step back.

"Yes, you play the trumpet, and he plays the accordion."

"I guess we do have something in common."

Up the brick walk we walked, no longer holding hands. I walked as quietly as I possibly could, while Theresa thumped upon the bricks in her high heels like a thundering buffalo.

"Theresa, where have you been?" asked Uncle Luigi with a definite nasal quality in his voice. "I was ready to come looking for you." When he rose from the shadows of the stoop, I noticed that he was as tall as I was.

"Out walking," she said very pleasantly, "and singing to myself."

Uncle Luigi chuckled. "Always singing."

"Yes, always singing." Seeing that I stayed behind, she gently nudged me to the forefront. "Uncle, this is Leo Skarbeck." I smiled. But in the dark, I doubt if Uncle Luigi noticed. "He's a great musician ... er ... with the local symphony, and I work with him ... uhh ... down town."

Uncle Luigi extended his hand, and I grasped it. "I wouldn't say *great*," I protested.

"I would," said Uncle Luigi, still pumping my hand. "You play trumpet with our symphony."

I was actually shocked that Uncle Luigi knew of me, an unheralded trumpet player. "I've been with Mr. Salini (the conductor since the orchestra's creation) for a long time."

"I know. I have followed your career closely over the years."

"He's now studying at Tioga," said Theresa with a tinge of pride in her voice.

"And you're at Julliard studying dance, drama, and music."

When Uncle Luigi informed me that Theresa was studying at Julliard, the most prestigious music school in the country, I almost

104

swallowed my tongue. "Ju-u-u-lli-i-ard! Wow!" Being quick witted and knowing that our group, The Hay Seeds, often discussed the need for a good female voice, I blurted out, "With all due respect, Theresa, my quartet is deeply in need of a female singer." I stole a peek at Uncle Luigi for his reaction and detected a wide smile on his Sicilian face. "And if it's okay with you and your family, we'd like you to join our little group tomorrow for a gig down at the Grantville Fire Company carnival."

"What do you say, Uncle?" said Theresa, pleading with folded hands and jumping up and down like a child. "May I?"

"Why of course. You have my blessing."

"Ahhh … I'm also in dire need of an assistant for my magic act," I said. "It's very easy to learn."

Without waiting for Uncle Luigi's approval Theresa exclaimed, "Yes! Yes! Yes! I'll be your assistant."

The following morning I telephoned Zeke, Harry, and Carl, the other three members of the quartet, to inform them of the altercation between Lily and myself. All three already knew of the quarrel. In Hancock bad news traveled very quickly. Not one in the group was sorry to see Lily depart. And when I explained that I had auditioned and then invited Theresa to join the group, they unanimously approved my decision.

To the uninitiated, a hayseed is a simple, unsophisticated person who lives in the country. All four of us not only resided in the country, but we were actually sons of farmers. And hence we called our group the Hay Seeds. To dress like country bumpkins caused some concern. In the end, we all decided to wear bib overalls, identical flannel shirts (purchased at Groves Country Store for seventy-five cents apiece), and straw hats.

Since the job began at two o'clock, we packed Carl's truck at noon. If you know anything about a Graham Brothers Truck, you are aware that only three people can sit in the front seat. Therefore, I always drove by myself in Dad's Maxwell. I had hoped that Theresa would join me. But since her aunt and uncle wished to see her perform, Uncle Luigi's chauffer was scheduled to transport them in the family automobile.

At precisely two o'clock, Carl struck his drum sticks together three times and we let go with our rendition of "Puttin' on the Ritz." The crowd quickly gathered in front of the raised stage and cheered us on.

Five seconds later, Theresa, dressed in a white-sequined dress and matching heels, wiggled onto the stage and began shimming to the music. The crowd went wild. Nonchalantly I scanned the crowd for

Theresa's aunt and uncle. I spotted them beaming and applauding happily under a giant poplar near one of the fire trucks. Judging from what I saw, Theresa got her looks from her aunt, who was quite younger than Luigi.

Lily may have been beautiful, but Theresa, in all honesty, matched her beauty. In addition, Theresa had a stage presence that Lily could never match. With her seductive eyes blazing and her hips vibrating, she captivated not only the audience but me as well.

As soon as the song ended, the band struck up "Brother, Can You Spare Me a Dime." Theresa, her body glistening and her tousled ringlets dangling like sausages in a butcher's shop, kicked off her high heels. She then jiggled her toes, padded to the mike, and crooned, "They ... used ... to tell ... me-e-e ... I was ... build-ing ... a ... dream---"

Before she could utter another word, the heavens opened and torrents of rain poured from the skies. "Pull the cord on the mike," called Zeke as the crowd scattered in every direction.

The first duty of a musician in such a situation is to protect his instrument. Harry and I, therefore, slipped our horns into their respective cases, while Carl tossed a tarp upon his drums and Zeke stowed his bass fiddle into its gig bag.

Since I was the leader, I always checked everything before the band left the site. And so while I made sure all of our equipment was secure, Carl, Harry, and Zeke raced across the vacant field to the fire station's social hall.

Dropping to my knees, I made one last check on the microphone cable and was satisfied. When I looked past the cord, I spied Theresa's ankles. Moving my eyes up past her ankles, I saw that her dress, completely drenched, clung to her body and highlighted her figure. "My God, you're built," I cried above the roar of the howling wind.

"Yes, I am," she said and winked.

Like a trooper she stood beside me and waited. Instinctively, I collected my trumpet, rose, and took her hand. "Come with me. I know the perfect place to ride out the storm."

"Lead on."

And I did. Remembering that the stage was actually built upon a storage room, which was no longer in use, we descended a staircase to a rusted steel door. With the rain cascading down my face in buckets, I clutched the door knob and turned. The knob creaked and balked. But it turned. I smiled to myself and put my shoulder to the door. By degrees it squeaked open. "A-haa!" Years of stagnate air assaulted our senses and rushed past us as we stepped inside. Soon gossamer cobwebs tickled our faces. Droplets of water dripped from the ceiling. "We'll be as snug as a bug in a rug ... ehh ... if you're not frightened by spiders and ants and dead bodies."

"With you by my side, Hon, I'm not afraid of anything." Slowly our eyes and noses grew acclimated to the darkness and the foul odors. "Ahhhh!"

"What's the matter?" I paused and stood stark still.

"I just tread on something cold and squishy."

"Probably the eyeballs and brains of old man Caruthers."

"O-o-old ... m-man ... Car-r-ruthers?"

"Yep." I gently took Theresa by the hand. "He was murdered in this room about ... mmmm ... twenty years ago, and..."

"And?" When Theresa drew closer to me, I pulled her even closer, lifted her face, and kissed her tenderly.

"And they never found his severed head until ... you just stomped into its pulpy remains."

"I'll tread in his entrails if you'll kiss me again." I kissed her again. More passionately. "Hon, it might be rainin' cats and dogs outside, but I'm havin' the best time of my life." She stood up on tiptoe and kissed me. "Please don't let this day end."

"Okay."

Ahead I observed a hazy streak of grayness. Onward we plod past the skeletal remains of one-armed bandits and splintered roulette tables and mildewed shreds of canvas scenery (probably used as backdrops for summer concerts). The gray light thickened, revealing antique music stands. And then before us, we observed a wall of lattice work that looked out to the fire house across the field. If anything the storm's intensity had increased.

"I guess we won't be going anywhere soon."

"Nope. I don't suppose so." I searched the area intensely and discovered exactly what I had hoped to find --- a wicker settee. I pointed to it. "Not too bad to sit on."

"No, not too bad." Taking the large, red bandana from around my neck, I dusted off the seat and sat. Theresa immediately plopped herself down next to me and drew her legs up beneath her dress. We embraced and kissed again and again and again. "Whew! I need some air." Theresa sat up and ran her finger across my lips. "Hon, what do you and the boys generally do after you're finished performing?"

I reflected for several seconds. "Well, since we're in Grantville, we always stop at the Grantville Diner and chow down."

"Could we do that today?"

"I don't see why we can't." Outside the wind shifted and blew icy-cold rain into the storage room. "Move closer and I'll warm you." She did, and I did my best to warm her shivering body.

About an hour later, the rain subsided enough for us to vacate the room. We judiciously retraced our steps, climbed up the staircase to the stage, and peered out over a landscape that had become a gigantic pond. Gone were all of people. Gone were Zeke, Carl, and Harry. Gone were the ten dollars that we should have earned that day.

I knew that if the guys had stopped at the diner, Carl's truck would be quite visible in the parking lot. However, when I eased the Maxwell into a parking space just in front of the Philadelphia trolley, which had been converted into an eatery by Jacob Zook, the only occupant was Jacob's horse and buggy.

"What is that?" asked Theresa as soon as she alighted from the automobile.

"That is the means of travel for an Amish man and his family," I said and opened the door for Theresa.

Once inside the long, narrow diner, we were greeted by two teenage girls dressed in long, purple dresses. On their heads they wore Amish bonnets. Both wore high-button shoes and pointed to Theresa's bare feet and disheveled attire. *"Arme seele,"* said the taller girl.

"Barfub und schwanger," said the other girl.

Theresa arched her brows and then latched onto my arm. "I wonder what they said," she whispered.

"Well, if my high school German serves me well, I believe that the first girl said that you were a poor soul, judging from how you look."

"Oh, my!"

"And the second girl said that as a good husband I should keep you barefoot and pregnant."

Theresa eyed me suspiciously. "She said all that in two words?"

I nodded several times. "Yes, she did."

"Well, I know you don't lie." Just then the taller girl pointed to a booth, recently vacated, and we seated ourselves. "Now ... as for being barefoot, that's no problem." Theresa reached over and stroked my hand. "As for being pregnant, there ... errr ... better be a wedding before you make me pregnant."

"I agree."

"Good!"

When the Amish girl handed us the menus, we pored over them for several minutes. Though I had frequented the diner on several occasions, I had never ordered anything except the *Wiener Schnitzel*, which was a breaded veal cutlet.

"I'll have what you have," said Theresa barely above a whisper. When the waitress arrived, I ordered two *Wiener Schnitzels* along with coffee, rolls, and butter. "You do know I am deeply in love with you."

"And how long has that been?"

"Ever since I first spied you at Mass."

"At Mass?"

"Yes. I sing in the choir, and from my vantage point in the loft, I see everything."

"Really!"

"Yep." Theresa released my hand when the waitress delivered our coffee and rolls. "You sit in the third pew in front of the pulpit at the nine o'clock Mass."

"My God! You're right." I added milk to my coffee, stirred it, and drank. "Is there anything about me that you don't know?"

"Have you ever been in love before, and do you have a girlfriend … presently?"

"Yes and no." When I offered Theresa a roll, she accepted one and buttered it slowly before setting it upon her plate. "I was in love with Hattie Hedgemeyer in the fourth grade, and I don't presently have a girlfriend." Taking my cup, I sipped once more.

"I have never been in love until you came along."

"That's gotta be a lie."

Theresa held up her cup with both hands, sipped, and sighed. "No, that's the truth." She set down her cup and ran her bare foot up my leg. "But I am betrothed to be married."

My palms grew clammy. My heart skipped several beats. My stomach rumbled. Theresa quickly noticed the sad expression of my face and placed her hand on top of mine. "Y-you're engaged? I thought you said you were never in love."

"I've never been in love until I met you." With her toes, she pulled down my sock and tickled my leg. "Uncle Luigi says that I have to marry an Italian from Sicily because I'm Italian. Anyone who is not Italian is out of the question. If I marry you, it's a mixed marriage according to him." We both chuckled at Uncle Luigi's warped mind-set. "Supposedly he has contacted some stiff by the name of Giulio Sardi and offered him a coupla bucks if he agrees to make me Mrs. Sardi."

"He's arranging a marriage for you?"

"Yep."

"What are you going to do? You can't marry a man that you don't love."

"You're right." Theresa now seized my cuff with her toes and pushed my pants leg up. "I doubt if this Sardi fellow will ever show." Higher and higher went my pants leg. "But if he does, will you run away with me and get married?"

I reached over, pulled Theresa closer, and kissed her. "Yes, I love you dearly. I had a friend who ran off to Elkton, Maryland, and married his high school sweetheart as soon as they graduated." I knew that I was upset with the news of Theresa being forced to marry another man

109

because my voice cracked and my ears burned. "In Maryland there's no waiting period and no blood test is required."

"Fine." When the waitress brought our entrees, we both nodded and smiled. "Now ... I don't hafta join the convent if this fellow ever shows." We both chuckled and then sampled our food.

"No, you don't."

"By the way, when's our next engagement?"

"Monday evening you make your debut as the Great Skarbeck's assistant."

On Monday Theresa and I took our magic act to Steepsville, where the Sons of Loki held their annual convention. Theresa, ever the enchantress, enthralled the entire male audience as soon as she pranced onto the stage as Erotica, the seductress. To say the least, the show with Theresa, as my assistant, was a huge success. As soon as the curtain fell, Billy Tompkins, Loki's president, rushed up and offered me a verbal commitment for the following year's dinner. He also intimated that the Hungry Club would be contacting me in the near future for a booking.

And the following day, I agreed to terms with Buddy Henderson of the Hungry Club. As to the quartet, which was now a quintet, bookings quadrupled. We barnstormed across the entire state, from West Norton to Kinklewood. Needless to say, our earnings were substantial. And three days before an engagement in Lewisville, a town in close proximity to three covered bridges, I purchased a Model T Ford. New it sold for $520.00. I bought it for a mere seventy-five dollars.

I was eager to give the Ford a good test ride. The drive down to the Christmas-in-July Festival in Lewisville and back assured me that I had made a good acquisition.

However, on that trip, I chipped the mouthpiece of my trumpet. And everyone knows that a damaged mouthpiece can cut or scratch the lips. As soon as I arrived home, I took the mouthpiece to Bennet's Music Store on Main Street for repairs.

Unfortunately the chip was too large to repair according to Mr. Bennet. A new mouthpiece set me back a few dollars, but it was worth the money.

With the two mouthpieces in my pocket, I hurried up Main Street and turned down Milkins Avenue, known to the locals as Millionaire's Row because of all the stately mansions lining the block.

I guess I was about to pass the Steagle Mansion, home of Gustav Steagle, the coal baron, when I noticed a late-model automobile parked near the curb. I thought it odd that an automobile, especially a La Salle, should be parked on the street. All of the mansions had garages in the rear. Additional parking for visitors was also available on the premises.

When I reached the La Salle, the rear door opened and a voice called, "Leo, come in and talk."

Somewhat startled, I paused and peered into the dark interior. "Hello," I said and squinted.

"It's me, Leo. Luigi Pizelli ... errr ... Theresa's uncle." Immediately a short, paunchy gentleman alighted from behind the steering wheel and motioned for me to join Mr. Pizelli, which I did.

I didn't know much about gangsters, but from what I had learned from my parents, siblings, and friends, respectable people didn't conduct business inside parked cars on dark streets. "Good to see you, Mr. Pizelli," I said, lying through my teeth and hoping that after my visit with him I still had a head full of teeth.

"It's also good to see you." After we shook hands, the driver closed the door and stood by the car. "I want to thank you for making my Theresa so happy this summer." He patted me good naturedly on my leg and caressed the material. I, personally, didn't mind the pat. But there was something peculiar about the caress that I disliked.

"Theresa is very talented, and I ... uhm ... was just happy to see her realize her potential this summer."

"Theresa is talented, but you, Leo, are an exceptional musician." Once more he caressed my pants leg, making me feel quite uneasy. "I am sure that when she marries later in the fall, she will look back upon this summer and you with fond memories."

"M-m-married." I said, feigning surprise at the news.

A third caress followed. "Yes, I have arranged a marriage for Theresa with an Italian nobleman from Sicily. He is a war hero."

"How nice."

When Mr. Pizelli mentioned that Theresa's fiancé was a war hero, I was perplexed. Had Italy entered into a war recently that I wasn't aware of? He couldn't have meant the Great War. That was too long ago. The man would have been my father's age. I docketed the information, but believed that Mr. Pizelli had his facts wrong.

After lighting a cigarette and puffing vigorously, he caressed me again. "Now ... I want to do something for you, my boy."

"Oh, there's no need to."

"Yes, there is." Another caress. "I have business connections in Chicago with other furniture dealers, and one fellow in particular is ... ugh ... associated with the Chicago Symphony Orchestra."

"No kidding."

"And this fellow has spoken to the conductor about you."

"Really!"

"The result is that the conductor wants you in his horn section." Mr. Pizelli sat back to allow me to process the offer in my mind. "Are you interested?"

"I'll have to think about it and discuss the offer with my parents."

"Yes, by all means. But don't take too long." Mr. Pizelli then tapped upon the window, and his chauffer immediately opened the door for me.

"Good night." As quickly as I could depart, I did. As soon as the chauffer slipped inside Mr. Pizelli's auto, the engine turned over, and the automobile crawled away from the curb. "What a cock-and-bull story. There's something rotten in the state of Denmark, and I think I know what it is," I said to the fire hydrant next to a utility pole.

The following day, when I related the conversation between Mr. Pizelli and myself to Theresa, she also agreed that it was a cock-and-bull tale.

"Uncle Luigi knows that I'm smitten by you, and he wants you out of the way."

"So ... he wants to send me to Chicago?"

"Exactly. I seriously believe that this Italian gigolo, Giulio Sardi, exists and will soon appear in Hancock," said Theresa, pursing her lips.

And he did come. That evening Giulio Sardi made his celebrated appearance at the Pizelli home. And the next day at work Theresa informed her co-workers and me of her fiancé's arrival. Sad to say, there was not a dry eye in the chamber. Judge Anderson went so far as to speak to the District Attorney about Luigi Pizelli's marriage intentions with regard to his niece.

In the days that followed, Theresa only spoke sparingly about Giulio. And then in a hushed voice. One day when Mrs. Potts pressed her for more information, she rolled her eyes and said, "I can sum up Giulio quite succinctly."

"Please do," said Judge Anderson, and we all gathered around Theresa.

She held up a dainty finger and strode to her desk, where she inhaled deeply from her nebulizer. "Now where were we?"

"Giulio Sardi."

"Oh, yes!" After ascertaining that all, including Pip Perkins, the law clerk, were present, she said, "First, but not foremost, is his filthy suit coat, which has three different buttons."

"So much for being an affluent nobleman." I said.

"You got that right." Theresa's cobalt eyes danced with anger. "Secondly, his skin is as wrinkled as a raisin." She took the newspaper from her desk, rolled it up, and repeatedly tapped it against her open palm. "He's old enough to be my father."

"No-o-o!" said the judge.

"And thirdly, he blows his nose by pressing one grimy finger against a nostril and blowing green mucous out of its mate." She promptly demonstrated his technique without actually blowing. Of course we all turned up our noses in disgust. "He then repeats the process with the other nostril." Shaking our heads in disbelief, we scattered to the four corners of the chamber.

Anything that took place in our work or we heard during the course of the day proved to be anticlimactic to Theresa's anecdotes.

The following morning everyone gathered around Theresa's desk promptly at eight o'clock and waited to be regaled with the latest tale about Giulio. We were not disappointed. And day after day, the tidbits kept coming. Then suddenly, after a span of two weeks, the stories stopped abruptly. When someone questioned her about Giulio, she informed us that her uncle and Giulio had gone to Philadelphia on business.

On the Feast of The Assumption of the Blessed Virgin Mary, Theresa arrived for work visibly shaken. "Are you okay?" I asked in a very low voice.

"Giulio's back," she said, switching on her nebulizer and adding a dose of medicine. "We had a heated argument this morning."

"Want to tell me about it?"

"Yes." She nodded to the Conference Room. "Inside ... from prying eyes."

With Theresa leading the way, I followed. Just as we reached the door, Uncle Luigi and Giulio burst into the room. "How dare you leave the house this morning ... when I am speaking to you," screamed Uncle Luigi, shaking his cigar at her. "I am your uncle, and you will do as I say."

While Theresa's eyes narrowed into two slits, I clenched my fists. "Mr. Pizelli, control yourself," I said very calmly, although I was raging inside. "This is Judge Anderson's chamber."

"Outta my way, Hunky."

My eyes bulged when Uncle Luigi's coat flapped away from his burly chest, revealing a pistol in a leather holster. I saw my life pass before my eyes, which wasn't supposed to happen to someone in the prime of life. "Calm down."

"I'm not calming down until Theresa goes with me and Giulio upstairs to the Marriage License Office and gets a license to marry Giulio ... tomorrow."

By now the entire staff had gathered around Theresa's desk like Conestoga wagons encircling a host of pioneers. A concerned Judge Anderson, attired in his robes, entered from his inner chamber and directed Mrs. Potts to call for security.

I'd rather go to hell than marry someone like Giulio," said

Theresa in an even voice. She turned and unsteadily headed for her desk and the nebulizer. From her breathing, I knew that her airways were closing. I glanced at the nebulizer. It purred like the engine in my Ford, which was a good sign. I grew concerned when Theresa's face turned ashen. She began to cough and stumble about. When she exhaled, there was a whistling sound. I had never seen her suffer such a serious attack.

When she reached her desk, her fingers reached out for the nebulizer. Suddenly her body grew ridged. Her eyes closed. Clutching at her chest, she tottered as if a marionette on broken strings and then crashed to the floor in a heap.

Everyone stood motionless and looked on. I immediately rushed to her side and felt for a pulse. "She's breathing," I said and noted that her face had suddenly turned from an unhealthy white color to the color of ripened grapes. Blood vessels surfaced on her face, which I surmised wasn't good."

"Give her an injection," said Uncle Luigi. "That always worked in the past."

"An injection would take too long." I glanced up at the nebulizer on the desk. It was Theresa's only chance for survival, but how would I dispense the needed medicine in time to save her life. "Pip, I want you to unplug that nebulizer and bring it to me."

"Gotcha," said Pip. Unceremoniously he yanked the plug from the outlet. But very carefully he carried the nebulizer across the room and deposited it by my side. "Here you are."

"Thanks." When I glanced down at Theresa, I saw that her very life was slipping away with each second. I had to act now, and my actions had to be correct. Lowering my head to the nebulizer, I sucked in the precious medicine once. While everyone drew closer and glanced at me as if I were demented, I closed my lips and knelt closer to the nebulizer once more. I then sucked in six more doses of the medicine. Excruciating pain tore the inside of my mouth. My heart thumped like a bass drum. But I concentrated as I never concentrated in my life. Sweating like a wedge of cheddar cheese, I lowered my face to Theresa, opened her mouth, and pinched her nose shut. I promptly and slowly blew the life-saving medicine into her mouth. For a split second, I thought she opened her eyes, but I wasn't sure.

"What the hell's he doing?" asked uncle Luigi. "That ain't gonna help her."

"Be quiet," said Judge Anderson.

Once more I filled my mouth with the medicine and blew it into Theresa's mouth. No sooner had I lifted my head, when I heard a popping sound. Everyone else also heard the popping noise, judging from my colleagues' cheers. When Theresa opened her eyes and smiled,

I lowered my mouth. This time it wasn't to dispense medicine. It was to kiss her. Though weak, she responded with her own kiss. "Your throat is open. You're going to be fine."

"I ... know."

"As soon as the Hunky is finished with my niece," said Uncle Luigi, "I'm marching her up to get a marriage license."

"No, you're not," I said emphatically. Reaching inside my coat pocket, I withdrew a folded sheet of paper and handed it to Judge Anderson.

"What's this?" asked the judge, accepting the paper and unfolding it.

"A reason why Giulio Sardi isn't going to marry Theresa."

"We'll see about that," exclaimed Luigi, shaking his fist at me.

"Leo's correct, Mr. Pizelli," said Judge Anderson. "This sheet of paper is a legal marriage license ... err ... issued by Cecil County, Maryland. I suppose in the town of Elkton." After waving the marriage license triumphantly for all to see, Judge Anderson read on. "It legally wed Leo to Theresa ... uhh ... let me see ... about three weeks ago."

With those words, the entire staff cheered once more. When I glanced down at my wife, I noticed that she had fully recovered from her asthmatic attack. Cautiously I raised her from the floor and hugged her.

"When did you get down to Elkton?" asked Mrs. Potts.

"We had a gig in a little town called Lewisville, which is about eight miles north of Elkton," announced Theresa, "and after the show, we drove down and were married ... unbeknownst to anyone."

The Pickwick Club

Grantville, population 3,012, is nestled in the northern tier of the commonwealth. Like other municipalities of its size, it supports civic associations such as the Lions Club, the Future Farmers of America, the Sertoma, and the Rotary. Unlike other towns in the vicinity, however, it also boasts a Pickwick Club.

Back when you read Charles Dickens's *Pickwick Papers*, you quickly learned that the venerable Pickwick Club was founded by Samuel Pickwick. Soon after the club was organized, Pickwick charged its members to travel about England, observe, and subsequently report their findings to the full membership.

The members of the Grantville Pickwick Club may have ventured over to Shippsville or down to Hancock on professional business. But none ever left town in the name of the organization to do any reconnoitering. No, sir-r-e-e-ee!

This association was actually a stay-at-home book club. They met as a body on the seventh day of each month (Dickens was born on the 7th day of February) at the home of Dr. and Mrs. Boris Brightbird on Main Street.

If the reader wonders why at the Brightbirds' home, the answer is quite simple. Mrs. Brightbird was the founder and president of the club. And since she was the first charter member, it was only correct (according to her) that her word was law with regard to membership, agenda, and dues.

As for Dr. Brightbird (the second charter member), don't jump to any rash conclusion that he was a famed neurosurgeon or a renowned internist or even a competent pathologist. The simple truth is that he was none of these. He never spent a single day in medical school. Dr. Brightbird was a charlatan. Oh, yes, an impressive-looking diploma hung on the wall of his office on the second floor of the Brunswick Building. But that diploma was a sham. It was purchased by Brightbird for the princely sum of $15.00 from the Hopewell Institute of Physical Adjustments.

His medical practice was limited to prescribing powdered starfish, skunk secretion, crushed bedbugs, powdered anthracite coal, and uric acid for all minor afflictions, such as the common cold and poison ivy.

As for serious illnesses such as cancer, Brightbird knew that in the 1920s very few people survived. As a matter of fact, most cancer patients died shortly after their diagnosis. But Brightbird decided that there were those afflicted souls who lingered at death's doorstep and would pay exorbitant sums of money for a miraculous cure. And it was to those people that Brightbird reached out. He reasoned that the deadly disease (whatever its structure) needed to be dislodged from its mooring and promptly purged from the body. After some thought, he devised a plan of attack. First, he had the patient wear a vibrating belt (cost $50.00) for twenty minutes each day. Then the patient jumped up and down upon a miniature trampoline (cost another $50.00) for three minutes. This treatment he named the Brightbird Electro-Acrobatic Regimen.

On the very first day of the program, the doctor enrolled eight patients and pocketed eight hundred dollars. At the end of a week, he deposited a total of three thousand dollars in his bank account. Seeing that the locals accepted his quackery without reservation, he decided to promote his cure outside of the area. And so he advertised his cancer cure in many metropolitan newspapers. At once folks arrived from near and far for the life-saving cure. However, Grantville with its single hotel couldn't accommodate the multitude of pilgrims.

Zelda Zigenfuzz, the headmistress of Chestnut Hill Finishing School for Girls and also a Pickwickian, rose to the occasion. She informed the Brightbirds that her institution could accommodate forty men and thirty women on its campus. And so the overflow of patients who arrived in Grantville were comfortably lodged, fed, and treated.

Sadly, though, none left cured. A few, under their own power, left town after a week of treatment. Others died during treatment. And still others left town in the last stages of their disease.

It was the folks in the latter two categories that Hortence Weidenheimer, the doctor's receptionist and paramour, ministered to. The dead she sent to Alonzo Buttercup, the town's undertaker. The walking-dead she personally escorted to the train station and sent home.

One morning, as the sun climbed atop the spire of Good Mercy Church, she waved good bye to a gaunt Myron Slocum as the eight o'clock train chugged out of the station en route to Philadelphia.

"Good bye," she cried as the last Pullman car clattered down the tracks, "and don't forget to wear your vibrating belt every day." Brushing away a layer of soot from her cloche, she straightened up and squinted at an approaching figure. "Roxy, is that you?"

"None other," said a tall, angular woman. As Hortence approached, the woman retrieved a flask from her pocket, screwed off the cap, and sipped. "Ahh-h-h-h! Nothing like my medicine to soothe my lumbago."

"I was about to call upon you."

"And why ... may I ask?"

"Amanda Brightbird is callin' a special meetin' tonight at ... uhhm ... at seven."

"Why are we meeting tonight? It isn't the seventh yet." After gazing about, Roxy lit a cigarette and puffed vigorously.

"Amanda's callin' the meetin' to find a replacement for Beatrice."

"That's right ... uhh ... the old biddy kicked the bucket last week." Roxy drank again, draining the bottle. "This tonic is so-o-o-o ... goo-o-o-od!"

Hortence smiled. "See you at seven o'clock."

The mantle clock in the Brightbird's library struck for the eighth time as Steegles, the butler, escorted a heavily rouged Roxy into the cluttered, musty sitting-room.

"I called the meeting for seven," said Amanda, arms folded across her flabby chest and eyes blazing with anger, "and ... and you show up an hour later ... and ... and ... quite looped."

"Put a sock in it, Amanda," said Roxy, swaying like the tall, ornamental grasses outside the Brightbird's home. "W-without ... uhmm ... me in this damn club ... ugh ... there would be no club." She raised a slender finger and shook it in Amanda's chubby face. "I pay for the refreshments and the guest speakers ... and never complain about it." With those words, Roxy plopped herself upon the sofa and claimed her flask from a pocket.

"I think ... errr ... we should cease with the unpleasantries," said Doctor Brightbird, "and get down to business."

"Quite so," said Amanda composing herself and forcing a faint smile to crease her chapped lips. "The only item on the agenda is to replace Beatrice." Having introduced the topic, she glanced at her husband, who threw back his head, causing his ill-fitting toupee to slide across his head and look like a clump of dry seaweed marooned atop a rock.

"Errr ... I think," said Dr. Brightbird as he rose to address the body with his thumbs thrust into his vest pockets, "that we should nominate a young person." He nodded to his wife, who smiled her approval. "Hmmmm ... someone," he pointed to Hortence, "with our values and education."

Roxy raised her hand and stood. When she was not acknowledged by Dr. Brightbird, she said in a loud, grating voice, "I nominate Hilda Hilgendorf."

"Not a chance," called out the other members in unison.

"She's your sister, and she runs a speakeasy," said a slight woman with a nose that resembled a parrot's beak. "I think that if you're lookin' for someone young and well-educated ... errr ... I got plenty of 'em at the finishing school."

"No, Zelda," said Hortence, "what Dr. Brightbird means is a person with university learning."

"Hhhmmm! My instructors may not know anything about algebra or history or Latin, but" the goiter in Zelda's neck bobbed with agitation as her face reddened, "you show me a university woman who can match Stella Snodgrass for grace, table manners, and poise."

"The problem," said Amanda, "is that the Club is short on people who can hold meaningful conversations with the likes of … a … a … Gertrude Stein or Robert Frost or … err … or Ezra Pound."

"Who in the hell is Gertrude Stein?" asked Roxy between puffs on her cigarette.

"And when are we ever gonna get some big cheese like Robert Frost to address our organization?" asked Hortence, rolling her eyes.

"Well, I don't think we're going to have Robert Frost talk to our group next week," said Amanda. Forming her bony fingers into a steeple and propping up her chin, she smiled. "But we have booked Delilah De Witt, the author of *Love in the Outhouse.*" At the mention of Miss De Witt's name and her latest book, a loud buzzing filled the room.

"Getting back to the topic at hand," said Dr. Brightbird, "I heard from Superintendent Gibbons that he's got a young lady on his faculty … ahh … who recently graduated from Penn State College with a degree in biology."

"I hope she's not a flapper," said Zelda, fingering the red mole on her nose. "We don't need anyone like that." She turned to the group for approval. All but Roxy nodded.

"I don't think Superintendent Gibbons would hire a flapper," said Amanda.

"Why not?" asked Roxy.

"Errr … because everyone knows that all flappers are heavy neckers," responded Hortence.

"I know some heavy neckers," Roxy giggled, "in our group who aren't flappers."

"Could we get back to the topic at hand?" said Amanda, tapping her manicured fingers upon her chair.

Dr. Brightbird cleared his throat. "Now … as I was saying, the teacher Superintendent Gibbons recommended is from down state, and … her name is Betsey Marak." Reaching into his coat pocket, he produced a photo. "This here is a photo of Miss Marak in high school." He promptly handed it to Hortence.

"Chubby little thing," said Zelda, straining her neck to look at the photo. "Instead of studying biology, she should have come to me."

"What would you have done with her?" asked Roxy. After snuffing out the embers of her cigarette, she took another from her case and lit it.

"I would have taught her better nutrition and showed her the value of exercise." Zelda accepted the photo, and after a cursory glance passed it to Roxy. "Poor thing."

When Roxy glanced at the photo, her eyes widened. A smile etched the corners of her mouth. "I know this young lady."

"That settles it," said Hortence. "If Roxy knows her, she's not the kind of person we want."

"No, I don't mean that I really know her." After sighing, Roxy wrinkled her brow. "Let me put it this way. This young lady lives over at Mrs. Sutter's boarding house, and … ugh … whenever we pass on the street, she always bids me the time of day."

"Whew!" exclaimed Dr. Brightbird, wiping his forehead with his soiled handkerchief. "I'm relieved. Thought for a second … er … she was a pavement princess."

"No, she seems quite respectable."

"Okay … then," said Amanda, "let's take a vote." Glancing about, she noticed that everyone, including Roxy, agreed with her. "Everyone … umm … who thinks that we should extend membership to Miss Betsey Marak … raise your hand." Everyone raised their hand except Roxy, who raised both her hands. "Four … five … six." Amanda winked at Dr. Brightbird and smiled. "It's unanimous." Slight applause followed. "Miss Marak has been accepted as a Pickwickian."

"What about getting her a copy of *Love in the Outhouse*?" said Zelda. When the youngest parlor maid offered her a cookie from a tray, she claimed the largest one. She then stole a peek at Amanda, whose back was turned to Dr. Brightbird. Noticing her hostesses' preoccupation, she seized three more cookies, wrapped them in a napkin, and stuffed them into her coat pocket. "Miss Marak really should have the opportunity to read *Love in the Outhouse* before the next meeting."

"That's only two days away," said Dr. Brightbird, "and it took me a month to interpret its sublime themes."

"I shall immediately pen Miss Marak a letter, asking her to accept an invitation to join us," said Amanda, "but how can I get a copy of *Love in the Outhouse* to her in such a short time?"

"No problem," said Roxy, rising to slip on her coat. "I see Miss Marak every day." She extended her hand to Amanda. "Give me the damn book, and I'll see that she gets it."

Amanda, probably wondering if Roxy would actually execute her commission, slowly handed Roxy her copy of the book. "Today is already Wednesday, and Friday afternoon Miss De Witt will join us for an exciting and informative afternoon."

"I think it's gonna snow on Friday," announced Zelda, "my bunions hurt."

Friday arrived bright and sunny with the temperature hovering in the low twenties. By one o'clock, however, the sun completely disappeared. And by two the sky turned sullen with flurries, the temperature plummeted into the teens.

Fifteen minutes later, Amanda directed Maggie and Jaime, the two parlor maids, and Steegles where to place the refreshments for the guests.

Since the guest speaker was expected within the hour, Dr. Brightbird and Hortence closed shop early and returned to his stately Victorian gingerbread house, which combined several styles of architecture. Soon after the doctor and Hortence arrived, Steegles placed a tureen of mock turtle soup (a cheaper imitation of green turtle soup) on the sideboard. And just as the doctor ladled a generous portion of broth into a bowl, Steegles announced the arrival of Zelda.

"Well, we're all here," said Amanda, fanning herself even though it was December, "except Miss De Witt, Miss Marak, and Roxy."

"I do believe that I see two felt cloches about to mount our front steps," said Dr. Brightbird. He raised the shade a mite, stepped away, and then studied it. Shaking his head, he returned to the shade and returned it to its former position. Because of his obsessiveness, he just had to adjust the shade once more. However, when Amanda scowled at him, he reddened and backed off.

"They're here!" cried Hortence and the four Pickwickians bumped into each other as they scurried into the drawing room.

Minutes later, when Steegles threw open the door of the sitting room, four necks craned forward as far as humanly possible. All eyes were riveted upon the exact spot where Miss Betsey Marak would make her celebrated entrance.

"I hope she can fit into the room," said Dr. Brightbird. Amanda shook an admonitory finger at him. The others giggled.

Steegles, tall and stately, entered first to announce the guests. "Mrs. Roxy Rheinsmith and Miss Betsey Marak," he said in his customary deep voice.

Steegles and Roxy blocked any view of Miss Marak, throwing the four Pickwickians into a tizzy. Steegles immediately peeled off to the right and Roxy to the left. All eyes bulged. Mouths gaped. Bodies twitched.

Betsey, wearing a simple straight-line chemise dress, strode into the room and smiled shyly. Dr. Brightbird, at once, fell in love with her. The three women instantly loathed her.

Dr. Brightbird instantly reached into his coat pocket, retrieved Betsey's high school photo, and compared the picture to the long-legged, nubile goddess before him. "Ohhh, my ... God!" he soliloquized. "I've died and gone to heaven. She's a doll."

121

Amanda must have heard him because she elbowed him in the ribs. "Shut up, you old fool," she whispered. "She's young enough to be your granddaughter."

Being the genial hostess, Amanda paraded up to Betsey, welcomed her, and warmly shook her hand. She then introduced her to all the club members, who smiled sweetly and fell over themselves pretending to be happy to make her acquaintance.

"Perhaps Miss Marak would like to partake of some nourishment and libation," said Dr. Brightbird. He took her under the arm in an attempt to spirit her away from the women.

"I would really like to freshen up a bit," said Betsey in a soft, soothing voice. "I've had a long day in school."

Hearing her request, Amanda latched onto her other arm and led her down the hall to a powder room. "I'm sure you will find everything inside that you need," she said, opening the door and pulling upon the light cord.

"Thank you." Once inside, Betsey took a washcloth, wet it, and dabbed her mouth and face. "Whew! What a day this has been." Just then she heard a door open on the other side of the powder room and several pairs of shoes clopping loudly like Clydesdale horses. "The wall is paper thin."

Betsey peeped into the mirror and was about to leave when she heard Hortence say, "Her eyes are too green, and her skin whiter than new milk." Someone snickered.

"And her teeth are too straight and white," said Zelda. Both women chuckled, and then the door opened once more, admitting someone else. "What do you think of Miss Marak, Amanda?"

"We made a big mistake by inviting her to join our little group," said Amanda. "She's too gosh darn attractive."

"I hate her."

"I do too," said Hortence. "We gotta make her life miserable."

"Make ... my life ... miserable," mouthed Betsey to the image in the mirror. "I don't need this." With cheeks burning and jaw set, she turned, opened the door, and stormed down the hall. Clenching and unclenching her fists, she marched rhythmically for her coat. "I'm out of here."

She was within steps of the cloak room when Roxy screamed, "Ohhh, my ... God!"

Hastening her step, she ran to the sitting room, where she had left Roxy. Opening the door, she burst into the room. Roxy, body trembling, reached out a thin hand for assistance. "Roxy!" screamed Betsey.

She rushed across the room to the stricken woman. But not before

Roxy collapsed upon the floor. "H-h-help!"

Falling to her knees, Betsey noticed that Roxy's chest was neither rising nor falling. Her eyes were vacant. Spittle dribbled down her chin. "It's her heart from all her smoking." Next Betsey sought air movement from the woman's mouth. Nothing.

"What is it?" called Dr. Brightbird, himself winded, as he waddled into the room. "Heart?"

"Yes, I think so." Betsey checked for a pulse. Nothing. She glanced up at the distraught doctor. "You're a doctor. Get down here and assist me."

"Errr ... I'm a cancer specialist. I'd like to help, but I know nothing about the heart." She glared at him and then turned her attention to Roxy. The doctor cautiously approached the inert body and watched the proceedings. Enthralled with Betsey's beauty, he grew embolden and ogled her from several angles. And when he noticed her dress ride up her exquisite gams, he decided to join her. He inched closer when the fragrance of her jasmine-scented neck stirred him. After glancing at Betsey's delicate features, he promptly moved even closer to her. She, realizing that his intentions were not exactly in the best interest of the patient, reddened and adjusted her position. "S-s-she's dead, Miss Marak!" The doctor threw up his hands in resignation. "She doesn't need a doctor. She needs an undertaker."

"It's cardiac arrest." Betsey raised Roxy's arms above her head and then pressed against her chest. "Come on, Roxy, respond. This is not the time to die."

"What are you doin' that for? She cashed in her chips." Hearing approaching steps and recognizing them as Amanda's, Dr. Brightbird climbed to his feet and distanced himself from Betsey.

"When I was a life guard, I learned that someone who experienced cardiac arrest from drowning ... err ... can be saved ... sometimes." Betsey pressed more vigorously upon Roxy's chest and counted, "Mmm ... one ... ehh ... two."

Suddenly Amanda appeared in the room. "Ohhhh!" she cried out at the sight of Betsey ministering to the lifeless Roxy. "D-d-did ... she faint from all the booze?"

"Nope. She's dead," said Dr. Brightbird. He glanced at his watch. "You've been at it for two minutes, Miss Marak. Isn't it about time you quit? You do know that she's D-E-A-D."

Betsey disregarded his comment. If anything, she worked more feverishly. "I got about five or ten more minutes before there's brain damage."

"What brain?" asked Amanda. "She was one of the stupidest people I ever met. And I, for one, won't miss her."

As she turned to leave, Zelda and Hortence appeared. "What happened to her?" asked Hortence.

"Bought the farm."

"I'm not surprised the way she drank." Hortence nonchalantly picked up Roxy's purse and rummaged through the contents. When she discovered something of value, she glanced about to ascertain if anyone was watching her. Of course, all eyes were focused on Betsey and her antics. And so Hortence calmly and quickly deposited the booty into her pocket.

"Miss De Witt has arrived," proclaimed Steegles, sticking his massive bald head into the room. "Oh, my. What have we here?"

"Roxy's dead," chorused the Pickwickians.

"Really!" He made the sign of the cross and raised his eyes to the ceiling.

With word of Miss De Witt's arrival, the Pickwickians fled from the room. Betsey, however, continued to exert pressure to the stomach. "I'm getting tired," she said, "and I'm running out of time."

"Yes, Miss Marak, you are." And with those words, Steegles's head vanished.

Betsey's effort slowed but did not cease. "Err ... uhm ... one ... two ... three-e-e-e." And then the shadow of a dove appeared on the floor beside her. When Betsey glanced up, she spied a young woman with a plunger in her hand. "Who are you?" asked Betsey, quite exhausted.

"I'm Angie," said the woman and thrust a sink plunger at her. "Try this. It might work."

"Thank you." Betsey reached up and took the plunger. "At this stage of the game, I'll try anything."

With renewed energy, Betsey placed the sink plunger over Roxy's heart, pushed down, and then pulled up. Nothing happened. "Up and down. Up ... and ... down. Upanddownupanddownupanddown." Like a plumber attacking a clogged sink, she set about her task. "Breathe ... darn it. Breathe!" Perspiration beaded upon her brow. Sweat rolled down her neck. But onward she labored as intensely as ever. "Upanddownupanddownupanddown."

And then, lo and behold, Betsey thought that she detected a slight pulse. "Dear Lord, don't mess with me." Betsey gazed up at the angel atop the decorated Christmas tree in the corner of the room. "I'm ... running ... on ... empty."

"Is ... that ... you, Mr. Barry ... more?" whispered Roxy, blinking.

"No-o-o, it's not." Tears of joy welled in Betsey's eyes. She reached down and kissed Roxy upon the head. "It's Betsey."

"Bets ... sey?"

"Betsey Marak." After patting her hand, Betsey raised Roxy's head. "You know. Betsey ... your neighbor."

"W-w-what ... happened?"

"Errrr ... you had a slight heart attack."

"N-n-no!"

"Would I lie to you?"

"I hope ... not." Roxy took her hand and held it tightly. "You're ... too ... pretty ... to lie."

"Thank you."

A loud clatter arose in the hallway. While Roxy arched her brows, Betsey arose and went to the doorway. "Where's the stiff?" called a gangly man, who was followed by Dr. Brightbird.

"We're in here." Betsey beckoned with her hand.

"Stiff," said Roxy. "I'm ... alive."

"Y-y-you sure are!" exclaimed Dr. Brightbird, amazed at the sight of a somewhat bedraggled but conscious Roxy. "Alonzo, can you run Roxy down to the hospital in Hancock?"

"No problem, Dr. Brightbird."

"Good." The doctor stared at Roxy and scratched his head, still doubting what he saw. "Very good."

"And I'll go with her," said Betsey.

"Thankee," said Roxy, her eyes misty.

In a matter of minutes, Alonzo, Betsey, and Dr. Brightbird loaded Roxy onto the stretcher and carried her out to the hearse, which also served the town as an ambulance.

Miss De Witt was still elaborating upon the symbolism in her latest novel when word of Roxy's resuscitation reached the Pickwickians in attendance. None believed that Roxy had returned from the dead. It was impossible. Hortence, increasingly bored with the speaker, twiddled her thumbs and stole a peek at Amanda, sitting behind a neglected Boston fern. Periodically Amanda parted the fronds of the fern and glanced at Zelda. The school mistress, in a state of lethargy from too much turtle soup, sat in a stupor with her legs spread. Occasionally she glanced at her watch before squinting across the room at Miss De Witt. Finally, as if on cue, the three Pickwickians shrugged their combined shoulders, rose simultaneously, and tramped to the sitting room. There Steegles informed them that Roxy was, indeed, alive. All shed crocodile tears before pursuing the cortege and the hearse.

Once Roxy was settled inside the hearse, Betsey excused herself and approached Amanda. "I wish to thank you for inviting me to join your little club," said Betsey.

"You are quite welcome," said Amanda, not meaning a word of what she said.

"But the truth is ... ehh ... I cannot accept membership at this time."

"Oh!"

"You see ... I have tests to grade and lab reports to read ... and four lesson preparations every evening."

"I see."

"Perhaps in a year or two my schedule will lighten."

"Perhaps."

"And would you please thank Angie for the sink plunger?"

"Angie!" Amanda's forehead furrowed. "Who's Angie?"

"One of your domestics."

"I have two domestics. Jaime and Karen. There is no one in the house by the name of Angie."

The Return of the Magi

Hopalong Cassidy always got his man. But today he was running out of time. The barrel-chested old man, sitting in front of his Dumont television set, glanced at the noisy Seth Thomas clock on the wall behind the front desk of his motel and impatiently drummed his fingers upon the arm of his swivel chair. Five minutes remained in the show, and Hoppy was still hunched atop his horse, Topper, pursuing the infamous Webster gang. And just as Hoppy drew closer to the gang and fired his six-shooter at Bucky Webster, the gang's leader, someone tapped loudly upon the front door.

"Nuts!" growled the old man. He rose with difficulty from his chair and pulled up his suspenders. Limping towards the door, he slapped his open palm upon the top of the check-in counter. "I'm coming." When he reached the door, he drew the shade away from the glazed window. Immediately the furrows on his mottled forehead vanished. "Walter!" Jiggling the key in the slot, he unlocked the door and opened it. "I thought you left town to spend Christmas with your boy."

"We were going to leave this morning," said Walter, stamping his shoes on the doormat, "but Anna's brother-in-law had a slight stroke last night."

"Is this Bobby Higgens you're talkin' about?"

"Yep." At once Walter entered the motel, padded across the room, and spat tobacco juice into a wastebasket. "You know him, Ski?"

"Know him!" Ski glanced over at the television set. Seeing that Hoppy had rounded up the Webster gang, he smiled and switched off the set. "I went to school with him. He's a peach of a guy."

"Well, since we're not going to Pittsburgh, I ... ayuh ... thought that ... maybe you'd like to go to church with me tonight?"

Ski removed a tawny-colored baseball from a shelf and examined it. He inhaled and released the air slowly, not permitting it to become a sigh. "These here signatures are all the guys on the 1941 Boston Red Sox. Your brother is always after me to sell him this ball. I keep telling him there ain't enough money in the bank to tempt me." Ski turned the ball over. "See ... there's Ted Williams's name ... and way over here ... that's my autograph next to Bobby Doerr's. They called me up from Minneapolis in August." Ski proudly tugged on his suspenders. "I won seven of eight starts." Recalling his youth, he stared past Walter's head at the yellowed snapshots on the wall. "Red Smith called me the next Dizzy Dean. Shucks! I never got a chance to pitch like old Dizzy." Ski sighed and bit his lower lip. "Next thing I know ... I'm drafted. The

Japanese took care of me. Got shot up so bad … the doctors didn't think I'd ever walk again, much less pitch." The veins in his neck bulged. His voice cracked. "Walter, let me tell you something. If there was a God, He would have taken better care of me." Ski snapped his fingers. "Jus' like that, my pitching career was snuffed out in the prime of my life. How can you stand there and ask me to go to church? If there was a God … my -- my wife would still be alive today." His eyes clouded with a misty bitterness. "My pitching career should have lasted more than three lousy months, and my daughter wouldn't be livin' three thousand miles away. No, sir-e-e-e! I don't believe there's a God, and I ain't going to church … ever again."

"I can see why you feel like you do, but if you change your mind … you're welcome to go along with me tonight." Walter removed his cap and scratched his thinning hair, causing a flurry of dandruff to cascade upon his jacket. "That's if we're not snowed in. Dan McMann, the weather man, is callin' for a doozy of a storm … startin' about noon."

"What does Dan McMann know?" He slapped Walter across the back good-naturedly and escorted him to the door. "Look." Ski pointed to the blue sky. "Not a cloud in the sky. And you say McMann is callin' fer snow by noon."

"Yep." Walter adjusted the flaps of his cap and zipped up his jacket. "I'll drop by tonight to see if you changed your mind."

Shortly after noon, when Ski ventured outdoors, he spied a desolate snowflake glide through the air and crash against his bifocals. The snowflake was an omen of what would follow. By two o'clock the sidewalk was covered with a winter blanket of white. And by three, the street was void of any traffic, except for an occasional pedestrian sliding along the sidewalk like a drunken sot.

"Looks like Walter ain't gonna go no place tonight," Ski said, peering out at the storm from his front window. He waddled across the room for his favorite pipe on the table when someone rapped on the door. "Nuts! Now what does Walter want?"

Long before he reached the door, the angular silhouette bobbing on the shade told him that it was not Walter. He nonchalantly switched on the *No Vacancy* sign below the neon lights advertising his motel. And then he unlocked the front door.

"Would it be possible for me to get a room for the night?" mumbled a snow-covered man as soon as Ski opened the door. Ski studied the man carefully and noticed that his eyes glittered with the raw fear of a doe.

"Nope," said Ski matter-of-factly. "I ain't open today. Don't you know it's Christmas Eve?"

"Yes, but----" Before the stranger could finish his sentence, the door closed in his face.

With shoulders slumped, the man trudged off and crawled behind the steering wheel of his Buick. Ski, watching the auto lunge out of the parking lot, was about to take his leave. Suddenly the Buick fishtailed on a patch of ice. Ski's eyes widened. His jaw dropped. The auto skidded across the parking lot and crashed into the neon sign. Sparks crackled. Smoke plumed. The sign hummed and then the lights periodically blinked off and on. Nauseating pangs shot through Ski's stomach. Why did people go out in such weather he wondered? Shaking his head in disbelief, he watched helplessly as the Buick slid and plowed into a snow bank. The driver promptly gunned the engine. But the harder he tread upon the gas pedal, the deeper the auto became imbedded in the drifting snow.

In despair the driver slammed the car door shut and lumbered back to the motel, his steps already covered by the swirling snow.

"Could I use your telephone to call a tow truck?" called the man through the window.

Ski said nothing. He didn't have to say anything. The smoke drifting up from the bowl of his pipe said everything. But he allowed the man to enter the motel and even pointed to the telephone on the counter. "Put your insurance agent's number on that pad and don't talk too long on the phone."

The stranger stared at Ski and then at the yellowed snapshots before calling after him. "Hey, I know you. You're Paul Barski." Ski stopped in his tracks and pivoted as well as old men pivot. "I played against you in '39 in the Sally League. Didn't you have a cup of coffee with Boston?"

"What did you say your name was?"

The traveler nodded. "I didn't."

"Oh!"

"I'm Joe Forbes. Played third base for Knoxville." Joe inched closer to the hissing radiator and warmed his chapped hands. "Didn't you win your first ten starts when the Red Sox called you up in '40?"

Ski wiped his hands against his shirt. "They called me up in '41, and I won my first seven starts." A faint smile tugged at the corners of Ski's floppy mouth. When he extended his hand, Joe pumped it several times. My God, Joe, that was a long time ago."

"Sure was."

"Say, would you care fer a cup of coffee while you wait fer the tow truck?"

"I'd like a cup of coffee very much."

Ski held up a gnarled finger and toddled off to the kitchen. And when he returned with two steaming cups of coffee, Joe informed him that he was unable to reach any emergency tow-truck service. Both men drank their coffee in silence. Joe finally broached the subject of the stranded Buick and asked Ski if he would help him dig his Buick out of the snow.

Without batting an eye, Ski dressed for the weather, armed himself with a shovel, and led the way to the Buick, which was now a shapeless snow sculpture. Together the two men cursed and dug and cindered. All to no avail. The Buick could not be dislodged.

Ski may not have been the first to realize that the Buick was captive to the elements, but he was the first to offer a short-term solution. "Joe, why don't you spend the night at my motel? I have ten vacant units, and I'm all alone. I'll throw a coupla of TV dinners into the oven, and we'll reminisce about the good old days in the Sally League."

"I'd like that, but first I'd like to lie down for about an hour."

"Sure. Sure."

An hour later when Tom Ward, the postman, delivered Ski's mail, he announced that the entire Lehigh Valley was being pummeled by a major snow storm. Ski turned on the radio as soon as Tom left and heard a disc jockey in Allentown plead with his listening audience to remain indoors. No sooner had he made his plea and spun Bing Crosby's "White Christmas" when Ski heard a faint knock at the door.

He expected to see a refreshed Joe Forbes. However, when he opened the door, he was quite surprised to find a tall brunette with rosy cheeks smile timidly at him.

"I ... errrr ... saw the *No Vacancy* sign outside, but ... I ... uhmm ... I thought ... I er ... might be able to come inside for a few minutes." When the snarling wind blew snow into the girl's pumps and obviously chilled her, she balanced herself upon one foot and then the other. "I'm on my way to Easton, and I think I lost my way in the storm."

"Miss--"

"Doyle." She offered her slender, shivering hand. "Maddie Doyle." Ski took her hand and led her inside.

"Maddie, the sign don't always work right." Taking her arm, he guided her to the radiator. "I have plenty of rooms, and you can stay as long as you like." Excusing himself, he flipped off the *NO* part of the sign. Ski didn't know much about the latest styles in women's apparel. But he did know that Maddie should be wearing more than a thin jacket in the middle of winter. And when she removed her jacket and revealed a gauzy summer dress, he suspected that she was wearing the best clothes she owned. "Would you like some hot coffee before supper?"

"Supper!"

"Ugh ... it's not gonna be a fancy supper." Ski's thin lips curved into a half-smile. "All I was gonna do is toss a coupla frozen TV dinners into the oven fer me and another guy."

"I'd love a TV dinner."

Ski liked her. Maddie reminded him of his daughter whenever she rolled her big black, animated eyes. It was good to have a young person such as Maddie present for Christmas. Approaching the mantel, he took the greeting card from his daughter and read each word again. Then he gazed at Maddie. "Have a cup of coffee in the kitchen while I fetch supper from the basement."

As Ski descended the steps to his basement, where he kept a freezer in his obsolete bomb shelter, he hoped that he would find three TV dinners. Much to his surprise, he discovered four dinners: a chicken, a turkey, a Salisbury steak, and one so old, the print on the box had faded beyond recognition. He didn't care what the others ate, but he smacked his lips in anticipation of the turkey dinner. In the end, he decided to lug all four dinners upstairs. And it was a good idea. In addition to Joe and Maddie sitting around the kitchen table, he discovered some kind of Asian man sitting in his favorite chair. When Joe introduced the man, Ski merely shrugged his broad shoulders and waddled over to the stove. The Asian would eat the mystery dinner. Ski didn't like any Asians since World War II. Had it not been for the Japanese, his baseball career may have lasted longer than eight games.

We totally defeated the Japanese, and then what did we do? We rebuilt their country. Allowed them to flood our nation with their calculators, radios, automobiles, and trinkets while American industry shut down. By gosh, he'd never buy anything made outside the United States. He slid his calloused hand over the oven and rubbed the decal that said: Made in the U.S.A.

Like clockwork, he inserted a frozen dinner into the oven, set the dial, withdrew the foil in a matter of minutes, and then repeated the procedure.

Within a short period of time, he prepared four dinners. In his absence, Maddie had set the table for four. She even placed a ceramic Christmas tree in the middle of the table. When Ski studied the Asian more closely, the fellow no longer looked as imposing. But he was still going to eat the mystery dinner, which turned out to be spaghetti and meatballs. On the radio Frank Sinatra, accompanied by Nancy, his daughter, sang the last few bars of "Silent Night." Some newscaster then mentioned another bank robbery down in Reading and a four-car accident up in the Poconos. Ski shook his head, switched off the radio, and proudly joined his guests for dinner.

"I thank God for allowing me to spend my last Christmas on this earth with three wonderful people," said Joe. While Joe fought back tears, Ski glanced across the table at Maddie and the Asian for some explanation.

"Joe, what on earth are you babblin' about?" Ski finally asked.

"Cancer. I got inoperable ... terminal cancer." Joe's Adam's apple quivered. "Went to see a specialist in Philly. Guy says ... I got six months ... maybe a year at the most." While Maddie fingered her five-and-dime necklace, the Asian patted Joe's hand. "That's how I got caught in this storm. I was on my home to Bangor. Got no family. Always spend the holidays ... alone." Joe stared at a piece of bread before he put it to his lips. "I prayed to God that I wouldn't hafta spend *this* Christmas Eve alone, and ... He heard my prayers."

"You're from Bangor?" asked Maddie.

"Yes."

"Me too." Maddie sat back and dabbed the corners of her delicate mouth. "Went to Kutztown and got a degree Elementary Education." Her eyebrows flickered a bit. "That was almost two years ago. I still haven't been able to land a steady job."

"How do you live?" asked Ski, leaning forward and setting his elbows upon the table.

"I waitress two days a week, but it's rough living on such a small paycheck."

"Have you written to many schools?"

"Everyone in the Lehigh Valley, but they're all looking for experience."

"How do you get experience if nobody gives you a chance?"

"Exactly. There's going to be an opening in town in the spring. I came down for an interview, but the storm chased everybody, including the superintendent, home. Guess I'll just have to wait and see if they contact me for another interview. If it wasn't for the blinking motel sign outside, I ... I don't know what I would have done."

"What about you, Ka ... high?" asked Joe.

The Asian smiled. "Not Ka ... high. It is Key, but everybody at factory call me Norman. So ... you, Mr. Joe, call me Norman, too. Hokay."

"Does your family live with you?" asked Maddie.

"No, Miss Maddie, I have no famle-e-e-e. Everybody kilt in Vietnam, 'cept me. I come dis country and get job in factory. Den I meet girl ... Hue To Do. She move to Hoboken. I go see her ... maybe marry her."

"How about that," said Joe, clasping the Vietnamese's narrow shoulders just as someone knocked loudly on the front door.

"More company," said Maddie.

"No, it's just Walter, my neighbor," announced Ski, rising from his chair. "He said he'd drop by before he went to church. Joe, let him in. I'll be right back."

"Church!" said Joe. "That's where I want to go."

"Me too," said Maddie. "I want to sing carols."

"Ca ... rolls?" asked the Vietnamese.

"Yes, we're going to take you along, too." Maddie turned and with mouth ajar, she stared at Ski, who had returned, holding a parka.

"Try it on," said Ski. "It was hardly ever worn."

"I ... I couldn't." Maddie shook her head but allowed Ski to slip the garment over her shoulders. "It's so-o-o-o warm." She ran her fingers upon the fleece lining. "How much would you want for it?" She arched one brow. "I could send you a couple of dollars every week."

Ski chuckled. "Take it" When she hugged him, he stiffened. He then felt warm all over and wondered if the heat flash was caused by his thyroid medicine or Maddie's caress. "It's yours. I ain't got no use fer it." Ski pulled at his suspenders. "Been wanting to give it away to the right person." From the expression on Ski's Slavic face, it was obvious that there was a Christmas spirit glowing warmly within his bosom.

"Snow's over," called Walter. The snowbound travelers rushed to the window to see for themselves. "I'm going to church, and you people are all welcome to come along with me."

In the next few minutes there was a bustle of activity as the guests set the kitchen in order, slipped on their winter gear, and filed outside to Walter's Ford. Ski took the baseball from the shelf and gripped it along the seams. "Walter, this is how I threw my round-house curve." He glanced about to make sure Walter and he were alone. "Is your brother still on the school board?"

"Yep, he was just elected to another term."

"Good." Ski folded his hands at his waist and looked over his shoulder as if he were checking the runner on first base. "Well, when you see him ... uhh ... give him this ball. Tell him that that he don't owe me a penny fer it." He handed Walter the ball and winked. Walter knew from the wink that Ski had more to say. "I don't want no money fer the ball ... but I do want a small favor from him."

"Oh!"

"That young lady you jus' saw in here ... is Maddie Doyle." Walter nodded. "She applied fer Schoochie Bumgardner's job."

"Really."

"A--a-ahuh." Even though they were quite alone, Ski took Walter by the elbow and pulled him closer to himself. "Ask him to scout around and see if there's any reason why she can't have Schoochie's job. Maddie looks like she'd make a good teacher."

"Sure, Ski! Sure. That's not askin' too much of a favor."

"And, Walter, one more thing."

"Anything you say, Ski."

"I'd like to go to church with you … errr … if there's room in your station wagon?"

Walter smiled, revealing a row of uneven, yellowed teeth. "There's room, Ski. The little Oriental fellow may have to sit in the middle, but there's plenty of room for you."

The Duke of Duncannon

Ever since a barnstormer by the name of Curly Armbruster visited our town in his Curtiss biplane and put on a thrilling show out at the fairgrounds, I knew that I wanted to be a pilot when I grew up. My parents, both bohemians, were quite supportive of my ambition. And so with their blessing I took flying lessons under the firm hand of Maurice Belanger at the Portland Airport as soon as I graduated from Bowdoin College. Not long after my initial lesson, I soloed over Casco Bay. When the day arrived that I earned my pilot's license, I celebrated the occasion by executing a perfect Immelmann turn over the Portland Head Light. I then buzzed the noonday crowd in downtown Portland. Of course, I was elated with my skills and accomplishment. However, the mayor wasn't. He registered a formal complaint with the Civil Aeronautics Board, the federal agency which oversees the licensing, training, and safety of all airplane pilots. That august bureaucracy immediately investigated the incident, heard the case, and subsequently suspended my newly acquired pilot's license for one year, subject to appeal. I implored the CAB to reverse its decision but to no avail. Needless to say, the CAB's action was tantamount to ripping the heart out of my chest cavity.

Soon after, I exhausted all of my appeals, I returned to the airport to clean out my locker. And while I stuffed my gear into a canvas bag, Maurice appeared with an impish glimmer in his cerulean eyes. From the twinkle, I knew that something was afoot. Maurice hemmed and hawed and shifted his weight from one foot to another before he informed me that I could continue to fly without a civilian pilot's license. And, to boot, I would be paid for my services.

While I stood fingering my logbook, my ears pricked up. The dapper Maurice smiled, revealing a mouthful of black stumps, reached into his pocket, and produced a crumpled leaflet. Unraveling the circular, I smoothed out the creases and read the contents. What Maurice said was true. I could, indeed, continue to fly without a civilian license. The catch was that I had to enlist in the British Air Force and fly combat missions against Hitler's Luftwaffe, which was terrorizing Europe in the name of fascism.

"This is it?" I asked, waving the leaflet. I quickly recalled that at dinner our family always listened attentively to the day's news on the Zenith radio and then discussed the war in Europe. My parents and I knew that sooner or later the United States would be drawn into the conflict. Did I wish to enter the service as an infantryman, or did I wish to choose my branch of service? "There are no other conditions?"

"Ayuh ... since you're an American ... umm ... you're bound by Roosevelt's Proclamation of Neutrality," said Maurice, removing his cap and brushing back his rumpled hair.

"What's that mean?"

"It means that if you're caught ... er ... you're subject to a fine and imprisonment."

"Hmmmm. That's not good." I breathed deeply and exhaled slowly. "Well, I gotta talk this over with my parents."

"Listen, Joe, talk it over with your mom and dad ... eh ... and then think it over ... hard. Your whole life may depend on what you decide?"

"You're right about that."

At dinner that evening, when I broached the subject of joining the Royal Air Force, both of my parents accepted and even promoted the idea.

"Since your mother is descended from the Duke of York, and my family's lineage can be traced back to the Tudors," explained my father, hacking away at his Salisbury steak with the gusto of a Cro-Magnon warrior, "the Brits may ask you to join a royal regiment."

"That's right," said my mother, forcing back a tear. "Nobility still has its place in a grand old country like England."

I nodded but said nothing. Many years later when I became interested in genealogy, I researched my parents' ancestry thoroughly. I found no blood relationship whatsoever between my mother and the Duke of York. It seems that her family, the Statiusks, were nothing more than Romanian gypsies and horse thieves. Their only intercourse with the Duke of York arose when they poached on his land and were evicted by the Sheriff of Nottingham.

As for my father, his ancestors were, for the most part, scullery maids and tinkers dating back to the reign of Henry VIII, who was a Tudor.

Buoyed by my parents' blessing to enlist in the RAF, I retrieved the rumpled leaflet from the glove compartment of my '39 Ford. No matter how diligently I scanned the bill, I failed to find the name of a contact, an address, or even a telephone number.

Perplexed by the dearth of information, I knew that I had to consult Maurice. Perhaps he saw the party who posted the flier and spoke to him. The fellow may even have given Maurice a telephone number or an address. Before slipping on my jacket, rushing out the door, and driving over to the airport, I checked my Timex. "Shucks!" I said despondently. "It's eight o'clock. Maurice is long gone to some gin mill and is half-looped by now." I unzipped my jacket. "I'll have to wait until tomorrow morning."

The following morning I arrived at the airport promptly at eight o'clock. As part-time mechanic and full-time flying instructor, Maurice was scheduled to begin work at eight. However, nine o'clock tolled on the watchtower and still there was no Maurice.

Just before ten, he tottered into the hangar, reeking of cigarettes and cheap whiskey. "Morning," he said, squinting through bloodshot eyes.

"I wanna join up," I said eagerly.

"Huh!" Maurice coughed and spat a greenish phlegm upon the concrete floor.

"I ... want ... to enlist ... in ... the British Air Force." After heaving a deep sigh, I held up the flier. "See."

"Oh, that." Even though there was high-octane gasoline in the area, Maurice lit a cigarette and puffed away like a chugging locomotive.

"Yes, that."

"You sure you wanna join up." Maurice rubbed his red eyes and inhaled on his Lucky Strike.

"Yes, I wish to enlist."

"Why didn't you say so?" He smiled and nodded to his desk along the near wall. "The enlistment papers are in the second drawer."

"You!" While my voice rose a full octave, my eyes narrowed like a cat's. "You're the one who ... who posted that flier."

"Yep." Maurice slipped his thumbs into his suspenders and tugged slightly. "I get a few bucks fer every guy I sign up."

"And how many recruits have you gotten so far?"

"None." He pointed to me. "You're the first."

"And probably the last."

"Pro ... bob ... ba ... ly."

Owing to the fact that this narrative is penned in the short story format, there is a need for an economy of words. I, therefore, shall not burden the reader with the trials and tribulations I encountered on the high seas when I set sail for England aboard the Canadian vessel *Arcadia.*

A week after I departed from Halifax, Nova Scotia, I disembarked in the bustling, somber metropolis of wartime London. At the dock, where flocks of sea gulls soared and dove relentlessly, a short, swarthy captain of the RAF met me, along with three other recruits from Canada and whisked us off to Hawardan, an advanced training base, near the city of Liverpool.

Since I had actually logged over a hundred hours in a Piper Cub, I was considered an experienced pilot. However, before I was allowed to climb into the cockpit of a Spitfire, one of the fastest airplanes in the world, I needed to demonstrate my proficiency by successfully flying a dual-controlled Miles Master plane, which I did without undue difficulty.

I quickly discovered that piloting a Spitfire was a thousand times more exhilarating than flying a Piper Cub. The Spitfire responded beautifully to the slightest touch of my hand. It soared high into the British sky at a speed of up to 350 miles per hour and then dove like an eagle in search of its prey.

In no time I felt comfortable in the Spitfire's cockpit. However, I could not master the art of gunnery for some unknown reason. I couldn't hit a drogue, a target towed by an airplane, to save my life. My marksmanship was so pathetic that I feared discharge and banishment to America, where prison awaited me. But I guess the Brits were desperate for pilots. And so after one month of training, I was commissioned a Pilot Officer on Christmas Eve and posted to a place called Wessex in Wales.

While most of my classmates knew something about their assignments -- Exeter, Biggin Hill, Pembrey, and Tangmere -- I knew nothing about Wessex.

In complete envy I watched as my former classmates packed their belongings, wished me the best of luck, and dispersed to their assignments. I was about to head over to see Major Higby, the Commanding Officer, when I spied him shuffling up the path toward me. "A fine day, isn't it, Lieutenant Moran," he called, surprising me that he knew my name.

"Yes, sir, it is," I said, saluting crisply.

After returning my salute, he studied me momentarily before he pointed to a sleek monoplane parked in the distance under an elaborate camouflaged tent. "That's your mount."

"Huh." I squinted and studied the airplane, which, except for the enlarged fuselage, bore a strong resemblance to the Piper Cub I had flown in Maine.

"It's a Miles Monarch. Seats three ... er ... comfortably."

"Really."

"I think it has a modified De Havilland engine in it." When I arched my eyebrows, he smiled and strutted toward the plane. "It's owned by Sir Cedric Mansfield of Wessex."

"Wes-s-s-ssex." As we approached the plane, I noted the name *Pegasus* painted upon the cowling. I knew that some pilots had the name of their sweetheart or wife stenciled on the fuselage. And if my memory served me correctly, Charles Lindbergh, the great American aviator, had his plane christened the *Spirit of St. Louis*.

"Sir Cedric is a recluse ... eh ... who lives in a sprawling mansion on Lake Manque with Elaine, his granddaughter, who Airman Richards tells me is uglier looking ... um ... than sin. Her parents, by the way, were killed in an air raid down in London ... eh ... a couple of months ago ... er ... so that's why she lives with Sir Cedric."

"And ... how do I ... a Royal Airforce pilot ... hmmmm ... fit into the equation?"

"In addition to being a top-notch scientist, Sir Cedric is also a crackerjack cryptographer."

"Cryptographer?"

"Yes, one of those fellows ... errr ... who tries to decipher the enemy's secret codes."

"Sounds like a very interesting man."

"He is."

When we finally reached the plane, Major Higby opened the door and invited me to glance inside the cabin, where I discovered a very luxurious interior.

Higby pointed to the yoke, which didn't appear any different from the yoke of a Piper Cub. I nodded and ran my hand over the cushioned seat, which was contoured and very plush. "Sir Cedric is also a very close friend of the Prime Minister, and ... Mr. Churchill often consults with him on defense issues."

"I take it ... my task is to fly Sir Cedric down to London from his estate in Wessex."

"Correct." Major Higby smiled and withdrew a stub of a Cuban cigar from his shirt pocket. After moistening his purple lips, he jammed it into his mouth. "Not only Sir Cedric ... but his granddaughter as well." The Major blew a wreath of blue smoke skyward and then paused in his tracks. "Now ... before you ask me what happened to the last fellow ... um ... who held your assignment, I'm going to tell you that he died of an apparent heart attack."

"Hamm ... interesting." I took a chicklet from a box, which was enclosed in a care package my parents had mailed to me, and tossed it into my mouth. "I'm sorry to hear that."

"Baker was a decorated pilot in the Great War, and still very competent at fifty." Higby puffed leisurely upon his cigar, enjoying it immensely. "A local doctor ... um ... by the name of Wallace was called in to certify Baker's death shortly after he collapsed. When I later spoke to Wallace about poor Baker, he told me that the corpse was soaking wet when he examined it. Almost ... as if he had just taken a shower."

I screwed up my face. "Soaking wet?"

"Yep, but that's not all. Wallace also told me that Baker had a horrible, terrified expression scrawled upon his face. Almost as if he had seen a ghost." Finally, Higby dropped the butt, tread upon it, extinguishing the glowing ashes. "When Baker was assigned to be Sir Cedric's pilot ... uh ... he underwent a strenuous physical examination before he was allowed to fly Sir Cedric's plane."

"Why doesn't Sir Cedric fly his own plane?"

"Oh, Sir Cedric is quite capable. He won quite a few races out in New Zealand in a De Havilland Comet ... er ... when he was a young man." When I offered him a Chicklet, he declined my offer. Instead, he held up a paper tote, peeked inside, and then produced a bonbon. Plopping the confection into his cavernous mouth, he chewed ravenously. "Sir Cedric no longer flies because of rheumatism in his fingers." Higby held up his hands. "Got it bad in his fingers."

"That's a shame."

"Sure is." Grunting and turning red and then crimson, Higby stooped and tapped a tank attached to the bottom of the fuselage. "Know what that is?"

I cocked my head and studied the tank. "An extra gasoline tank."

Higby nodded. "That's what I thought, too." He grabbed hold of the cowling and slowly, painstakingly rose to his full height. "It's a contraption that's supposed to allow the pilot to skywrite."

"Does it work?"

"Don't know." Higby helped himself to another bonbon. After chewing for several seconds, he thrust his index finger into his mouth to dislodge a nut or a raisin. "He should have installed an auxiliary gas tank instead." Above us, the sky thundered with the roar of approaching aircraft. We both paused, shaded our eyes, and gazed at a trio of Spitfires, returning from a mission. A ribbon of smoke and tongues of fire snaked from the tail of the last plane in the formation.

When Higby turned and strode purposely toward the barracks, I knew that I had been dismissed. Once we reached the parade grounds, we paused and shook hands. "All you have to do is pilot Sir Cedric down to London to visit the Prime Minister whenever he desires it."

"No problem."

"Merry Christmas."

"And a Merry Christmas to you." Once more I saluted, and then we parted. I watched Higby clop away like a Clydesdale pony until his stout form finally disappeared between two hangars into a copse of scrubby pine trees. I glanced again at the Monarch and decided that she was a very beautiful airplane. I also knew that a new chapter in my life was about to unfold -- for better or worse.

In less than fifteen minutes I packed my personal effects, seven Bing Crosby records, three wallet-girl photos (the term for pinups before World War II), spare clothes, and a Colt revolver. After pausing momentarily to take one last look at the room I had so recently shared with another man, I headed for the door. Outside, on the company street, a bone-chilling zephyr buffeted my face before roaring toward the runway, where the Monarch sat proudly with its engine purring.

"You're the last pilot to leave," called Airman Willie Hope, the rigger, through cupped hands when I approached him. Steadying himself against the wind, he lit a cigarette and inhaled.

As soon as I opened the door, he took my bag and tossed it onto a compartment behind the rear seat. "Will you be spending Christmas on the base?" I asked, knowing that Willie hailed from Australia.

"No." When I showed Willie my Crosby records, he pointed to a metal chest in the rear. I nodded. When I raised the lid, my eyes bulged, and Willie's jaw dropped. I expected to find a first-aid kit or a blanket or at least a flare. Instead, I spied a pair of spiked heels, a dress, and one nylon stocking. We both chuckled. Either Sir Cedric was a sly old fox, or Elaine was a vamp. I didn't know the true story behind the apparel, but I was dying to find out. After retrieving the party dress, I folded it and set it neatly on the seat. As for the solitary nylon stocking, I stuffed it inside the toe of one of the shoes. I then deposited my records inside the chest. "I'm sorry to hear that."

"Oh, don't feel sorry for me." Willie blew a steady stream of smoke through his nose and took one more drag before field-stripping the butt. "My girl over at Birney invited me for Christmas dinner with her parents."

"Great." After strapping on my holster and zipping up my flight jacket, I slipped into the cabin, gazed about, and familiarized myself with the instrument panel. "All set." I adjusted and tightened my harness. "Everything looks good."

When I gestured with my raised thumb, Willie saluted and stepped back. I waved.

"Merry Christmas and good luck."

"And ... the same to you."

Grabbing hold of the throttle with a gloved hand, I brushed my tongue against the back of my teeth and shoved the throttle forward. The engine responded in kind. Relaxing, I smiled contentedly. When I taxied down the grassy runway, the Monarch bounced, skipped, and jitterbugged. "You're doing fine, Joe," I said to my shadow. As was my habit, I checked my gauges once more. Utility poles, trees, and the base's infirmary sped by me. *Whrrrrrrr!* screamed the engine. The Monarch's nose rose slightly when I tugged on the yoke. Whether piloting a Spitfire or a Piper Cub or a Monarch, the experience was always the same -- exhilarating. In my immediate forefront a cluster of pine trees appeared and stood sentinel over a charred truck and an abandoned outhouse. Suddenly the needle on the altimeter jumped. And when I looked outside, I noted that the Monarch was airborne, and I was cruising along at one angel or a thousand feet. "Next stop ... Sussex."

Since the Monarch was unarmed, and my top speed was only 145 miles per hour, I maintained a vigilant eye for bandits. All too often marauding Messerschmitts or Junkers or Heinkels, returning from a mission, were only too happy to swoop down out of the sun and pounce upon a target of opportunity such as a defenseless Monarch.

In less than an hour, the tawny patchwork terrain of the English countryside gave way to the rugged, majestic mountains of Wales. I was about to drop down five hundred feet when my radio crackled. "Robin Hood, this is Merlin," called a raspy, wheezing voice.

"Merlin, I hear you loud and clear ... over," I called into my mouthpiece and promptly checked my bearings.

"According to my radar ... er ... you're about ten minutes from Sherwood Grange ... over."

"Good ... over." I pulled on the throttle and checked my altimeter.

"Must fly down to Camelot ... pronto ... with Maid Marian to confer with King Arthur on delicate matter. How does your fuel tank look?"

"No problem ... over."

"Excellent. Marian and I shall board as soon as you land."

"Roger ... out."

I banked the Monarch and began my descent. "Easy does it." In less than a minute, I spied my destination, an Edwardian-style dwelling, situated on a large lake. "Nice place." Just as I reduced speed and eased the Monarch down, I beheld my passengers, a tall, gaunt gentleman, attired in an ulster, and a petite woman, bundled up in a swagger coat. "Touch down ... just like they taught you." I pulled back gently on the yoke and executed a perfect landing. "Good! Very ... good." Taxing across the lawn, I cut the engine and parked several feet from my passengers. "I'm ready if you are."

As soon as I jumped out of the cabin, the gentleman extended his bony hand, which was spotted with brown liver marks. "Cedric Mansfield," he said, sniffling and coughing from an obvious head cold. "Honored to meet you, Lieutenant Moran." When we shook hands, I was impressed with the strength of his grip. "And this is Elaine Mansfield, my granddaughter."

"We've been waiting to meet you," said Elaine in a rich, sweet voice. She offered her slender, delicate hand. I took it and held it for several seconds before I relinquished it.

At once I knew that Elaine was not the owner of the apparel I had discovered in the chest. She was far too small to wear any of the clothing. Perhaps the dress, the shoes, and the nylon stocking belonged to one of Sir Cedric's ladies. "I just found out about you this morning … um … when the assignments were announced," I said.

"Well, when Gramps requested the best pilot, Major Higby recommended you."

When Elaine smiled up at me, my pulse quickened, and my knees turned to jelly. On the spot I decided that her ruby-red lips were too full and sensuous. Her creamy skin too perfect. And her auburn hair far too glossy for a mere mortal. I hadn't been so totally smitten by a female since I proposed to Annie Gilders in the fourth grade. I slyly studied Elaine more critically from a different angle and wagged my head. I didn't know Airman Richards. Perhaps he had actually dated Elaine, and she rejected his overtures. To get even, he let it be known that she was not very attractive. Stranger things have been known to occur.

No sooner had I conducted her to a seat and slipped on her seat belt when her face flushed angrily. Her voice hardened. "Look at this!" She held up the shoes and dress and waved them. "That scoundrel, Baker, was using the *Pegasus* as … as his own private bordello."

"Now … now," said Sir Cedric, adjusting his harness. When he turned toward Elaine, he scrutinized the clothing. "Say … doesn't that dress belong to Mildred Hillish, the mayor's wife?"

"It does, and so does everything else back here."

"I always thought that Mildred had a wandering eye."

"Humph!"

Somewhat relieved that I had so quickly learned of the identity of the person who abandoned the clothing, I raised my eyes, whispered a prayer of thanksgiving, and switched on the magneto. *R-r-r-r-r-h-h-h-mmmm!* wailed the engine. Smiling like a Cheshire cat, I leaned back and pushed the throttle. Within seconds we were lumbering down the field. "Hang on!" The lake and mansion and carriage house shot by, and then we were climbing above a majestic forest into the sky, leaving the bleak, gray heath behind us.

While Elaine still seethed and Sir Cedric dabbed at his red, runny nose with his handkerchief, I set a course for London. With my spirits sustained by the fact that Major Higby considered me an excellent pilot and an infatuation smoldered deep within my heart, I checked my airspeed and scanned the sky. Nothing. Not a plane in sight. I decided to relax and enjoy the ride when suddenly a glowing, white tracer shot past my left wing. "Ohhh, cripes!"

"What's the matter?" asked Sir Cedric, wiping tears from his watery eyes.

"Company." Though I sounded calm, I was terrified. *Wooooosh!*

Another tracer rushed past. A bit closer to the wing. "Damn!" When I tugged on the yoke, the Monarch reacted perfectly and climbed faster than I expected.

"Isn't there any evasive action you can take?" Sir Cedric slouched further in his seat and pulled a battered fedora down on his massive head. "Elaine, I strongly encourage you to lie low back there."

"Yes, sir," said Elaine with an edge in her sultry voice.

I knew that sooner or later the Monarch would be destroyed by a volley of bullets, and we would all perish. But since an overwhelming desire to live another day and grow better acquainted with Elaine was paramount, I needed to do something. I quickly discovered that extreme fear didn't impair my ability to think. Actually, I was somewhat relieved when I spied an ocean of stratus clouds below us. *Zin-n-n-ng!* Another tracer flashed by the starboard wing. This shell passed far wide of its mark, buoying my spirits. The enemy gunner was a far poorer shot than I was. When I cackled in delight at his lack of marksmanship, I was sure that my passengers believed me deranged or worse.

Within seconds our nemesis, a Henschel, zoomed past and veered off to the right. "Did you see the smirk on the face of that arrogant Hun?" I asked, pointing to the open cockpit of the gray biplane some distance below us?"

"Isn't that a World War I plane with those two wings on top of each other?" asked Elaine, craning her neck for a better view.

"No." I tugged on the yoke, and the Monarch dove and raced for the safety of the clouds. "It's only about five or six years old."

"Looks older."

"Its scary feature is the noisy engine … er … which sends panic through those on the ground when they hear it diving down at them."

"So that was a Henschel," said Sir Cedric, somewhat more composed as he stole a peek out the window.

"Sure is." Tugging on the throttle, I was pleasantly surprised by the response of the engine. And I was truly impressed with my speed. "I can't believe it. We're flying at about two hundred miles per hour."

"Over the years I rebuilt the engine and tweaked it considerably to increase its speed."

"Nice job." In a matter of seconds we dove into the dull-gray stratus clouds. From my studies at Bowdoin College, I knew that these clouds would offer us sufficient cover from the Henschel. "I think we're safe." I wiped my beaded forehead with my handkerchief and unzipped my jacket. "In about thirty minutes we'll reach our destination."

"Wonderful." Sir Cedric, his brows rising in obvious pleasure, rubbed his hands together and then formed a steeple with his fingertips.

"Major Higby is an excellent judge of character and ability," said

Elaine. And when a gust of turbulence suddenly rocked the Monarch and tossed her forward, she brushed a gossamer kiss across my cheek, allowing the sweet scent of her perfume to further addle my senses.

"Er … what is the red knob for?" I asked, tapping my finger against a square projection.

"That's the skywriting facilitator," instructed Sir Cedric proudly.

"Does it work?"

"No," said Elaine, stifling a chuckle. It only belches out puffs of black smoke like St. George's dragon."

"She's quite right," said Sir Cedric. "I haven't perfected it as yet."

After checking my gauges once more, I offered my guests a Chicklet. Both accepted my offer.

As I suspected, the stratus clouds soon dissipated, leaving a bright December sun at our backs. "Look there!" I uttered through clenched teeth, throwing a nod with my head. The Henschel, unaware of our presence, cruised directly below us.

"Ohhhh, no!" cried Elaine, her voice choked with fear.

"Hold on." Grasping the yoke, I nosed the Monarch down towards the unsuspecting Hun, who was busily strafing a flock of sheep in a field below. Hunched over, he randomly sprayed the helpless sheep. "Gonna … get you … now." Steadying the Monarch, I bit my lower lip until it bled. The Hun, his yellow scarf trailing in the wind as if it were a pennant, was too engrossed to see us. And if he had glanced up, I doubt if he would have seen us in the blazing sun.

When I grabbed the skywriting knob, Sir Cedric's eyes widened in dismay. "W-w-what … are you going to do?" stuttered Sir Cedric, watching with keen interest.

"Just watch." I eased the Monarch down to within yards of the open cockpit and waited. Finally, when I was over the Henschel, I pulled on the knob. It balked and hissed initially. But when I twisted the knob, it spewed a jet of black smoke into the cockpit. The pilot turned and flailed wildly with his arms.

"Eureka!" screamed Elaine happily. Unflinching, she lunged forward and breathed a kiss upon my neck. "That's for saving our lives and being a hero."

"Good shooting," called Sir Cedric, rubbing his thin fingers together in delight.

"Gottcha-a-a-a!" I called enthusiastically and watched a thick stream of black smoke envelope the bewildered pilot. I paused and studied my handiwork, a blackened cockpit and its occupant, who resembled a chimney sweep.

Once more I pulled on the knob, blasting the choking Hun. He tipped his wings, but I continued to spray him. More smoke billowed out of the cowling. I squirted once more before the Hun finally realized that his only option was to land immediately.

Down he glided. I followed. Probably because of the turmoil the smoke caused within the cockpit, the Hun failed to drop his landing gear. He belly flopped on a grassy dale, bounced several times, spun around and around, and struck a haystack.

Being in total control of my emotions, I touched down gently, taxied away from the smoking Henschel, and shut off my engine. "Stay here!" I instructed and meant it.

Leaping out of the Monarch, I raced toward the disabled enemy plane with a drawn revolver. *"Draussen!"* I screamed at the disoriented pilot, who was already stumbling out of the cockpit with his hands held high. *"Sprechen sie Englisch?"*

"Yah, I speak English ... little."

"Walk." I stepped aside and motioned with my revolver.

"No shoot."

With my prisoner leading the way, I followed close behind, not knowing where we were headed or what I would do with him. However, within seconds I spotted three members of the Home Guard, all armed with ancient battle axes, trudging toward us. And across the road, a farmer, pitchfork in hand, tramped out to meet us. "That way." I pointed to an official-looking man bicycling in our direction.

Initially, I was as frightened of my prisoner, a hooked-nose chap with bovine eyes, as much as he was of me. However, with the arrival of reinforcements, I gained more courage and marched more confidently.

"Good job, Governor," called the official on the bicycle, who was the first to reach us.

"He's all yours." I waved my prisoner toward the cyclist with my revolver.

Seconds later a high-pitched siren wailed in the distance. The British version of a paddy wagon shimmied across the rocky, uneven field and ground to a sudden halt before us. Out scampered two Bobbies. After frisking the German and finding no weapons, they imprisoned him in the rear of the wagon and sped away.

"You were marvelous," said Elaine, rushing up, slipping her hand through the crook of my arm, and squeezing.

"I think there's a medal being cast for you ... right this minute," called Sir Cedric, huffing and puffing, as he climbed up the hill and tiptoed around the carcasses of three dead sheep.

"Just doing my duty," I exclaimed, slipping my revolver into its holster. "Anyone of you would have done the same."

In the next few minutes the area assumed a carnival atmosphere with scores of people pouring out of their thatched cottages to inspect the wrecked Henschel, sympathize with the farmer on the loss of so many fine sheep, and congratulate me on a job well-done.

"Who's going to pay for my sheep?" asked the farmer, thrusting his pitchfork into the sod. "That's what I want to know."

"The Air Ministry," called a voice from beyond a knoll. "Just send them the bill."

The voice did not sound familiar to me, but when I glanced at Elaine's face, I detected a total look of surprise. Her eyes sparkled in disbelief; her lips quivered. "L-o-o-o-k!" she stammered. "It's ... it's ... the Prime Minister."

Indeed, it was Mr. Churchill, the Prime Minister. Clad in his customary greatcoat with the astrakhan collar turned up, he exuded confidence as he flashed his well-known victory sign to the assembled crowd and paused to shake every hand offered him. "We shall persevere and defeat our enemy," he exclaimed, raising his hand and brandishing his familiar victory sign once more. The crowd responded with a thundering round of applause. He continued to mingle amongst and chat with his adoring constituents until every man and woman had been recognized.

"I think his presence ... eh ... might just save us a trip to London," said Sir Cedric, joining us in front of the Monarch. Elaine and I merely nodded and munched on sandwiches, which had been provided by the farmer's wife.

"You're correct about that," called the Prime Minister, excusing himself from a departing admirer. He hurried over to the Monarch and extended his hand to me, which I pumped warmly. "Lieutenant Moran, is it?"

"Yes, sir," I said, wondering if I was expected to genuflect.

"You not only saved the lives of Sir Cedric and his granddaughter, but you also captured a German aircraft."

"How did you know we were here?" asked Sir Cedric, tamping a wad of tobacco into his pipe and pointing it at the Prime Minister as if it were a pistol.

"Heard it on my radio." The Prime Minister accepted a sandwich handed him and rammed it into his mouth. "I was on my way to London, but when I heard that an unarmed British plane had captured a Henschel, I hurried over to see for myself what a Henschel looks like."

"Could we confer here ... now?"

"The back of my Rolls Royce is as fine a place as any." The Prime Minister turned and waddled off to his automobile. "We won't take long, Elaine, I promise."

"Take as long as you like, Mr. Prime Minister," said Elaine, latching onto my arm once more and swinging it back and forth like a school girl. "I have something very important ... er ... that I wish to discuss with Lieutenant Moran."

"Lieutenant Moran!" I said, feigning displeasure at the use of my surname by a woman who had so very recently kissed me twice.

Happy to finally be alone, Elaine and I drifted closer to the Monarch's fuselage, where I checked the plane's integrity, ending with a kick of the tires. Satisfied that the Monarch had suffered no structural damage in the encounter with the Henschel, I glanced up at Elaine. And when our gazes met, I noted that her emerald eyes were warm and radiant, bubbling with joy. Pointing to the grass, which was dotted with animal droppings, I strongly recommended that she seek the comfort of the Monarch's cabin. She agreed. Taking her under the arm, I led her inside the plane. And when I was sure that she was comfortable, I switched on the heater.

I was about to initiate the conversation when she slid her icy-cold hand over my mouth. "Joe, before you say another word, I want to tell you that I have fallen in love with you." Coloring from her disclosure, she removed her hand and stared into my eyes for a sign of my affection for her.

When I reached over and took her hand, she squeezed mine and lowered her eyes. "I fell in love with you as soon as I saw you ... standing on that frozen grass with Sir Cedric." When she released my hand, I gently tickled her palm. She leaned into me and purred like a tabby. "If ... we weren't sitting here with that Rolls Royce parked directly in front of us, and," I paused to heave a deep sigh, "I'd kiss you."

"Look." She shifted her eyes toward the Rolls Royce. "Gramps and the Prime Minister are watching us as we speak."

"I know. They've been watching our every move."

"Yes, but tonight ... after Sir Reginald Dunston disappears, hmmmm ... we shall find a very secluded place to get to know each other ... better."

I tilted a brow at the mention of another man's name. "Is Sir Reginald Dunston one of your boyfriends?"

"Jolly, no. He's a ghost." Elaine's tone was very casual.

"A ghost?"

"Oh, yes." She wrinkled up her nose. "He has been haunting the house since my arrival."

Cocking my ear, I took Elaine's hand once more and held it. "Do you know why he has only surfaced since your arrival?" To say the least, I grew more interested in her ghost. "Where was he before your arrival?"

"I ... I think he was dormant."

"Huh!" I scratched my head and tapped my fingers upon the yoke. "Can a ghost be inactive?"

"This one was." Elaine swallowed hard and tossed her auburn mane over her shoulder. "He ... errrr ... thinks I'm the first mistress of Sherwood, who, by the way, was my great-grandmother."

"And in addition to resembling you, uh ... I'll bet that her name was Lady Elaine Mansfield, and he was in love with her ... umm ... a century ago."

Elaine took a small compact from her purse, studied her image, and powdered her shiny nose. "You're correct on all points."

"So-o-o-o-o ... let me get this straight ... a ghost suddenly appears at Sir Cedric's house because he believes that his long-lost love has returned."

"True." From the expression upon her patrician face, I knew that she spoke the truth. I giggled, recalling that my own mother maintained that our house was haunted. Mother insisted that she sometimes caught a glimpse of our ghost in the attic. That ghost only visited on nights when it rained. And then she vanished as quickly as she appeared. Mother conducted several séances in an attempt to communicate with her ghost but failed miserably.

"How many people have seen Sir Reginald?"

"Thank God ... only Gramps and Baker have ever seen him."

"And did Baker die from fright?"

"Yes." When she noted that I was receptive to her disclosure, her tense body relaxed. "Baker, slightly drunk, strolled into the study one night when the ghost was present, took one look at him, and keeled over."

"Dead."

Her hand darted downwards. "Dead before he hit the floor."

"Was Baker sweating profusely when he unexpectedly dropped in on the ghost and you?"

"If you're wondering why Baker was soaking wet when the doctor examined him, it was because the ghost is a water spirit and doused him. He wets everything he comes in contact with."

"A water ghost." I stroked my jowls. "That's very interesting."

"Yes, he's a water ghost who committed suicide over a hundred years ago --"

"Because your great-grandmother would not return his love and marry him."

"Err ... right." Elaine withdrew a handkerchief and twisted it into knots. "When Gran spurned him, he drowned himself in one of the

149

springs underneath the mansion. We believe ... er ... that's where he gets his energy."

"And his water."

Elaine nodded. "I'm telling you about Sir Reginald because Gramps and I need help." Elaine peered out at the tawny field, where several men were collecting the dead sheep and tossing them into a truck. "The ghost really hasn't harmed anyone ... except ... maybe contribute to Baker's demise, but the mansion is crumbling from all the water damage he's caused by his mere presence."

"Hmmmm." I had to admit that ever since I learned of a ghost in my own home, I harbored an interest in paranormal phenomena. Now I wished to learn more about Sir Reginald in order to exorcise him to the underworld. "What have you done to rid the house of this water ghost?"

"Well, the very first thing that Gramps did was ask the local vicar to pray for Sir Reginald's soul."

"And that didn't work."

"No way. Reginald must be an atheist." We both chuckled.

"Following the exorcism, Gramps hired a man to caulk all the cracks in the floor and around the windows and doors."

"No luck."

"None. The ghost showed up two hours after the workman left."

"Was that the last time you tried to dispatch the ghost?"

"Oh, no." Elaine blew out her cheeks. "Since Gramps is an obstinate old man, who loves his home, he asked the servants to turn up the heat in the furnace and set fires in all of the fireplaces. He thought that heat would dry the ghost up."

"I would have thought that would have solved the problem."

"It didn't even slow him down."

I shook my head. "I really don't know what to tell you." Just then I noticed that there was a stirring in the Rolls Royce. "But ... together ... we can rid the house of Sir Reginald."

"Well, if there isn't soon a satisfactory conclusion to this little conundrum, Gramps will sell Sherwood and move down to London."

Elaine's words caught my undivided attention. My jaw dropped; my body stiffened as if a poker had seared my very skin. "That would mean that you'd be living in close proximity to the Prime Minister."

"True. Gramps could simply drive over to 10 Downing Street every day to see him."

"Ah-ha." I reached out, took Elaine's hand, and stared into her green eyes. "You do know that we really have to rid the mansion of Sir Reginald." I punched my fist into the palm of my hand. "And ... starting right now, we have to formulate a plan."

"Wonderful!" Elaine threw her arms around me and kissed me

150

once more. This kiss was more affectionate. "What do you suggest ... uh ... we do to rid Sherwood of Sir Reginald?"

"I don't know, but ... er ... right now I see Sir Cedric heading our way ... so let's get back to Sherwood and celebrate Christmas ... together."

After glancing at her watch, she patted my knee. "Just wait until you see the grandeur of Sherwood at Christmas time."

With the sun setting quickly, I wished for nothing more than an uneventful flight back to Sherwood. "I hope no more Germans shoot at us." I received my wish. And after an uneventful flight, I touched down at Sir Cedric's private runway, where a sleek Bentley awaited us. "As soon as I put the Monarch to bed, I'll join you."

"Perhaps Elaine would like to show you a shortcut from the hangar to the house," said Sir Cedric, handing his briefcase to the chauffeur.

"That's a jolly good idea," said Elaine, already ensconced in the front seat.

Minutes later the Monarch was sitting snugly and safely in the wooden hangar, and Elaine and I, hand in hand, were strolling up a gentle incline to the brightly lit manor house. "It's a beautiful night to be alive and in love," I said as we passed the carriage house.

"Look!" Elaine stopped in her tracks and pointed to the sky. "The first star of the evening."

"So."

"So ... you must kiss me ... according to legend ... or you turn into a frog."

"Humph!" Without another word, I embraced her and kissed her icy-cold lips. She moaned and ground her hips into my body. "How I have fallen for you ... in just one day." I kissed her again, more passionately. She cooed and returned my kiss, threefold.

While the house loomed in our immediate forefront, we didn't seem to get any closer to the front door. Each time we reached a tree along the path, I found a reason to pin Elaine against its trunk and kiss her. Eventually we approached a marble statue of some sort of pagan god or goddess atop a pedestal of white stone. At that point, I scooped her up into my arms and carried her up the incline.

In due time we reached the giant oak door beneath an iron portico. While a copper-colored moon tossed silvery beams between the naked branches of the gnarled poplars, I glanced at the cornices for signs of spitting gargoyles or hissing dragons. I found nothing of the sort. Even the door knocker disappointed me. No head of Jacob Marley snarled back at me. There was only a simple metal ring.

At once I set the statuesque Elaine down. While she blew

disheveled hair out of her face and buttoned her coat, I rapped upon the massive door. By and large, it was only a matter of seconds before a squat, obese manservant, wearing horn-rims and looking quite owlish, threw open the door and invited us into the foyer, an elegant vestibule with flanking mahogany staircases.

"May I take your things?" said the servant, holding out his pudgy hands. "Sir Cedric awaits you in the dining room."

"Thank you, Peters," said Elaine, already handing him her coat, gloves, scarf, and my flight jacket. "Put Lieutenant Moran's things in the vacant room next to mine."

Peters bowed. "I shall attend to Lieutenant Moran's possessions immediately."

"Wonderful." After smoothing her dress in the wall mirror, Elaine applied a coat of fresh lipstick. "Now ... I'm a bit more presentable."

"Lead the way," I said, allowing her to slip her arm around mine.

Since I had never been inside a mansion such as Sherwood, I was quite impressed by the opulence surrounding me. The interior was Edwardian par excellence. Well, it was quite majestic, save for the water marks on the white ceilings, the mildew on the beige walls, and the decaying parquet floors. Every room we strolled past had been vandalized by Sir Reginald's meanderings. As we strolled down a long corridor, I noticed that the ceiling above us had been bloated with water at some recent point and cracked under the pressure. Warped floorboards creaked under our feet, and once elegant chandeliers were tarnished by water stains and beyond repair.

The center piece of the dining room was an overwhelming fireplace, where a gigantic Yule log glowed and blazed and spat, sending out volumes of heat and light. Sir Cedric, already dressed in his dinner jacket, sat at the head of the table, sipping brandy.

"Welcome to Sherwood," he called, rising as Elaine and I entered. The dining room had not been spared by Sir Reginald. The carpet showed water marks, as did the ceiling. And when I gazed at a bulge in the ceiling, Sir Cedric sadly followed my line of vision. "We've had some plumbing problems, but all will be repaired after the holidays."

"Gramps, Joe knows about Sir Reginald," said Elaine, squeezing my hand.

"Oh, does he?"

"His home in America was haunted by a ghost." Elaine gazed up into my eyes. "And he's going to help us rid Sherwood of that awful water spirit ... so you won't have to sell."

A tear welled in one of the old man's eyes. "Bless you, Joseph, for trying to help us." Sir Cedric plopped down in his chair and sighed expansively. "I … just don't think that there's anything that can be done … short of selling Sherwood."

"I don't want to disclose my hand because Sir Reginald might be listening, but I think that I can rid Sherwood of him," I said, not having any idea whatsoever how to deal with Sir Reginald.

"See, Gramps, there's hope," said Elaine enthusiastically. "Now … Let's eat. I'm starved."

Sir Cedric rang a bell and shortly thereafter the headwaiter, a tall, lean gentleman with a Vandyke beard, carried in a robust turkey. He, of course, was followed by subordinates, who carried bowls of steaming vegetables, plates of cold meats, and trays of breads of all varieties.

Though a good portion of the house had been damaged by the reckless ravages of Sir Reginald, my guests put aside their predicament and celebrated the Christmas Eve meal with the warmth of the season. The meal, to say the least, was the best I had eaten since I left Maine. Being an American, I had never sampled plum pudding, a boiled treat containing fruits and spices. But the very last dish served was the traditional plum pudding along with spiked eggnog. I was somewhat leery of the confection when I first spied it, but one taste assured me that it was a delicacy fit for kings.

I didn't know if it was the grandeur of the meal or a combination of the brandy and the spiked eggnog that Sir Cedric consumed, but soon after he downed his second snifter, he retired for the evening.

With Elaine and me left to our own pursuits, we gravitated to the confines of the drawing room, a formal reception room, at the far end of the corridor.

In all twenty-two years of life back in Maine, I had never seen a drawing room. Our family considered themselves well positioned in the community. However, we only had a parlor for entertainment. No drawing room. Even the Thompsons, the wealthiest family in the area, had no drawing room.

Sir Cedric's drawing room was a mixture of overstuffed chairs, solid oak bookcases, and the acrid smell of stale cigars. "This is where Sir Reginald has appeared most often," said Elaine, pointing to a waterlogged bear rug. Upon closer examination of the rug, I thought that it resembled a poorly woven toupee, which had recently been invaded by an army of moths.

"And all the shoes?" I asked, noticing at least two pairs of opera pumps and a pair of men's wing-tipped shoes drying before a raging fire in the marble fireplace.

"The room fills with water every time the ghost appears, and our shoes get wet." Elaine took my hand and led me to the near wall, where several portraits hung. "The one … er … all the way to the right is my great-grandmother."

"My word … you bear a remarkable resemblance to her."

"Don't I?" She held up a dainty finger as the grandfather clock in the corner tolled the hour. "Love, if you will excuse me, I shall run upstairs and check with Beatrice to see if she has completed my charwoman's outfit for Boxing Day."

"What is Boxing Day?"

"On Boxing Day … ummm … which is the day after Christmas … er … two of the staff exchange places with Gramps and me."

"Really."

"Gramps will spend the day as a manservant, and yours truly will assume the duties of a charwoman."

"And what are the duties of a charwoman?"

"A charwoman scrubs the floors on her hands and knees and then cleans out the grease pit in the kitchen. Not a very glamorous job." Elaine seized a copy of Scott's *Ivanhoe* from the table and returned it to the bookshelf. "Thank God that Boxing Day only comes once a year."

"Doesn't sound too bad."

"That's easy for you to say." Elaine blew me a kiss and wiggled away. Her stiletto heels thumped upon the parquet floor in syncopation to the incessant tapping of an errant tree branch against the dormer window.

Since I had never read any novels written by Sir Walter Scott, I retrieved the volume from the shelf and seated myself before the roaring fireplace, which cast a ludicrous yellow image on the ceiling of a *shagimaw,* the fictitious critter of northern Maine, which, according to legend, was a cross between a moose and a bear.

Once I opened the book, I actually became quite engrossed in my reading and did not stir until I heard the door squeak open and detected a presence in the room.

I raised my eyes slowly from the passage where Gurth and Wamba encountered Prior Aymer and peeked at the stout Yule candle on the sideboard. The taper flickered uncontrollably, slithered, and then expired as if extinguished by a supernatural breath of air. I sat up with a start as all the window panes in the room rattled simultaneously, and the floor boards creaked. I was sure that Sir Reginald was present.

When I turned toward the door, my eyes grew as large as saucers. It wasn't Sir Reginald, who had entered the room, but a blushing Elaine. She smiled coquettishly in the shadow of a full suite of German armor, curtsied, and threw me a hip-cocked pose. I heaved a sigh of extreme relief and set the book aside.

Elaine no longer wore the modest dress and patent-leather pumps of a respectable English lady. In addition to being barefoot, she was now wearing a skimpy, tight-fitting halter, exposing the swell of her large breasts, and a sackcloth skirt, barely reaching her dimpled knees. I supposed that the English took Boxing Day very seriously, and so her charwoman's costume was quite authentic. As for traipsing around barefoot, I remembered her saying that she would be scrubbing floors on her hands and knees like Cinderella and then crawling around in a grease pit. Prancing around in high heels would not have been comfortable or practical. Besides, she looked quite sexy barefoot.

"Your wench awaits you," she said in a seductive voice. Pirouetting on sooty toes, she tugged at the scarlet ribbon atop her head and tousled her hair mightily with both hands. The aforementioned agitation coaxed an abundance of Titian curls to plummet past her creamy-white shoulders. "Do you like me barefoot and half-naked?"

"Yes, very much," I said.

Rising from the three-seat settee, I held out my hand. She brushed it aside. In her eyes stirred a glint of mischief. "If you want me … you have to catch me." Giggling, she dashed around the edge of a table. I feinted. She stopped, pivoted, and retreated. I easily corralled her, swept her up into my arms, and kissed her mouth with long, hard kisses. With a heaving bosom, she clung to me and buried her head in my chest. When I gazed into her blazing green eyes, I spied the reflection of a figure helping himself to one of Sir Cedric's cigars.

"Lady Elaine, what is the meaning of this?" called a gurgling voice. "Who is this scallywag?" When I turned, I beheld the ghost, attired in a nineteenth-century frock coat and matching slacks. "Your conduct is not becoming a lady, and your dress is scandalous … to say the least." The damp and dewy ghost pointed a bony finger, dripping with seaweed, at me.

"This," exclaimed Elaine, snuggling closer to me, "is my fiancé … Lieutenant Joseph Moran of the Royal British Air Force." Upon hearing the word *fiancé,* I gently set Elaine down and kissed her tenderly.

"What is this rubbish I hear, you … you hussy?" The ghost rippled in obvious agitation, drenching the rug. "You are betrothed to me, and I have come to claim you."

"Nonsense … you … you … aqueous refugee from a cesspool." Taking a copy of Shakespeare's sonnets from an ottoman, she reared back like Bob Feller, kicked high with a bare foot, and hurled it at the apparition. The volume sailed through the opaque ghost, crashed against the mantel, and fell harmlessly among Sir Cedric's drying shoes.

"Ha-a-a-a!" The ghost, unfazed by Elaine's burst of anger, dragged vigorously upon his cigar, sending noxious gray clouds of smoke in every direction.

"Whew!" I exclaimed and threw open the window behind Sir Reginald. "Stinks in here."

"D-d-d-don't … d-d-do … t-t-that." Distressed, judging from the ghost's halting speech, he promptly crossed the room and shut the window with a thud. When he turned, I discerned a hoary frost nipping at his curls and ice crystals clinging to his bulbous nose.

Suddenly, a plan, so simple I never contemplated it, unveiled before me. I immediately lifted the unsuspecting Elaine from the floor, sat her upon the oak card table, and peered into her jade eyes. "Elaine Mansfield, you stated that I was your fiancé."

"True," she said with a smile on her rosebud lips.

"Then … if I am your fiancé, and we truly love each other, I … I offer you my hand in marriage."

"I accept!" She clasped her hands together in her lap and swung her dangling feet back and forth. "I accept without reservation."

"I object," cried the ghost, puddling the floor at an alarming rate.

"Well, sir, if you have any objections to our union, I propose that we settle it by dueling."

"A duel?" While Elaine gave me an anxious look, the ghost inclined his head and deliberated. After some seconds he turned and pointed to a rusted blunderbuss, hanging over the fireplace. "I accept your challenge." He tossed his cigar into the fire. "And … let the best man win and claim Lady Elaine's hand."

"Agreed." Fingering my revolver, I pointed to the door. "Outside, Sir Reginald."

"Outside?" The ghost stole a peek through the frosted window.

"Outside." I slipped on my jacket and zipped it up.

"Very well." The ghost bowed, and I led the way.

Though the moon shined brightly, the piercing wind howled and caterwauled around our heads. Underfoot, our steps, or at least mine, crushed the frozen turf. Retreating deeper into my jacket like a turtle withdraws into its shell, I exhaled, blowing out a wreath of steam.

After only a short distance from the house, the ghost huffed and puffed and exhibited signs of distress. "Come you wretched mass of recycled elements."

"P-p-pleeeease," croaked the ghost, pausing in his steps. "M-my … kneeeees … stiiiiffen." He hung his head and stumbled along.

"Come!" I thrust my hands more deeply into my pockets and plod on.

"M-m-merccccy, Lieuuuutenant." The ghost wheezed and whistled through his nose. "Liiight … a fire … p-p-p-pleeeease."

"Come!" When I paused and glanced over my shoulder, I noticed that the ghost had grown rigid. "Hurry!"

"S-s-s-s-stop!" His movements were now quite mechanical and much labored. "I c-c-congeal."

"You had your last drench."

"W-w-w-what … is-s-s … h-h-happeniiiing?"

"You are freezing."

"F-f-f-reeeeezing?"

"Yes, and when you finally turn into an ice-bound form, I shall have you placed into a refrigerator, where you will never again threaten anyone of the Mansfield family." Since all was now quiet, save for the mischievous wind's churning and soughing, I returned to the still figure. All that remained of Sir Reginald Dunston, the Duke of Duncannon, was a statue sculptured in clear, transparent ice.

Of course, Elaine and Sir Cedric were overjoyed with my Herculean accomplishment. On the eve after Boxing Day, Sir Cedric announced plans to have a permanent refrigerator erected deep inside the bowels of his estate. According to his plans, the temperature inside Sir Reginald's new home would always be hundreds of degrees below zero.

Elaine., of course, held me to my proposal of marriage. Sir Cedric concurred with the union. And so on the Feast of the Epiphany of the Lord, Elaine and I exchanged vows in the village church some miles from Sherwood. Though my parents also agreed to our marriage, they never met Elaine until our twins, Winnie and Churchill, were six years of age.

Flight

So after thirteen months of combat, I was about to fly my fiftieth and final mission in the European Theater of Operations. And this last flight was to Berlin, the German capital, no less. I recalled how fiercely the dogfights were waged over the skies of France and Italy. The intensity and the abundance of the flak bursting above, below, and about my Mustang were more intense than I thought humanly possible. I could only imagine the welcome we would receive in Berlin. But the city's marshaling yards had to be bombed in order to destroy Hitler's war machine. And so our squadron was awarded the honor of demolishing the rail yards, as Major Reynolds, the Operations Officer, put it at our morning briefing.

"Humph! Some honor," I said to myself as our flight of pilots drove out to the airfield in a two-and-a-half-ton truck that wheezed and coughed as if tubercular.

I glanced at my watch and then at my three comrades. Most of the time, on these excursions out to the airfield, there was a fair amount of good-natured teasing going on. Today there was none. Abbott, our flight leader, sat hunched over, praying. I knew that he was praying because his lips moved silently. And every time he petitioned Jesus, he bowed his head in reverence.

Connors, a wingman and a native of California, stared blankly at his boots. Periodically he gnawed on the heal of his hand.

Next to him, Williams sat with his eyes closed and his hands folded upon his lap. Though he said nothing, I knew that he was thinking of his newly born son back in Cleveland.

When I parted the canvas flap, I noticed that we had reached the control tower. In the distance, the fuselages of the silver Mustangs gleamed in the early morning sun. Each engine purred in readiness for take-off.

As we neared the first plane, which was my machine, I spied Sergeant Conley, the crew's chief, spitting upon a rag and polishing my canopy.

Suddenly the truck braked and rolled to a screeching stop, allowing Colonel Beauchamp's jeep to cross our path. Our driver grumbled incoherently and shifted gears smoothly. The truck then lumbered down the road and passed the scorched remains of Dugan's plane. Across the road waited our Mustangs.

"All out!" cried the driver as soon as we reached the flight line.

Tossing my chute over my shoulder, I jumped from the truck and trudged towards the sleek, deadly fighters.

"Good luck," called Abbott, slipping his hand into his pocket and fingering the crucifix on his rosary.

"Same to you," I said and zipped up my jacket against a biting wind.

"It might not be a milk run," said Connors, trying to sound optimistic, "but it might not be so bad."

"I hope you're right." Taking a last drag on my Camel, I exhaled and snuffed out the butt.

"I really envy you, Joe," said Williams, hastening his step to catch up with us.

"Why's that?"

"Because ... by tomorrow at this time, you'll be heading home to Connecticut to spend Christmas with your parents."

"Hey!" I stopped and tapped my finger repeatedly upon Williams's arm for emphasis. "After we wipe out that rail yard today, the Fuhrer will see just how futile his predicament is, and ... and he'll sue for peace."

"Think so?"

"I do." I looked into his baby-blue eyes and smiled. "I also think that within a very short time you'll be heading home to see your new son."

"Gee-e-e! That would be great."

I nodded in agreement and strolled past Williams to my plane. The dapper Sergeant Conley had already kicked the chocks away from the tires and was making one last check of the Mustang before take-off.

"She's a beautiful lady," said Conley, "except fer the fact that she don't have no name on her."

I smiled and nodded. Most of the guys had names or pictures painted on the fuselage. Some even had small Swastikas stenciled below the cockpit to show how many enemy airplanes they had shot down. My ship had neither a name nor the number of kills displayed below the cockpit.

I reasoned that if my plane bore a fancy name or the number of planes I had bagged, the enemy might consider me a hot shot. And then I might be singled out for immediate extermination.

In all honesty, I simply wished to be known as an ordinary guy who was just doing his part for the war effort. Truth be told, I had downed six German aircraft and was considered an Ace.

After strapping me in and shutting my canopy, Conley hopped over to my right wingtip. There he directed me with his hand signals. Watching him, I taxied for my takeoff. He jumped off when I approached the runway and gave me the thumbs-up for good luck. I nodded and returned his gesture.

Taking a deep breath, I revved my engine and checked my mags. The tachometer showed full power. I then drove out to the runway. Praying until I received permission from the tower to take-off, I waited.

"There it is," I said when the green light flashed from the control tower. "Here we go!" Shoving the throttle, the Mustang roared down the runway and soared into the air, barely clearing the tops of a copse of conifers. "Up! Up! And away!" Retracting the wheels, I assumed the element leader's position and joined Abbott.

In due time the squadron climbed above the North Sea and entered into the Netherlands. At ten thousand feet I attached my oxygen mask. It was well past the German city of Hannover when I spied the initial burst of flak in the distance. But on the outskirts of Berlin, the flak grew heavy. On we flew, searching the landscape below for the elusive train yards.

"There's the marshaling yards," called Abbott several minutes later. "Let's go!"

Abbott peeled off. We followed and began our dive out of the sun at about ten thousand feet. I reached zero feet in a hurry and pulled up at about two hundred feet. My eyes bulged in their sockets. Dead ahead, I spotted a big, black locomotive chugging out of the yard. It was a troop train, heading west. Biting my lower lip, I held my breath and gently squeezed off a short burst. *Rat-a-tat-tat* screamed my machine guns. Judging from the tracers, the bullets found their target. Seconds later the locomotive caught fire and exploded, sending shrapnel in every direction. I barreled through the explosion and tugged on the stick. Skyward I soared, relieved that my ship had not been damaged by any of the debris.

"Good shooting. Let's make another pass and see what else I can line up in my gun sights." Perspiration dripped into my eyes and chilled me. Glancing over my shoulder, I noticed a fiery red ball rising from the train I had so recently strafed. Passenger cars derailed. Soldiers hurtled through the windows. Secondary explosions erupted from flatcars.

Satisfied with my marksmanship, I scanned the sky for Abbott, Connors, and Williams. Much to my surprise, they were nowhere to be seen.

Air combat was always like that. All hell broke loose for a few minutes. And then there were complete peace and quiet. Suddenly, without explanation, the dials on my gauges vibrated. The plane shook. My radio went dead. Apparently I had taken a hit from the exploding train. "Damn! What luck. Stinkin' last mission."

Pulling frantically on the stick, I was able to climb several thousand feet. The engine, though sounding rough, had responded to my command. Perhaps I could nurse the Mustang back to England and miraculously escape time in a POW camp.

A minute later the engine coughed and sputtered. Smoke filled the cockpit. "Oh, crap!" Seconds later the engine stalled. Frantically I tried to restart the engine. All my efforts failed. "Gonna hafta bail out." My eyes watered, and I coughed as the smoke grew more acrid. "Damn! No Christmas in Connecticut this year."

After releasing my seat and shoulder harness, I disconnected my headphone and jettisoned the canopy. "Dear Lord, please take care of me." Rolling the Mustang over upon its back, I made the sign of the cross. "Gotta clear the tail section, or I'm chopped liver." I then popped out of the plane like a cork from a champagne bottle.

In all the movies I ever saw, a paratrooper always screamed, "Ge-r-r-ron-n-ni-m-o-o!" whenever he parachuted from his plane. But as I plummeted helter-skelter, like a rag doll, to the patchwork earth below, I was much too frightened to utter anything. I couldn't even bring myself to tug at the ripcord of my chute.

While spinning and tumbling, my brief life flashed before me. I then reflected upon my early days back at flight school. Vaguely I recalled some instructor informing me that if my chute didn't open by the time I was a mere five hundred feet from the ground, it was too late. I was toast.

In all honesty, I was more concerned with the reception awaiting me below. In the last letter from home, my mother mentioned that Tommy Hornak, a classmate of mine at St. Ambrose's School, was killed in the Normandy Invasion.

Tommy, always a hellion in school, had joined the airborne infantry shortly after I had enlisted. In his first jump on D-Day, his chute opened, and he glided down to earth, ready to do battle. About a hundred yards from the ground, a Nazi riddled his body with several blasts from his machine gun. So much for poor Tommy.

Once more I was traumatized by the fear of being shot to death or being taken prisoner. But as the earth neared, I realized that if I didn't do something quickly, there would be no need to worry about being shot or hustled off to a POW camp. I would be joining Tommy.

Coming to grips with my dire situation, I reached for the ripcord with my right hand. Locating it, I pulled with all my strength. *Whump!* The chute opened. I grinned sheepishly. The salt-and-pepper earth no longer rushed up to greet me.

No longer was I falling as if I were a meteor. I now drifted with the air currents. When I peered down, I noted a grove of sycamore trees surrounded by islands of melting snow and a meandering river. Much to my pleasure, no enemy soldier awaited me with his carbine poised at my chest.

Thump! I touched down feet first on a patch of snow. My momentum carried me for about ten more feet before I stopped next to a gigantic pine tree. A textbook landing to say the least. Glancing about I saw nothing. At least I saw nothing in the immediate area that intimidated me. "The chute," I said softly. "You gotta get rid of the chute."

Though my heart raced, and my bladder emptied, chilling me, I was able to gather the chute up into a bundle of white silk. "Now ... I gotta ditch this thing."

Standing stark still, I listened and heard the gurgling river that I had so recently soared across. At that moment I knew where I would discard the chute. I looked to the right. Then to the left. Nothing. Gaining courage by the seconds, I dashed across an open field, seeking the river. "How am I going to submerge it when I get there?"

When I reached the river bank, my conundrum was quickly resolved. There, under my feet, lay several boulders. Glancing about again, which was becoming a habit, I still saw nothing but the brackish, babbling water. "Here ... goes." Reaching down, I gathered up about six boulders and then waded into the icy-cold river. "F-f-fre-e-eezing!" I dropped the chute to its watery grave and promptly piled the rocks upon it. "There!" Much to my delight the chute bubbled but remained submerged.

Satisfied with my accomplishment, I turned and plodded back to the bank. "So far ... so good."

In the forefront of my mind dwelled that fact that a German patrol would be searching for me very shortly, if not already. It was imperative that I find concealment until nightfall. And then, under the cover of darkness, I would travel. But where would I go? I had no idea. Later, after I had time to think, I would formulate a plan. At the present time, I simply needed to hide somewhere. Any old place would do.

Before me rose a steep hill, which, since I was in the prime of my life, I decided to scale at an energetic trot. However, after about thirty yards of steady jogging, I grew tired and winded. "Damn cigarettes," I muttered and slowed to a walk. Painful cramps doubled me over. But I stumbled on like the town drunk.

At the top of the knoll, I paused, scanned the terrain below, and spotted the burned-out shell of an Heinkel, a twin-engine bomber. "Ahaaa! My hiding place."

Inhaling the frigid December air, I coughed and slid down a wide furrow, excavated by the descending bomber. Sweat poured down my face. "Gotta quit smoking those stinkin' Camels and switch to another brand." Reaching into my pocket, I withdrew a pack of Camels. I actually arched my pitching arm with the intention of tossing the cigarettes away. Sanity, thank God, prevailed in the end. I gently slipped the package back into my pocket and moved on.

When I finally reached the Heinkel, I studied the charred wreck from all angles. Only one of the elliptical wings was still intact. The other wing, bent like Quasimodo's back, reposed in a ditch, some sixty feet away. Judging from the dried blood splattered about the inside of the Plexiglas nose, I seriously doubted if the pilot and the navigator survived the trip down the hill. And from the woodbine creeping out of the hull and the dormant thistle licking the tail section, I guessed that the plane had been decomposing for quite some time.

Sidestepping a twisted propeller, I squeezed myself through a jagged opening in the fuselage. The interior was dark, dank, and depressing. From the caked footprints on the floor, I knew that I wasn't the first visitor inside the bomber.

Navigational charts, oxygen masks, and empty ammunition boxes lay underfoot and forced me to step gingerly. Searching about cautiously, I finally caught sight of the former radio room. "Maybe I can hide there."

When I peeked inside, I was mildly surprised. The area, though confining, afforded adequate concealment. "This will do." Ducking into the area, I dropped to my knees and then sat against the remnants of an overturned table. Relaxing for the first time since breakfast, I closed my eyes and listened. Except for a mournful, sighing wind and the staccato dripping of water somewhere aft, there was relative silence.

"Guess I oughta see what's in my survival kit." Carefully I placed each item on the floor. "Hmmmm can use the compass." Unfolding a silk handkerchief, I discovered a map of Germany on one side. On the opposite side was France. "Very valuable."

A photo of me, dressed in civilian clothes, absolutely worthless. I considered discarding it. In the end, I jammed it into a pocket.

"Mmmmm! What's this?" I fingered a chocolate bar and sniffed it. "Ahhh! Smells so-o-o-o ... good." Famished, I tore off the wrapper but ate only a bit. "If I don't find anything to eat, I'll ... at least ... have a piece of chocolate to nibble on."

With the exception of some French money, I regarded everything else as useless. No sooner had I stuffed the currency into my pocket, when I detected a rustling outside the bomber. My heart pounded. My hands shook. My throat dried. "Don't panic, Joe." Cocking my head, I listened. "Stay calm."

Crawling on all fours, I inched my way across the room to where there was a slit of daylight between the walls. I squinted and saw a roly-poly soldier sitting on the wing. His ruddy, pocked-marked face was creased like cheap leather. When he removed his helmet, snow-white curls fringed his bald head.

From all indications, it was obvious that the Third Reich was exhausting its supply of vibrant, young fighting men. My spirits soared at the sight of this old codger, who was now sipping from a flask between puffs on his cigarette.

I grew cautiously optimistic of my immediate future. Truly, I was the master of my fate. By stealth, God's help, and sheer perseverance, I might avoid capture and return to my base in England.

I waited patiently and watched Methuselah. In due time, he drained the contents of his flask and snuffed out his butt. Rising slowly, he slung the stock of his antique fowling piece over his shoulder and shuffled off.

I crossed myself and heaved a deep sigh of relief when the soldier disappeared over the horizon. With his departure, a stiff wind settled in and gray clouds completely obliterated the sun. I should have felt chilled as the temperature plummeted. But having avoided capture, made me as buoyant as a school boy on summer vacation. "What the hell." I took another bite of my chocolate bar and settled back to reflect upon my situation. I did little thinking, serious or other. In a matter of seconds, I was fast asleep.

I had no idea how long I slept, but when I awakened, it was pitch-dark outside. "A good time to move on," I said and meant it.

Stepping outside the bomber, I tugged my service cap down onto my head and raised the collar of my jacket. Taking the tiny compass from my pocket, I noticed that three green dots glowed. Two of the dots at the end of the compass needle indicated north. The single dot at the other end of the needle stood for south.

I suddenly recalled from the map on the wall of the Briefing Room that Berlin was situated in the eastern section of Germany. I was positive that I strafed the rail yard from the west. And so, therefore, I ditched the Mustang and parachuted east of the city.

Captain Bernard, the Intelligence Officer, always said that if shot down, we should avoid the big cities. In order to bypass Berlin, I had to travel north. And so I trudged north.

I walked for several hours, seeing nothing. No houses. No vehicles on the road. No fellow travelers. Nothing.

When hunger pangs rattled around in my stomach, I ate the rest of the chocolate bar. But I was still hungry. And then it began to rain. On I walked, feeling quite uncomfortable.

The wind blew harder. Naturally, the intensity of the rain increased. And somewhere a horse neighed. I stopped in my tracks and listened. The horse cried again -- louder.

There before me, in the slanting rain, stood a ramshackled barn.

As I neared the structure, I observed that it was, indeed, quite rickety. Raising my face to the rain, I prayed. "Thank you, God."

When I nudged the barn door open, it squeaked rather sadly. Once I passed inside, the horse squawked again. Growing up as the son of a fisherman, I was acquainted with lobster traps and fishing boats and yellow slickers.

But I knew nothing about horses. Never petted one. Never rode one. Never wanted one. The only horse in my life was Tony, Tom Mix's steed. I initially encountered Tony in the movies when Tom Mix, my favorite cowboy, galloped across the screen atop Tony and captured a gang of rustlers or arrested a bank robber.

"Easy," I said to the massive horse in the stall when it whinnied softly. "Jus' wanna get out of the rain. I won't hurt you." The horse gently nodded and stamped its foot. "Gooood."

With my night vision firmly established, I gazed about my shadowy, foul-smelling surroundings and noted that there were several other stalls in the barn. All unoccupied. I also discovered that there was an abundance of hay in one of the stalls.

Tiptoeing into the hay-filled stall, I immediately burrowed into the hay like a badger. By and by, the hay warmed me. I decided to stay put until the rain slackened. Only then would I resume my journey. However, the rain intensified. Snuggling deeper under the hay, I listened to the pattering rain upon the roof and dozed off.

When my stable mate kicked at his door, I awoke with a start. Sitting up, I felt refreshed. Looking around, I knew why. It was early morning of Christmas Eve day. The winter sun, though weak, poured into the barn through the only window. "Screwed up big time, Joe." Break-neck speed in traveling through Germany was my only hope of avoiding capture and imprisonment in a POW camp. And now I had eliminated that one advantage by sleeping when I should have been traveling. Shaking my head in disgust, I punched my fist into my open palm. "Damn!" Rising from the floor, I brushed the hay from my clothing.

Since I had no contingency plan, I was at my wit's end. "What am I gonna do? I'm nowhere near Berlin." That all changed quickly. From somewhere outside the barn, there came a rushing of determined footsteps. A woman's steps. Glancing up, I caught sight of a hayloft. Without hesitating, I climbed the four steps into the loft and waited and watched.

Seconds later the door flung open. A woman, wearing a babushka and a frayed woolen coat, strolled into the barn. At once she grabbed a pitchfork and went to work, feeding the horse a generous amount of hay.

When she passed out of the shadow of the stall and stepped into the sun light, I was smitten by her celestial bearing. Though her eyes were too large and her skin too smooth and her hair too blonde, I was attracted to her like lodestone to a magnet.

"Get a grip on yourself. She's a German," I whispered to a yoke hanging upon the wall. Inching closer to the ladder, I watched her discharge her duties with great care and devotion.

As soon as she fed the horse, she picked up a broom and began sweeping the dirt floor. My eyes followed her every step across the room. And when she set the broom aside and shoveled up the manure, I craned my neck, dangled my body over the side like a bat hanging from the ceiling of a cave, and glared. What sensuousness. What grace. What vitality.

And then I did a very foolish thing. In my exuberance, I leaned out a little too far, lost my balance, and hung in midair for a split second. "Ohhh, God!" Back at the Alliance Technical Institute, I was a member of the gymnastic team. As a matter of fact, I performed quite proficiently on the rings. Remembering my former days of glory on the rings, I reached out and caught hold of a pipe overhead. *"Ohhhh,"* I screamed as I swung back and forth, trying to regain my footing.

The girl, terror stricken at the sight of my sudden, unannounced appearance, dropped the shovel and looked up in awe. Her head twitched back and forth with my every move.

While my eyes widened, her lower lip trembled. *"Amerykanski!"* she shouted and held her arms open to catch me.

"Ahhhh!" I felt my fingers slipping. Finally I lost my grip and fell several feet into her waiting arms. Down we both went in a heap. I on top of her.

When I stole a peek at her, I noticed that her eyes were shut tightly. Her head was flung back, and her rosebud mouth set at a distorted angle. Panic overtook me. I held my breath, but when she stirred and opened her eyes, I exhaled.

Neither of us uttered a word. The girl then smiled and whispered the word *Amerykanski* once more. I nodded but remained silent. Suddenly it dawned upon me. Back at Central High School, I studied the German language for two years. In all honesty, I didn't learn much. However, I did learn that the German word for American was *Amerikaner.* The young lady pinned under me said *Amerykanski*, and she said it twice. It finally dawned upon me that she wasn't German; she was Polish.

"Pani Polska jest?" I asked, taking her slender fingers into my hand.

"Yes, I Polish." she said, amazing me with her command of the English language. "And you?"

"Well, I was born in the United States, but my parents were born right here in Poland."

"Then ... you Polish too." She smiled and tightened her grip upon my hand.

"Where did you learn to speak English?"

"My father was official doctor to Polish ambassador in Washington. I born there."

"Hmmm ... how about that." I lowered my head and gently kissed her waiting, ruby-red lips. "And what is your name?"

"Anna Novak." Anna raised her head and kissed me passionately. "And you are?"

"Joe Gatski."

"Many Gatski families in Poland."

When I attempted to kiss Anna again, she turned her head. "No more kisses. You stink from cigarettes."

"If I quit smoking, may I kiss you again?"

"Yes, only one kiss because we must hide you before soldiers come looking for you."

With my right hand, I reached into my pocket, retrieved my package of Camels, and tossed them across the floor. "I quit ... so I'm collecting my kiss." Looking into Anna's green eyes, I lowered my head and kissed her tender lips lovingly.

"Whew!" Anna fanned herself. "How they say ... all bells ring like crazy. What good kiss."

Rising, I took hold of Anna's hands and pulled her to her feet. "There are more kisses like that for you."

"Later." Anna took my arm and led me out of the barn and into the frigid morning air. "We go to convent and make plans to hide you and then escape later."

"What convent?" From my tone of speech, I must have sounded perplexed.

Anna pointed to a thicket of Norway Pines. "See." I squinted and saw nothing but trees. No convent in sight. On we trudged for another two minutes. And then, to my right, I spotted a clapboard building surrounded by the most majestic conifers imaginable. The convent, needless to say, was not as pleasing to the naked eye as the trees. It was weather-beaten and listed like a schooner in a storm.

"How many sisters live at the convent?" From the size of the structure, it couldn't have housed more than four or five nuns.

"One ... er ... Sister Zygmunta." At the crumbling portico, Anna lifted her coat and stepped upon a cracked, marble tombstone, which served as the front step.

"Only one lives here." I followed but paused to read the name on the gravestone. "Casmir ... Byk."

"Other four sisters shot to death by Nazi soldiers." With a gigantic step, Anna climbed to the stoop, turned the doorknob, and entered the convent.

When my turn came to enter the building, I dawdled to count the bullet holes in the door before entering. "How did Sister Zygmunta escape the Nazi firing squad?"

"She in forest chopping down tree for fire wood."

Glancing about for a German patrol and seeing nothing out of the ordinary, I followed Anna into the foyer, a dark, damp room, which was no warmer than the outdoors we had so recently left behind.

"Isn't she afraid that they'll come back and shoot her?"

"That was four years ago." Removing her babushka, Anna dipped her fingers into a stoup of holy water and made the sign of the cross. I did the same. "And they not come back ... yet."

"I ... see."

My eyes leaped out of their sockets. There standing in the shadows was Sister Zygmunta, all six feet and two hundred pounds of her. From her coarse brown habit, headdress, and wooden crucifix suspended from a cord, I recognized her as a Sister of the Order of St. John Kanty.

This particular order of nuns had a provincial house back near Bridgeport, Connecticut. As a callow youth, I thought that the Order was a strange brood because they all took the vow of silence. And, according to my way of thinking, if they were all silent ---- all the time ---- they never accomplished anything. I assumed that they couldn't even ask each other to pass the salt or butter at dinner.

When I grew older and wiser, I realized that our world was composed of many diverse people. The Sisters of St. John Kanty no longer appeared quite so strange. And though I never completely understood their ascetic philosophy, I respected their lifestyle.

Hoping not to offend Sister Zygmunta, I genuflected as if she were royalty and nodded. Zygmunta, her massive hand clutching a dead duck's neck, which I knew was to become *Czarnina*, a soup, using the late duck's blood for the stock, nodded and retreated.

"Now, Joe, we make plans," said Anna with a warm smile on her patrician face.

"Uhmmm ... before we make plans ... ayuh ... I need something to eat. My stomach is gurgling like ... hell."

"You poor man." Anna threw off her coat, revealing a nubile figure entrapped in a bulky sweater and a skirt cut of the identical material as Sister Zygmunta's habit. Somehow on Anna that same cloth looked absolutely smashing. "Come." She beckoned with her finger.

"We go to kitchen."

I rubbed my cold hands together in glee. "I'm right behind you."

Down a narrow corridor, whose whitewashed walls were decorated with faded icons representing the Stations of the Cross, I followed Anna to the kitchen. In one end of the primitive kitchen sat Sister Zygmunta plucking the downy feathers from the duck's carcass. With extreme care, she dropped each precious feather into a tote. From my past experience at home, I knew that those feathers would become the stuffing of a mighty fine pillow.

At the other end of the kitchen stood a massive fireplace, hissing and spitting and serving as the convent's stove.

Growing up in a family of five, my parents always stressed the fact that, even though we were poor, there was always someone a mite poorer. And to those people, we children were expected to show respect and love. Above all, we were never to degrade them.

From all outward appearances, I knew that Anna and Sister Zygmunta owned few material possessions. Their country had been at war since 1939. During that span of time, they had suffered horribly at the hands of the Nazis.

Though hungry, I reminded myself, before I sat at the table, that I would eat only enough to subsist upon and no more. But when Anna produced a large platter of poppy-seed rolls and a steaming pot of coffee, my constitution wavered. In the end, my conscience prevailed. I ate only one roll and refused a second cup of coffee.

Retiring to the formal dining room, where a simple rough-hewn table was surrounded by eight mismatched, wooden chairs, Anna unfolded a tattered map of Poland.

"This is where we are," said Anna, pointing to Glodscz, a town which seemed to be located in the middle of nowhere.

"I can't believe I flew this far into Poland." I said, concerned with the great distance I had flown from Berlin. "We're no place near Berlin."

Anna arched her tawny eyebrows. "That is correct." She ran her finger in a northerly fashion to the Baltic Sea. "If we can get to town of Tyln, on the Baltic, we can get help from Dingus."

"Dingus!"

"Yes, Dingus is … uh … member of Polish Underground."

"Is he trustworthy?" I reached into my pocket for a cigarette and quickly remembered that I had quit smoking about an hour ago. "Have you worked with him?"

"Yes, on two occasions I take one Gypsy and a Jew to Tyln."

"And Dingus got them out of Poland?"

"Yes." Anna beamed with pride at her role in both incidents.

"Dingus took them to safety."

"Are you also going to be my guide?" I slipped my arm around Anna's slim waist. She snuggled up to me. Naturally I kissed her upon the cheek.

"I be your guide this afternoon. We go by train."

"On Christmas Eve?"

"Yes, best time to travel."

"Do we jus' walk out of here dressed as we are and board a train for Tyln?"

Anna chuckled. "No, you crazy Mohegan. I will pose as doctor." She then stood back and gazed into my eyes. "And you be old man ... uh ... who had stroke in brain."

I folded my arms across my chest and stepped back. "Why must I be an old man ... er ... who had a stroke, and you the doctor?"

"Very simple." Her eyes brightened like a clever terrier's. "Because as young man ... soldiers ask why you not in Army." Smiling, she formed a church steeple with her slender fingers and touched her lips. "And man wid stroke cannot always talk so good."

I nodded in agreement with her sound logic. "Sounds good to me."

"Also ... I have studied medicine at university."

"So you really are a doctor?"

"Not yet." Folding up the map, Anna strode across the room and claimed a doctor's satchel from a shelf on a cupboard. She then opened the bag and concealed the map in the false bottom. "I only spend one year at university before it close down because of war."

"And how did you end up at the convent?"

"Come back here to live with my parents." A salty tear streamed down Anna's face and plopped upon her sweater. I reached out and held her icy-cold hand. "But they ... dead." Staring out the window at the swaying conifers, she sniffled. Before she could wipe her eyes with her sleeve, I forced my handkerchief upon her. "After wiping away the tears and blowing her nose, she sighed. "Hanged by the Gestapo."

"And so you came here to live with the nuns?"

"Yes, I have no place else to go. Zygmunta take me in, and I join the Polish Underground."

"How awful!" I shook my head. "War is hell, isn't it?"

"Yes, it is." Anna sighed and returned to her work at hand. Watching with interest, my eyes widened when she hid a Derringer in the compartment with the map. Nonchalantly, she placed vials of pills, a stethoscope, several bandages, and a syringe atop the false bottom. "Now ... we prepare our costumes for long journey."

"Lead the way."

Just as we entered into the corridor, the front door swung open and thumped loudly against the wall. A small, thin soldier with menacing yellow eyes and a scraggly moustache charged into the room with his Mauser rifle aimed at us. He gestured for us to raise our hands above our heads, which we did without question.

"Zigaretten!" he exclaimed, brandishing the pack of Camels I had discarded. I should have hidden the butts. By my reckless behavior, I had jeopardized not only my life, but the lives of two innocent women.

Glancing about the hallway furtively, the soldier seemed to be considering his next move. Finally he marched us back into the dining room. When he spied the doctor's bag sitting upon the table, he confiscated it and tucked it under his arm. Apparently nothing else in the room interested him, for he nodded and prodded us with the barrel of his rifle to move on.

We bypassed the library, which housed nothing but books. I assumed that he was not a reader. But at the chapel he paused and then marched us inside. Since I was a dunce, it took some time for me to realize that he was searching for artifacts of value -- the tabernacle, the chalice, the paten, and even the golden candlesticks.

Had my command of the German language been better, I would have informed him that he was too late. I was sure that after the four nuns were slaughtered, the Nazis took anything that was of value.

His beady eyes, nonetheless, scrutinized every inch of the chapel. However, he found nothing but a desecrated altar and two blackened pews. Disgusted at finding no booty, he motioned for us to exit the room.

Once more he marched us down the corridor to the kitchen. When I stole a peek at Anna, she calmly winked. I wondered how she could be so unruffled at a time like this. Didn't she realize how close to death we drew with each step?

"O-o-o-o-weee-e-e!" screamed the Nazi as we passed the butler's pantry. Spinning on my heels, I watched the soldier rise up on his toes in mortal pain. Zygmunta, wielding a poker like a baseball bat, repeatedly struck him across his back and neck. His rifle took flight, then ricocheted against the ceiling, and finally skidded along the polished floor. The helmet shot off his misshapen head like a missile and clanged against the eleventh Station of the Cross.

The soldier, his mouth skewed and his arms thrashing at the empty air, fell to his knees. Zygmunta, her face filled with hatred and contempt, wound up like Ben Hogan at Augusta and swung from her heels. In the next second, the poker pulverized his head. While blood and sinew squirted in every direction, human brain matter oozed down the wall.

While I stood in awe and gaped at the gooey mass of pulp, Anna casually stepped over the prostrate form and seized my hand. "Come. It's getting late," she instructed. "Sister Zygmunta will dispose of the body."

I guessed that Anna would take me to her bedroom, where we would prepare for our journey north. How wrong I was. Instead, she led me up three flights of steps to the attic, a room containing at least fifteen steamer trunks and various other pieces of antique furniture.

"Sit," commanded Anna, positioning a hall chair next to a dressing table that, from all appearances, dated back to the last century. "You look too young and too healthy."

"Hmmm." I looked into the hazy mirror and agreed with Anna.

"We fix that." Scooping gel from a jar, Anna vigorously rubbed the concoction not only into my hair but onto my eye brows as well. Within minutes my jet-black hair took on a donkey-gray hue. And then my brows turned gray, matching my hair. "Now ... you mouth." As far as I was concerned, the transformation was complete. Not to Anna, though. Again she rummaged through one of the trunks until she located another jar. Dipping her hand into the container, she withdrew only a tiny glob. This she kneaded feverishly with her fingers. "It is wax. Open up mouth." I did as she requested. While humming some Polish folk tune, she worked diligently. No sooner had she attached the wax above my teeth when it solidified. "Now look in mirror."

"Holy crap!" I exclaimed when I glanced into the streaked mirror. The dye added at least another thirty years to my age. But it didn't stop there. The wax turned up one side of my upper lip. My once handsome face appeared paralyzed, which, of course, was Anna's objective.

"Pretty good ... huh?"

"I'll say." I just couldn't take my eyes off my image. "Where did you learn to do this?"

"Teach myself." Anna handed me a pile of men's clothing. "Now you go behind screen and find old man's clothes to wear."

"And what are you going to dress like?"

"Beautiful young doctor." She gently pushed me toward the screen. "Go! You see me ... soon."

"Humph!" Though I hadn't worn anything except military uniforms for almost two years, I wasn't ecstatic about the Polish mufti. Especially when it reeked of mothballs.

Of all my new clothing, I coveted the one-piece union suit most of all. Though moth- eaten, it fit well. I also knew it would be welcome in the frigid weather.

As for the remainder of the clothing, I was able to fit into a pair of checkered slacks and a striped suit coat. If Spike Jones needed a drummer for his orchestra, I would have auditioned for the job.

With the exception of my GI boots, I looked and felt quite continental. However, when I ripped off the top section, the shoes looked like the typical footwear of the people in occupied countries I was set to travel.

Hoping that I had allowed Anna sufficient time to change her clothes, I casually strode out from behind the screen.

Anna, attired in a long woolen dress, similar to that worn by my grandmother, no longer looked like the radiant young girl I had met that morning. She had also dyed her hair gray. And with make-up, she created a fine network of lines and shadows around her eyes and neck. In all honesty, she looked quite matronly.

Hand in hand, we descended the three flights of stairs to the dining room. In our absence Zygmunta had pitched the dead Hun into an abandoned well on the property and set the hallway in order. She had also placed holly boughs on the table and decorated the windowsills with pine cones. Even though I wasn't home in Connecticut, I had to admit there was a Christmas spirit glowing inside my breast.

"Merry Christmas!" I said, thankful for everything that Anna and Sister Zygmunta had done for me.

"Merry Christmas to you," replied Anna with a smile on her lips and a glint of happiness in her eye.

Suddenly my nostrils detected the aroma of simmering *czarnina.* And seconds later, a beaming Sister Zygmunta waddled into the room with a tureen of soup and freshly baked black bread.

At once we seated ourselves at the table and said grace. Anna then excused herself. Minutes later she returned with an *oplatek,* a blessed wafer. She promptly shared the wafer with us. According to Polish tradition, we then wished each other the best for the New Year.

The broth, complimented with slivers of prunes, homemade noodles called *kluski,* and chunks of succulent duck meat, was equal to my mother's soup. Perhaps better.

When Sister Zygmunta offered me a second cup of coffee, I accepted it. I refused more bread and soup though. From Anna's anxious glances at the wall clock, I knew that she wished to get underway.

In the deep recesses of my mind, however, lurked a very real dilemma. Outerwear. In all honesty, I couldn't venture outdoors as I was attired. Oh, I could have worn my flight jacket over my outlandish garb. But, in truth, that was courting disaster. Zygmunta must have read my mind. Holding up a chubby finger, she motioned for me to stay put. I complied. All my fear was quickly put to rest. Smiling broadly, she returned with an overcoat, a scarf, and a *Homburg*. The coat, though threadbare, fit well. Most importantly, it contained several well-concealed pockets. The *Homburg* was another story. It not only covered my head, but my ears as well. Not to worry. Anna immediately remedied the situation. She strategically stuffed newspaper inside the headband.

Following a tearful departure, Anna and I, at long last, slipped out the back door of the convent and launched our overland trek to Glodscz. There we would board a train for Tyln, a fishing village on the Baltic Sea.

Though the main highway was a shorter route, Anna reasoned that it would be heavily traveled and thus more dangerous. She decided that we should travel a more circuitous route and follow a dried-up river bed. I agreed whole heartedly with her logic.

And so while a bone-chilling wind buffeted our faces, we lowered our heads and trudged along a frozen creek and then across an expanse littered with the smoldering ruins of peasant huts, a roofless grist mill, and a sacked abbey.

Occasionally we happened upon the rusted hulk of an Heinkel bomber or a Stuka dive-bomber or even an Henschel biplane. More often than not, however, we passed the remnants of the outmoded P-11, a gull-winged fighter of the Polish Air Force.

Back at the barracks in England, I often informed my mates that if Poland had been equipped with the Mustang in 1939, the Poles would have very easily beaten back the Nazis. No one disagreed with me.

At a point in our travels, where a bluff loomed forbiddingly on our right, a single gunshot exploded in the distance. Seconds later, another shot broke the silence. Anna stopped and turned to face me. Her face was white. Her hands trembled. "Germans," she whispered. I nodded in agreement.

"Stay here," I said. "I wanna see what's up ahead." Shuffling ahead as Anna instructed me to do as part of my new character, I dragged my feet as if a feeble, old pensioner. Scanning the immediate area, I saw nothing out of the ordinary. More importantly, I heard no more gun shots. Shuffling back to where Anna awaited with her rosary beads in her hand, I took her icy-cold hand into mine. "I didn't see anyone."

"That is good."

"Those woods over there." I pointed to a stand of pine. "If we walked through them, would it take us out of our way?"

"No."

"Let's go then."

Across the open field Anna walked nimbly, while I wobbled along at a much slower and unsure pace. When we finally reached the tree line, another shot rang out. We froze in our tracks. From the expression upon Anna's wind-burned face, I knew that her heart skipped a beat. As for me, I almost swallowed the wax inside my mouth.

With a train to catch, we couldn't simply hide in the timberline. We had to move on. And so we bravely entered the dark forest, hoping for the best. Though the wind howled, I perspired freely. As for Anna, she smiled meekly and led the way. On we walked, careful not to step upon any twigs and reveal our presence. Eventually the light of day appeared in our foreground. We had successfully walked through the woods.

I sighed in relief as we passed out of the tree line. And then it happened. A tall German grenadier, shouldering a double-barrel shot gun towered in our path. He seemed to be as surprised as we were. Anna nodded. He nodded. But when he caught sight of my disfigurement, he winced. Reaching into a bag, he retrieved a dead goose and pressed it upon me.

"Dankuu," I said, realizing that as the temperature dropped, it grew more difficult to speak with the wax in my mouth.

Anna, always the actress, dropped to her knees and kissed the soldier's hand. *"Danke schon,"* she whispered.

Our silent benefactor merely smiled, revealing a mouthful of blackened stumps, and tramped on.

We watched in silence and then resumed our journey. Up a hill and across a knoll we walked. At least Anna walked. I tottered on behind her. At long last, there in the distance, stood Glodscz. All of Glodscz seemed to consist of one frame building, which I hoped was the train station.

"What do we do when we get there?" I asked Anna, limping along in my most casual manner.

"You sit on bench wid you goose and wait," said Anna, "while I buy tickets. No talk to any person. Understand?"

"Yes."

"Good." Taking me under the arm, Anna escorted me down a hill to the main road. As we neared the train station, I discovered that, save for a German major and his wife, who was quite pregnant, there were no other people awaiting the train.

The major, his florid face a series of angles, circles, and rhombuses, scowled at us as we neared him. Anna curtsied. I bowed. Playing the role of the devoted physician, Anna seated me and raised the collar of my coat. She then walked to the ticket window, while I gazed down at my dead goose and prayed.

When the train whistled, belched black smoke skyward, and charged around the bend, I sat mutely and waited. Anna returned and assisted me from the bench. Arm in arm we boarded the train.

Up until I enlisted in the Army, I had never ridden on a train of any kind. Once I left Connecticut, however, that changed ... dramatically. While in flight school I crisscrossed the United States several time by train. Then in England I rode the train to London whenever I had a pass.

I must confess that the trains I rode were state-of-the-art models of transportation. Glancing up at the locomotive and two passenger cars before me took my breath away. And not in a good way. The locomotive was a nineteen century replica of the *Stourbridge Lion,* the first locomotive built in the United States. The two wooden passenger cars it pulled were riddled with bullet holes. The roofs and sides of the coaches bore large red crosses. Apparently the crosses had little impact upon the Allied fliers. Most of the windows had been blasted away and replaced by sheets of plywood.

Since the first coach was occupied by a company of German storm troopers, Anna and I entered the second car along with the major and his pregnant spouse.

In addition to the major and his wife, two aged couples, one outgoing and the other reserve, occupied seats in the second coach. Since the elderly couples had boarded the train at an earlier point, they were already seated in the area of a potbellied stove, the only source of heat in the car.

The seating arrangements changed rather quickly. The major, a runt with the disposition of a bantam rooster, immediately berated the passengers sitting in the seats next to the stove. Waving his Luger at both couples, his face colored as red as a beet. He then shouted in German and pointed to the other end of the car.

While I could not understand a word he said, Anna's quivering mouth and frightened eyes, revealed the gist of his tirade. Meekly the old folks rose on stiff joints and retreated to the very rear of the coach.

The major, reveling in his accomplishment, settled his wife into the seat behind the stove. He, of course, sat next to her.

As soon as the locomotive pulled out of the station, I knew that we were destined for a gut-wrenching ride. If the coach had shock absorbers, they were old and worn. I also knew that the major's pregnant wife would suffer most on this trip. Having only time on my hands, my eyes roamed about the coach. For some unexplainable reason, however, they always returned to the major's wife With every jarring motion and vibrating sensation of the coach, her body jerked, her eyes rolled, and her Adam's apple twitched. From the patina of sweat and soot on her brow and the ashen hue on her cheeks, I was sure that she felt quite ill from the constant agitation that her bloated body endured.

She finally received a reprieve when the train rolled to a stop at Nowa Tylka, which unlike Godscz was a bona fide town with buildings and a cemetery and a working bridge.

Nowa Tylka was also the destination of the troops in the lead coach. Whistles blew. Voices bellowed orders. Guidons unfurled. Wave after wave of soldiers swarmed out of the car and stood at attention in the cobbled-stoned street. Within minutes the troopers were shouldering their Mausers and goose-stepping down the street toward their bivouac area   Unlike Glodscz, where only four people boarded the train, a score of people dribbled into the two passenger cars at Nowa Tylka.

About four miles out of town, the pregnant woman screamed something in German to her husband. The major immediately panicked. And, of course, not being able to resolve his wife's dilemma, he frantically beckoned to the conductor, a wizened man with a clubfoot.

After the conductor conferred with the major at some length, he took leave and limped down the aisle. When he reached Anna's side, he bent over and whispered into her ear. Anna craned her neck in the direction of the major's wife and nodded. The conductor thanked Anna profusely and tottered back to the major's side.

Anna retrieved her medical bag from the floor and leaned into me. "You play baseball in America?" she whispered into my ear.

"Yes," I said, thinking it was not the time nor the place to be discussing baseball.

"Good." She squeezed my hand tenderly. "I be coach. You catch." Perplexed, I glanced at her. An uneasy smile surfaced at the corners of her mouth. "Come."

Together we arose from our seats and walked unsteadily to the end of the coach, where the major's wife moaned pitifully. From all indication, her water had burst, and she was about to give birth to her baby.

Anna, after surveying the situation, knelt by the woman's side. She then motioned for me to position myself between the woman's extended legs. The major's eyes bulged. At once he unsheathed his pistol from its holster. This time he shoved the Luger in my face. No one was going to see or touch his baby before he did.

"*Nein!*" he shouted. Shoving me aside, he crouched before his wife with cupped hands as if he were about to field a ground ball.

Anna calmly unbuttoned the woman's coat, hiked up her dress, and cut away her undergarment. "*Stossen,*" commanded Anna authoritatively. With all the strength the woman could muster, she pushed as requested. Seconds later the baby's bloody head slithered out of the womb like toothpaste from the tube.

The major, hands trembling, stood up and swayed like the pendulum on a clock. He promptly fainted and crashed against the potbellied stove. Had he fallen anywhere else, he would have been out of harm's way. However, when he collided with the cast-iron stove, he loosened the pipes leading from the stove to the vent in the ceiling.

Initially, there was only a shower of soot raining down upon the stricken major. But then the pipes fell away. Finally the iron elbow dislodged itself, dropped like an anchor, and cut the major's forehead, leaving behind a six-inch gash and much blood.

We all looked on in horror. Only Anna, who was now supporting the sooty baby and guiding it out of the mother's body spoke. *"Psa krew!"* she shouted angrily.

In the Polish language the words *psa krew*, as I understood their translation meant *dog's blood*. As a child, I occasionally heard my parents utter them. I knew that the words were some sort of Polish vulgarity. But what? Whenever I asked my parents what the words actually meant, they simply glared at me and dismissed my inquiry.

"Ohhh!" cried the mother when the baby was finally out. Anna, at once, showed it to the proud mother. She then cleaned it up and wrapped it in the major's coat.

And while everyone huddled about the mother and baby, the major lay bleeding profusely. Anna quietly handed the baby to its mother. She then turned her attention to the major. Taking her medical bag, she rummaged about for several minutes. Her eyes shined when she found a large bandage. After administering to the wound for several minutes, she was able to stanch the bleeding. I watched in silence and knew that the wound had to be closed. Anna also knew it. Breathing deeply, she let out a long sigh. Had she owned catgut, she probably possessed the skill to suture the wound. Of course there was no catgut in the bag. Only pills, bandages, and a lonely syringe.

Her eyes wandered about the coach, which was slowing to a stop. Finally her emerald eyes lit up when she spied the stove. Motioning for me to join her, she took my fingers and placed them upon the major's forehead. I pressed the flesh together and awaited Anna's return. When she joined me, she held a red-hot poker in her hand. My eyes watered. Then legions of goose bumps swarmed across my flesh. I screwed up my face in anticipation of what was about to happen. Anna, unflinching and determined, approached the soldier. She then thrust with the poker, cauterizing the wound. "Ahhhh!" screamed the major, falling back unconscious once more. The stench of human flesh immediately filled the air, prompting the conductor to open several windows.

While the baby was being delivered and Anna had saved the

father's life, a crowd of people had gathered about to watch the proceedings. The train, in the meantime, had arrived at Kotyn, the last stop before Tyln.

As soon as the train halted, the conductor seized the opportunity to relay news of the activity in our coach to the engineer and to two guards at the depot.

Anna dressed the mother, placed the baby in her arms, and handed both over to the conductor. The conductor, laboring mightily under the woman's weight, managed to escort mother and child to the train station.

By the time the conductor returned from his mercy mission, the two soldiers were carrying the disoriented major down the aisle and off the train.

After reclaiming my seat by the window, I noticed that most of the passengers had disembarked at Kotyn. These travelers were replaced by an octet of musicians, toting their instruments and luggage.

On the purple horizon, the sun was already setting on this Christmas Eve of 1944. I wondered what the future held for Anna and me. Though I only knew this remarkable girl for a very short time, I wanted to spend the rest of my life with her. I truly hoped that she possessed some feelings for me.

Again the locomotive groaned and coughed as we chugged along in the plum-colored dusk. Glancing out the window, I caught sight of a band of soldiers surrounded by Nazi guards with submachine guns. Initially I thought the captured soldiers were British. But, no, they were American airman. My palms grew clammy. My heart raced. I pressed my nose to the window. The Americans, to a man, stood dejectedly. As the train rattled along, I stared. My eyes widened. Before me huddled Abbott, Connors, and Williams. All three looked quite miserable. Our entire flight group had been shot down by the Germans. Though all four of us had survived, I was the only one still free. Silently I mumbled a prayer for my three friends. I also prayed that the war would soon end. Anna, sensing my discomfort at seeing the Americans awaiting their trip to a POW camp, reached over and touched my hand. I wanted to kiss her inviting mouth, but it might be a foolish mistake. I knew nothing of the musicians sitting behind me. For all I knew, they might be Nazis. Or worse. We had come too far to slip up now. There was no way I wanted to abandon Anna's side. I winked and patted her slender hand.

I had no idea the distance between Glodscz and Tyln. But I did know that Tyln was the last stop on the route. After sitting on a narrow wooden bench for many hours and bobbing about like a cork in water, my buttocks were quite sore. However, when I thought about Abbott, Connors, and Williams spending their first night in a German POW camp, I assured myself that the ride wasn't all that bad.

179

And just as I was consoling myself, the train braked and slowed considerably. We had arrived at Tyln. The wheels squeaked and squawked for several minutes. But we rolled on. Finally the locomotive discharged a cloud of steam. Our coach lunged forward, pitching everyone. And then it stopped.

Peering out the streaked window, I spotted a soldier, armed with a carbine. He approached our car and waited. I nudged Anna. "What's he doing here?" I asked, holding my handkerchief up to my mouth. Anna simply shook her head and shrugged her narrow shoulders.

While the boisterous musicians bustled about, claiming their instruments and suitcases and buttoning up their outerwear, Anna and I watched the soldier. The guard requested identification from the first passenger who stepped off the coach. Of course, the man handed it to him, waited for its return, and then walked toward the exit. "I never saw the Germans check papers on this line before," said Anna, trying to remain calm. At once I saw myself joining Abbott, Connors, and Williams in *Stalag* 22.

"You go," I said to Anna, knowing that, as a Polish citizen, she possessed the proper papers.

"No!" She stamped her foot. "I stay wid you."

"Pomoc nam," called a gravel voice, asking for our assistance. When I looked up, I beheld a rotund man in his mid-sixties, who I judged to be the leader of the musicians. He didn't wait for our reply. He handed me a bass drum and Anna a stack of sheet music. I clasped his shoulder firmly and bestowed my goose upon him.

The man, with fowl in hand, turned and threaded his way through the musicians to the head of the line. Clearing his throat, he politely drew the guard aside and handed him the goose and a bottle of wine. Pointing to the musicians and mimicking a flutist, he spoke at some length to the soldier. The soldier stuffed both the goose and the bottle into his pack and pointed to the exit. In response the leader whistled shrilly and directed the musicians, including Anna and me, past the smiling guard and into the silhouetted town of Tyln. We marched along with the musicians until they reached their destination, a concert hall of some sort. I immediately handed over my drum, while Anna relieved herself of the bundle of sheet music. Before Anna could utter a word of thanks, the leader put a finger to his lips, shook our hands, and led his musicians inside the building for their Christmas Eve gig.

Standing alone in the dark, cold evening, we presently detected the sound of a sentry's slow, measured footsteps. Wisely we retreated into the shadow of the hall and took refuge behind three trash cans. With baited breath, we waited. The footsteps grew louder. Then stopped. A shadow of a helmeted soldier appeared on the wall above us.

I held my breath and squeezed Anna closer to me. A nervous cat snarled and scampered under my legs to the street. At once the footsteps resumed and faded away down the street. Relieved and happy, I embraced Anna, lifted her off her feet, and kissed her frozen mouth.

Setting Anna down, we composed ourselves, strolled out of the alley, and checked both directions before continuing our journey. Satisfied that it was safe, we headed for Dingus's house.

As we walked, I recalled that Christmas Eve in Bridgeport, Connecticut, was a very festive occasion. Carolers were always out and about spreading good cheer. Decorated trees twinkled in every window. Store fronts gleamed with animated displays. Not so in Tyln. The streets were dark and desolate. Store windows were shuttered. Houses stood somber and silent.

Within a short time, we approached Dingus's home, which, according to Anna, consisted of two tiny rooms above his restaurant. At least it was an eatery until the Nazis invaded Poland and shut it down. Soon after it closed, Dingus joined the Polish Underground.

Unlike so many of the buildings I had seen in Poland, Dingus's place was not a drab clapboard structure. Constructed mainly of brick, it was actually quite pleasing to the naked eye.

Anna, removing one of her tattered mittens, boldly strode up to the front door and rapped steadily upon the window pane. She then glanced up at a second-story window, which was shuttered. "Humph!" She knocked once more. "He is always home."

Just then a Baltic zephyr streaked across the street and whistled through the stately maples dotting the curbside. Of course, a smattering of dried leaves fluttered down upon us. For no reason at all, I peeped up at the falling leaves. And then something caught my attention. I rubbed my weary eyes and squinted. Much to my surprise, a man's body and head bowed and tongue hanging out, dangled from a rope. When the wind howled once more, the limp body swayed slightly. A lump grew in my throat, preventing me from calling out to Anna, who was peering into the darkened restaurant. Clearing my throat, I finally called out, "Anna." With my eyes glued onto the body, I inched closer to Anna and tapped her upon the shoulder. "Is ... ehhh ... that Dingus ... er ... swinging from that tree?"

Anna at once raised her head and followed my pointing finger. Her eyes teared. "Yes, that is Dingus." She made the sign of the cross. "I would know him anywhere."

"Let's move on." I took her hand and led her away. "Now we must make new plans."

I grew up in the area of Long Island Sound, where the sights, sounds, and smells of the sea surrounded and shaped me. As soon as I stepped off the train, the briny sea air reminded me of home. And now as Anna and I strolled through the town, the salty air grew more pungent; the outline of the seawall more vivid; the sound of charging water louder.

"How do we get to the dock?" I asked Anna as we approached the only house in town where lights blazed in every window and three Opels were parked in haphazard patterns in the driveway. Against the drawn shades of the parlor, animated figures came and went. We hurried on when sounds of "O Tannenbaum" wafted forth from a tar-papered outhouse. "At least we know where the Germans are celebrating Christmas."

Anna latched onto my arm and chuckled. "The dock is around the corner."

Down a gravel path we walked to a wooden dock that creaked and swayed with every gust of wind. And whenever one of the rowboats, tethered to a piling, bobbed, the entire pier vibrated. "Rowboats! Rowboats! Rowboats!" I exclaimed to Anna, swinging my arms over my head as if I were a conductor directing his orchestra.

"Rowboats ... no good?" asked Anna timidly.

I pointed to her and then to myself. "We need a boat with a gas engine so we can travel a great distance." As I spoke, we must have passed some five additional rowboats. "My father was a fisherman, and he took me to work with him, during the summer months, when I was a little boy. By the time I turned sixteen, I could sail the boat and even repair the engine. If we find the right kind of boat, I'm sure I can sail it."

On we trudged, bracing ourselves against the wind and searching for my elusive gas-powered boat. I had a feeling that the pier would soon end, and our search would be fruitless. But at the very end of the dock, sat the very vessel I sought -- a fishing boat similar to my father's lobster boat.

"Look!" whispered Anna, hugging my arm. "Big boat."

"Yes, just what we need to sail to Sweden."

"We go to Sweden?" Ann stopped abruptly and clasped her hands together. The excitement in her voice told me that she approved of my decision. "No war there. Only peace."

"That's true." I cautiously stepped from the dock onto the deck of the rocking boat. The feeling of the sturdy wood under my feet felt good. I promptly turned and lifted Anna onto the deck. With Anna on board, I made a cursory inspection of the craft and pronounced her seaworthy.

I was sure that the door of the pilot house was locked. And it was. I could have broken the door down to gain entry. That, however, would have been foolish. The noise would have brought every soldier in the area to the dock to investigate. The situation called for Yankee stealth and ingenuity.

I needed to pick the lock and frisked myself thoroughly for something that would unlock the door. Unfortunately I found nothing useful.

"What you look for?" asked Anna curiously.

"I need something to slip into the lock and spring it open."

"I have hair pin." Anna reached into her coat pocket and produced a bobby pin. "Here."

Taking the pin, I dropped to my knees, inserted it into the key hole, and jiggled it ever so slightly. *Click!* Smiling like a Cheshire cat, I turned the knob slowly. Noisily the door swung open. At once the smell of schnapps and cigarettes rushed out from the pilot house. "Good odors." Delighted, I rubbed the palms of my hands together. "Means someone's been sailing the boat recently."

"A-a-hum," said Anna, not knowing what I was jabbering about.

I took Anna by the hand and led her inside. Being familiar with the typical fishing boat, I didn't need a light to find the steering wheel, the compass, the charts, and the primer. Besides, any glimmer of light would have betrayed our incursion.

Of course I needed to know if the vessel had sufficient gasoline for an extended trip. That question was answered when I accidentally kicked a gas can. By the sound of the can, I knew that it was full of gasoline. Dropping to my knees, I touched the can and ran my fingers over it. Much to my surprise and delight, I discovered another can. And another. And another. All three cans were filled with gasoline. I wondered how a fisherman was able to get his hands on so much gasoline. It suddenly crossed my mind that the owner of the boat might be a member of the Underground. He, too, might be planning a trip to Sweden. I decided that if he arrived within the next two minutes, he was welcome to join us. If he failed to show, we sailed alone.

"Anna, come here," I whispered and held out my hand. As soon as our hands touched, I gently pulled Anna to the floor, where we sat under a moonless sky. "Where does this body of water go?"

"This is the end of Lalka River. It goes very fast to the Baltic Sea."

"Are there any German sentries in the area?"

"Yes." Anna pointed past my ear. "There is a train bridge with German soldiers guarding it."

"M-m-m-m!" I stroked my unshaven jowls. "Interesting."

Chances were excellent that the engine would start as soon as I turned the key. However, if the motor was as loud as the one in my father's boat, the noise would draw attention to the dock. I gave it much thought but decided that it would be best to sail down the river with the current. Once the vessel was past the bridge, I would engage the engine.

After casting off the dock lines, I returned to the pilot house and, with Anna by my side, gently turned the wheel. The boat, reacting to my touch, slipped away from the pier. By degrees it gained speed until it raced down the river under a smutty darkness.

"The bridge is ahead," whispered Anna. I saw nothing. No soldiers. No bridge. Nothing. We flashed past the shore, and still I saw no bridge. Around the bend, we thundered.

Unexpectedly my eyes bulged. Before me blazed greens and yellows and blues. "The aurora borealis!" cried Anna, digging her fingers into my arm. A red streamer slithered before our very eyes like a sea serpent. "Never see one on Christmas Eve."

"Look ... over there," I blurted as blue lace curtains fluttered and danced down upon the silvery water. And then we sailed under a trestle bridge and spotted a horseshoe arch rise and dip on the horizon. "Did you see the bridge back there?"

"We go under it, but I see no soldiers wid guns."

"Probably home drinking beer and eating *schnitzel*."

Anna nodded. "Pro-bob-bubbly so."

With all the excitement generated by the appearance of the spectacular northern lights, I failed to realize that we had finally sailed out into the open sea.

Our lives now depended upon me starting the engine and sailing to Sweden, a neutral country, where we would be welcome.

Since I didn't smell any gasoline, I knew that it was safe to start the engine. In the darkness my hand fumbled blindly until I found the gearshift. I promptly wiggled the lever, hoping that the drive gears were set in neutral. I advanced the throttle slightly. "Here ... goes." I waited several seconds for the motor to start. I heard nothing but our collective breathing. Not even a cough from the engine. "Shoot!" Panic hadn't set in, but it was hovering above us. "Didn't hear a click when I shifted the lever into neutral." I breathed deeply and held my breath. "Bet ... that's it." Once more I slipped the drive gears into the neutral position. *Taa-clink!* I exhaled. Again I started the engine. *Va-a-a-a-rooom* cooed the motor.

"She good boat?" asked Anna, squeezing my arm until it hurt.

"She's a very good boat," I answered and shoved the throttle forward. The engine responded, and the craft shot through the water. "Anna, I've only known you for a short time, but ... err ... when we get to Sweden ... would you marry me?"

"Yes!" screamed Anna." She let go of my arm and jumped up

184

and down. "When you knock me down in barn and fall on me, I decide I want to be you wife."

With one hand on the wheel, I reached out and pulled Anna close to me. "I love you, Anna Novak."

"I love you, Joe Gatski."

To Tell or Not to Tell

As soon as her shift ended, Samantha burst out of the Elm City Library and drove home. Of course, she failed to stop at the only stop sign in town and parked too close to the curb, scraping her white walls in the process. On any other occasion she would have been outraged at herself for scuffing the white band on her tires. Today was different, however. Today it was tolerated because the library was closed until after Christmas. Furthermore, tonight she was going to a dance at St. Elizabeth's Church in Kingston.

There certainly weren't many places where a single girl could meet a man except in a bar. And often when a girl did meet an *eligible* bachelor in a bar, he really wasn't *eligible*. She also recalled that many men who frequented the bars were looking for a one-night stand. At this time in her life she was seeking a meaningful relationship. And so she was pleased that the church periodically held dances.

In November she attended the Thanksgiving Day dance and met several young men. None impressed her until she met a slim, well-built man who spoke with a slight lisp. He asked her to dance, clutched her tightly, and kissed her on the cheek tenderly when the dance ended. If there was any such phenomena as love at first kiss, she was in love. Gazing into his cobalt eyes, she mumbled incoherently while he excused himself to take a telephone call. Dreams of being crushed within his embrace danced before her eyes. But he never returned, not even to tell her his name. She guessed it was a pressing matter which called him away.

Days later she decided to telephone the church rectory and describe her mystery man to Monsignor Gimbol, the pastor. She hoped that he could shed light on the man's identity. The priest confessed that he couldn't identify the man. He did, however, inform her that a Christmas dance was scheduled on the twenty-third. Perhaps her mystery man would be present then.

She was still thinking about her mystery man when she fumbled about in her purse for her apartment key. And as usual, the key stuck in the lock. But before she could kick at the door, as was her custom, Jo, her roommate of two days, heard the scratching and clamoring and rushed to investigate the noise.

Jo quickly and quietly opened the door, much to Samantha's delight. Sheepishly, Samantha sidled past Jo, removed her coat, and hung it upon a hook in the foyer. Jo followed her into the living room, pausing only when Samantha screeched to a halt in front of the hazy mirror on the wall. And while Samantha rifled through her mail on a table, Jo adjusted her bodice in the mirror with one eye while she studied Samantha with the other. "So tonight's the big night."

"I've been waiting for this night for weeks... er ... ever since I spoke to Father Gimbol on the phone." After tossing her mail into a wastebasket, she kicked off her spiked heels, surrendering three inches of height. "Wild horses couldn't keep me from that dance."

"Not even a chance of a snowstorm?"

"Not even a blizzard."

Jo, her expression growing concerned, took her coat from a chair and slipped it on. "I can't believe that you're going to drive twenty miles to a dance in the hope of meeting some guy who walked out on you and didn't even have the courtesy to inform you that he was leaving. I'm glad my Charlie isn't like that." She shook a manicured finger in Samantha's face. "You'll see what I mean when you meet him." After patting her hair, she pulled a ski cap down over an abundance of sable curls. "You're a hopeless romantic." She nodded emphatically. "No, you're crazy. You won't give a guy in a bar the time of day, b-but you're going to travel all the way to Kingston when the weather bureau's predicting snow tonight." She zipped up her jacket, punctuating her words with a stubby finger. "Promise me at least one thing ... that you'll dress sensibly."

"If I listened to you ... you'd dress me in a union suit, *mukluks*, and a *babushka*." Samantha unhooked her skirt and let it glide to the floor. After retrieving it, she tossed the garment over her shoulder in a gesture of bravado. "I'm going to wear that new dress -- the one with the plunging neckline --- and knock their socks off. You've got an engagement ring ... so-o-o you don't have to worry about being an old maid."

"You're only twenty-two. I'm seven years older." She turned and captured both of Samantha's eyes. "Look, I've tried my best to talk some sense into you, but if you must go, I'm going to wait up and hear you tell me that I was right." She smiled and was gone, leaving Samantha alone with a small, squat spruce tree that they had both decorated the previous evening.

Samantha glanced at her watch and decided there was still time to wrap the Christmas presents she had purchased the previous evening. She would then deposit them in her trunk when she left for the dance. They would be safe there. And tomorrow when she left for her parents' home in Wellington, she wouldn't have to fret about both the packages and her luggage. She hoped that little Lucy would like the toys she had selected for her. Likewise she wanted Grandfather McGee to like the tie and her mother the Avon necklace. She wrapped each gift with care, taking great pains to choose the perfect bow for each package.

If she took great pains to choose the best bow for each gift, she was even more finicky about selecting her clothing for the evening. Everything had to be just perfect from the new dress to the sequined pumps to the white panty hose with the red rhinestones. She wondered if the panty hose were too gaudy, and she even returned them to the dresser drawer. However, something told her that she must be bold, daring, and brash. She succumbed to her intuition, retrieved the hose from the dresser, and set them on the bed next to her bra and panties.

After bathing for the second time that day, she anointed her body with an expensive French body splash, the name of which she could neither pronounce nor spell. For all the primping, she truly hoped that it would be a memorable evening. "Samantha McGee, you look marvelous ... errr ... if I do say myself." She pirouetted before the mirror, noting how her breasts pointed immodestly. Once she gathered her coat from the ottoman and snatched the shopping bag, filled with the Christmas gifts, she departed.

Outside, the wind danced like breath exhaled. And the street light reflected off last week's snow. Samantha pranced through the sooty snow, careful not to get her feet wet, and deposited her treasures in the trunk.

The ride down Route #9 was a panorama of long, thin trees, spooky in their nakedness. She switched on the radio and joined Kenny Rogers and Dolly Parton in their rendition of "Silent Night."

Samantha wondered what Dolly Parton had besides a terrific voice and a generous bosom. She would have liked a better singing voice. But she had no interest in a larger bust. She was satisfied with the mold used to cast her body. Well ... almost satisfied. To be a mite taller would be nice, but she made do with the height she had.

When she crossed the old railroad tracks in Ringleville and headed for Kingston, she noticed the needle on her fuel gauge had crept towards *Empty*. It was also beginning to snow. She knew that she'd still find a service station open for business, but it was another ten minutes before she spied a Texaco sign swinging in the wind like a metronome. After checking her rear-view mirror, she eased the Ford into a combination general store and gas station. Once she switched off the ignition, she waited for the attendant. Anxiously she tapped her finger nails rhythmically upon the steering wheel and watched her breath cloud the window. After several minutes of waiting, she grew impatient and popped out of the auto into the snow-muffled world.

"Hello-o-o-o," she called and waited but only heard the wind spanking the corn stalks across the road. "Anybody ... here?" Her steps creaked in the virgin snow, leaving distinct prints. Seconds later the angry, whistling wind followed her and obliterated each print. Once she reached the station, she shielded her eyes and stared into the store. Slowly a thick tangle of curls and inquiring eyes rose above the window sill. "Is your daddy home, little girl?"

"No, and Mommy's sick," answered the thin, intense face through the pane. "Can you fix her up?"

Samantha pulled the collar to her face and padded across the walk to a glass door that was decorated with an assortment of stickers, ranging from STP to Pepsi to Goodrich. All of the decals seemed to deal with automobile care or food. A clanging cow bell and the acrid smell of kerosene greeted her once inside the building.

She followed the child down a dimly lit corridor to the family kitchen, where an antique water pump supplied the family's needs. Passing through the kitchen, her spiked heels clopped loudly upon the discolored linoleum floor. "Shhhhhh," whispered the child, holding her tiny finger to her lips. "Mommy's sick."

Samantha nodded and followed on tiptoe to a bedroom, where a pregnant woman reposed upon a bed. "How long has Mommy been sick?"

"I don't know."

The woman opened her eyes at the sound of the voices. "My water busted," she said softly, apologizing.

"Oh-h-h-h ... my ... word," said Samantha, tossing her coat upon a chair. She approached the bed and stared at the woman whose broad features were bathed in sweat. Instantly she realized that it was too late to drive to the nearest hospital. She had never witnessed a child's birth. The closest encounter she had ever had with child birth occurred at the library when she discovered two teenage boys giggling over graphically depicted pictures of a birth in a nurse's textbook. After she confiscated the book, she paused to glance at the pictures. However, looking at pictures and actually delivering a baby were two entirely different things. "Look, you're going to be fine. I'll boil some water."

The woman arched her thick brows. "Why are you gonna boil water. You gonna drink coffee at a time like this?"

"They always boil water in the movies when a woman's going to deliver."

"Trust me, lady, you don't need to boil no water. Those guys in the movies don't know what it's like to have a baby."

"Well, I'm still going to help you." And true to her word, she helped deliver a tiny, baby boy, shriveled and red.

"He's so beautiful," whispered the woman, cradling the baby in her arms. Samantha, hose and dress stained with blood, smiled and winked at the little girl, who was holding her brother's hand. "Me and my hubby ain't doin' so good, so he drives a truck besides runnin' this here place." Suddenly the woman's breath caught in her lungs. "He should be home pronto." When the woman moaned, Samantha's mouth dropped. "Ohhhh! I think ... ahhhh ... I'm going into labor again." And so she gave birth to a second child, a girl, a bit redder and a mite smaller than her brother.

Samantha heaved a long, audible sigh before putting both mother and twins to bed. Satisfied with her evening's work, she tiptoed down the hall and found the eldest child sleeping on the sofa. She gently covered the child with a quilt that displayed a tear shaped like the state of California in the very middle.

She yawned happily and then spotted a silver tree, forlorn and bare, sitting in the corner. Beneath the tree sat one, small box, addressed to Connie. "Kind of a bleak Christmas." She pulled on her coat and returned several minutes later with a bag of packages -- Christmas gifts she had intended for her family. "Connie, I hope you like this doll and book." She rummaged about in her bag once more. "Let see ... here's a box of socks for Father and a pair of gloves for Mother." She dipped her hand into the box but came up empty. "I don't have anything for the twins, but nobody in our family had a new baby." She finally switched off the light. "Merry Christmas."

Outside the snow had abated. But the wind howled, creating snow ghosts that swirled and charged the gas pumps with intense fervor and then whipped themselves into powder. She walked briskly. Her unsure steps crunched the brittle snow. Once she settled behind the wheel, she wondered if it was too late to drive to the dance. She pondered the question for several minutes. Then she drove her Ford off the lot, past walls of snow left behind by the departed plows.

The sensible thing to do was to head home. But deep down something told her to seize the opportunity with reckless abandon. Fifty feet up the road, she cut a perfect *U* and headed towards Kingston, singing "Jingle Bells" at the top of her voice.

By the time John Denver, the Muppets, and she finished singing, she had passed a sign that read *Kingston -- Next Two Exits.* She downshifted and negotiated the hairpin turn, spewing snow onto the remedial strip.

On Main Street, she drove west and passed a snow plow that was creating a snow castle fir for Ymir, the snow giant. St. Elizabeth's Church was on the corner of Fourth Street. When she neared the Parish Center, her heart pounded with joy at the sight of the lights gleaming from the basement. After parking, she tramped through the snow, wincing as the wind stabbed her. The snow, softer and deeper near the Center, forced her to high-step through the drifts all the way to the stoop. Her frown, though, changed quickly to a broad smile when she opened the door and stepped inside.

"Can I help you?" called a man as big and as round and as strong as the oak trees in her grandfather's backyard.

"I'm here for the dance," she said, brushing the snow from her coat.

"I'm sorry, but the dance is over." He waddled away to a table, returned with two pieces of cake, wrapped in party napkins, and pressed them upon her. "It's been over for an hour." He held up his hands, open palms extended. "I'm sorry. If you want more cake, you're welcome to it."

Her bottom lip looked as if she had a weight in it. "I -- I guess I'd better be going."

The drive home was uneventful. Occasionally a gust of snow danced across the hood and settled on the windshield only to be swooshed away by the relentless wipers. It wasn't so much the fact that she missed the dance as it was the fact that she would have to face Jo's I-told-you-not-to-go speech with all of its ramifications.

At 1:00 A.M. Fat Franky Fabian, a local disc jockey, played the "Star Spangled Banner" before the station signed off for the day. Fifteen minutes later her car coughed and sputtered and rolled to a dead stop on the shoulder of the road. "What!" She turned the ignition key and pumped the gas pedal. "Come on." In anger she pounded her fist against the steering wheel. "No! No! No! I forgot to get gas. I'm out of gas in the middle of nowhere."

She had to find something -- anything that she could tie to the antenna to attract the attention of a passing motorist ... should there be one. She hadn't seen a car pass since she drifted onto the shoulder of the road. She also knew that there wasn't anything in the trunk or on the rear seat to attract someone's interest. But she had seen a rag in the glove compartment last summer. Feverishly she rummaged through the contents. She found nothing but a map and a badly stained coffee mug. She needed something white. But the only white items were her undergarments -- bra, panties, and panty hose. There was no way she would shed her bra and hoist it up the antenna like the Stars and Stripes. She considered her panties, but they were too frilly and much too scanty. As for the panty hose, they were brand new. She weighed her options and decided that if she froze to death, she'd do so clad properly. The panty hose, however, were already soiled with blood. Yes, that was it. The panty hose could be sacrificed. They didn't really look as beguiling on her legs as she had hoped. "Well, here goes," she said and deftly slipped off her pumps. Quickly she discovered that her coat restricted her movement. After unbuttoning her coat, she realized that she would have to hike her dress past her hips to remove the hose. Reluctantly, she shucked the coat and reclined on her back and flapped her legs as if an overturned tortoise. "I can't believe that a girl could strip in a car and have sex. All those stories are pure fabrication by over-active imaginations." Gasping and snorting, she finally managed to slide the panty hose past her thighs. In the process, however, she managed to wedge herself between the steering column and the seat. "Oh, no! I'm going to choke." Breathing deeply, she tugged at the panty hose, scraping her bare knuckles upon the icy seat. "S-stay c-c-calm." She arched her back and then without warning she capsized, crashing to the floor. Now her feet were entombed in a cocoon of rhinestones and acrylic. "Take care of them, and you get a thousand runners. But try to get them off, and they're like leg irons." She finally sat up, crawled onto the seat, and peeled away the gauzy hose just as panic set in. She lost her panties, and there was no way she would continue until she found them. Groping about in the dark, she finally located them, rumpled and damp, between the seat and the door. Wet or not, she hauled them up her legs, whining when they touched her flesh.

She bundled herself as best she could, opened the car door, and hazarded a step into the knee-deep snow. Immediately she lost her shoe. Her toes jiggled in the snow, probing and searching. When she finally found the shoe, it was filled with snow. She recovered it and tapped it against the fender before jamming her foot into it. Cursing, she tied the hose to the antenna. Before she returned to her car, she paused to kick at the snow and decried the elements.

Once she trudged back inside, she huddled in a corner, hugging and fondling her bare, coltish legs. "C-c-c-cold out there." The wind wailed through the silver forest around her, churning the snow into a white fog. She knew that she must not become alarmed. Help would come ... but when? She recalled a story about a prospector who froze to death because he barged out into the sub-zero temperatures. Kicking off her shoes, she pinched her feet. "O-o-ouch! N-no, frostbite as ... y-yet." She wiggled her toes and decided to cover her legs with the map. If only she hadn't given away those socks, her feet would now be warm. "T-that prospector in the story ... f-froze to death when he dropped off to sleep. C-can't sleep. G-gotta s-stay awake." The map fell away to the floor. Instinctively she crooked her toes. "M-make small talk. S-stay awake." She shivered and kneaded her calves, thinking before she blurted:

"W--who-whose woods these are, I -- I think I know.
H-his house is in t-the town of Stowe.
I -- I s-shall now m-mind his fallow d-deer
Because t-there is n-no gas p-pump n-near."

Her head slumped against her chest. When a wolf's cry wafted through the pines, she sat bolt upright. Within seconds, she was fully aware of her surroundings. Embracing herself, she fell deeper into despair. She accepted the fact that surely she would freeze to death. Something in the back of her mind told her that she could not just sit and wait for death. "I -- I don't wanna die!" She opened the door and shut it, declining to venture out into the night. Her fingers were now numb. Her toes tingled. And her nose had no feeling. "J-just like t-that p-prospector in the story." She reclined on the seat and pumped her legs as if she were pedaling a bicycle. "W-whose w-woods these are ...."

After a few minutes a woodpecker tapped against a distant tree in syncopation to her grunts. She wondered what a woodpecker would be doing out at this hour. How could he possibly see what he was pecking unless he had a flashlight? The tapping persisted. It grew louder and louder. Then she realized that the tapping was not that of an aberrant woodpecker. It was someone rapping against her window. She rolled down the window and beheld a tall, stooped man about her grandfather's age, displaying the remnants of her panty hose.

"Is this yours?" he asked in a deep, graveled voice that made her jump.

"It's just an old rag." He shined a flashlight, revealing a face whose folds resembled a relief map of the local mountains. "I -- I ran out of gas." Her breath escaped in clouds like a puffing locomotive.

"Listen, I got some gasoline in my trunk that you may have." He scratched a head of thinning, red hair. "Got me a granddaughter as young as you, and she does the same darn thing. Ran out of gas jus' last week."

In a matter of minutes he emptied the can of gasoline into her tank, and she was speeding along Route #9, reflecting on the bizarre turn of events that had filled her evening. True, she missed the dance and ran out of gas. But the evening wasn't a complete disaster. She aided in the birth of twins. And that single miracle provided her with more satisfaction than she would have gotten at the dance. She hoped that Jo would be asleep when she arrived home. But as soon as she entered town and turned the corner at Sampson Street, she spied a silhouette a la Norman Bates framed in her second story window. She conjured up thoughts of how Janet Leigh must have felt.

Scrambling out of the Ford, she dashed up the steps, stamping her feet on the last step. The front door always betrayed her when she opened it, but it only sighed when she turned the knob. "Thank God, I'm finally home." She paused to remove her shoes and tiptoed across the floor. "Gotta be careful ... not to wake the neighbors." No sooner had she reached the stairway, when the door to Mrs. List's apartment opened ever so slightly. Samantha stopped abruptly and wondered why she was sneaking about. After all, she was twenty-two years of age and owed no one any explanation for her actions. Balancing herself on one leg as if a flamingo, she dusted off her dirty sole and slipped on one shoe. After repeating the procedure with the other shoe, she marched across the hardwood floor, her heels clacking loudly.

"So-o-o-o ... you're still up, are you?" she said, parading through the door. Before Jo reminded her how foolish she had been for traveling on such an abominable night, she seized the initiative. Turning, she thrust two pieces of cake into Jo's hand. "Before you tell me how dumb I was to go all the way to Kingston on a night like this, I want you to know that I had the greatest time of my life." She embraced a pillow and chassed across the room like she had seen Ginger Rogers do in some old movie with Fred Astaire.

"Did your mystery man show his face?"

"You mean Bob?" She tossed the pillow onto the sofa and turned away. "Yes, he did." She raised a finger and tapped it against Jo's chest. "And ... he apologized for leaving so abruptly on Thanksgiving. Seems he's in the service, and he's home on emergency leave because his mother's very ill ... errr ... was very ill." She swallowed hard. "She's better now. And ... so he's sailing for Japan the day after Christmas ... ugh ... with the fleet. And ... he won't be home for two years."

"Really! He's a sailor?" Jo stuffed another piece of cake into her cavernous mouth, resembling a chipmunk with bulging cheeks. "Are you going to write to him?"

"No, two years is too long a time." She smiled mischievously and walked to the closet with a spring in her step, allowing the soft blonde hair to dance about her face. "I'm too young to sit and wait for a man for two years. I really think that I've got to meet more men before I finally decide to settle down."

"Y-you do?"

"I do. I don't want to rush into anything." After shedding her coat, she stepped out of her shoes and fanned her toes. "Like you said ... I'm only twenty-two."

"Say ... you didn't do anything -- errr -- brazen tonight, did you?"

"No, why do you ask?"

"It's just that you're not wearing any hose, and I can't believe that you went out in the middle of winter without anything on your legs."

Samantha blushed like a school girl who had been caught in her own lie. "You know ... mmmm ... you were right about those rhinestone panty hose."

"Huh! I don't understand."

194

"You said that they were too big for me when we saw them over at K-Mart, and they were." She struck up a dancing pose. "There I am dancing with Bob, and I feel this tickling sensation around my ankles. I glanced down at my feet, and there are my panty hose sliding down my legs." She shrugged her shoulders. "So-o-o-o ... I went to the lavatory, took 'em off, and threw them away. See ... you were correct. I should have listened to you."

"I'm glad that you realize that. Say, this is good cake. You should have taken more."

Samantha smiled demurely. "I would have, but I was so busy dancing with Bob ... uhm ... that when I finally got to the punch bowl and cake, there were only these two pieces left. I'm sure you understand how it is when you're dancing up a storm."

"Listen, Samantha, in all the excitement, I forgot to tell you that my Charlie stopped by. He was ready to leave, but I insisted that he stay and meet you. I hope you don't mind."

"No, I don't mind. From all you've told me, he sounds perfectly divine."

"Oh, he truly is." Jo folded her hands and nodded. "He's in the kitchen."

"Well, I've got to meet him." Padding on bare feet, Samantha threw open the kitchen door. She stopped in her tracks. Her mouth fell open when she discovered her mystery man sitting before her in the person of Charlie.

"Hi, Thamantha," he said, "I've heard tho much about you."

195

E = mc²

After Sherlock Holmes retired as a consulting detective and moved to Sussex, he spent his time meditating and tending his bee colony. Needless to say, our friendship endured. Hardly a week passed when I did not receive a letter by post in which he extolled the beauty of the English Channel or noted the superiority of the Italian bee over the Syrian bee or bemoaned the rising cost of American tobacco.

Long after Holmes had withdrawn to Sussex and immediately preceding the onset of World War I, he was persuaded to accept a clandestine assignment in his country's service. He acquiesced only when the Foreign Minister and the Prime Minister petitioned him to infiltrate and unmask the German espionage ring that was encircling the British defense system.

Proud to say, I joined Holmes briefly at the climax when Von Bork, the German spy, was apprehended.

Since the Von Bork affair, I had not seen Holmes until the wake of Mrs. Hudson, our former housekeeper.

On the day of the funeral, I took an early train from London. And at the internment, which was held at the tiny, wind-swept cemetery in Wessex, I expressed my condolences to Mrs. Hudson's sister, Mrs. Emily Turner, who informed me that she had recently assumed ownership of the Baker Street property.

Holmes and I had met Mrs. Turner years ago when she spent a fortnight caring for our needs while Mrs. Hudson enjoyed a brief holiday. It was during the time that Holmes was retained by the King of Bohemia in the Irene Adler caper.

Holmes always called Miss Adler *the* woman. On my train ride back to London after the funeral, I found myself yearning for those days when Holmes and I were hot on the scent of Professor James Moriarity or John Clay or Colonel Sebastian Moran or even Irene Adler. I sighed as the locomotive, spewing great, black clouds of soot everywhere, coating everything in its path, wheezed and lumbered into Paddington Station.

Being a mature, realistic man, I knew that I couldn't live in the past. But as I hurried home, past the quaint, little shops festooned with Christmas garland, I was depressed and quite dissatisfied with my present life. Something was sorely missing.

As the winter sun dipped into the western horizon, I quickened my pace in the hope of arriving home before the impending snow squall transformed the streets into a white quagmire, making travel treacherous, if not impossible.

Once home my fingers, numb from the bone-chilling cold, fumbled with the keyhole. After several seconds, I finally managed to insert the key into the latch and push open the door, barely escaping another arctic blast.

The frigid vestibule hardly thawed my frozen limbs, prompting me to delay shedding my ulster and cravat. I started upstairs to my lodgings when my eye caught sight of an envelope addressed to me, lying on the candle stand. At once, I tore it open and read the message.

> Watson,
> Meet me at our old digs tomorrow at 9:00 A.M.
> Holmes

"I wonder what Holmes wants." I climbed the ancient, creaking stairs, and the following morning the clock tolled nine as I was again mounting the stairs. But these stairs were at 221B Baker Street. I still wondered why Holmes sought me. A twinge of excitement raced up my spine.

I quickened my pace at the top of the landing and was about to knock on the door of our old quarters when a familiar voice shouted, "Come in, Watson."

Once inside, I was astounded by the appearance of the sitting room. Everything had remained intact from our former days, including the framed picture of General Gordon, which adorned the far wall and had been used for target practice by Holmes.

"Watson, you know Mrs. Turner." His bony fingers pointed to the stout, ruddy-faced landlady. "And this is Mr. Leyland Reyton, her guest."

Mr. Reyton, reclining on the settee, clad in a faded-gray nightshirt, which was spotted with phlegm, extended an emaciated, alabaster hand. And when I pumped it, it felt as if I were grasping a bag of dried twigs.

"Glad to meet you," whispered the gaunt man. He struggled to raise his head from a pillow, which was littered with strands of his coarse, chestnut hair. "I know that I'm dying, but I must tell someone about the mad plot of Professor Joseph Heywood ... before it's too late."

"Too late ... for what?" asked Holmes, drawing closer.

"Too late to keep him from destroying London with his atomic bomb."

"Atomic bomb," I said, laughing at the suggestion. "How preposterous. Sounds like something that fellow Jules Verne would write."

"No, it's not, Dr. Watson." Reyton paused to catch his breath. "I know that Verne has predicted a bomb made from atoms, but Professor Heywood has actually devised such a bomb."

"Pray tell, Mr. Reyton, what is the theory behind Heywood's bomb?" asked Holmes. Puffing on his pipe, he sent a mushroom-like cloud of smoke skyward, where it danced along the ceiling.

Reyton dropped his head upon the pillow to rest momentarily, gaining strength before he spoke again. "Professor Heywood is a German terrorist. I -- I didn't know he was a terrorist until recently. With his atomic bomb ... he's going to obliterate all of London and force the English to sue for peace ... thus ending the war in Germany's favor. Some time ago Heywood found a French scientific article in which it stated that uranium atoms give off rays ... ugh ... which are unstable. According to the theory, these atoms give off an emanation, and the splitting of the atoms produce much energy, causing the atomic blast."

Reyton sipped from a glass and then propped himself up like a teddy bear in a shop window at Christmas time. "Gentlemen, this atomic bomb will be like no other bomb ever created." His purple lips quivered. "One bomb will kill millions of people."

Holmes, always the master of his emotions, puffed calmly upon his pipe and folded his hands upon his chest. Taking the pipe from his mouth, he leaned forward and tapped the bowl upon an ashtray, emptying it. He set his gaze upon Reyton. "Mr. Reyton, where's Heywood?"

"In ... hiding.

"Humph!" Satisfied that the bowl was clean, Holmes slipped the pipe into his pocket. "We must find Heywood before it's too late." I watched as Holmes strode across the room and peered out the window at the house across the street where we had captured the diabolical Colonel Sebastian Moran. "How's the bomb to be delivered?"

"By--" Reyton recoiled in a paroxysm of violent coughing and spitting. His face reddened. His eyes watered. His arms flailed wildly. "By ... a ... camel," he stammered through the side of his mouth. He then fell back, dead, his eyes staring at the ceiling.

Mrs. Turner gasped as I rushed forward to check the man's pulse. "Poor devil," I said, dropping his limp wrist and closing his eyes.

"Does he have any kin?" asked Holmes.

"I don't know, Mr. Holmes," answered Ms. Turner. "He arrived a few days ago, and from his appearance, I knew he was ill." She clasped and unclasped her hands nervously. "I don't believe that he ever went out. He seemed to get worse, and yesterday, when I returned from Wessex, he informed me that he was dying. Said London was in great danger." When she swallowed, her Adam's apple bobbed like a mallard on a pond. "But he didn't want to speak to the police. He said that Scotland Yard would never believe him."

"And that's when you suggested that he speak to me?"

"Yes."

"It sounds like one of those science-fiction tales that Jules Verne writes," I said, stroking my jowls. Neither Mrs. Turner nor Holmes said anything. Holmes, however, withdrew a lens from his pocket, approached the corpse, and studied, with great interest, a burn on the man's arm. "Who ever heard of a bomb made from atoms?"

Mrs. Turner, in the process of gathering together Reyton's possessions, paused and nodded in agreement. "Will you be leaving tonight, Mr. Holmes?" she asked.

"With your permission, Mrs. Turner, the good doctor and I shall be staying with you for a few days." Holmes was now sniffing about the man's mouth. "That is ... hmmm ... if my friend will once more aid me in my investigation?"

"Certainly, I shall, Holmes." I rubbed my hands together in sheer delight. "But I truly believe Reyton's story about an atomic bomb is pure balderdash."

"Maybe so, but with millions of lives at stake, we can't assume anything." Holmes immediately donned his deerstalker's cap and ulster before he turned to me, his eyes twinkling. I have some business to address, Watson, and I am sure that you have patients to visit today. However, if you will return later today, we shall resolve this conundrum." With those words, Holmes turned and departed.

Lately, my practice had kept me occupied without any respite. And today was no exception. Some folk always seem to succumb to real or imaginary illnesses during the holiday season. Therefore, I found myself treating all sorts of ailments, from gout to rheumatism.

It was well after seven o'clock when I prescribed the last dosage of aspirin and returned to Baker Street, where I joined Holmes and our old friend, Inspector Lestrade of Scotland yard, over a cold supper of duck and cheese.

"Inspector Lestrade discovered that I was in town, Watson, and he dropped by to share a glass of Christmas cheer with us." Holmes raised a goblet of brandy to Lestrade.

"London certainly isn't the same without you, Mr. Holmes," announced Lestrade with a tinge of sadness in his voice. "We just don't seem to have those interesting crimes these days. Gone are the murderer, the bank robber, and the counterfeiter." The little man's shoulders drooped. "Today ... someone stole a camel." Lestrade waved his hands wildly about his head. "The other day there was a drunk driving his horseless carriage up the museum steps, and last week someone reported the theft of a shipment of pitchblende."

I roared with laughter. "What's this world coming to?" I asked, unable to control myself as tears rolled down my cheeks. "Stealing pitchblende. What would you do with pitchblende?"

Lestrade shook his head in bewilderment. "I don't know. I think you make tar out of it."

"Maybe the thief wanted to tar his roof." Both Lestrade and I laughed again.

"It's so very good to see both of you again." Rising from his chair, Lestrade reached for his hat. "There's a bit of jollification going on down at the Yard tonight, and I must be going." He extended his hand to both of us. "Merry Christmas to two of the finest gentlemen I ever had the pleasure of knowing."

Holmes patted Lestrade on the back and opened the door. The inspector pulled up his collar and disappeared down the steps. His salutations ended only when the door closed after him.

When I lifted the mug to my mouth, I caught Holmes's gaze. It was a look I had seen several times before in our professional relationship -- once, when Trelawny Hope, the Secretary for European Affairs, had lost a very valuable letter. And the second time being when Colonel Valentine Walter sold the highly classified submarine patent to Hugo Oberstein.

On both occasions the nation teetered on the brink of catastrophe, only to be rescued by Holmes's amazing powers.

"Holmes, what's the matter?"

"Pitchblende."

"Pitchblende?"

"Yes, pitchblende is an ore from which uranium is extracted, and uranium is a very unstable element." Holmes thrust his hands deeply into his pockets and stared through the frosted windows into the starless night. "Watson, have you ever heard of the equation E=mc squared?"

"No, I can't say that I have."

"A young physicist ... errr ... over in Switzerland, by the name of Einstein, developed the equation back around 1904." E stands for energy; m the loss of mass, and c the velocity of light."

I raised my hands, palms extended. "So--"

Holmes tapped his pipe against the ashtray and smiled. "So, my dear Watson, what Professor Einstein said, in effect, was that matter and energy are the same thing. And ... one thing can be changed into the other. It also implies that a very small amount of mass can be transformed into an immense amount of energy."

My jaw dropped. And I swallowed hard before I could speak. "So what you're saying, Holmes, is that Professor Heywood has built an atomic bomb."

"It is quite possible that Heywood surmised after reading the French article that uranium is the very substance for an atomic explosion since the atoms are so unstable." Holmes folded his hand and placed them under his chin for a brief second. "And, therefore, he is the one who pilfered the pitchblende ... uhm ... because—"

"Because uranium is found in pitchblende." I dreaded the conclusion I reached because it might doom London in the near future.

Holmes in a rare display of emotion patted me across the back. "Excellent, Watson."

"Reyton said that the bomb would be delivered by a camel, and ... earlier this evening Lestrade said mentioned that a camel had been stolen."

Holmes, now pacing about the room, heaved a long sigh. "I truly wonder if a dromedary could convey anything as gigantic as an atomic bomb." He stopped in his tracks and screwed up his face. "And secondly, where is he going to deliver it? Since the pitchblende was stolen last week, I believe that Heywood's bomb might be near completion."

Outside the sound of carolers filled the air as the revelers passed by our window. I couldn't help but wonder how those same people would react if they knew how close to death they were.

I was frustrated and angry -- frustrated because I was of little help to Holmes and angry at myself for making light of such a disastrous situation earlier in the evening.

"Holmes, is there anything that we can do tonight?"

"No, Watson. The only thing we can do is retire and hope that Heywood trips up before we all blow up. You may as well get a good night's sleep."

I retired to my old room, where I had always slept. But I lay awake and counted the church bells, ushering in the birth of Christ. I simply could not sleep. I tossed. I turned. I wrestled with the blanket. I finally dozed off in the wee hours of the morning. It was still pitch-black when Holmes, fully dressed, entered and towered over my bed with a guttering candle in hand.

"Watson, arise." He glanced at his pocket watch. "The game is afoot. There's a pot of coffee downstairs. I'll give you twenty minutes."

"I'll be down in fifteen minutes." It was ten minutes later when I appeared in the sitting room. The air was stale from tobacco smoke. And because it was so thick, I knew that Holmes had spent the night pondering the situation.

From our many years of collaborating on some hundreds of

investigations, I knew it was Holmes's custom to place himself in the perpetrator's psyche. He did so in order to learn what the criminal mind was scheming. However, before I could question him, he tossed the *Daily Telegraph* onto the sideboard. "Read the headlines."

"Sopwith Camel bags two Fokkers." Suddenly a smile creased my lips, while my mouth formed a little *o*.

"Aeroplane, Watson. The Camel is an aeroplane." Holmes waved the newspaper above his head. "Professor Heywood is going to drop the atomic bomb by aeroplane."

I gulped down the coffee and then followed Holmes down the stairs and out the front door. In the amber glow from the gas lamppost, I noticed that my Model-T Ford stood clad in ice as if it were a piece of black onyx. And in the passenger seat, I spied Holmes already perched rigidly. Plumed steam rushed from his nostrils. "Where to?"

"Parkhill. That's where the army keeps its aeroplanes."

While Holmes waited impatiently, I cranked the Ford. Nothing happened. I cranked once more and stood back. Suddenly the Ford sprang to life and vibrated, shedding icicles. I grinned and then jumped inside. "Holmes, what makes you think that Heywood will drop his atomic bomb today? Why not tomorrow or next week?"

I tread upon the gas pedal gingerly. By inches the Ford drifted away from the paving. Timidly it chugged along Baker Street. The humming of the combustion engine frightened a gaggle of Christmas geese in their cage atop a wagon. And later a horse tied to a pole was spooked when the Ford's engine backfired. In both incidents, I incurred the wrath of the animals' owners.

"Today is Christmas, Watson. Look about you. There's no one on the streets." And then he shook a finger in my face. "There's probably not a soldier at the aerodrome. All the army personnel are celebrating Christmas in London."

Holmes was correct. The road was a ribbon of frozen turf, which we traveled alone. Of course there was an occasional dray, which we passed without undue difficulty thanks to the mechanized horse power.

Sometime later, when we sped into the aerodrome at the speed of nine kilometers per hour, we discovered the area deserted. There were hangars to the right of us. And there was a water tank to our left. Suddenly Holmes nudged me. "There!" he exclaimed and pointed to a serpentine-like column of smoke that snaked its way skyward from a building behind the tank.

As soon as I switched off the motor, Holmes and I climbed out of the Ford and marched across a brown, grassy knoll toward a frame building marked *Headquarters*. When we drew closer, the purring of a gramophone needle, stuck in a record groove, assaulted our ears. I wondered why someone had not lifted the gramophone arm to relieve the cacophony. It was not a difficult task.

We strode up to the door and knocked. No answer. Holmes rapped again -- more authoritatively. Still no answer. Clutching the doorknob and turning it, the door creaked open. We entered tentatively and glanced about. Scanning the immediate area, we quickly discovered why the gramophone needle had not been adjusted. There, on the floor, a soldier reposed. He was either dead or unconscious.

"Look to him, Watson, while I look about."

I dropped to my knees and examined the soldier. "He's suffered a nasty bruise to the head, but the skull has not been injured. He should be fine."

"Let him be."

Just then there arose a loud roar outside. The entire room shook. And before my eyes, the coffee cups on the table rattled; the suspended paraffin lamp shimmied, and a framed picture of King George fell from the wall. I could not hear a word above the commotion. We rushed to the door and caught a fleeting glimpse of a silver-and- green bi-plane taxing past the barracks. It rushed toward the open pasture. Atop the fuselage sat the atomic bomb, secured by cable and hemp.

"It's got to be the atomic bomb," I said, holding onto my bowler. "It's huge." I glanced at Holmes. He said nothing, but sped after the plane. I, in turn, chased after Holmes. After four steps I gasped for fresh air. Right then and there, I vowed never to indulge myself in another cigarette.

Across a muddy field we dashed toward a bi-plane with a double cockpit. In a matter of seconds Holmes, stern and glaring, was poised in the front cockpit. Intuitively, he seized a pair of goggles and slipped them over his deerstalker cap.

"Give the propeller a try, Watson." I did as Holmes instructed, but nothing happened. "Try again." I gave a second tug. The propeller hummed. The engine whistled, emitting a cloud of malodorous fumes. "Get in."

Tearing my trousers in the process, I crawled into the rear cockpit. However, before I could acclimate myself to my new surroundings, Holmes had the contraption speeding across the frozen field in pursuit of Professor Heywood, who was not airborne, as yet.

I righted myself just as the plane skidded on an icy patch. The aeroplane veered, hurling me against the machine gun. "Ooouch!" Instinctively I touched my forehead and discovered a welt, the size of a bantam egg.

Dazed, I focused my sights upon the Camel once more. "The atomic bomb's too heavy. He can't take off," I shouted just as Heywood left the ground and skimmed above a farmer's barn, almost detaching the cupola. "Holmes, are you sure you want to try to navigate this blasted death trap?"

"I've got to, Watson. You and I've lived good, long lives, but if we don't stop the professor, there are many people who won't have the lives to live, which we've had."

Down the field we thundered, bounding and quaking. When Holmes pulled on the joystick, we climbed into the atmosphere, the wind thrashing our faces. My stomach rumbled. I knew I would become ill very shortly.

I had no idea what Holmes would do next. But I knew what I intended to do -- pray. I closed my eyes. When I opened them, Professor Heywood was ahead of us, the squat atomic bomb, sitting like Buddha, scowled at us.

Above the tree tops we soared, gaining on the Camel. "Watson, when I get closer, you fire the machine gun."

The Camel swerved to the right. We followed in pursuit. It dove. We dove, and my new bowler flew away, a whirling dervish. I peered over the side and watched it crash into the Thames below.

"Where is he headed?" I asked.

"Buckingham Palace." Holmes studied the Camel as we drew closer. "Now ... shoot him out of the sky."

Rat-a-tat-tat-rat-a-tat-tat screamed the Vickers machine gun when I squeezed the trigger, filling the air with a volley that sheared the steeple of a church below.

"Not the church, Watson, the plane."

I pulled the trigger again, but the gun jammed.

"Damn it!" I smashed my fist against the gun. "Now we can't stop him. He's free to drop his atomic bomb and kill us all."

Professor Heywood pulled on the stick. Obediently the Camel climbed into the air and settled on our tail. I glanced back and watched as the professor, beady eyes and handle-bar moustache, sighted us with his machine gun. We were now the prey. I shuddered, waiting to be blown out of the sky.

Closer and closer the Camel inched until I could hear the click of his machine gun. I slouched down into the cockpit, waiting ... waiting for a deadly burst, which would end my life.

When several seconds passed, and nothing happened, I grew bold and peeked back. I noticed that the Camel's engine had stalled. Its propeller had quit spinning. Heywood was cursing and pummeling the gauges but to no avail.

The Camel wavered in midair. In the very next second I watched the nose arch forward. Down, down, down the aeroplane sped with its atomic bomb, and with it the destruction of London, one of the finest cities ever built by mankind.

I leaned over the side and watched, bracing myself for the greatest explosion that humanity had ever experienced. When the Camel dove into the Thames, splitting the water, like an Olympic diver, I closed my eyes and cringed. I waited. But there was no explosion.

"Holmes, there is no atomic bomb." Tears welled in my eyes.

Holmes, who was now quite adept as a pilot, circled the crash site several times. Nothing surfaced, except for a few bubbles. Professor Heywood had gone to his watery grave.

"It's time to celebrate Christmas, Watson." Holmes banked the aeroplane and headed back to the field. "I hope you're hungry for goose," and several hours later Holmes and I visited the Grand Hotel. There we feasted upon the largest goose I had ever seen.

After our Christmas pudding, I lit a cigarette and drew in the toxic smoke. Certainly, I was aware that I was probably hastening my demise. But after the harrowing morning, I did not care.

"Holmes, do you, in your infinite wisdom, believe that it is possible to build a weapon as destructive as an atomic bomb?"

"I do, Watson. I do." Holmes lifted his glass and gazed afar, as though transfixed. "I don't believe that we shall see an atomic bomb within our life time. We simply do not possess the means. Someday, however, long after we're gone, man may develop the technology to unleash an atomic bomb." I nodded. "It will be so deadly, it may destroy civilization as we know it."

And It Came to Pass

Many people believe that elves only live at the North Pole and serve as Santa Claus's helpers. Though the greatest number call the North Pole home, there are elves living all over the world. Most lead sedentary lives. But some do migrate from one area to another.

Occasionally, Santa will need an elf with a certain skill. And on one such day, Santa came to me and announced, "Trippett, I need an apothecary at once. With winter coming on, there's bound to be some colds and sore throats and ... errrr ... pulled muscles among the men, and I'd like a good apothecary to be able to mix a few home remedies."

"Good idea, Santa," I said, wondering if it would be difficult to recruit an apothecary, and a good one at that. "I'll put out a request for one this moment." I glanced at Santa, and something in his pale, blue eyes told me that it was more than the normal winter maladies that concerned him. "Boss, is there something that you're not telling me?"

Santa nodded and raised a stubby finger to his lips. "Constipation," he whispered, peeking about to see if anyone overheard us. "I've had it for several weeks, and if I don't soon go ... I --I feel as though I'm gonna explode."

"Why don't you eat some prunes? They always work for me."

"I've eaten prunes and licorice and raisins and beans and apples, but nothing has worked." Santa stroked his jowls and heaved a troubled sigh. "With Christmas coming, I can't afford to get sick because so many children are depending upon me." He threw up his hands in resignation. "I thought that if we could get an apothecary up here, he might be able to do something for me." Santa grasped my shoulder firmly. "Trippett, you have to get me help."

I ran my teeth across my lower lip, removed my cap, and scratched my bald head. "Santa, I'll see what I can do."

"You got to do more than try, my boy. There are going to be a lot sad children in the world if I miss Christmas."

"I'll put out an urgent request for an apothecary to STEPS -- Santa's Temporary Elf Placement Service."

"E-r-r-r-r ... do you think STEPS is a good idea? The last time we used STEPS to get a replacement for Skrugg, the candy maker, it took them so long to find someone ... we had to work the poor man day and night just so we could meet our seasonal demand."

I shrugged my shoulders helplessly. "What other choice do we have?"

"I guess you're right, my boy." Santa winced and rubbed his stomach I obvious distress. "Better do it as soon as possible."

I glanced out the window at the new blanket of snow that had transformed familiar landmarks into deformed gargoyles. With some reluctance I slipped on my tunic and headed for the office, cursing the wind that pummeled my face.

Winter at the North Pole can be downright brutal. Often it snows for fifty days without respite. This winter, however, had been mild in comparison. The temperature had dipped to minus ninety degrees on only ten or eleven night. And as I trudged down Candy Lane, the snow crying underfoot, I could hear the carols and the banter, drifting over the snow from the toy factory before me. There would be no rejoicing in the world, though, if Christmas had to be canceled because Santa didn't feel well.

The office was dark, save for the eerie silhouettes on the ceiling that were created by the yellow flames jitterbugging across the logs in the fireplace. I paused tom warm my hands before I approached the teletype and sent out my urgent request for help. Deep down, I wondered if my message would travel unimpeded and be answered. My heart suddenly skipped a beat when I thought that my message might go unanswered, knowing that if we couldn't get assistance for Santa, Christmas would surely be canceled.

Outside the blizzard intensified. I, however, was deeply engrossed in reverie and failed to observe the snow cascading past the window. I only returned to reality when a gust of powdery snow crashed into the window, splattering into thousands of sparkling diamonds.

I peered out at the naked sign marker, shivering in the wind, and wondered how soon our apothecary would arrive. Three days later the snow still pelted the village. The sign marker metamorphosed into a gigantic mushroom, but our apothecary had still not arrived.

Santa's crestfallen spirits had now infected the entire settlement. More and more talk centered around the cancellation of Christmas.

"Drat! Where's that apothecary?" called Santa as he pounded his fist on a counter, scattering a trio of cavaliers, Humpty Dumpty, and a ballerina. "Trippet, I thought that you said you contacted STEPS."

"I did, Santa. I don't know --" I began to say when suddenly there was a knock at the door.

"If that's Percey again, tell him to check Donder's hooves."

"Y-yes," I stammered, but when I threw open the door, there standing before me was an elf; his beard and eyebrows frozen with ice, but his gray eyes twinkled with joy.

"Uhm ... I'm Buck ... your chemist. STEPS sent me."

"You mean apothecary," I said. "A druggist."

"No, I'm a chemist. I mix chemicals." He brushed the snow from his smock and stamped his clogs. "I'm sorry to say, chaps, but I don't know anything about pharmacology."

"STEPS sent us the wrong man," cried Santa, holding his stomach in excruciating pain. "Christmas is ruined."

"What's wrong with him?" asked Buck. "He doesn't look well at all."

"He's constipated," I said, "and if something doesn't happen soon … Christmas will be canceled this year."

Buck scratched his bald head. "M-m-m-m … has Santa tried castor oil or mineral oil?"

"I tried 'em all," explained Santa. "Nothing works. I was hoping that you'd be an apothecary, and you'd be able to mix an excellent laxative for me."

"Well, I'm not. I'm a chemist. My specialty is chocolate." Buck wrinkled his forehead and smacked his lips. "I make dark chocolate and light chocolate and semi-sweet chocolate."

Santa dismissed the chemist with a wave of the hand. "Here at the North Pole, we only make one kind of chocolate. You may as well go back to where you came from."

"Couldn't I stay for the night?" There arose a trace of sadness in Buck's voice. "I've always wanted to see Santa's workshop."

I look at Santa, who only nodded and lumbered off towards a display case. "Well, Santa's workshop isn't really a workshop. It's really a series of factories, all specializing in particular toys, candies, or tree ornaments."

Buck, still shivering, followed me through the office, where several elves were already dismantling the Christmas tree and pulling down the garland in anticipation of canceling the greatest holiday of the year.

"On any other Christmas season the North Pole's ablaze with excitement and good cheer, but this year it's different. There's no song, no last-minute bustle, and no filling of Santa's bag for his Christmas Eve ride," I explained to Buck, his eyes bedazzled by the magnitude of our operation.

"It's so sad. I wish I could do something," said Buck as we passed the Wood Shop, where hundreds of multi-colored horses would never fine homes.

"There's nothing you can do, so don't worry about it. You say you're a chemist …."

"I make chocolate -- all kinds."

"So you said." The smell of cocoa suddenly tantalized my nostrils. "We only make one kind of chocolate, as Santa stated, but I … errr … want you to take a look at our operation."

"I'd be glad to look around."

Buck followed me into a large room, where thousands of potted dandelion plants stood growing under a battalion of bright lights.

"Dandelion growing at the North Pole," he said in disbelief.

"*Taraxacum Officinale* is its official name. Here at the North Pole this weed has many uses. The flowers are used to brew wine, which we all indulge in from time to time. And of course ... uhm ... the milky juice of the roots has medicinal value. Mmmmm ... the leaves are eaten in a salad."

"I see," said Buck, admiring a tall, robust plant.

"Through this door is the Chocolate Room." As I pushed open the massive oak door, out rushed Zork, the union steward, his face besmirched with chocolate.

"T-t-tippet-t-t-t," he stuttered. "T-t-there's something wrong. I c-c-can't turn off the main valve."

"No problem," said Buck, pushing me aside. "I've worked around chocolate all my life."

We followed Buck into the room, past the vats. All around us chocolate bonbons raced along on conveyor belts and leaped off the edge, splattering upon the floor like water balloons dropped from a great height. Hapless workers scurried about frantically. Some cursed. Other prayed. And still others tried to set the operation right.

"All I hafta do is turn this knob ... I think," said buck, twisting until his face turned beet-red.

"No! Don't touch that knob," pleaded Zork. "it controls the temperature of the main kettle." Zork glanced at me with trepidation. In the next second I reached for Buck, but not before there was an earth-shattering explosion. Molten chocolate thundered through the door, covering everything in its path.

The upheaval tossed me into a cauldron of chocolate, from which I tried to escape. But the sea of chocolate propelled me through the door past the chocolate covered dandelion, which now resembled grotesque shrubs of a subterranean world.

"Help me!" cried Buck as he sailed past, his arms clinging to an exhaust pipe. "I turned the wrong valve. I'm sorry," he apologized to me. Hours later, he was still apologizing -- this time to Santa.

"Look at this mess," Santa said in a voice so weak I knew his health had deteriorated vastly since I had last seen him. I knew that the explosion wasn't his primary concern. We had blown things up before. "The dandelion plants have all been ruined." Santa fingered a large plant. It crumbled into pieces. The chocolate melted in his fingers, prompting him to toss it into his mouth. "My ... that's good."

He retrieved another plant and ate it, smacking his lips in delight.

"Very tasty." Suddenly flatulence broke the silence.

When Santa looked at me, I pointed to the dandelion. He quickly devoured any plant within his grasp. His hands and mouth became soiled with chocolate. His breath reeked from chocolate. But he never stopped eating until the flatulence increased in volume. "It's going to happen." He pumped Buck's hand in delight. "Chocolate-covered dandelion is an excellent laxative." The long-lost smile, at last, tugged at the corners of Santa's mouth.

Buck, my boy, you have saved Christmas," called Santa over his shoulder as he sped away as quickly as a man of his age and girth could run.

Yes, Buck had truly saved Christmas with his EXCELLENT LAXATIVE, which he sold to a New York firm. Of course the firm, as everybody knows, marketed his invention as the world famous *Ex-Lax*.

Like Father, Like Son

Since my great-grandfather served as the personal physician for General Felix Ruttlidge of the Army of the Potomac, and my father was a surgeon with the American Expeditionary Forces in France during World War I, I volunteered to serve with the Army as soon as I received my medical degree in June of 1944.

Commissioned a Captain, I was assigned to serve in the Third Army, which was locked in mortal combat in Northern France at the time.

In medical school I studied about all sorts of maladies, ranging from blood disorders to cancer to accidents and injuries. But when I joined the 3rd Armored Division, I was stationed at a field hospital behind the lines and performed meatball surgery, which is nothing more than medicine performed to stabilize the wounded soldier as quickly as possible.

When I wasn't operating on a poor tanker or an infantryman, I tended to cases of frostbite, trench foot, and venereal disease.

By the spring of '45 everyone, including the Germans, knew that the war was over. And as a result, I no longer spent long hours in surgery, laboring under the most primitive of conditions.

On the seventh of May, while I was checking our plasma supply in the operating room, which was simply a canvas tent, Major Reynolds, the unit's chief surgeon, poked his massive head into the tent and informed me that the Germans were about to surrender.

Ecstatic over the fact that I had actually survived the war, I poured myself a cup of tepid coffee and dropped into a chair in the corner of the room.

No sooner had I wrapped my long, slender fingers around the cup and sipped when the tent flaps parted once more, and Corporal Simmons, a medic, burst into the room with a wide smile on his pock-marked face.

"Captain Krol," he said, removing his steel pot and revealing a crop of matted blonde curls, "they say the war is over." Spying the pot of coffee, he strode across the room and helped himself to a cup.

"I heard that rumor, too," I said. As he drank, I watched his Adam's apple bob like a baked pear in a punch bowl of eggnog.

"As soon as I finish this joe, I'm going souvenir hunting. Wanna come along?"

"Hell no-o-o-o-o!" I took a long swig and set the cup aside. "I don't get a thrill out of scavenging for dented helmets and Nazi flags and … and pilfering some corpse's Iron Cross."

Simmons's jaw dropped; his eyes widened. "You got me all wrong." From the tone of his voice, I knew that I had touched a raw nerve. He pointed to himself with his thumb. "I ... I don't go after that kinda stuff."

"Ohhh!"

"Not me." He drained his cup and wiped his mouth with his sleeve. "I only go after Lugers."

"Guns!"

"They're German guns, and I'll sell them for a fortune back home in Indiana."

"How many Lugers do you have?"

Simmons gazed up at the holes in the ceiling and counted on his fingers. "Mmmm ... twelve." Finishing his coffee, he rinsed his mug in the sink and returned it to the instrument table, which also served as our desk and card table "The next one I find is gonna be lucky thirteen."

"Is that so?"

"Yep." After plopping his helmet upon his head, he executed a snappy about-face and disappeared into the balmy spring afternoon.

"Good hunting." Alone at last, I retrieved a Dear John letter from my pocket. I had received it earlier in the day from Lillian Williams. Shifting my position so that I sat directly under a lamp, I read it, once more, in its entirety. Lillian and I had been dating on and off since my residency days at North Wales General Hospital. Now she was going to marry a plumber and move to Ohio.

I thought about our courtship briefly, assured myself that Lillian really wasn't the girl for me, and tossed the letter into a nearby trash can. "Better fish in the ocean."

According to the inventory I conducted on the plasma, the supply was low. However, if Major Reynolds was right and the Germans had, in fact, surrendered, there would be no need for more blood.

Nevertheless, blood was a very valuable commodity. I gulped down the last of my coffee and decided to organize the plasma according to type and age. Just as I had gathered all of the oldest plasma and moved it aside, Major Reynolds, smelling of whisky, returned. "It's official, Tom," he said, "some Kraut general by the name of Jodl unconditionally surrendered."

W--w-w-w-w-r-r-r-rump!

"What ... in the hell ... was that?" I heaved a deep sigh. "Thought this damn war was over."

The major peeked out the window and scanned the distant hill. "I don't see anything." Turning toward me, he seized a pile of blankets from a cot and stashed them inside a footlocker. "Probably some dogface firing his carbine in celebration of the end of the war."

212

"Hmmm … sounded more like some sort of explosion."

"I don't think so."

Deciding not to pursue the issue, I let it rest. After all, did it really matter if the noise was created by a rifle or a mortar? I returned to my task. And in no time all of the plasma was organized according to type and age and returned to the refrigerator. With my work completed, I reflected upon my tour of duty, thankful that the war was finally over. As a result of my deep, serious thought, which slipped into a bit of reverie, I never heard the squealing of the tires outside the tent or the squawking of the loud, garbled voices that followed.

But when the tent flaps parted and two soldiers, bearing a stretcher, strode in with a body, I jumped to my feet. Approaching the soldier, my eyes bulged at the sight of Corporal Simmons. His head was flung back at an angle and his jaw twitched. Upon closer inspection, I spied his gaping stomach wound. "Holy cow!" I exclaimed.

"Scrub up," ordered the major, tossing me a gown. While I slipped on the gown, he doused his face with water and poured himself a mug of coffee. "You're the best damn surgeon in the outfit." Taking the cup into his hand, he drained it. "If anybody can save Simmons, you can."

"You going to assist?" I motioned to the stretcher bearers to place Simmons upon the operating table.

"I'll be right by your side." While I placed my surgical tools upon the table and checked the catheter attached to the suction machine, which removed excessive blood from the patient's wound, the major rolled up his sleeves and lathered his hands with soap.

Taking a deep breath and praying silently for guidance, I approached Simmons and snipped away the remnants of his shirt. "My … word." Shaking my head, I bit my lower lip. "His aorta's spouting blood like a geyser."

"Any of you guys know how this happened?" asked Major Reynolds, addressing the stretcher bearers.

Holding masks over their faces, they watched my every move. "Simmons is the best souvenir hunter in the unit," said the taller soldier, "and after some searching in no-man's-land … out yonder, he spotted a dead Kraut with a Luger … er … clenched in his fist."

"And when he lifted the Luger from the German's grasp … it was booby-trapped," said the shorter soldier, waving his arms like a soap-box orator. "Ka-a-a-boo-o-o-m!"

"His lucky thirteen," I mumbled under my breath as I soaked up the blood in order to get to the wound.

"What was that?" asked the major, handing me a sponge.

"Eh … nothing." At long last, I made some headway. The

213

bleeding subsided, which was good.

"I think you're going to save him." Somewhere another explosion erupted. This one was closer, prompting the utensils on the cabinet to jiggle.

"Sure hope so." Suddenly, without any explanation, the aorta ruptured in another spot. "Oh, damn!" Blood filled the chest cavity once more. "Back to square one."

"His pulse is dropping."

"More suction." I bent over Simmons and worked feverishly for several minutes.

The major inched closer to me. "We're losing him."

"Come on, Simmons." I aimed the catheter at a fresh pool of blood. "Don't you dare quit on me ... now." Another explosion, and the light above flickered. But I never looked up from my work.

Simmons's lips parted, and then he went rigid. "Tom, he's dead." The major pulled off his mask and gloves. "You did all you could."

"If Simmons is dead ... I didn't do enough."

"I never saw an aorta in that bad a shape." Covering Simmons up with a blanket, the major motioned to the two soldiers to remove the body.

"I failed Simmons."

The major lit a cigarette and puffed leisurely. "Don't blame yourself. We save many more than we lose."

I nodded. "I guess you're right." Slipping off my gown, I tossed it aside and stretched.

"Of course I'm right." The major reached into the cabinet and produced a deck of cards. "Want to play?"

"Naw. Not in the mood." Taking a rag and a bottle of rubbing alcohol, I commenced to wipe down the operating table.

"Well, I got some news that's really going to put you in a good mood."

"Oh."

The major drew closer and put his arm around my shoulder. "Between you and me ... eh ... the unit's being sent back to the States within the next two weeks."

"Now ... that's good news."

Because the major always knew the latest scuttlebutt, I honestly believed that we'd all be going home shortly. However, he was only partially correct. Since he had served in the Army since Roosevelt declared war back in '41, he had accumulated sufficient rotation points and was honorably discharged within a week. The fact that his father-in-law was a Congressman back in Illinois probably also had something to do with his departure.

214

As for the rest of us in the unit, we were all assigned to the Occupational Army and scattered across Europe. Some of the guys were sent to Italy. Others went to France. And as for me, I was transferred to an outfit stationed at Berchtesgaden in the Alps. I had never heard of Berchtesgaden, but I quickly learned that it was the location of Hitler's mountaintop retreat, the Eagle's Nest.

Ensconced in a chalet, which had once belonged to a high-ranking Nazi official, I now treated bee stings, lanced an occasional boil, and prescribed ointments for sunburn.

On the second of August, rumors surfaced about our being sent to the Pacific to battle the Japanese. Two days later, I was instructed to close shop and prepare for departure to an unknown site. Of course, I knew that I was headed to the Pacific.

And then on the fourteenth of August, President Truman announced that Japan had surrendered after the cities of Hiroshima and Nagasaki had been leveled by atomic bombs.

A day later, I unpacked all of the medical equipment. But as I reorganized my medical supplies, scores of comrades were notified of their impending discharge from the Army.

In the weeks that followed, most of the old-timers bid adieu and left for home. I stayed behind with a skeletal contingent of men. Thanksgiving came and went. And then, a few days before Christmas, when I checked the bulletin board outside Headquarters, I discovered my name listed for discharge from the United States Army.

Since this narrative form insists upon an economy of words, I shall not weary the faithful reader with the details of my discharge and the subsequent humdrum voyage to New York City aboard the *Ira P. Nicholson,* a 790-foot troop transport, commissioned in 1927.

From my boyhood excursions to New York City with my parents, I knew that I could reach my home in Pennsylvania if I could locate the Port Authority Bus Terminal.

And so as soon as the ship docked at the wharf and I marched proudly down the steep gangplank, I scanned the joyous crowd below for a policeman. Lo and behold, I spotted a roly-poly patrolman standing next to a well-dressed gentleman and his lady.

The sergeant was only too happy to assist me. With his expert directions, I was able to easily find my way to the bus terminal. And in less than four hours, I stepped off a Greyhound bus across the street from the post office, the exact location where I was inducted into the Army less than two years ago.

Hoisting my duffel bag onto my shoulder, for what I hoped was the last time in my life, I trudged up Main Street. I took three steps when the clock atop the belfry of St. Anthony's Church tolled twelve.

Somewhere a cur barked, welcoming me home, and then every mongrel in the neighborhood yelped and howled. But nowhere on the street did I encounter a single, solitary soul. The streets were as empty as the Polo Grounds in February.

When I reached Beechwood Street, I thought that I detected a figure lurking in the grocer's alley between Rossi's Camera Shop and Wagner's Bakery. However, as I neared those establishments, I discovered that the Peeping Tom was merely the battered remnants of a folding camera sitting atop a tripod, missing one of its legs.

The Rossi family had been professional photographers ever since old Livio Rossi came to this country back in the 1890s. I wondered if the camera had belonged to Livio and why the family was now discarding it. Even if the camera no longer functioned, surely there was sentimental value attached to it.

Shrugging my shoulders, I marched on. In the distance I spied my home, sitting atop a knoll on the corner of Grant Street. Though my father was the chief surgeon at the local hospital, my mother and he lived in a modest Tudor-style dwelling, which they had built before the Great Depression.

When I hastened my step, my shoes squeaked like sled runners on virgin snow. At long last I was home. My pulse quickened. I knew that my parents were asleep because Dad had to be at the hospital early, and Mom always shopped at the local farmers' market as soon as the doors opened. But as I neared the driveway, I noticed that the lights burned brightly in the living room. Up the concrete steps I climbed. Glancing through the bay window, I saw Dad wrestling with a set of tangled Christmas tree lights. As he tugged and passed a light through a loop, his moon-shaped face reddened. His lips moved. I knew he wasn't praying. He was cussing the lights. Mom was nowhere in sight. I guessed that she was in the kitchen making out her shopping list.

Being as stealthy as Sheeba, our cat, I gently wrapped my hand around the doorknob and turned. By degrees the door opened, permitting the warm air inside to escape out into the frigid evening.

With a minimum of motion, I stepped into the foyer, still shouldering my barracks bag, and then strode into the living room. "Where ... in the hell ... does this light go?" said my father, hunched over. I dropped my bag with a thud. Pop looked up. "Oh, my word!" My father was never a demonstrative man. However, when he saw me, he wept. "Thomas!" He dropped the string of lights. "Mary, look who's here."

"If it's Buddy, tell him it's too late, and he should go home to Anna," called my mother from the kitchen.

"No, it's not Buddy." My dad shook my hand and then hugged

me. "It's Tommy."

"Tom-m-m-m-my!" I heard the refrigerator door close. "I'm coming." The floor boards squeaked under her weight. The startled tabby meowed and then scurried between the sofa and the upright piano. And then Mom, her arms outstretched, rushed into the room and embraced me. After smothering me with scores of kisses, she gazed at the crucifix on the wall. Though her lips didn't move, I knew that she was thanking the Lord for my safe delivery. "Are you hungry?"

"Of course he's hungry." When Dad shoved a box of ornaments aside, I knew that the tree would have to wait until tomorrow to be trimmed. "They never feed you right in the service."

"How about a *kielbasa* sandwich, a cup of coffee, and a piece of cake?"

"Sounds good to me," I said and followed my parents into the kitchen, which hadn't changed one iota since my departure, save for the blue-star banner hanging on the far wall. The blue star signified that I was alive and serving in the armed forces. Had I been killed, my parents would have changed the color of the star to gold.

"You're home for good?" asked my father, reaching into the cabinet for three cups.

"Sure am." Slipping off my overcoat, I brushed away a tad of lint before draping it over a chair. Right then and there I swore that I'd never wear any clothing that was either olive drab or brown in color. Navy blue was fine. Black was even better. Gray would also do. But no shade of brown or green.

"Good." Pop set the cups on the table and filled each with hot coffee. "Murphy the surgeon ... eh ... who took over for Perkins quit."

"Oh, I'm sorry to hear that." I sipped the coffee and realized how good my mother's coffee tasted. "That's going to put a strain on you, isn't it?"

My father smiled and stirred his coffee. "Not now." He drank and then added more sugar. "I'm offering you Murphy's job."

I breathed deeply and exhaled. "Errr ... to tell you the truth, Dad, I'm not interested in your offer."

"You wanna work in a big hospital, don't you?" said my mother, placing a sandwich before me.

"No, I don't want to practice medicine ... anywhere." Biting into the freshly baked pumpernickel bread, I chewed enthusiastically before swallowing. "Hmmm ... I think I'd like to become a chef or a short-order cook."

"Like you did down at Pep's while you were a college student."

"Exactly." After two more bites, the sandwich was consumed, and I turned my attention to Mom's chocolate cake.

"I understand," said my father, dabbing the corners of his mouth. "Pep needs a second-shift cook."

"Why don't you go down tomorrow morning and apply for the position," said my mother. "I'm sure he'll hire you."

Ever since I lost poor Simmons on the operating table, I was convinced that I would not return to medicine once I became a civilian. I knew that I just wasn't good enough to be a surgeon. In truth, I should never have lost Simmons.

Back in the operating room, when I stared at Simmons's corpse and made the decision to give up medicine, I knew the biggest obstacle lay in informing my parents, especially my father. Before I entered medical school, we often talked about working together down at the hospital. And now I was embarking upon a totally new career.

In all honesty, however, my parents took my decision very well. I was quite relieved when both supported my choice to sling hash down at Pep's Diner.

"I hope that the coffee and *kielbasa* don't keep you up," said my father, aware that the meal was quite heavy before bedtime.

"He's young," said my mother, "he can sleep through anything."

And sleep I did. As soon as my head hit the pillow, I was soundly asleep. My parents were always early risers. But neither one was ever quiet. Pop would hum some Rudy Vallee tune while he showered and dressed. And Mom was always clanging pots against each other or reprimanding the cat.

If they did, in fact, follow their conventional routine the following morning, I never heard a sound. I was dead to the world. Only when the church clock tolled eight times, did I stir. And then I didn't move for another fifteen minutes.

By the time I shaved, showered, and dressed, it was nine o'clock. Famished, I marched into the kitchen for breakfast. "Mom," I called. No response. I guessed that she was still out shopping. And since it was Christmas Eve, I knew that after she had visited the market, she stopped at Zerby's Emporium to buy a piece of fresh fish, probably smoked herring.

Since it was still Advent, a season of penance, the Christmas Eve meal would be meatless. I'm sure that most of our neighbors dined on turkey or ham. But our family followed the Church's teachings, and dinner's entrée would consist of fish.

Reaching into the closet and grabbing my topcoat, which no longer fit me very well, I decided to eat breakfast down at Pep's Diner. For about thirty cents, I could order a hearty meal. And over my second cup of coffee, I would chat with Pep about employment.

After locking the front door, I stepped off the porch and was greeted by a sunny December morning. Though chilly, the wind and temperature were nothing like the past two winters I had spent in Europe.

Nodding to friends and to neighbors as I strolled down the street, I decided that I would work at Pep's for a year or two. That experience would enable me to establish my own restaurant. Since I had once eaten in an authentic Parisian eatery, I would specialize in French cuisine. By the time I reached Peach Street, I had decided upon the entire menu, including the wine list.

"Docto-o-or Kr-r-r-oll!" called a silky-soft, feminine voice from behind me. "Tom, yoo- hoo." When I paused and glanced over my shoulder, I recognized the finely chiseled facial features and flowing auburn hair of Noel Lubin. "She smiled and waved frantically. After turning up my collar, I thrust my hands into my coat pockets. "Wait there."

Noel and I went back to our school days at St. Anthony's Grammar School. Actually, I initially met Noel when she moved to town during the first week of eighth grade. Immediately, I fell in love with her. She, however, never noticed me. To her, I didn't exist.

When we entered high school, I played the piano and joined the school's orchestra. Noel became a cheerleader. Since we had diverse interests, we gravitated toward different social circles. Until today, our paths never crossed again.

Dressed in a black swagger coat and matching heels, Noel pranced down the street like Miss Folk County, which she was crowned four years ago at the local fair.

"Merry Christmas," I said, not knowing what else to say.

She looked more ravishing than ever. I was about to tell her so when she rose up on her toes, planted her hands on my shoulders, and kissed me on the cheek. "And ... a wonderful New Year to you." Even after kissing me, she still held onto my hand. "I'm so glad I ran into you."

"Oh!"

"Yes." She gently squeezed my hand. "Tomorrow's my birthday, and I'm having a little get together at my house."

"Really." Since we were not close friends, I wondered why she was informing me of her plans. "That's nice."

"Well, if you're not too busy ... errrr ... I'd like for you to come to my birthday party." She gazed into my eyes and held them like a sorceress, which I truly believed she was. "Eh ... eight o'clock ... uh ... if you can make it."

Swallowing hard and perspiring profusely, I blinked like an owl. Regaining my composure quickly, I took both her hands into mine. "I'll be there only … if you agree to go out to dinner and a movie with me on New Year's Eve."

Noel's jaw dropped. Her brows arched in dismay. I knew that I had overstepped my bounds. I had no right to ask her out. Waiting for her rejection, I lowered my head and licked my parched lips. "I'd love to go out with you."

"You would?"

She inched closer and raised her head. "You know, Tom, I've been waiting for you to ask me out ever since I moved to town."

"No kidding." I shook my head. "That long?"

"I've had a crush on you ever since Sister Constance introduced me to the class back in eighth grade."

"Really!"

"You have no idea how happy you've made me this morning." She heaved a deep sigh just as the church bells tolled. "Now … if you'll excuse me, I must run over to Wagner's Bakery and pick up my birthday cake."

"Maybe I'll see you at Mass tonight and be the first to wish you a happy birthday."

"I'd like that." Growing bolder, I scooped Noel up into my arms and kissed her icy-cold lips. She cooed like a pigeon and then returned my kisses. "Must run, Dear, but we can continue kissing … eh … later tonight … on my sofa." After tossing her reddish-brown mane over her shoulder in a very sexy manner, she wiped away the lipstick from my cheek.

I watched her strut across the street with a slight wiggle and slink around the corner. "It's beginning to fee-e-e-e-el a lot like Chariss-s-s-mu-us."

Suddenly hunger pangs gnawed at my stomach like never before in my life. At long last I continued my journey up the street until I spotted Pep's Diner nestled between Brady's Tailor Shop and the Bijou.

Pep's Diner, an original Philadelphia trolley car, opened for business in 1916 when Luigi Pepiconti arrived in town from New York City. The converted trolley car, a twelve-stool restaurant, was open twenty-four hours a day and served some of the best Italian food in the area.

Unbuttoning my coat, I mounted the three steps of the diner and threw open the door. At once the aroma of freshly brewed coffee assailed my nostrils.

"Rita, look who's here," bellowed Pep, brandishing his antiquated spatula like a saber. "Good to see you, Tom."

"Merry Christmas," called Rita, an octoroon with wide hips, who Pep hired fifteen minutes before he opened for business back in 1916.

Sniffling, she poured me a cup of coffee.

"Good to be home," I said and meant it.

Since the last breakfast patrons were long gone, I had my choice of stools and plopped myself down next to an elderly gentleman known near and far as Count Pulaski. The man's actual name was Stanley Aloysius Pulaski. However, Stanley explained to anyone, who cared to listen, that his surname was identical to that of the Revolutionary War hero. Hence, he reasoned, he must be related to the Polish general. Stanley also pointed out that Count Casimir Pulaski's title was hereditary. And, therefore, since Casimir Pulaski was a nobleman, so was he. Case closed. No one argued with Stanley. Standing well over six feet and weighing approximately two hundred pounds, the former professional prize fighter was accepted, without question, as Count Pulaski in the community.

"Ain't it nice to be home for Christmas?" said the Count, not waiting for my reply. He returned to his plate and methodically stuffed ham, eggs, toast, and potatoes into his cavernous mouth.

"What will it be?" asked Rita, setting eating utensils before me.

"The usual," I said, glancing up at the menu on the chalkboard, which hadn't changed since my departure.

"Adam and Eve on a raft for the doctor."

"Gottcha," said Pep, already pouring the batter onto the griddle. "Gonna work for your dad down at the hospital?"

"No," I said and cleared my throat. "Actually ... err ... I'd like to fill that vacant position you have here."

"Can you start the day after Christmas?"

"Yes."

"Job's yours." After tossing two sausages onto the griddle, Pep flipped my pancake. When the Count coughed, he looked up. "For cripes sakes, Count, don't fill your mouth like that."

"One of these days ... you're gonna choke," said Rita. Shaking her head, she placed a bottle of maple syrup before me. "Slow down. Nobody's gonna steal your food."

"Hmmmm!" exclaimed the Count. Awkwardly he rose, wheezed, and flailed at the air with his open hands.

"Count!" called Pep, watching the scene unfold. "Sit down and drink some water.'

"Ahhhhh!" screamed a hysterical Rita as the Count tottered about like a spinning top on the edge of a table.

Catching him under the arms, I slapped him on the back. "Spit it out," I instructed. I slapped him again, harder.

"He's turnin' purple."

After two more unsuccessful slaps between the shoulder blades, I wrapped my arms around his waist and pressed inward. "Vomit, Count."

"He's looking worse," said Pep, tossing his apron aside and joining us.

When repeated attempts at dislodging the food failed, I eased the Count to the floor. "He's not breathing."

"What are you going to do?"

"Pep, get me a very sharp knife and a straw." Flexing my fingers, I reached out with a finger and sought the Count's Adam's apple. "Rita, call for an ambulance."

"Will do," said Rita, hurrying away to the public telephone in the rear of the diner.

I traced my finger down the Count's neck, searching for the cricoid cartilage. "Got it."

"What do you have?" asked Pep, watching my every move.

"The exact spot ... eh ... where I'm going to make an incision." When I held out my hand, Pep handed me a razor and the straw. He then patted me upon the back. Opening the straight razor, I made a very neat half-inch horizontal incision. "Good. Very ... good."

"Gee ... you're so damn steady."

"Gotta be. His life's on the line." The half-an-inch-deep cut barely bled, which was excellent. "So far ... so good." After pinching the incision open, I slid my finger inside the slit and opened it.

"Wow!"

Taking the straw, I cut it into half with the razor blade. "Now ... the tricky part."

"Why's that?"

"I have to insert the straw into his neck and get him to breathe." With deft hands, I slipped the straw into the incision and pushed. My action prompted Pep to look away. "A ... little more. There." Lowering my head, I breathed into the tube. Nothing happened. "Damn!" I blew again, twice. Still nothing. Outside a siren blared, and then the ambulance came to a screeching halt in the parking lot. I breathed again into the tube. Miraculously, the Count's chest rose. He was breathing on his own. Opening his eyes, he smiled.

"Uhh," moaned the Count. He tried to raise his head when he heard the two ambulance attendants enter the diner. Naturally, I held him down.

"Don't talk or move." I loosened his tie. "You're going to be fine."

"Litter coming" said one of the attendants, who I recognized as Stubby Hinkle, my old Scout leader. "Tommy, what do we have here?"

"Throat obstruction." I rose and wiped the perspiration from my brow with my handkerchief. "I performed a simple tracheotomy."

"Not so simple," said Pep. "You should have seen him operate. Cool as a cucumber."

"If I need an operation," explained Rita, "I want Tom to do it."

I felt my neck redden. "You people are too kind." I watched as Stubby and his assistant placed the Count on the stretcher and wheeled him toward the door. "Stubby."

"Yes," said Stubby, pausing. "When you get to the hospital, tell my dad ... eh ... that I'll be down to start working ... err ... as soon as I finish my breakfast."

"Will do, Tom."

As soon as the ambulance backed out of the driveway and sped down Main Street, I returned to my stool and awaited my fare. "What smells?" I sniffed and realized that my sausages and pancake had burned on the griddle.

"The boss burned your breakfast to a cinder," said Rita, tossing the charred remains into a can.

"Like father ... like son," announced Pep, handing the spatula to Rita.

"What's that mean?" I asked, interested in Pep's comment.

"You're just like your dad."

"Really." From the inflection in my voice, I knew that I sounded proud as a peacock.

"At least he lasted a whole week."

"You're talking in circles." I beckoned for more coffee, which Pep poured into my cup. "What are you jabbering about?"

"Back in 1918, when the war ended, your father came in and asked me for a job as an assistant cook."

"I didn't know that." I leaned forward and listened with a keen interest.

"Your dad said that he was a surgeon in the war, but didn't want to do any more doctoring." Pep took a plate from Rita and placed it before me. "Said he was fed up with people dying on him. Wanted to start over ... some other line of work ... uh ... because he stank as a surgeon."

"Really!" I poured syrup upon my pancake and cut a sausage into half. "He said that." When I bit into the sausage, I chewed and savored the spicy flavor, realizing how the Army had mistreated my taste buds. "How'd he do as a cook?"

Pep stroked his jowl. "To tell you the truth, he was pretty damn good for a beginner."

"I'm not surprised."

"He worked a full week and then told me that he was going back to doctoring."

"How about that." Finishing the last of my breakfast, I reached into my pocket for my wallet. "Did he give any other reason for quitting?"

"He said that he missed doctoring, and then ... ur ... there was also your mom."

"My mom!"

"He had met your mom a few days before, and they were in love."

"You do know that ... uhmm ... in the valley courtships only last a few weeks before the happy couple decides on getting hitched," added Rita with a wink.

"And what does that wink mean?" I asked, slapping a dollar upon the counter.

"Errr ... our spies," explained Pep, "have already reported seeing you smooching it up pretty good with Noel Lubin ... eh ... this morning in front of Sears."

"That filly is the best catch in town and nobody has ever been able to corral her," said Rita with a smile. She collected my soiled plate and offered me more coffee, which I welcomed.

"The same spies said that she literally floated into Wagner's Bakery after she left you." Pep removed his spectacles and polished them with his apron. "Mark my word." He paused for affect. "In about a month, she's gonna be marching down the aisle as Mrs. Thomas Krol."

Blushing, I said nothing because I knew that Pep was right. Pep was also correct about my father and me. We were alike in many respects. Taking up my cup, I drained it. Pep smiled and extended his swarthy hand. I grasped it and shook it firmly. "Merry Christmas," I said.

"Merry Christmas."

"Like father ... like son."

"Yep, in so many ways."

ABOUT THE AUTHOR

Ted Kuzminski graduated from Alliance College (located in the snow belt of northwestern Pennsylvania) in 1962 with a degree in English. Soon after his graduation, he served in the United States Army at Fort Jackson, South Carolina, and at Fort Knox, Kentucky. In May of 1973, he received his Master of Science degree from Temple University. A month later he married a science teacher (Karen Sitlinger) in his building. That winter Karen prodded him into writing her a short story as a Christmas present. Forty-two years later, he is still writing stories for Karen. *Karen's Stories*, a compilation of fifteen stories, is his first published collection.